PENGUIN BOOKS

Wars of the Roses

Book Three: Bloodline

'Iggulden is in a class of his own when it comes to epic, historical fiction' *Daily Mirror*

'Superbly plotted and paced' *Times*

'Conn breathes new life into the darkest and most dramatic of times, with a flair for both the huge scale and human interest of it all' *Star*

'Exceptionally well-written and gripping' *Stylist*

'Compelling reading' *Woman and Home*

'A page-turning thriller' *Mail on Sunday*

'Pacey and juicy, and packed with action' *Sunday Times*

'Energetic, competent stuff; Iggulden knows his material and his audience' *Independent*

'Conn Iggulden is a master storyteller and makes our blood flow faster' *Sunday Express*

ABOUT THE AUTHOR

Conn Iggulden is one of the most successful authors of historical fiction writing today. Following the *Sunday Times* bestsellers *Stormbird* and *Trinity*, *Bloodline* is the third book in his superb new series set during the Wars of the Roses, a remarkable period of British history. His previous two series, on Julius Caesar and on the Mongol khans of Central Asia, describe the founding of the greatest empires of their day and were number one bestsellers. Conn Iggulden lives in H

Wars of the Roses

Book Three: Bloodline

CONN IGGULDEN

PENGUIN BOOKS

PENGUIN BOOKS

UK | USA | Canada | Ireland | Australia
India | New Zealand | South Africa

Penguin Books is part of the Penguin Random House group of companies
whose addresses can be found at global.penguinrandomhouse.com.

First published by Michael Joseph 2015
Published in Penguin Books 2016
001

Copyright © Conn Iggulden, 2015

Inside cover map and insignias copyright © Andrew Farmer, 2013

The moral right of the author has been asserted

Typeset by Jouve (UK), Milton Keynes
Printed in Great Britain by Clays Ltd, St Ives plc

A CIP catalogue record for this book is available from the British Library

ISBN: 978–0–718–19642–4

To my father, for his patience and humour.

Acknowledgements

The loss of my father in September 2014 was a terrible blow. Given that he was ninety-one, it should not have been unexpected, but it was. The trees of your childhood don't just fall – until they do, and the world no longer holds them.

Without the support of a few key people, this book would certainly never have been finished. With their support, I think it could be the best I've written. It helped that I was writing Edward of York and Richard, Earl Warwick, right after they lost their fathers, five hundred years ago.

I give thanks then, for my agent, Victoria Hobbs, my brother David Iggulden, my friend Clive Room and chief of all, my wife Ella.

Conn Iggulden

Map and Family Trees

England at the time of the Wars of the Roses

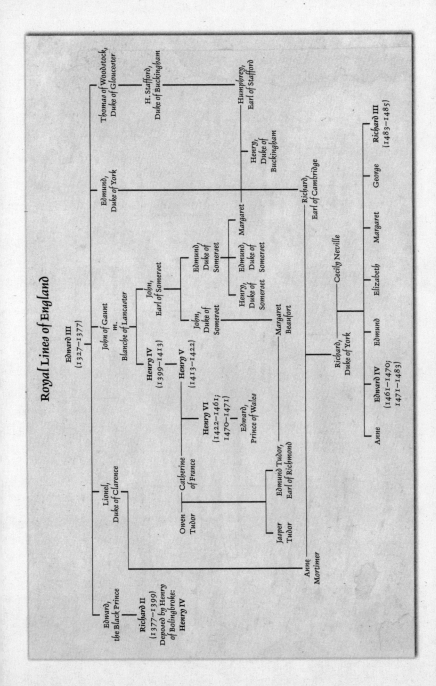

Royal Lines of England

Edward III
(1327–1377)

Edward, the Black Prince

Richard II
(1377–1399)
Deposed by Henry of Bolingbroke:
Henry IV

Lionel, Duke of Clarence

Anne Mortimer

John of Gaunt
m.
Blanche of Lancaster

Henry IV
(1399–1413)

Henry V
(1413–1422)

Catherine of France

Owen Tudor

Henry VI
(1422–1461;
1470–1471)

Edward, Prince of Wales

Edmund Tudor, Earl of Richmond

Jasper Tudor

John, Earl of Somerset

John, Duke of Somerset

Edmund, Duke of Somerset

Margaret Beaufort

Henry, Duke of Somerset

Edmund, Duke of Somerset

Margaret

Henry, Duke of Buckingham

Edmund, Duke of York

Richard, Earl of Cambridge

Richard, Duke of York

Cecily Neville

Anne

Edward IV
(1461–1470;
1471–1483)

Edmund

Elizabeth

Margaret

George

Richard III
(1483–1485)

Thomas of Woodstock, Duke of Gloucester

H. Stafford, Duke of Buckingham

Humphrey, Earl of Stafford

House of Lancaster

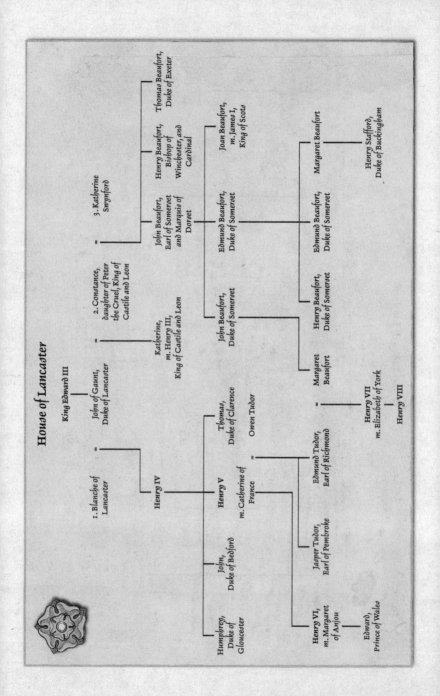

King Edward III

John of Gaunt, Duke of Lancaster

1. Blanche of Lancaster =

2. Constance, daughter of Peter the Cruel, King of Castile and Leon =

3. Katherine Swynford =

Henry IV

Katherine, m. Henry III, King of Castile and Leon

John Beaufort, Earl of Somerset and Marquis of Dorset

Henry Beaufort, Bishop of Winchester, and Cardinal

Thomas Beaufort, Duke of Exeter

Humphrey, Duke of Gloucester

John, Duke of Bedford

Henry V m. Catherine of France

Thomas, Duke of Clarence

Owen Tudor =

John Beaufort, Duke of Somerset

Edmund Beaufort, Duke of Somerset

Joan Beaufort, m. James I, King of Scots

Henry VI, m. Margaret of Anjou

Jasper Tudor, Earl of Pembroke

Edmund Tudor, Earl of Richmond =

Margaret Beaufort

Henry Beaufort, Duke of Somerset

Edmund Beaufort, Duke of Somerset

Margaret Beaufort

Henry Stafford, Duke of Buckingham

Edward, Prince of Wales

Henry VII m. Elizabeth of York

Henry VIII

House of York

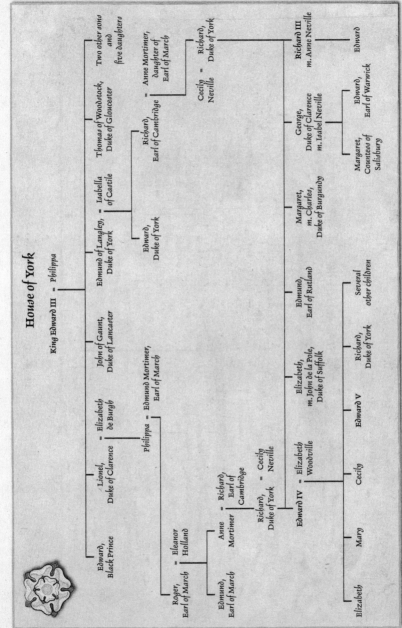

King Edward III = Philippa

Edward, Black Prince

Lionel, Duke of Clarence = Elizabeth de Burgh

Philippa = Edmund Mortimer, Earl of March

Roger, Earl of March = Eleanor Holland

Edmund, Earl of March

Anne Mortimer = Richard, Earl of Cambridge

Richard, Duke of York = Cecily Neville

John of Gaunt, Duke of Lancaster

Edmund of Langley, Duke of York = Isabella of Castile

Edward, Duke of York

Richard, Earl of Cambridge = Anne Mortimer, daughter of Earl of March

Thomas of Woodstock, Duke of Gloucester

Two other sons and five daughters

Cecily Neville = **Richard, Duke of York**

Edward IV = Elizabeth Woodville

Edmund, Earl of Rutland

Elizabeth, m. John de la Pole, Duke of Suffolk

Margaret, m. Charles, Duke of Burgundy

George, Duke of Clarence m. Isabel Neville

Richard III m. Anne Neville

Elizabeth | Mary | Cecily | **Edward V** | Richard, Duke of York | Several other children

Margaret, Countess of Salisbury

Edward, Earl of Warwick

Edward

House of Neville

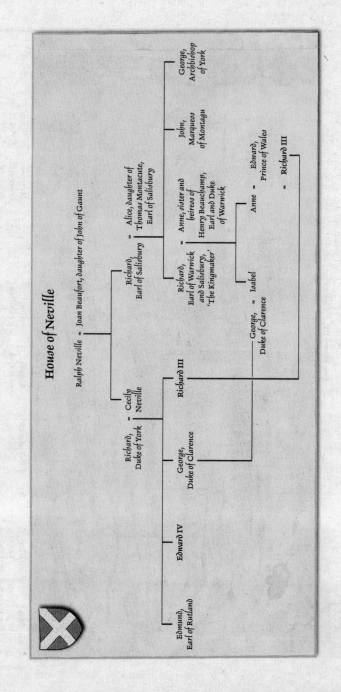

Ralph Neville = Joan Beaufort, daughter of John of Gaunt

Richard, Earl of Salisbury = Alice, daughter of Thomas Montacute, Earl of Salisbury

Richard, Duke of York = Cecily Neville

Richard, Earl of Warwick and Salisbury, 'The Kingmaker' = Anne, sister and heiress of Henry Beauchamp, Earl and Duke of Warwick

John, Marqueas of Montagu

George, Archbishop of York

Edmund, Earl of Rutland

Edward IV

George, Duke of Clarence

Richard III

George, Duke of Clarence = Isabel

Anne = Edward, Prince of Wales

= Richard III

House of Percy

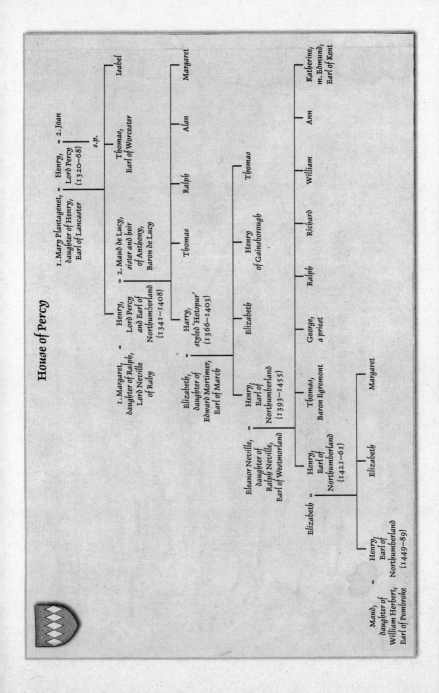

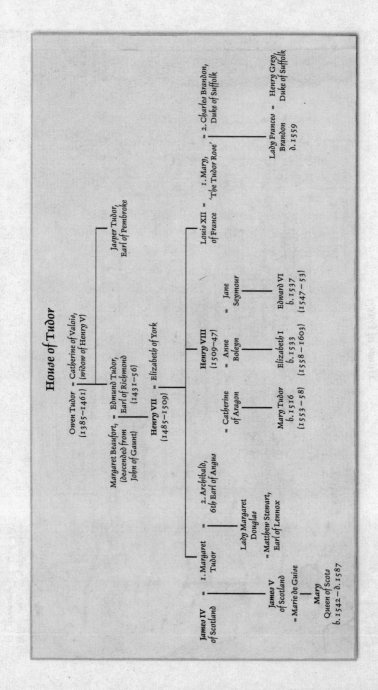

House of Tudor

Owen Tudor = Catherine of Valois,
(1385–1461)   (widow of Henry V)

Jasper Tudor,
Earl of Pembroke

Margaret Beaufort, = Edmund Tudor,
(descended from   Earl of Richmond
John of Gaunt)   (1431–56)

Henry VII = Elizabeth of York
(1485–1509)

1. Margaret Tudor = 2. Archibald,
                     6th Earl of Angus

Henry VIII
(1509–47)

Louis XII = 1. Mary, = 2. Charles Brandon,
of France   'The Tudor Rose' Duke of Suffolk

James IV =
of Scotland

Lady Margaret
Douglas
= Matthew Stewart,
Earl of Lennox

= Catherine   = Anne   = Jane
of Aragon   Boleyn   Seymour

James V
of Scotland
= Marie de Guise

Mary Tudor   Elizabeth I   Edward VI
b. 1516   b. 1533   b. 1537
(1553–58)   (1558–1603)   (1547–53)

Lady Frances = Henry Grey,
Brandon   Duke of Suffolk
d. 1559

Mary
Queen of Scots
b. 1542–d. 1587

List of Characters

- *Queen Margaret/Margaret of Anjou*: Wife of Henry VI, daughter of René of Anjou
- *Derry Brewer*: Spymaster of Henry VI and Queen Margaret
- *George, Duke of Clarence*: Brother of Edward IV and Richard, Duke of Gloucester
- *John Clifford, Baron Clifford*: Supporter of Henry VI, killer of Richard of York's son Edmund
- *Andrew Douglas*: Scottish laird and ally of Henry VI
- *Edward IV*: King of England, son of Richard Plantagenet, Duke of York
- *William Neville, Lord Fauconberg*: Uncle of Earl of Warwick
- *Richard of Gloucester*: Son of Richard of York, brother of Edward IV and George, Duke of Clarence
- *Sir John Grey*: Supporter of Henry VI, first husband of Elizabeth Woodville
- *Mary of Guelders*: Widow of James II of Scotland
- *Henry VI*: King of England, son of Henry V
- *Sir Thomas Kyriell*: Bodyguard of captured Henry VI
- *Albert Lalonde*: Chancellor to King Louis
- *King Louis XI*: King of France, cousin of Queen Margaret
- *John Neville, Baron Montagu*: Brother of Earl of Warwick
- *Anne Neville*: Daughter of Earl of Warwick

- *George Neville*: Archbishop of York, brother of Earl of Warwick
- *Isabel Neville*: Daughter of Earl of Warwick
- *John de Mowbray, Duke of Norfolk*: Supporter of Edward IV
- *Henry Percy, Earl of Northumberland*: Head of Percy family, supporter of Henry VI
- *Henry Percy*: Disinherited heir to Earl of Northumberland
- *Hugh Poucher*: Chief steward of Richard of York, factor of Edward IV
- *Richard Woodville, Baron Rivers*: Father of Elizabeth Woodville
- *Edmund, Earl of Rutland*: Son of Richard, Duke of York; killed at battle of Sandal Castle
- *Alice Montacute, Countess of Salisbury*: Wife of Earl of Salisbury, mother of Earl of Warwick
- *Richard Neville, Earl of Salisbury*: Grandson of John of Gaunt, father of Earl of Warwick; killed at battle of Sandal Castle
- *Henry Beaufort, Duke of Somerset*: Supporter of Queen Margaret; inherited title after his father's death at the first battle of St Alban's
- *Owen Tudor*: Second husband of Catherine de Valois (widow of Henry V); killed after battle of Mortimer's Cross
- *Anne Beauchamp, Countess of Warwick*: Wife of Earl of Warwick
- *Richard Neville, Earl of Warwick*: Head of the Neville family after the death of the Earl of Salisbury, later known as the Kingmaker
- *Edward of Westminster*: Prince of Wales, son of Henry VI and Queen Margaret

- *Abbot Whethamstede*: Abbot of St Alban's
- *Anthony Woodville*: Brother of Elizabeth Woodville
- *Elizabeth Woodville/Grey*: Wife of Edward IV
- *John Woodville*: Brother of Elizabeth Woodville
- *Cecily Neville, Duchess of York*: Wife of Richard, Duke of York, granddaughter of John of Gaunt, mother of Edward IV
- *Cecily of York*: Daughter of Edward IV and Elizabeth Woodville
- *Elizabeth of York*: Daughter of Edward IV and Elizabeth Woodville
- *Richard Plantagenet, Duke of York*: Great-grandson of Edward III; killed at battle of Sandal Castle

Prologue

The wind snatched at them, alive and full of malice. It filled their chests in sudden gusts and made their mouths ache with cold. The two men shuddered under the assault, yet continued to climb, on iron rungs that stung their hands. Though they did not look down, they could sense the watching crowd below.

Both men had been raised far to the south, in the same village of the county of Middlesex. They were a long, long way from home, but with their master, they'd been given a task by Queen Margaret herself. That was what mattered. They'd ridden further north from Sandal Castle, leaving behind the bloody ground and the pale, stripped bodies lying on it. They'd taken cloth sacks to the city of York, with the gales rising around them.

Sir Stephen Reddes watched from below, one hand raised against ice flecks on the wind. The choice of Micklegate Bar was no accident. English kings had always used that tower to enter York from the south. It did not matter that hail stung his men or that darkness was thick as dust in the air. They had their charge, their orders – and all three were loyal.

Godwin Halywell and Ted Kerch reached a narrow wooden ledge above the crowd. They edged out on to it, leaning back when they feared a wild gust might snatch them off. The crowd thickened beneath them, gleaming just a little with white hail resting on dark hair. Shuffling figures still came out of houses and inns, some of them demanding answers from the local men on the walls. There were no replies called back. The guards had not been told.

Short iron spikes had been set a dozen feet above the ground, too high for friends of executed men to reach. There were six in all, driven deep in good Roman mortar to lean out over the city. Four of them bore rotted heads, gaping at the night.

'What do we do with these?' Halywell called. He gestured helplessly to Kerch over the row of heads between them. There'd been no orders about the remains of criminals. Halywell swore under his breath. His temper was shortening and the hail seemed to blow even harder, a lash against his skin.

He let anger smother his revulsion, reaching out to the first head and taking hold. Its mouth was full of white beads of ice, shifting. Though he knew it was idiocy, a fear of being bitten meant he could not bring himself to put his hand between the jaws. Instead, he hooked his fingers under and just heaved the thing off its spike into the darkness. The lurching effort almost sent Godwin Halywell after it. He grasped the stones with white fingers, panting. Voices cried out below and the crowd surged back and forth, shocked at the idea that heavy, dangerous things might come flying down amongst them from the gatehouse tower.

Halywell looked along the wall to Kerch and they exchanged a glance of grim resignation, just two men getting on with unpleasant work while others watched and judged them from relative safety. It took time to remove and throw down the remaining heads. One of them all but shattered on the stones below, with a noise like pottery breaking.

Halywell supposed they did not *have* to clear all the spikes. They carried only three heads in the two sacks they bore, but somehow it did not seem right to set their charges alongside common criminals. He had a sudden thought of Christ sharing the hill of skulls with thieves, but he shook his head, concentrating on the job at hand.

While the wind howled, Halywell brought his sack up to his right shoulder, fumbling in its depths to wrap his fingers around locks of hair. Blood had stuck the heads to the cloth, so he had to wrestle the sack half inside out, almost tumbling off the wall again with his efforts. Gasping in fear and weariness, Halywell held it steady enough to snatch out the head of Richard Neville, Earl of Salisbury.

The hair wound around his fingers was iron-grey and the eyes had not rolled up, so that the slack face seemed to peer at him in the torchlight. Halywell muttered a prayer he had almost forgotten, wanting to cross himself, or at least to close the eyes. He had thought he was inured to horrors, but having a dead man watch him was something new.

It was no small task to spike a head. Halywell had received no instructions, as if every man of sense would have known immediately how it should be done. As it happened, he'd spent a summer of his childhood slaughtering pigs and sheep with a dozen other lads, earning the odd silver farthing or a bit of glistening liver to take home. He had a vague idea of there being a space at the base of a skull, but he couldn't seem to find it in the dark. He was almost sobbing as he worked the head back and forth, his hands slipping and his teeth chattering. All the time, the crowd were watching, murmuring names of men.

The iron rod sank in suddenly, piercing the brain and running up against the inside of the skull. Halywell sighed

3

in relief. Below his feet, many in the crowd crossed themselves, like a flutter of wings.

He pulled out the second head on good, dark hair, much thicker than the grey locks of the first. Richard, Duke of York, had been clean-shaven at the moment of his death, though Halywell had heard bristles would keep growing for a time, after. Sure enough, he could feel an unpleasant roughness on the jaw. He tried not to look at the face and jammed the head down on to its own iron point with his eyes pressed shut.

With hands smeared in seeping muck, Halywell made the sign of the cross. Along the line, Kerch had spiked the third head alongside York. That had been an evil thing, everyone said. The rumour was that York's son Edmund had been fleeing the battlefield. Baron Clifford had caught him and cut the boy down, just to spite his father.

All the heads were fresh, with their jaws sagging open. Halywell had heard of undertakers who sewed the lower jaw to the cheek or stuck it shut with a mouthful of tar. He didn't think it mattered. Dead was dead.

He saw Kerch was turning back to the iron rungs set in the stone, their work done. Halywell was about to do the same when he heard Sir Stephen calling up to him. He could barely make out words over the wind, but the memory sprang alive and he swore aloud.

A paper crown nestled at the bottom of his sack, stiff and dark with dried blood. Halywell unfolded it, looking askance at the head of York. He had a handful of thin split-pegs in a pouch at his waist, cut from dry reeds. Muttering about foolishness, he bent to the head and fixed the thing on to the dark hair, lock by lock. He thought it might remain for a while, in the shelter of the tower, or be blown across the city by the time he was down on solid ground. He didn't much care. Dead was *dead*, that was what mattered. All the hosts of heaven wouldn't care if you'd worn gold or paper, not then. Whatever the insult was meant to be, Halywell couldn't see it.

With care, he swung on to the ladder and climbed down the first couple of steps. As his eyes came level with the row of spiked heads, he paused, looking across them. York had been a good man, a brave man, so he'd heard. Salisbury too. Between them, they'd challenged for the throne and they'd lost it all. Halywell thought about telling his grandchildren he was the one who'd spiked York's head on the walls of the city.

For an instant, he had a sense of presence, of a breath on his neck. The wind seemed to fall away in a lull and he was staring across three humiliated men in silence.

'God be with you all,' he whispered. 'May He forgive your sins, if you had no time to ask at the end. Let Him welcome you lads. And bless you all. Amen.'

Halywell descended then, away from the moment of terrifying stillness, back into the heaving crowd and all the noise of men and cold of winter.

PART

PART ONE

1461

The smylere with the knyf under the cloke.

Geoffrey Chaucer, 'The Knight's Tale'

I

'You make too much of it, Brewer!' Somerset snapped, raising his face into the wind as he rode. '"The Lord went before them in a pillar of cloud", yes? *"Columna nubis"*, if you knew your Exodus. Black threads in the air, Brewer! It puts the fear of Almighty God into those who might yet stand against us. And there is nothing wrong with *that.*' The young duke turned to look over his shoulder at the greasy trails still rising behind them. 'The men must be fed: that's the long and the short of it. What are a few peasant villages now, after all we have accomplished? I'd scorch the sky black if it meant the lads ate well. Eh? Anyway, in this cold, you'd think they'd welcome a good fire.'

'Yet the news will run ahead of us, my lord,' Derry Brewer said, ignoring the rough humour. He was striving for politeness, though his stomach felt as if it touched his backbone and hunger gnawed at him. At moments like this, he missed Somerset's father, for the old man's subtlety and understanding. The son was quick and clever enough. But there was no depth to him. At twenty-five, Henry Beaufort had some of the military confidence men liked to follow. He would have made an excellent captain. Unfortunately, he was in sole command of the queen's army. With that in mind, Derry tried again to make his point.

'My lord, it's bad enough that messengers run south with news of York's death, while we stop for supplies in

9

every town. Our skirmishers loot and murder and the men spend the full day catching up to them – while local lads race to warn the next village in our path. It is harder and harder to find food, my lord, when those who prefer to keep their goods have hidden them all away. And I'm sure you know why the men set fires. If they cover up crimes in each village we pass, we'll have the whole country in arms before we even see London. I do not believe that is your intention, my lord.'

'I'm sure you could persuade a man to sell you his own children. I do not doubt it, Brewer,' Somerset replied. 'You always seem to have a fine argument ready. Yet you have been too long a *queen*'s man.' So confident was Somerset in his own rank and strength that he thought nothing of adding a certain insulting emphasis to the words. 'Yes, that is the trouble, I think. There are times for your long plans, of a certainty, for your . . . French whispers, Brewer. Perhaps when we reach London. I don't doubt you would have us wait patiently at all the local markets, bargaining or begging for bowls of stew or a fine capon or two. And you would see us *starve*.' His voice rose in volume to carry to the marching ranks around. 'Today is for these men, do you follow? See our lads march a stripe down the country – miles wide of archers and men-at-arms, fresh from victory. With their weapons held ready! You can see by looking at them, they have had a fine battle. See their pride!'

The crescendo in his voice demanded a response and the men around him cheered his words. Somerset looked smug as he faced Derry Brewer once again.

'They have been blooded, Brewer. They have brought enemies down. Now we'll feed them on red beef and mutton and turn them loose on London, d'you see? We'll make

Earl Warwick bring out King Henry and humbly beg our pardon for all the trouble he's made.'

Somerset laughed at the thought, carried away by his own imaginings. 'I tell you, we'll put the world to rights again. Do you understand, Brewer? If the men ran a little wild in Grantham and Stamford, or Peterborough, or Luton, it doesn't matter! If they take the winter hams they come across, well, perhaps those men who owned them should have been *with* us, making sure of York!' He had the sense to drop his voice to a murmur as he went on. 'If they cut a few throats or steal the virtue of a few country maids, I imagine it will fire their blood all the more. We are the *victors*, Brewer, and you are not least among us. Let your blood seethe for once, without spoiling it all with fears and plots.'

Derry looked back at the young duke, his anger poorly hidden. Henry Beaufort was charming and handsome – and he could speak in a great flow of words to bend someone to his will. Yet he was such a *young* man! Somerset had rested and eaten well while towns that had belonged to the Duke of York had been burned to the ground. Grantham and Stamford had been torn down and Derry had witnessed horrors in those streets as cruel as anything he'd seen in France. It galled him to have a cocky young nobleman tell him the men deserved their reward.

Derry glanced to where Queen Margaret rode ahead in a cloak of dark blue, her head bowed towards Earl Percy as they talked. Her seven-year-old son Edward trotted a pony on her other side, the boy's pale curls dipping with weariness.

Somerset saw the spymaster's glance and smiled wolf-ishly, confident in his youth compared with the older man.

'Queen Margaret wants her husband back, Master Brewer, not to hear your womanish concerns over the conduct of the men. Perhaps you should let her be the queen, eh? In this one instance?'

Somerset took a breath to throw back his head and guffaw at his own humour. As he did so, Derry reached down to the man's boot and gripped the shank of his spur with his gloved hand, giving a heave. The duke vanished over his horse's side with a roar, making the animal skitter back and forth as the reins sawed. One ducal leg pointed almost straight up to the sky and Somerset struggled madly to regain his seat. For a few stupefied instants, his head jogged along with a good view of the horse's leathery genitals swinging below.

'Careful there, my lord,' Derry called, prodding his own nag to trot a little distance between them. 'The road is most uneven.'

The greater part of his irritation was at himself, for losing his temper, but Derry was infuriated at the duke as well. The source of Margaret's strength, the source of a large part of her authority, lay in her being *right*. The whole country knew that King Henry was held prisoner by the Yorkist faction, traitors to a man. There was sympathy for the queen and her young son, forced to roam the land and find support for her cause. It was a romantic view, perhaps, but it had swayed good men like Owen Tudor and brought armies to the field that might otherwise have stayed at home. It had given them the victory at the end, with the house of Lancaster rising up, after so long with its face pressed down.

Letting an army of Scots and northerners murder, rape and loot their way to London would not help Margaret's cause or bring one more man to her side. They were fresh from their triumph, still half drunk on it. They had all seen Richard Plantagenet, Duke of York, forced to his knees and killed. They had seen the heads of their most powerful enemies taken away to be spiked on the walls of the city of York. For fifteen thousand men, after the rage and wild panic of battle had settled, they still had the victory like coins in a purse. Ten years of struggle had come to an end and York was dead on the field, his ambitions broken. The victory was *everything*, won hard. The men who had bared York's head for the blade expected rewards – food, wine and gold altar cups, whatever they came across.

Behind Brewer, the column stretched into a haze, farther than the eye could see on a winter's day. Bare-legged Scots stalked along with short Welsh archers and tall English swordsmen, all grown thin, with ragged cloaks, but still walking, still proud.

Some forty yards back, the red-faced young Duke of Somerset had regained his seat with the help of one of his men. Both glared at Derry Brewer as he touched his forehead in false respect. Armoured knights had always raised their visors when their lords passed, showing their faces. The gesture had become a salute of sorts. Derry could see it hadn't eased the outrage in the pompous young man he'd unseated, however. Once more, Derry cursed his own temper, a rush of red that could overwhelm him so completely and suddenly that he'd lash out without a moment's thought. It had always been a weakness in him, though it was true that the abandonment of all caution could be quite satisfying. He was too old for it, though, he thought. He'd get himself killed by a younger cock if he wasn't more careful.

Derry half expected Somerset to come charging over to demand redress, but he could see the man's companion speaking urgently into his ear. There was no dignity in petty squabbling, not for one of Somerset's station. Derry sighed to himself, knowing he'd better choose his sleeping spots carefully for a few nights – and avoid going anywhere alone. He'd dealt with the arrogance of lords all his life and knew only too well how they considered it their right, almost their primary occupation, to demand redress for a grudge, openly or on the sly. Somehow, those they offended were meant to play along, to duck and weave as best they could until the natural order was restored and they were found beaten senseless, or perhaps with fingers or ears cropped short.

There was something about getting older that had stolen away Derry's patience with that sort of game. He knew if Somerset sent a couple of rough lads to liven him up a little, his reply would be to cut the duke's throat one night. If Derry Brewer had learned anything in the years of war, it was that dukes and earls died as easily as commoners.

That thought brought a vision of Somerset's father, cut down in the street at St Albans. The old duke had been a lion. They'd had to break him, because he would not yield.

'God keep you, old son,' Derry muttered. 'Damn it. All *right*, for you, he's safe from me. Just keep the preening bugger out of my way, though, would you?' He raised his eyes to the sky and breathed deeply, hoping the soul of his old friend could hear him.

Derry could smell char and ash on the air, touching him in the back of the throat like a waxed finger. Their outriders made new lines of smoke and pain rise ahead of them, dragging joints and salted heads from barns, or prodding forth live bulls to be slaughtered in the road. At the end of each day, the queen's column would reach the furthest points of the sweeps ahead. They'd have marched eighteen or twenty miles, and for the sight of a flapping capon to be cooked and gnawed to the split bones, they'd be blind to a few more manors or villages burned, with all sins hidden in flames and soot. Fifteen thousand men had to eat, Derry knew that, or the queen's army would dwindle away on the road, deserting and dying in the green ditches. Still, it sat hard with him.

The spymaster glowered as he rode along, reaching down to pat the neck of Retribution, the first and only horse he had ever owned. The elderly animal turned its head to peer up at him, looking for a carrot. Derry showed his empty hands and Retribution lost interest. Ahead, the queen and her son rode with a dozen lords, still stiff with pride, though it had been weeks since the fall of York at Wakefield. The sweep to the south was no great rush to vengeance, but a measured movement of forces, with letters borne away to supporters and enemies every morning. London lay ahead and Margaret did not want her husband quietly murdered as she approached.

Getting the king back alive would be no easy task, Derry was certain of that much. Earl Warwick had lost his father at Sandal Castle. As the land was still frozen and the nights long, Warwick would still be about as raw with grief as York's own son, Edward. Two angry young men had lost their fathers in the same battle – and King Henry's fate lay in their hands.

Derry shuddered, remembering York's cry at the moment of his execution: that all they had done was unleash the sons. He shook his head, wiping cold snot from where it had dribbled on to his top lip and set hard. The old guard was passing from the world, one by one. Those left to stand in their places were not so fine a breed, as far as Derry Brewer could tell. The best men were all in the ground.

A gusting wind battered the sides of the tent as Warwick faced his two brothers, raising his cup.

'To our father,' he said.

John Neville and Bishop George Neville echoed the words and drank, though the wine was cold and the day colder. Warwick closed his eyes in brief prayer for his father's soul. All around them, the wind snapped and fluttered the canvas, making it seem as if they were assailed on all sides, the very centre of the gale.

'What sort of a madman goes to war in winter, eh?' Warwick said. 'This wine is poor stuff, but the rest is all drunk. At least it gives me joy to be with you two great louts, with no *pretence*. I *miss* the old man.'

He had intended to continue, but a sudden wave of grief tightened his throat, so that his voice cracked. Despite his efforts to breathe, the air huffed out of his lungs until they were empty and his eyes suddenly blurred. With a huge effort, Warwick pulled in a long, slow breath through his teeth, then another as he found he could speak again. In all that time, his two brothers had said not a word.

'I miss his counsel and his affection,' Warwick went on. 'I miss his pride and even his disappointment in me, for at least he was there to feel it.' The other two chuckled at that, something they had both known. 'Now it's all set, with no more change. I cannot take back one word or have him know one more thing I have done in his name.'

'God will hear your prayers, Richard,' his brother George said. 'Beyond that is a sacred mystery. It would be the sin of pride to think you might discover God's plan for us – or for this family. You never can, Brother – and you must not grieve for those who feel only joy.'

Warwick reached out and gripped the bishop by the back of the neck in affection. To his surprise, the words had brought him a little comfort, and he was proud of his younger brother.

'Have you news of York?' George Neville went on, his voice calm.

Of the three Neville sons, the bishop seemed to have taken their father's death with the least turbulence, with no sign of the rage that ate at John, or the grim spite that opened Warwick's eyes each morning. Whatever else lay ahead, there was a price owed, for all the troubles, all the pain they had endured.

'Edward writes nothing,' Warwick said, showing his irritation. 'I would not even know he had defeated the Tudors without their own ragged refugees, taken up and questioned by my people. The last I heard, Edward of York was sitting on a mound of dead Welsh archers and drinking away the loss of his father and brother. He has ignored the messages I've sent telling him how sorely he is needed here. I know he is only eighteen, but at his age . . .' Warwick sighed. 'I think sometimes, the great size of him conceals what a boy he still is. I can't understand how he can delay in Wales and revel in his grief, while Queen Margaret comes against me here! His concern is only with himself, with his own noble grief and rage. It's my feeling that he cares nothing for us, or our father. Understand me, lads: I say this to you, to no one else.'

John Neville had been made Baron Montagu by his father's death. The elevation showed in the richness of his new cloak, the thick hose and fine boots, bought on credit from tailors and cobblers who lent to a lord as they never had to a knight. Despite the layers of warm cloth, Montagu glanced at the billowing walls and shivered. It was difficult to imagine any spy being able to hear over the thrum and whistle of the wind, but it cost nothing to show caution.

'If this gale grows any more fierce, this tent'll be snatched up and taken over the army like a hawk,' Montagu said. 'Brother, we need that York boy, for all his youth. I sat with King Henry this morning while he sang hymns and plainsong under the oak. Did you know some smith has put a rope on his leg?' Warwick looked up from his thoughts and John Neville raised both palms to ease his concern. 'Not a shackle, Brother. Just a knotted rope, a hobble, to stop our royal innocent from wandering away. You talk of the boy in Edward, but at least it is a fine, strong boy, given to temper and firm action! This Henry is a mewling child. I could not follow him.'

'Hush, John,' Warwick said. 'Henry is the king anointed, whether he be blind or deaf, or crippled, or . . . simple. There is no evil in him. He is like Adam before the Fall, no – like Abel, before Cain murdered him for spite and jealousy. Telling me he has been tied brings shame on all of us. I will order him freed.'

Warwick crossed to the lacings of the tent, tugging at the cords until a widening flap brought the wind in. Papers in a corner flung themselves into the air like birds, escaping the lead weights that held them down.

As the entrance yawned open, the brothers looked out

on a night scene that might have been a painting of hell. St Albans lay just to the south of them. Before the town, in the torchlit dark, ten thousand men worked all around that spot, building defences in three great armoured 'battles' of men. Fires and forges stretched in all directions, like the stars above, though they gave a sullen light. Rain fell across that multitude in gusts and swooping slaps of damp, delighting in their misery. Over its noise could be heard the shouts of men, bowed down under beams and weights, driving lowing oxen as they heaved carts along the tracks.

Warwick felt his two brothers come to his side, staring out with him. Perhaps two hundred round tents formed the heart of the camp, all facing north, from where they knew Queen Margaret's army would come.

Warwick had been returning from Kent when he'd heard of his father's death at Sandal. He'd had a month and a half from that hard day to prepare for the queen's army. She wanted her husband, Warwick knew that well enough. For all Henry's blank eyes and frailty, he was the king still. There was but one crown and one man to rule, even if he knew nothing of it.

'Every time the sun rises, I see new strips of spikes and ditches and . . .'

Bishop George Neville waved his hand, lacking the words to describe the tools and machines of death his brother had gathered. The rows of cannon were just a part of it. Warwick had consulted the armouries in London, seeking out any vicious device that had ever proved its worth in war – back to the seven kingdoms of the Britons and the Roman invaders. Their combined gaze swept out across spiked nets, caltrops, ditch traps and towers. It was a field of death, ready for a great host to come against it.

2

Margaret stood at the door of her tent, watching her son fight a local lad. No one had any idea where the black-eyed urchin had come from, but he had fastened himself to Edward's side and now they rolled with sticks held like swords, clacking and grunting on the damp ground. The struggling pair crashed against a rack of weapons and shields, bright-coloured in the twilight, with the breeze catching the banners of a dozen lords.

Margaret saw Derry Brewer approach, her spymaster looking fit as he jogged through the long grass. They had chosen a meadow for that day's camp, close by a river and with few hills in sight. Fifteen thousand men were just about a city on the move, with all the horses, carts and equipment taking up a vast space. In late summer, they would have stripped orchards and walled gardens, but there was little to steal as February began. The fields were dark, life hidden deep. The men had begun to look like beggars as their clothes wore to rags and their bellies and muscles wasted away. No one fought in winter, unless it was to rescue a king. The reason was all around her, in the frosted earth.

Derry Brewer reached the entrance of the queen's tent and bowed. Margaret raised a hand to make him wait and he turned to observe the Prince of Wales vanquishing his opponent, knocking the weaker boy on to his back. The other lad screeched like a cat being strangled.

Neither Derry nor the queen said anything to interrupt and Prince Edward changed his grip on the stick and jabbed it past the boy's defence, sinking it hard into his chest. The boy curled up and lost all interest while the prince raised his stick like a lance, cupping one hand and mimicking a wolf. Derry grinned at him, both amused and surprised. The boy's royal father had not shown an ounce of martial fervour his entire life, and yet there was the son, feeling the rush of excitement that came only from standing over a beaten man. Derry remembered the feeling well. He saw Edward reach down to help the other boy to his feet and spoke quickly.

'Prince Edward, you should perhaps let him rise on his own.' Derry had been thinking about the fight pits of London and had spoken without thought.

'Master Brewer?' Margaret asked, her eyes bright with pride.

'Ah. My lady, men have different views. Some call it honour, to show grace to those you've defeated. I think it is just another sort of pride myself.'

'I see – so they *would* have my son raise this lad to his feet? *You* – stay where you are.'

The last was aimed with a pointing finger at the urchin in question, who was trying to struggle up, his face burning from the attention. The boy was appalled to be spoken to by such a noble lady and slumped back on to the mud.

Derry smiled at her.

'They would, my lady. They would clasp arms with an enemy and show their greatness in forgiving sins against them. Your husband's father was wont to do that, my lady. And it's true his men loved him for it. There's greatness to such an act, something beyond most of us.'

'What about you, Derry? What would you do?' Margaret asked softly.

'Oh, I am not such a great man, my lady. I would break a bone, perhaps, or tickle him up with my knife – there are places that won't kill a fellow, though they will spoil his year.' He smiled at his own wit, the expression slowly fading under the queen's gaze. He shrugged. 'If I've won, my lady, I do not want an enemy to come to his feet, perhaps even angrier than before. I've found it best to make sure they stay down.'

Margaret inclined her head, pleased at his honesty.

'I think that is why I trust you, Master Brewer. You understand such things. I will *never* lose to my enemies but hold my honour, if honour is the price. I would choose victory – and pay the price.'

Derry closed his eyes for a moment, his head dipping as he understood. He had known Margaret as a young girl, but she had been tempered in plots and battles and negotiations into a subtle and vengeful woman.

'I believe you may have spoken to Lord Somerset, my lady.'

'I did, Derry! I chose him to lead my army – and I did not choose a fool. Oh, I know he does not like to ask for my counsel, but he will do so if you force his hand. Young Somerset is a fierce bird, I think, strong in sinew and heart. The men adore him for his roaring. But would his father have made a fool? No. He believes you would have us delay in the north, to gather food rather than to take it, some such concern. My lord Somerset thinks only of reaching London and keeping the men strong. There is nothing wrong with having such a care for my army, Derry.'

As the queen spoke, Derry hid his surprise. He had not

22

expected Somerset to swallow his young man's pride and ask Margaret to rule on the matter. It suggested a loyalty and maturity that, oddly enough, gave Derry hope.

'My lady, Warwick is strongest in the south. His followers are Kent and Sussex men for the most part, those godforsaken, rebellious counties. We must overcome them and either recapture your husband or . . .'

His eyes strayed to the two boys as the sticks suddenly clacked again. If King Henry did not survive, almost the entire house of Lancaster would be the seven-year-old prince with a lump over one eye, a boy who was at that moment trying very hard to strangle his opponent to death.

Margaret's gaze went with his and then back, her eyebrows raised in question.

'However it turns out,' Derry said, 'the king will have to rule England in peace from that day, my lady. With the right tale in the right ears, King Henry could be . . . Arthur back from Avalon, Richard from the Crusades. He could be the anointed king restored – or another King John Lackland, my lady, with dark tales dogging his steps like shadows. We have left a strip of destruction half the length of England. Hundreds of miles of death and theft, and all those who cursed us will starve now. Children like these boys will die because our men stole their animals and ate their seed crops, leaving them nothing to plant in spring!'

In his indignation, Derry broke off at the pressure of the queen's hand on his forearm. He had been watching the boys tumbling in the mud as he spoke, rather than plead with Margaret directly. He turned to her then, seeing both certainty and resignation in her eyes.

'I . . . cannot pay the men, Derry. That is still true until

23

we reach London, and perhaps not even then. They must surely fight again before I will see coins enough to fill their purses, and who knows how that will turn out? While they are not paid, you know they expect to be turned loose, like hunting dogs. They expect to take plunder as they go, in lieu of payment.'

'Is that what Somerset said?' Derry replied, his voice cold. 'If he is such a fine master, let him take those dogs by the scruff of their necks . . .'

'No, Derry. You are my most trusted counsellor, you know it. This one time, you ask too much. I am blinkered, Derry. I see only London ahead and nothing else.'

'You don't smell the smoke on the air, then, or hear the women screaming?' Derry asked.

It was reckless to challenge her in such a way, for all their long association. He saw pink spots appear high on her cheeks, spreading to a flush that stained her skin right to her neck. All the time, she looked into his eyes as if he held the secrets of the world.

'This is a hard winter, Master Brewer – and it goes on. If I have to look away from evil to gain back my husband and my husband's throne, I will be blind and deaf. And you will be mute.'

Derry took a long breath.

'My lady, I am growing old. I think, at times, that my work is better suited to a younger man.'

'Derry, please. I did not mean for you to take offence.'

The spymaster held up his hand.

'And I have not; nor would I leave you without the web I have spent so long weaving. My lady, I am sometimes in great danger in my service. I say it not as a boast, but merely to acknowledge a truth. I meet hard men in dark places and I do it every day. If the day comes when I do *not* return, you should know all I have arranged to follow.'

Margaret watched him with large, dark eyes, fascinated by his discomfort. He stood before her like a nervous boy, his hands twisting together at his waist.

'There is a chance you will be in peril yourself, my lady, if they take me. Another will come to you then, bearing words you will know.'

'What will he look like, this man of yours?' Margaret whispered.

'I cannot say, my lady. There are three in all. Young and sharp and utterly loyal. One of them will survive the other two and take up the reins if I drop them.'

'You would have them murder one another to stand at my side?' Margaret asked.

'Of course, my lady. Nothing has value unless it is hard won.'

'Very well. And how will I know to trust your man?'

Derry smiled at the quickness of her thought.

'A few words, my lady, that mean something to me.'

He paused, looking through her to the past – and ahead as he imagined his own death. He shook his head, disturbed.

'William de la Pole's wife Alice still lives, my lady. Her grandfather was perhaps the first man of letters in all England, though I never had the chance to meet old Chaucer. She used a line of his about me, once. When I asked her what she had meant, she said it was an idle thought and I was not to take offence. Yet it stayed with me. She said I was "the smiler with the knife beneath the cloak". I find it a fair description of my work, my lady.'

Margaret shivered in turn, rubbing one arm with the other.

'You make my flesh creep with such a line, Derry, but it will be as you say. If one comes to me and says those words, I will listen to him.' Her eyes glittered, her face hardening. 'On your *honour*, Derry Brewer. You have earned my trust, though it is not lightly given.'

Derry bowed his head, remembering the young French girl who had come across the Channel to marry king Henry. At thirty, Margaret was still slim and clear-skinned, with long, brown hair bound into a single tress with red ribbon. With the rarity of just one pregnancy, she was no broken-backed old dray-mare like so many of her age. She had not lost the slender-muscled waist that made her lithe. For one who had known such pain and loss, Margaret had aged well, to any eye. Yet Derry saw with the experience of sixteen years at her side. There was a hardness in her, and he did not know whether to regret or rejoice in it. The loss of innocence was a powerful thing, especially to a woman. Yet what came after was always better cloth, for all the single red stains. Derry knew women hid such things each month. Perhaps that was the heart of women's secrets and their inner lives. They had to hide blood – and they understood it.

Derry Brewer felt the spiced wine warm his stomach and chest, easing some of his aches. The knight facing him nodded slowly and leaned back on his stool, fully aware of the importance of the news. They sat in the corner of a heaving taproom, with standing soldiers pressing in on all sides. The tavern was already down to foul beer and dregs, while hopeful men still looked in from the road.

Derry had chosen the public inn for his meeting, knowing his noble masters understood little of his work. It did not appear to occur to them that a man might ride from one army to another and pass on absolutely vital information. Derry leaned back against the corner of oak boards, looking at Sir Arthur Lovelace, certainly his most prideful informant. Under Derry's scrutiny, the little man smoothed down an ornate moustache that drooped over his lips and must have made every mouthful of food at least one part hair. They had met after the battle of Sandal, when Lovelace had been one of a hundred downcast knights and captains Derry had taken aside. He'd given a few coins to those who had none and a few words of advice to anyone who would listen. It helped that the spymaster was a retainer of King Henry. No one could doubt Brewer's loyalty – or question the rightness of his cause, not after that victory.

As a result of Derry's encouragement, more than a few of York's soldiers had been persuaded to loiter at Sheffield for the queen's army, joining the very men they had been fighting against. It might have seemed madness, if men didn't need to eat and to be paid. When it turned out they would not be paid, perhaps it was revealed as madness after all. Hundreds in that army had helped to sack towns loyal to York, just to fill their own bellies and pouches.

Lovelace wore no colours, no surcoat or painted armour that would have had him marked and perhaps reported as he came through the camp. He'd been given a password and he knew to ask for Derry Brewer. That would have been enough to get him past inquisitive guards, but the truth was he'd come to the heart of Queen Margaret's army without being challenged even once. On another day, it would have galled Derry Brewer and had him calling out the army captains to explain once *again* the importance of keeping spies and assassins from where they might do untold damage.

Lovelace leaned forward, his voice an excited murmur. Derry could smell the man's sweat as heat came off him almost as a glow. The knight had ridden hard to reach the king's spymaster with what he knew.

'What I have told you is *vital*, Master Brewer, do you understand? I have delivered Warwick to you, plucked and greased and tied in cords – all ready for the turning spit.'

'The Sailor,' Derry said absently as he thought. Warwick had been Captain of Calais for years at a time and was said to love the sea and the ships that sailed it. Lovelace had agreed not to use the names of important men, but of course the knight kept forgetting. At such times, Derry preferred to act as if his worst enemy was standing at his shoulder, ready to pass on whatever he could learn.

The inn was growing less friendly as soldiers drank it

dry. In the heave and crush, a red-haired stranger suddenly fell across their small table, lurching at Derry and saving himself with both arms held before him. The man gave a great shout of laughter. He was turning to complain to whoever had pushed him when he felt the line of cold metal Derry held across his throat and his voice choked off.

'Careful there, son,' Derry murmured in his ear. 'On your way.'

He gave the soldier a push and watched carefully as he vanished back into the crowd, eyes wide. Just an accident, then. Not one of those 'accidents' that are so tragic but ultimately the will of God, and what bad luck to have fallen on the blade, and Brewer's in the cold, cold ground and we must go on with our happy lives, recalling him often and with fondness . . .

'Brewer?' Lovelace said, snapping his fingers in the air.

Derry blinked irritably at him.

'What is it? You've passed on your news – and if you're telling the truth, it's useful to me.'

Lovelace leaned closer still, so that Derry could smell onions on his breath.

'I did not betray "The Sailor" for nothing, Master Brewer. When you and I met at that tavern in Sheffield, you were very free with silver coins and promises.' Lovelace took a deep breath, his voice trembling with hope. 'I recall you mentioned the Earldom of Kent, as yet vacant, with no loyal man there to pass on taxes and tithes to the king. You told me then that even such a fine, sweet plum as that might be the reward for a man who delivered Warwick.'

'I see,' Derry replied. He waited just for devilment, as if he had not understood. In part it was because the foolish knight had used Warwick's name yet again, even though they were so crowded about that men loomed over them and one had nearly ended up in Derry's lap.

'And I have done so!' Lovelace said, growing red and swelling slightly about the neck and face. 'Are your promises mere straws, then?'

'I warned you to come to this camp with no banner, no surcoat or painted shield to be remembered. You walked through ten thousand men to reach this inn. Did even one of them take you by the arm and demand to know who you were?'

Lovelace shook his head, unnerved by the intensity of the spymaster's words.

'And good knight, did it cross your mind that if you could come to me, I might have men wandering the camp you left behind? That I might have a number of fellows in the south, all carrying water and polishing armour – just watching and counting and remembering all the while? What, did you think I was blind without your eyes?'

Derry watched the hope drain out of the knight in front of him, so that Lovelace sagged in his seat. To be made an earl, a king's companion, well, it would have been an impossible fantasy for a common soldier, or even a knight with a manor house and a few tenant farms. Yet in times of war, stranger things had happened. Derry imagined Lovelace had a wife and children somewhere, all depending on his pay, his wits and perhaps a little luck.

Poverty was a hard master. Derry regarded the crest-fallen knight more closely, seeing the wear on his coat. He wondered if the straggling beard was just the result of not having coin to have it trimmed. Derry sighed to himself. When he'd been young, he'd have stood then, patted Lovelace on the shoulder and left him there to be beaten and robbed on his way out, or whatever might befall him.

Instead, infuriatingly, Derry knew age had softened his hardest edges, so that he had begun to see and hear the pain of others – and hardly ever laugh at it any more. Perhaps it was time to retire. His three younger men were all ready to fight it out if he failed to come home one night. In theory, none of them knew the names of the others, but he would bet the last coin in his purse that they'd all found out. One good way to dodge a blow is to kill the man holding the blade. Men in Derry's trade knew that best of all was to kill the man before he even knew he was your enemy.

None of his thoughts showed in his expression as Derry regarded Lovelace, the man still coming to terms with having sold Warwick for no more than a pint of dark ale. The spymaster didn't dare drop silver or gold on the table with so many soldiers about. If he did that, he knew he might as well knock Lovelace out himself and save a coin. Instead, he reached out and clasped Lovelace's hand, pressing a gold half-noble between them. He saw the poor knight's eyes tighten with embarrassment and relief as he glanced into his hand. The coin was small, but it would buy a dozen meals, or perhaps a new cloak.

'God be with you, son,' Derry said, rising to leave. 'Trust in the king and you won't go wrong.'

The moon was new and hidden, but Edward of York could see his hands in starlight. He turned the left in front of his face, watching his fingers move like a white wing. York sat on a Welsh crag and he had not bothered to ask

31

its name. His feet dangled over emptiness, and when he dislodged a stone, it fell for ever and never seemed to strike. Depths yawned below his feet and yet the darkness was so thick he felt he could almost step out on to it.

He smiled drunkenly at the thought, reaching with one foot and padding it around as if he might find a bridge of shadows to take him across the valley. The action shifted his weight from the lip of the crag and he scrambled suddenly, kicking in a spasm, the panic gone as soon as it had come. He would *not* fall, he knew it. He might have drunk enough to kill a smaller man, but God would keep him from tumbling down some Welsh rock. His ending was not there, not with all he still had to do. Edward nodded to himself, his head so heavy it continued to sway up and down long after he intended it.

He heard the footsteps and murmuring voices of two of his men as they began to speak, barely a dozen paces behind him. Slowly, Edward raised his head, realizing they could not see him in the blackness by the ground. With his limbs lit such a bone-white, he thought he must resemble some spirit. In another mood, he might have lurched up with a great howl, just to make them cry out, but he was too dark for that. The night around him sank in when it touched his arms. No doubt that was why he saw the white skin – because it had drawn in the darkness and was still drawing, filling him up until his seams would creak with it. The idea was beautiful, and he sat and wondered at it while the men talked behind him.

'I don't like this place, Bron. I don't like the hills, the rain or the bloody Welsh. Scowling out at us from their little huts. Thieves, too, like as not to steal anything that isn't tied down. Old Noseless lost a saddle two days back and it did not walk off on its own. This is not a place to stay – but here we still are.'

'Well, if you were a duke, mate, perhaps you'd take us back to England. Until then, we wait until Master York says we move. I'm content, I'd say. No, mate, more than content. I'd rather be sat here than marching or fighting in England. Let the big lad drown his grief for his father and brother. The old duke was a fine man. If he'd been my dad, I'd be drinking away the days as well. He'll come right in the end, or burst his heart from it. There's no point worrying which it will be.'

Edward of York squinted in the direction of the pair. One was leaning against a rock, blending into it like one great shadow. The other was standing, looking out and up at the field of stars blazing around the north as the night crept on. York had a feeling of irritation that his grief, his private pain, should be discussed by mere knights and pike-men as if it were no more than the weather or the price of a loaf. He began to scramble up, very nearly toppling off the edge as he came to his feet and stood swaying. At four inches over six feet, York was a huge figure, by far the largest man in his army. He blotted out a fair section of the sky and the two speakers froze as they became aware of the silent apparition just standing there, looming dark against dark, outlined by stars.

'Who are you to tell me? Eh? How to show my sorrow?' Edward demanded, slurring.

The men reacted in utter panic, turning away as one and scrambling over the crest of the hill and down the easier slope on the other side. Edward roared incoherently behind them, staggering a few steps and then falling as he turned his foot on some unseen stone. Vomit spilled from his mouth, old wine and clear spirit mixed in acid so rough that it stung his broken skin.

'I'll find you! Find *you*, insolent whoresons . . .'

Rolling on to his back, he slipped into sleep, half aware that he would not know them again. York snored noisily, with a Welsh mountain under him, anchoring him to the earth as the sky turned above.

It was raining as Margaret's lords gathered, the downpour hissing on the canvas and making the poles creak with the weight of sodden cloth. Derry Brewer folded his arms, looking across the faces of the queen's most senior commanders. Henry Percy had lost more than anyone else in that great pavilion. The Earl of Northumberland wore his family on his face, the great blade of the Percy nose marking him out in any group. The price the Percy family had paid gave the young earl a certain gravity among them – in Derry's eyes, the loss of his father and brother had matured him, so that he rarely spoke without thought and wore his dignity like a cloak around his shoulders. Earl Percy could easily have led them against Warwick, but it was the even less experienced Somerset who had been put in command. Derry allowed himself to glance over at the queen sitting so demurely in the corner, still rose-cheeked and slim. If it was true she had turned to Somerset in the months of her husband's absence, she had been remarkably discreet about it. Somerset remained unmarried at twenty-five, which was sufficiently rare to raise eyebrows on its own. Derry knew he should counsel the duke to marry some willing heifer and produce fine, fat babies before too many tongues wagged.

Half a dozen minor barons had gathered at the queen's

summons. It pleased Derry that Lord Clifford had been placed among them on the benches, where they sat like squirming schoolboys called to their lessons. Clifford had killed York's son at Wakefield and then waved a bloody dagger at the father in spiteful triumph. It would have been hard to like the man after that, even if he'd been a paragon of virtue. As it happened, Derry thought Clifford was both pompous and weak – a hollow fool.

It was strange how far and fast the story of York's son being cut down had spread, on its own wings almost, so that Derry's web of informers had reported being told it many times since. The queen was also coming south with an army of howling, barking northerners, accompanied by painted savages from the Scots mountains. She had apparently taken heads and marked her men with the blood of York, delighting in the destruction of innocent boys. The stories were well planted and Derry could only wonder if there was a mind like his behind them, or if it was just the careless cruelty of rumour and gossip.

Derry's clerk had finished reading the long description of Warwick's forces, culled from a dozen men like Lovelace to build a picture Derry believed was fairly accurate. Positions would change, and certainly the movement of armies could alter an entire battle before it began, but for once he was confident. Warwick had dug in. He *could* not move again. The spymaster nodded to his man in thanks, waiting to discuss or defend his conclusions.

It was Baron Clifford who chose to reply, the man's braying voice enough to make Derry grit his teeth.

'You would have us move the army like pieces on a board, Brewer? Is that how you think war should be fought?'

Derry noted the 'us'. For six years, Clifford had been

trying to include himself in the ranks of nobles who had lost their fathers – along with Earl Percy of Northumberland and Somerset. Those two seemed to bear no malice towards him, but neither did they show Clifford especial warmth, as far as Derry could see. He had not answered Clifford's first questions, suspecting they were rhetorical. He decided to let the baron blow himself out.

'Well? Should spies and sneaking cutpurses decide how a royal army takes the field?' Clifford demanded. 'I do not believe I have ever heard the like! From what you say, it seems that *Warwick* is the one who understands honour, even if you do not! You say he has placed himself across the road to London, there to challenge us. Yes! *That* is how men of honour go to war, Brewer: without sneaking subterfuge, without lies and treacheries. I am appalled at what I have heard here today, I really am.'

To Derry's irritation, Margaret kept silent. She had experienced some of the joy and grief of direct command in the far north and she had not found it to her liking. More, he thought Somerset had made some private argument for her to defer to his authority. Somerset was the man he had to persuade, not Clifford, or even Earl Percy, though it would be easier if one of those agreed the course Derry had laid out.

'My lord Clifford,' Derry began. He could not say the man was a pompous simpleton, though he slowed his words to be understood. 'With your training and experience, you know battles have been fought where one side manoeuvred before the clash of arms. Fortresses have been taken in the flank before, my lord. That is all I have proposed. My task, my charge, is to provide my lords with all the information they might require.'

Clifford opened his mouth to speak but Derry went on, forcing an even chillier calm.

'My lord, Warwick has made a fortress of the road to London, with cannon and spiked nets and ditches and ramparts and all the other things the men must overcome to take one step past him. All my reports . . .' He paused as Clifford snorted. '*All* my reports say he faces north, my lords. That he has set his spears and cannon to destroy an enemy coming from the north. It is, I suggest, the *merest* common sense to swing past him and avoid the most vicious part of his defence.'

'And show *fear* to a smaller force!' Clifford said in exasperation. 'To show our fellows that we take the Neville dogs seriously, that we respect traitors and treat them as equals rather than dead wasps to be swept away and burned. By those same reports, Master Brewer, we have five *thousand* more men in the field! Do you deny it? Ours are the victors against York! We outnumber Warwick's Kent farmers and London beggars – and you would have us dodge and weave like a boy stealing apples? I say to you all – where is the *honour* in that?'

'You do have a fine turn of phrase, my lord Clifford,' Derry replied, his voice and smile growing tighter, 'but there is a chance here to keep the lives of those men you command – to damage Warwick or even destroy him, without breaking your ranks on the defences he has set up. My lord, I see *little* honour in . . .'

'I believe that will do, Master Brewer,' Somerset murmured, raising his hand. 'Your argument does not grow stronger by repeating it. I am certain we have understood the main thrust.'

'Yes, my lord.' Derry said. 'Thank you.'

He sat down on a chair that wobbled, wincing as his right knee twinged and threatened to cramp. He was cold, aching and fed up with arguing with fools and younger men who outranked him. He had been so long away from King Henry that the font of his authority had run dry. There had been a time when all men had feared Derry Brewer, for his connections to men of power – and to the fountainhead itself. These days, he had to argue his points with asses like Clifford who needed to have their noses pulled down from where they had been lifted into the air.

'I do not fear Warwick's army,' Somerset said.

'Of course not!' Clifford muttered, silenced by a warning glance.

'It is true that they have had a month or so to prepare a defence, while we marched as slowly south as any group of washerwomen.' Somerset held up his hand to quell a rising grumble of objection. 'Peace, gentlemen. I know the men had to be fed, but the result is that Warwick has been given time – and with his wealth, I do not doubt he enjoyed the resources of London. More, he has King Henry and a strange sort of . . . influence from that. Though the king is a prisoner, I believe we are all aware he will not be crying out or attempting to escape. Yet, despite all such things, they are too small a force of Kentish, London, some Sussex and Essex lads. I do not fear *that* army – but of course there is another.'

Somerset looked around at the gathered men, his gaze resting briefly on Margaret, though she did not look up from where her hands lay in her lap.

'York's son, Edward, shall I call him York now? He who was the Earl of March, who had no more than a few thousand in Wales and still managed to break the forces of three Tudors, killing the father and scattering the sons. Perhaps he has not recruited others to his banners after that victory, though there are angry men all over the country who might walk to him if called. York is a royal house and he could threaten us. If York joins Warwick, they are almost our match – certainly too close in number for any comfort.' He shook his head. 'Like Warwick, I might wish for an enemy in front of me, ready to fight and die, but York's son will surely come against us in time – and he could strike our flank.'

Somerset paused to take a breath, looking around at them all.

'My lords, my lady, Master Brewer, we cannot dance with Warwick and be caught between them. We cannot let him call the tune. If Master Brewer's informers have brought news of a fortress with a weak flank, my orders will be to take any advantage we have been offered. I do not see the especial honour of sending thousands of men to die against a well-fortified position, Lord Clifford. Caesar manoeuvred on the field, I believe. In these very fields perhaps, John!'

Derry saw Clifford smile and dip his head. For some reason, he suddenly could not bear to see the man relaxed in such company. It might have been another aspect of growing older, but he could not let the moment pass.

'If I might explain it to Baron Clifford, my lord, there is a difference between killing a wounded boy as he runs away and attacking a solid defence that has . . .'

'Brewer! Hold your *tongue!*' Somerset snapped at him before Clifford could do more than stare in shock. 'No, get out! How *dare* you speak in such a way before me! I will consider your punishment. *Out!*'

Derry bowed deeply to Margaret, seething more at him-self than anyone in that tent. He found some grim satisfaction that he had given voice to Clifford's crime. York's son had been seventeen and no threat to anyone as he tried to run from the field at Sandal. Derry didn't know if the boy had been wounded, but he'd added the detail to make Clifford all the more the spiteful bully he actually was. That was how stories grew.

Derry kept his back stiff as he left the tent, knowing he had gone too far. In the colder air, as his anger seeped away, he felt old and weary. Clifford could call him out, though Derry suspected the man would neither lower himself nor take the risk of a duel before witnesses. Der-ry's best years were behind him, of a certainty, but he'd still bash Clifford to a brainless pulp if he had the chance, and the man would know it. No, it would be a knife in the dark, or chopped cat whiskers in his food to make him puke blood.

Derry looked up miserably to the spire of the village chapel, built on land owned by the Stokker family of Wyboston. It was not high enough to protect him from hard men seeking him in the night. He'd just have to stay awake and in company. He did not curse himself for aggra-vating Clifford or even Somerset. There was an absence of power around Margaret, ever since the death of York. With her chief enemy dead and her husband still in captiv-ity, she had lost some of the fierceness that had driven her for years, almost as if she did not know exactly how to go on. Into that emptiness had stepped men like Somerset, bright and ambitious young fellows, looking far to the future. Weaker sods like Clifford were doing no more than choosing a champion to flatter.

It was hard not to hope, Derry knew. York was dead, Salisbury with him, after years of having their hands on the throne as if they had a damned right to it. The loss of King Henry was the only itch still to be scratched – one poor innocent held by men with every reason to hate him. The truth was that if Henry had been killed, his queen would not grieve for too long. Derry could see how her eyes brightened when they rested on Somerset. It was hard to miss, if you looked for it.

4

Nightfall brought a freezing wind, even colder than the day. Hunched into the icy blast, the queen's army swung away from the London road. At Somerset's order, they left the wide, flat stones, cutting west, the men's boots crunching frosty earth. Scouts waited for them on horses, waving torches to keep them on the right path, close by the town of Dunstable. That had been Derry's suggestion, to make fifteen thousand men disappear overnight while Warwick's scouts waited in vain for the first glimpse on the road south.

In the days since Derry had seen Lord Clifford reduced to red-faced frustration, no one had sidled close or even threatened the spymaster. He had not relaxed his vigil, knowing men like Clifford and their spite rather well. There had been no word from Somerset either, as if the young duke preferred just to ignore and forget any insult he had witnessed. Derry knew if Somerset changed his mind, the result would be something like a public flogging – carried out without embarrassment, in full view of the men. Clifford had neither the authority nor the manhood to arrange such a thing. From him, Derry expected an attack when he was distracted. As a result, without a solid and definite intention, Derry had begun to plan for the man's quiet disappearance. Yet even for a spymaster, removing a king's baron from the world was no small task.

The ranks of marching men woke the terrified inhabitants of Dunstable with a parade of torches and what had already become a weary demand to 'bring out victuals or livestock'. It wasn't as if the people of the town had much left by the end of winter. The bulk of their stores had been consumed during the hard months.

For once, Queen Margaret and her son were there on horseback to oversee the army's passage through the town. There would be no destruction in her presence, at least under the light of the torches. Derry had no doubt the gleanings would be much poorer as a result. He heard someone begin shrieking in a back street and would have sent a few lads over with cudgels, if Somerset hadn't reacted first and given the order. A dozen men were brought back to the main road, yelping as they were struck and lashed along. Some raised their voices in complaint, until one of the captains snapped furiously that he could, if he wished, treat them all as deserters. That shut them up like a scold's bridle. The penalties for desertion were meant to discourage men who might consider it, perhaps over the cold, dark hours of a winter watch. There was much mention of iron and fire in those traditions, learned and recited by men who could not read or write.

The nights in February were long enough to hide most sins. By the time the army had flooded through Dunstable, all the shops and houses on the main street had been stripped of food. Wailing voices filled the air and the last of the soldiers trudged head down against the wind, weapons clutched in numb hands.

Outside the town, the darkness became paler. An ancient forest of oak, holly and white birch lay thick there, able to swallow even such a host. In the gloom under its boughs, the men were allowed to rest and eat, knowing that they merely gathered strength to fight. Blades were sharpened and leather oiled. Rotten teeth were pulled by blacksmiths with their pincers of black iron. Serjeants and camp servants simmered cauldrons of onions and stiff threads of venison. For most, the share was little more than a thin, greasy water. They still filled mugs with jealous care, watching every drop and smacking their lips.

Those who could hunt loped away to seek out grouse and rabbit, foxes or still-hibernating hedgepigs, anything at all. The hunters had been paid for their efforts in the beginning. When there were no more coins, they had continued the work, taking a larger share for themselves instead. There had been one hunter who made a point of keeping everything he snared, once there was no money to pay him. He'd spent a night eating a fine hare over a small fire, watched by many. His body had been found hanging the following morning and no one had even heard a cry. Men died on a long march, that was all there was to it. They fell down or wandered away, blank-faced from hunger or exhaustion. Some were flogged back into line. Others were left where they fell, to breathe their last as the rest marched by and stared without shame at an interesting sight on the road.

Once the queen's army had some soup in their bellies, they set off, striking out into a grey dawn, heading towards the horizon as the sun began to rise. They were still strong enough, still hard enough. They had swung right round St Albans in the night, so that they came from the southwest. Some of them showed their teeth as they loped along, imagining the surprise and fear in Warwick's men when they saw an entire ragged army just a-strolling up behind them.

*

Sitting high on a fine black gelding, Warwick stared at the road stretching north. The sun was rising into a clear sky, though the wind was chill and blew right through him. The hill and town of St Albans lay at his back, topped over all by the abbey. That thought brought a twinge of irritation as he recalled Abbot Whethamstede in his finery, giving sage advice as one who had witnessed the battle on the hill six years before. As Warwick had played his own vital part in that victory for York, he could hardly understand how the older man thought it was reasonable to lecture him on the details yet again. The abbot had taken up a good portion of the previous evening with grisly descriptions, related with what appeared to be great fondness.

Warwick shook his head to clear it. His only concern was the queen and the army coming south against him. The wonder was that they had not arrived already. Somehow, Margaret had allowed him time – and he had used it, twisting his rage and grief into ditches and ramparts. There was no road to London any more. His army had dug the land into deep clefts to ruin any cavalry charge against them. Nets of rope studded with spikes had come out of the London foundries, each upright blade twisted into the knots by hand. It was not that no one could breach such defences, but that in doing so they would have the heart torn out of them. Warwick's plan was to whittle the queen's larger army down, rank by rank, until the remnant was exhausted and bloody. Only then would he send in his three battles, ten thousand men to break the will and last hopes of Lancaster. He frowned at the thought, considering how little will remained in King Henry himself.

Henry rested not far away from where Warwick surveyed the great sprawling camp. The king sat in the shade of a bare oak tree, staring upwards through the branches, crossing in patterns above his head. The king seemed entranced. He was no longer tied, but then there was no need.

When he had first encountered the king's simple innocence, Warwick had wondered for a time if the man was gulling him, so perfectly did Henry play his part. Five years before, there had been tales of the young king returning from his sleeping state with something like a man's vigour. Warwick shrugged at the thought. If it had been so once, it was not so any longer. As he stared, some noise caught the king's attention. Henry gripped the earth in his hands and watched the bustle around him in fascination. Warwick knew if he approached, Henry would ask questions and appear to understand the answers, but no spark of will could make him rise from a spot once he was settled. He was a broken thing. Warwick might even have felt pity once, if that amiable child had not caused the death of his father. As it was, he knew only a cold scorn. The house of Lancaster did not deserve a throne, not if Henry was all they had to put on it.

Warwick turned his horse with a gentle clicking in his cheek and a twitch of the reins. He had seen three figures riding along the edge of the camp and trotted to intercept them. Two of the group were his brother John and their uncle Fauconberg, Neville men wedded to the cause. The third was less of a rock than Warwick might have desired, though de Mowbray, Duke of Norfolk, had done nothing to excite his suspicion. Still, the man outranked him and was his senior by a decade. It was true Norfolk had a Neville mother, but the same had been true for the Percy brothers – and they had chosen to support King Henry. Warwick sighed to himself. War made strange allies. For Norfolk's rank and experience, Warwick had given him the prestigious right wing, standing slightly ahead of the rest of the army in the great staggered line of squares. Of course, it was a co-incidence that Norfolk would meet the enemy first in the vanguard. If the duke planned anything like treachery, he would do least damage there and still allow Warwick to fight a desperate defence from further back.

Warwick shook his head a fraction as the three men reined in. His father's death had stolen some of the joy from the entire world, tainting things he had once taken for granted, without question. The old man's absence was a hole in his life, a loss so great he had not done more than peer over the edges of it. Warwick looked at friends and allies, looked even at brothers and uncles – and saw only how they might betray him.

He inclined his head courteously to William, Lord Fauconberg, but the man walked his horse closer, extending his arm until Warwick was forced to grip it and then drawing them together into a stiff embrace. It did not give Warwick pleasure to see aspects of his father's face in his uncle. It made the man hard to look upon, and there was always a smouldering resentment when Fauconberg talked intimately of his older brother, almost claiming some ownership out of his much longer knowledge. In some effort to comfort the sons, Fauconberg had told many tales of their father's childhood, but none of them trusted his versions without their father to confirm or deny the truth of them. In Warwick's eyes, his uncle was the lesser man. The three sons all honoured him in public, but Fauconberg assumed a far greater love from his nephews than they felt themselves.

47

Warwick could sense the man's dark-eyed gaze on him at that moment, like a hand touching his face. He had not particularly minded Fauconberg before, but since his father's death, wet-eyed Uncle William could drive him to rage with his mawkish pity and his damned touching.

Seeing thunder gathering in Warwick, John Neville reached out and clapped Fauconberg roughly on the shoulder. The brothers had agreed the gesture as a signal of private irritation, to be made when one or the other could not bear their uncle's pale reflection of their father any longer. Fauconberg took it all in good stead, of course, assuming he was being included in some manly gesture of family support. Between them, they had come close to knocking him out of his saddle more than once.

Warwick smiled for John, though his eyes remained cold. At least, in Montagu, John Neville had the title he had long desired, falling on him at the moment of their father's death. The Earldom of Salisbury had become Warwick's inheritance, another few dozen manors, castles and great houses, including his childhood estate of Middleham, where his mother still lived and wore black. Warwick cared nothing for any of it, though he knew John envied him lands that made him the richest man in England. Not even the house of York could match him then. Yet it was all tin, at least while his father's murderers lived and drank and whored and smiled. It was not right that the severed head of Salisbury should stare down from the walls of the city of York while his enemies prospered. Warwick dared not speak of that, though he felt it like an open wound. Any attempt to retrieve their father's head would see them all killed. It had to stay there, in the wind and rain, while his sons laboured on.

Warwick's gaze turned again to the distant figure of King Henry, sitting and dreaming away the short winter's day. John had called for his death, of course, the younger man seeing only an eye for an eye, a father for a father. Yet in Henry's case, Warwick suspected the king was not much loved even among his own people. While he remained alive, Henry was a weakness in the queen and her loyal lords. Henry was the piece of fat in the wolf-trap, and his followers could not ignore such a fine and royal bait. Warwick knew the king's death would simply set Queen Margaret free to raise the man's son and try again.

Wind gusted into Warwick like a tongue in his mouth, making him gasp. He looked up into the pale face of the Duke of Norfolk, realizing the man had been staring and weighing him without saying a word. They had come together while Warwick had been torn and raw with grief, and no man could say they were friends. Yet Norfolk had done him no wrong – and that counted for something after the treachery of so many.

The duke was thickset, his head more square than round and shaved to stubble from his crown to the point of his jaw. At forty-five, he showed the marks and scars of old battles on his face – and no trace of weakness at all, just a cold assessment. Warwick knew the man was related by blood to both York and Lancaster. There were just too many cousins standing on opposite sides, he thought. Looking at the man's powerful build as he sat so comfortably on his horse, Warwick gave thanks that Norfolk's Neville blood had run true.

'Well met, my lord,' Warwick said to Norfolk.

The older man dipped his head and smiled in response.

'I thought it could not hurt to ride across to you, Richard,' Norfolk said. 'Your uncle worries about you.'

There was a suggestion of a light in Norfolk's eyes as Fauconberg nodded solemnly. Warwick snorted air from his nose. There was no malice in Fauconberg, he was certain. It was beneath Warwick to find honest pity so cloying, but it had somehow become the very focus of his anger. Perhaps Norfolk was not such a block after all, if he had noticed what had escaped Fauconberg.

'Any reports from the scouts?' Warwick said, his mouth quirking on one side as he breathed out.

Norfolk shook his head, instantly stern at the business of the camp.

'None. No word at all, beyond a trickle of the dispossessed coming south, with all their complaints.' He saw Warwick open his mouth to speak and went on. 'Yes, as you ordered, Richard. They are fed and made warm, given a small purse and sent south to London. Strong lads are made to remain and join our ranks, of course, but there are enough old men and children wending their way to London with tales of horror. The queen will not be welcome in the south as word spreads.'

'No small thing,' Warwick's brother John added. 'To have her seen as she truly is? I would the whole country could know her as we do. As an honourless, faithless whore.'

Warwick winced slightly. It was not that he didn't agree with every word, but his younger brother was as brash and bluff in his way as Edward of York. There were times when neither man seemed to understand subtlety, as if a loud voice and a strong right arm were all a man needed. Warwick thought then of Derry Brewer and wondered if he still lived.

'John,' Warwick said, then added the title for a formal matter, 'Lord Montagu – perhaps you should oversee the hand-gun training for your men. There is a new batch of eighty come in and I have no experts yet to teach the others. They are still too slow to load after a shot.'

He saw his brother's eyebrows rise in interest, the younger man intrigued by the extraordinary weapons coming out of the city. Warwick had spent silver in a vast torrent, with half the forges and foundries of London working all hours to supply his men. The results were still causing awe each morning as carts arrived by the dozen, often with some new contrivance of blades or black powder. Every day before dawn, ranks of his new 'gunners' trooped out with long weapons of iron and wood over their shoulders. They stood in ranks, pouring in heavy-grained powder, ramming home a ball, or pellets of lead, and then blocking the muzzle with a plug of wool to stop it all rolling back out. They were learning as they went, and God knew the weapons didn't have anything like the range of a longbow. Warwick's redcoat archers had been amongst the first to volunteer to try the guns, but by the end of the first day, to a man they had handed them all back and returned to their old weapons. It was the time between shots that had worried them, compared with stroking out arrows breath by breath. Yet Warwick had hopes for the guns as a defensive tool, to break a massed attack, say, or to unhorse a group of officers. He saw potential for them, used at exactly the right moment. The roar of sound they made was simply astonishing at close range. His first test-firing rank had dropped their own guns and bolted for cover at the thunder and fog. For that alone, he thought they might have a place on the field of war.

John, Lord Montagu, touched his hand to his forelock. Warwick dipped his head in response, wishing he could feel the same excitement he saw in his brother. He had a stronger bond to John since their father's death, that was undeniable. As affection for their uncle drained away, so the friendship between Richard, John and Bishop George Neville grew more firmly rooted. They had common cause, after all.

Warwick and Norfolk turned almost together as a horn sounded behind them, high on the hill of St Albans. Norfolk twisted his head to favour a sharper ear, then stiffened as the bell of St Peter's Church began to toll across the town.

'What does that mean?' John Neville asked his uncle, not yet experienced enough to understand the shock in the others. Fauconberg shook his head, speechless. It was Warwick who answered, crushing down his own panic to speak calmly.

'It is an attack. The bell would not sound for anything else. John, your men are closest. Send a dozen knights and a hundred of your lads to check the town. I have just a few archers up by the abbey – wounded men, recovering from strains or broken bones. Go, John! The bell won't have been rung for nothing. They're coming. Until we know numbers and positions, I'm blind down here.'

Warwick looked bleak for a moment as John raced away. He had spent a month building a great palisade of spikes and guns and men across the north road – and the bastards had come from behind him. He felt his face burn as Norfolk and his uncle waited for orders.

'Gentlemen, return to your positions,' Warwick said. 'I'll send word as I hear.'

To his irritation, his uncle nudged his horse close and clapped him on the shoulder. There were tears in the older man's eyes, gleaming.

'For your father, Richard,' Fauconberg said. 'We won't fail.'

5

The massed ranks of the queen's army raced uphill towards the great abbey. Derry saw no hesitation in Somerset or Percy when it came to using the advantage his reports and spies had provided. The men were alive with excitement, shrugging off weariness at the chance to charge up behind an enemy army, to fall on them like a hawk stooping to crush some small animal into the ground. Many of them had punched another man without warning at some point in their lives, when some rogue or merchant had not been expecting a blow. There might have been little honour in it, but surprise was one of the great factors of war and counted almost as much as strength of arms. Derry found his own heart pounding as he rode Retribution along a street. He looked out on the rising sun and saw Warwick's great camp below, in three huge squares across the north road.

The men around him did not pause to take in the view. Their task was to tear out the heels of the rearmost battle of men, standing under the banners of Lord Montagu. Those soldiers would be the weakest in supplies and quality; every man there knew it. The left battle would often be the last to engage, if they fought at all. For the men streaming down towards them through the shocked and empty streets of St Albans, that body of soldiers looked like the limping stag left behind by the herd.

Derry had no particular desire to follow them down.

His work ended when the fighting began, as far as he was concerned. He had brought Somerset and Earl Percy to the right spot. It was up to them to drive the knife home. He considered making a sketch of the great squares of men stretching away from St Albans, at least the ditches and main groups, but thought better of it as panicky voices began roaring somewhere close, echoing back from the walls of the abbey.

'Watch it there, you clumsy sod! There!' Derry heard, turning his horse on a tight rein to listen and find the source. He did not know the voice.

'Archers! 'Ware archers!' another yelled, higher, more afraid.

Derry swallowed nervously, suddenly sensing he was a nice target for any bowman who came across him. He hunched down in the saddle, ready to kick with his heels and risk bolting.

A side door creaked open in the abbey, revealing a thick mop of dark hair and deathly white skin, darting out and looking around. The sight of Derry Brewer staring did not seem to worry the man and he gave a low whistle. As Derry watched, a dozen others came out, some hobbling and limping, but carrying unsheathed knives and strung yew bows. Each one had some part of him stitched or bound in blood-stained cloth. They looked feverish: red-faced and eye-bright beyond even strong emotion. When they looked up at Derry Brewer, he quailed. It was already too late to run, he realized. A man who ran from archers needed to start when he was half a mile away, not twenty yards or so.

Derry understood that Abbot Whethamstede had allowed wounded men into the abbey for the monks to treat and heal. There were always accidents when men and fire and iron blades came together. With his mind spinning, Derry recalled how his old friend William de la Pole used to say that 'Stupidity' was the fifth horseman of the Apocalypse, from the Book of St John of Patmos. Without Latin or Greek, Derry had never been able to read the passage, to see if he'd been telling the truth. Under the gaze of enemy soldiers, he had the feeling he might be meeting that horseman, with its braying laughter. He shuddered.

The group of injured men had come to an end, just thirteen of them, with eight archers, though one of those had lost an eye and surely much of his accuracy. Derry's mind tended to focus on small things when he was afraid. The simple fact of it was that these men would kill him in a heartbeat if they knew which side he was on.

'You lads are not to fight,' he said suddenly. 'You've been told to rest and heal. What good are you wounded?'

'More good than killed in our beds,' one of them snapped, suspicious. 'Who are you?'

'Master Peter Ambrose. I am an aide to my lord Norfolk,' Derry said indignantly. 'I have some knowledge of the physic and I was sent to observe the Gentle Brothers in their work, perhaps to learn a balm or an unguent.'

He stopped himself, knowing that liars ramble. His heart was trying to shrink in his chest as he realized he'd made himself useful to such men. Still, they would have no desire to see him dead if he might help with their wounds and dressings.

'You'll come with us, then, down the hill,' the same man said, glowering at him.

He carried a yew bow lightly in his right hand, rocking it at the balance point. The man's thumb rubbed the wood back and forth and Derry could see a whiter patch there, from years of the same motion. The archer was ready for him to run, he was suddenly certain. To turn away would mean an arrow in his back. They stared at each other coldly.

'Down, Brewer!' came a voice from his right.

Derry dropped from the saddle, risking his neck by simply going limp and sliding off like a dead man. He heard Retribution snort and used the animal's bulk as cover while he wormed swiftly away on his elbows, tense with expectation of an arrow pinning him to the earth. Thumps and cries diminished behind him, cut short in savagery. Derry kept going, head down, until he heard footsteps running up behind him, loping along with a young man's easy balance.

Unseen, Derry slid a dagger from his coat, drawing his legs under him and coming up ready to launch himself. He was slow, he could feel it. Movement that in his youth had been cat-fast had become clumsy, thick-bodied and just *slow*. For one who had once revelled in his strength and agility, the self-awareness was hugely depressing.

The soldier who stood over him held up both hands, one with a bloodied hatchet in it. He was disgustingly young and visibly amused by Derry's dusty, puffing anger.

'Easy there, Master Brewer! We're pax, or whatever you say. Same side.'

Derry looked past him to where a heaped group of bodies wore new quills fletched in good white feathers. One or two still moved, their legs shifting on the flagstones as if they were trying to rise. Somerset's archers were among them already, cutting out the shafts with ruthless efficiency. Each arrow had been the labour of an expert hand and was far too valuable to be left behind. Derry felt a twinge of regret for those wounded men. Sometimes, whether a man lived or died was down to luck. He did not know if that realization made him value his own life more or less. If death could come because you chose the wrong door leading out into the sun, perhaps there was no sense to any of it – just the fifth horseman. He shrugged to himself, putting such thoughts aside. One thing about his life that he did enjoy – there was always someone he wanted to die before him. No matter what else happened, Derry Brewer wanted to die *last*. That was the path to happiness, right there – to outlive every last one of the bastards.

His horse, Retribution, had lost a bit of hide. An arrow had torn a stretch of his haunch and still hung from a strip of skin, snagged and dripping bright blood. With a wince, Derry worked it free, patting the torn skin back into place and soothing the animal with his voice. At least there were no flies in winter to settle on wounds.

More ranks of archers and swordsmen marched past him, joining the throng heading downhill to the squares of men below. He could hear the crash of arms and high-called orders at the foot of the hill, where he'd once stared down at Richard of York's much smaller army. Derry could hear Warwick's drummers rattling death at the queen's men, at that moment and six years before, the memories mingling as the wind tried to freeze his eyes open.

The drummers could not hold back the attack. As Derry watched, he could see a great bite appear in the leftmost square as it was charged and rolled up. A nimble army might have turned to face the queen's forces – perhaps some had. Yet half Warwick's men were standing in trenches and ditches facing north, unable to deploy quickly to a new direction.

Duke Somerset, Earl Percy of Northumberland, even Lord Clifford and the other barons took their men in at a reckless pace, recognizing an opportunity. Warwick's squares *would* turn; his archers would scramble back to slow the queen's army down while they did so. The outcome of the battle hung on how much damage and destruction could be done to that rear square before Warwick's forces re-formed to face their tormentors.

Derry rested his cheek against the whiskery soft muzzle of Retribution and stared across miles of farmland, pleased to be out of the fray. It might have been a moment of calm and beauty if two armies hadn't been clashing on the open fields. At such a distance, Derry could barely see the banners. It was certainly too far off to mark individual men, or anything more than the main sweeps and charges, like herds moving across the earth.

He had stood in a few lines of that kind, when he'd been young. Derry jerked his head, feeling a shiver run the length of his back as if his skin wanted to leap off him. He knew there was awful slaughter going on below, the final gasping instants when it comes down to two men rushing at each other with a club or a blade, with the will to stand until one of them dropped. And then again, and then again, until a man could hardly raise his sword as yet another young fellow steps up, all fresh and smiling, beckoning him in.

Warwick sat with his hands numb on the reins, his fingers half frozen as they gripped the leather. His breath was visible, but with a thick wool coat under his armour, he was warm enough, a heat fed by both anger and embarrassment. He could hear his captains yelling orders to turn and face the enemy, but over them all, clearly visible, the streets of St Albans had become rushing streams of soldiers, pouring out on to the plain and biting into Montagu's ranks like a devouring acid. Warwick shook his head, so furious with himself and with them that he could hardly summon his wits to command. Yet he did so. His horse and personal guard became the centre of galloping messengers, racing in to hear his orders, then charging away with cries for others to get out of their way. His captains knew their trade, but the Kent and London soldiers were raw, not used to quick manoeuvres on the field. It was one reason why Warwick had depended so heavily on a fortified position against the queen's more experienced army. He knew his men had courage, but they had to be told when to stand or to retreat, when to flank and bolster a line, when to attack. The grand movements were the concern of the most senior officers, while big-handed labourers and fighting men decided the details with sharp iron.

Warwick sent all his archers back in two trotting groups along the flanks. He clenched one fist as they began to send looping volleys soaring against the men still streaming down the hill. Not one in a score would strike at that range, but the queen's forces would come with more caution under that whirring, hissing barrage.

Warwick sent a boy to give his compliments to Norfolk. Through no fault of its own, the duke's vanguard was as far as it could possibly be from the fighting. Norfolk had not moved at all since he had returned to his men. Warwick had no idea if his colleague had frozen in shock or was simply waiting to see the best use of his forces. The runner went with no orders, simply the expectation of some word from the duke to bring back.

With that done, Warwick shook off the last of the lethargy that had made his thoughts slow. His own square of three thousand men had turned as best it could, climbing out of trenches and ramparts. It broke his heart to see it, but half the obstacles he had set for the enemy had become irritations to his own men forced to walk over them. Caltrops strewn across the ground sank in partway, making them invisible in the mud. Horses had to go wide around any field of those, for fear of ruining the animal for the price of a couple of iron nails bound together and tossed down. It was slow work and Warwick continued to command and harangue his officers. His brother John was deep in the thick of the fighting, his banners seeming to hold back a tide that threatened to spill right around him.

Warwick thought then of King Henry. He could still see the tree where the king sat, unshackled. The man was close enough to stroll to his wife's forces if he'd had the wit or the will. Warwick raised a gauntlet to his bare forehead, pressing hard enough over his closed eyes to leave a print of scales. His hand-gunners were assembling in awkward ranks. His archers had slowed the enemy. His men-at-arms were ready to march.

Warwick sent one simple order to Norfolk, calling him in. He did not know if he could save his brother John, or even the left wing, but he could still turn the battle and prevent a rout. He muttered the words to himself in growing desperation.

6

King Henry came to his feet as a flood of marching men raced past him. His knees were aching, but he wished to confess to Abbot Whethamstede. The old man heard his sins every morning, a ceremony of great pomp and splendour, with a silent heart to it as Henry whispered his failings and his guilts. He knew he had lost good men through his weakness and poor health, men like William de la Pole, Duke of Suffolk; men like Richard, Duke of York, and Earl Salisbury. Henry felt every death like another coin on the scales of his shoulders, twisting his bones, bearing him down. He had liked Richard of York, very much. He had enjoyed their conversations. That good man had not known the danger of standing against the king. Heaven cried out against blasphemy, and Henry knew York had been broken for his pride – yet the sin was also the king's, as one who had not forced York to understand. Perhaps if Henry had made that truth ring in York's ears, the man would live yet.

The king had heard the talk in the camp, heard the fate of York and Salisbury and York's son Edmund. He had witnessed the pain and hatred caused by those deaths, the ragged need for vengeance that took them all into darker lands, beginning to spiral together faster and faster like leaves in a gale. Under that weight of guilt, Henry was little more than one bright spot in the void, weak and flickering.

Around his oak, thousands of the queen's men were

trotting, jingling, riding, spilling out of the town with faces still flushed from descending the hill. Two knights remained by the king, a tiny island of stillness left behind as Neville lines retreated. The most senior, Sir Thomas Kyriell, was a great bear of a man, a grey-haired veteran of two dozen years at war. His moustaches and beard were oiled and about as heavy as his appalled expression.

Henry wondered if he should call to one of the passing men-at-arms, to say he would like to be taken up to the abbot. He took great breaths of the cold air, knowing that it sharpened his thoughts to do so. As he watched the men, many of them turned their heads to the lone figure, standing with one hand on the trunk of an ancient tree, smiling at them while they marched to the killing. One or two gestured back aggressively, somehow irritated by the peace and good humour they saw in him, so out of place on that field. They drew thumbs across their throats, raised fists, touched their teeth or jerked two fingers at the small group of three men. The movements reminded Henry of his music master at Windsor, who would cut the air with his hands for silence before every tune. It was a happier memory and he began at first to hum and then to sing a simple folk song, almost to the rhythm of the marching ranks.

Sir Kyriell cleared his throat, going a deeper shade of red.

'Your Grace, though that is a fine, strong tune, perhaps it is not suited for today. It is too sweet for soldiers' ears, I think. Certes too sweet for mine.'

The knight was sweating as the king laughed and continued to sing. The chorus was close and no song should be denied its chorus – old Kyriell would see that when he heard it.

'And *when* the green is seen again, and the larks give song to *spring*...'

One of the passing men in armour turned his head at the sound of a cheerful voice in such a place. The fighting was not far ahead, with screams and rushing arrows and the clamour of metal on metal mingling with men's growling voices. They knew that music well, all of them. The high tenor calling out a song of spring was enough to make the knight rein in and raise his helmet.

Sir Edwin de Lise felt his heart thump beneath his breastplate as he stared beneath the stark oak branches. The great tree looked dead, but it spread in twisting boughs for fifty feet in all directions, waiting for the green to return. At the foot of a massive trunk, two knights stood to flank one man, with their swords drawn and resting on the ground before them. They resembled stone effigies, still and dignified.

Sir Edwin had seen King Henry once before, at Kenilworth, though at a distance. With care, he dismounted and pulled the reins over his horse's head to lead the animal. As he ducked under the outermost branches, the knight removed his helmet completely, revealing a young face, flushed with awe. Sir Edwin was blond and wore a straggling moustache and beard, gone untrimmed for an age on the march and the campaign. He tucked the helmet under his arm and approached the three men, seeing tension in the pair who flanked their unarmoured charge. Sir Edwin noted the dirt that marred clothes of great quality.

'King Henry ...?' he murmured in wonder. 'Your Majesty?'

Henry broke off his singing at the words. He looked up, his eyes as blank as a child's.

'Yes? Have you come to take me to confession?'

'Your Grace, if you will permit it, I will take you to your wife, Queen Margaret – and to your son.'

If the knight had expected a rush of gratitude, he was disappointed. Henry tilted his head, frowning.

'And Abbot Whethamstede? For my confession.'

'Of course, Your Grace, whatever is your will,' Sir Edwin replied. He looked up, sensing a subtle shift in the way the older knight stood.

Sir Kyriell shook his head slowly.

'I cannot let you take him.'

Sir Edwin was twenty-two years old and certain of his strength and right.

'Don't be a fool, sir. Look around you,' he said. 'I am Sir Edwin de Lise of Bristol. What is your name?'

'Sir Thomas Kyriell. My companion is Sir William Bonville.'

'You are men of honour?'

The question drew a spark of anger from Sir Kyriell's eyes, but he smiled even so.

'I have been called so, lad, yes.'

'I see. Yet you hold the *rightful king* of England as a prisoner. Give His Grace into my care and I will see him returned to his family and his loyal lords. Or I must kill you.'

Sir Kyriell sighed, feeling his age in the face of the younger man's simple faith.

'I gave my word I would not give him up. I cannot do as you ask.'

He knew the blow was coming before it began. A more experienced warrior than the young man might have called for support from the ranks, perhaps even a few archers to grant him overwhelming force. Yet in his youth and power, Sir Edwin de Lise had not imagined a future where he could possibly fail.

As Sir Edwin began to draw his sword, Kyriell stepped in quickly and jammed a narrow blade into his throat, then stepped back with sorrow written deep in the lines of his face. The young knight's sword clicked back into its scabbard. The two stared at each other, Sir Edwin's eyes widening in shock as he felt his warm blood spilling and his breath spattering droplets from his throat.

'I am truly sorry, Sir Edwin de Lise of Bristol,' Kyriell said softly. 'Go to God now. I will pray for your soul.'

The action had not gone unnoticed. As Sir Edwin fell with a crash, voices shouted in anger and warning. Those walking by were ready to fight, their pulses racing, their faces flushed. They were like wild dogs scenting blood in the air, and yet they did not rush the grey-haired figure in silver armour glaring at them all. More than a few of those men chose to look away from him, leaving the task to another. Yet there were enough. Men with billhooks stepped out and approached the tree, rushing the armoured knight who had killed one of theirs. Above them all, it began to rain, sheeting down across the field and making them all cold and sodden in an instant.

Sir Thomas Kyriell did not raise his sword again. In grief and shame, he only turned his head a fraction to present his neck, so that the first swinging blow struck him dead. His companion struggled and roared until he was battered from his feet and his throat gorget hammered in with an axe-handle, so that Sir William Bonville choked to death in his armour.

Resting one shoulder against the oak, King Henry shivered

slightly, though it was the cold and the rain that raised his skin like a Christmas goose. He watched the deaths of his captors with no more horror or interest than he would have shown at the plucking of such a bird for the table. When the violence came to an end and those present turned to him, the king asked quietly once again to be taken to the abbot for confession. More senior men came then to bear him away, awed by their fortune. They had come to rescue the king and he had fallen into their hands in the first moments of the fighting. If there had ever been a sign that God was on the side of Lancaster, it was surely then.

John Neville, Lord Montagu, staggered, breathing so hard he could feel his lungs curling like kidneys on a spit. There was blood running in veins on his armour, sliding and changing paths in the oil. He looked at the lines of red in confusion, slowly recalling a great blow that had rung his bell for him. Sparks of white shone at the edges of his vision, fading as the noise of fighting returned. One of his personal guard was staring at him, pointing to his eye.

'Can you see, my lord?' the man was asking, his voice oddly muffled.

John nodded irritably. Of course he could see! He shook himself again and saw that his shield had fallen to the ground. The rain was turning everything to mud, but the fighting went on. Montagu blinked, the dimness fading away, to be replaced by cries and clashes. He understood he'd taken some sort of blow to his helmet. He could see it by his feet, with a great dent in its crest and dome. Montagu looked up as a boy skidded to a stop at his feet. He'd come through marching lines like a rabbit through gorse, holding a spare helmet up to his lord and master.

The boy bowed his head as he presented the polished helm, panting visibly.

'Thank you,' Montagu managed.

He jammed it down over his head, feeling blood unstick from his cheek and fresh pain sharpen him further. He drew his sword and looked at the blade, standing perfectly still while all around him the forces of the queen pushed on and on.

'My lord, *please*, come with me now. We must fall back for a time.'

The knight had taken him by the elbow and was tugging at him. Montagu shook him off, feeling weak but angry once again. He swallowed vomit, almost choking on it as it rose without warning into his throat, burning the inside of his nose. Head wounds were strange things. He'd known one man who had lost his sense of smell after such a blow, and another who lost all kindness, even to his own family.

As a young knight of good form, John Neville had known for years that rage could let a man perform wondrous feats. He thought nothing of standing to face armed ranks. He had done so before in St Albans, when the lords Somerset and Percy had fallen. Their sons were lesser men – and they would not make him afraid. Though the sudden appearance of the queen's battle ranks had surprised him, the month of waiting and building his brother's defences had worn heavily. It had been almost a relief to hear the church bells, for all the shock of an attack coming from the south. John Neville gripped the leather wrap of his hilt, feeling he had the strength. This was still his chance to take a sword and smash it into the face of an enemy, perhaps the very man who had butchered his father. Dazed and in pain, he remembered roaring orders and sending messengers back for support. He could taste blood and felt it gumming his lips. They'd broken through his first ragged lines by then, rushing and howling.

Thousands of men had pounded down the hill towards his position, a flood of queen's soldiers carrying axes, swords and bows. His hatred had given way to a sense of dread as the massed ranks had torn his standing flank apart. He recalled a dying knight dragging him down and the roar and heave he had made to fling that man away. Another had come running in, depending on speed and the weight of armour to break through the shields held to stop him. John Neville's knights were sent tumbling, though they hammered his attacker into the ground. Two more lads with heavy billhooks had come at a sprint and the rain had begun to fall.

Montagu remembered that moment as clearly as any other, when the sky had suddenly filled with pale drops as far as he could see, so that the hill of St Albans blurred. In the wet and the mud, men slipped and went down, with limbs wrenched the wrong way, their screeching more pitiful than a death cry.

John Neville shook his head again, realizing he had been standing still for too long, like a bloodied statue. He could feel his scalp throbbing, but his spinning thoughts were slowing, growing clearer. He was John Neville. He was Lord Montagu. He could move. At his back, horns sounded and he knew Warwick was turning the army, bringing the main centre square out of its embankments and trenches. Norfolk would be riding along the open flanks, treading carefully across the trapped and spiked ground, to reach what had been the camp and the baggage and the safest spot on the field.

John Neville blinked rain and blood out of his eyes. His guards seemed to have gone; he stood alone. He turned to see the enemy and in that moment he was borne down, knocked on to his back in the mud with an axe half buried in his armoured chest and a man's heavy foot pressing down on his head.

'Pax! I am Montagu!' he shouted over the pain, spitting mud and foulness. 'John Neville. Pax.'

He was not sure if he had said the call for mercy and ransom aloud or just in the echoing vault of his head. His eyes rolled up and he did not feel his body lifted with the axe, crashing back into the soft mud as the blade came free from the metal.

7

Standing in his stirrups, Warwick watched in horror as his brother's position was engulfed. The furthest wing was overrun, but Warwick could see John standing alone. It could not have been more than a few heartbeats, yet it seemed an age, with the battle swirling around that one, still spot.

All his brother's guards had run or been slaughtered, the Montagu banners thrown down and trampled. Warwick found himself breathing shallowly, unable to look away as he gripped his reins and waited to see his young brother killed. The moment grew quiet, with all the clamour of his messengers and captains going unanswered. Warwick sucked in a sudden breath of freezing air, almost sobbing as he saw a line of roaring axemen thump John from his feet. Over a distance of six hundred yards, they were separated by thousands of soldiers, with trenches, carts and cannon. He could see nothing else.

Warwick squeezed his eyes closed. He opened them bloodshot, his lips pressed to nothing. The rain fell harder, sculpting his cloak in sopping folds and making his horse snort, flinging drops into the air.

He turned to his captains and saw his uncle Fauconberg had ridden up, a look of honest anger on his ruddy face. Warwick began to give a stream of orders, seeing the picture of the battlefield in his mind's eye and issuing commands to individual units that would hold the ground. Half the queen's forces were still coming down the hill. If he could shore up John's broken ranks, he might yet steady the lines. Margaret's northern savages would be like sheep running at a line of slaughtermen. It would not matter then how many she had been able to bring to the field. He would grind them up rank by rank – and he had the weapons to do it.

'Uncle, this for you. Bring up the cannon,' he called to Fauconberg. 'Have my crossbowmen and hand-gunners stand in support. Choose a line and set them ready. You understand? Braziers and supplies. Organ guns, bombards, culverins. When I give the order, I do not want the rate of fire to slow until we have pushed them back in *rags*.'

'We'll stop them here, Richard,' his uncle said. 'I swear it.'

Warwick stared coldly back until the man had turned his horse with a flourish and raced off, gathering a wake of serjeants and men-at-arms to carry out the orders.

The fighting continued on Warwick's left shoulder as John's reeling soldiers were forced back over their own dead. It was not edifying. Those men knew they were the worst of the York army – the old men and the boys and the one-eyed and the criminals. It was true they were not cowards, but no commander would risk his defence on whether or not such men would hold. They did not have much pride – and pride mattered.

Warwick looked up at the sound of longbows clattering, breathing in relief when he saw his red-coated archers still visible in long ranks. He knew they would be swearing and cursing the rain, hating the damp that warped their bows and stretched the linen cords. Those men had pride to spare. They'd stand for ever, in righteous fury against the men who were causing them to stand. He nodded to himself, taking heart from the constant rattle of shafts.

The assault was slowing, bogging down, giving his captains the time they needed to form a line of cannon. Whether iron or bronze, the big weapons were brutally heavy. Some had been mounted on wheeled gun carriages, while others had to be dragged on a keeled wooden sled like a boat, with groaning oxen under yoke. The weapons used a huge number of fighting men, sometimes as many as twenty to move, load and fire just *one* – men who would otherwise have been standing in line with the rest. Yet those guns were his joy – his pride.

Warwick wiped sweat and rain from his brow. For all his outward confidence, he was still staring at disaster. He could not allow himself to think of John falling. So soon after the loss of their father, it was too much to take in.

Seeing his cannon dragged across the field was enough to make a man weep, Warwick thought. They had been snug in structures of turf and brick, propped and aimed and surrounded by sheltered awnings for their precious stores of powder and shot. All that had been dug up and torn down. The tubes of black and bronze were shining in the rain, half covered by canvas that was as likely to snag under a wheel and be yanked clear as it was to protect the touch-hole in the breech. Still, a dozen of the largest bombard cannon made a terrifying sight when they were lined up together, heaved into place, with smaller culverins in between. The braziers were brought up by groups of four, carrying beams like oars, with the iron cage full of coals gripped between them. Warwick could hear the fires hissing and crackling as the rain increased. Some were spilled in their hurry, to rush a great wave of steam across the wet ground.

Behind the cannon teams came hundreds of his hand-gunners, trotting along with strained faces and their weapons wrapped in cloth, resting on their shoulders. Some of them had already loaded the long guns, pouring in black grains and lighting the slow fuse that coiled like a snake ready to be lowered in. The weapons were much cheaper than crossbows and the men needed only a day to learn their use. Warwick shook his head in dismay as the rain increased, the clouds thickening overhead as they poured across the sky. The new guns would be a wonder to behold, if they could be made to fire at all.

Rank by ragged rank, Warwick's army turned towards the sounds of iron. The red-coated archers bought them time on the wings, while Montagu's left wing fell back without their commander, stopping to gasp and swear and bleed once they were through the line of cannon.

The hand-gun ranks came out then to meet the enemy, standing with their heads bowed in the rain. The ground was slippery and men skidded and cursed as they brought their weapons to their shoulders and squinted down the iron barrels.

'Fire,' Warwick whispered.

His serjeants bellowed the order and puffs of smoke spread along the line as men touched fuses to damp powder. The ranks of the queen's soldiers did not flinch as they came forward in good order. They saw no threat in those facing them.

The rippling crack was more hiss than thunder. Rushing, stinging smoke shocked some of the queen's men to a halt. Gaps appeared as soldiers fell back, struck and dying. Before the rest of them could react, Warwick's gunners were turning their backs and running past the line of heavy guns to reload. A great roar of confusion and anger went up amongst the queen's forces – and the line of cannon replied. At no range at all, even a weakened shot tore through their ranks in a great welter of bone and limbs. With the enemy right upon them, Warwick's gun teams touched a hot wire or a taper to the powder in the touch-hole and then just ran, as the world shook.

Warwick felt his heart beating madly as gold flashed in the smoke and dirt amidst the queen's soldiers, hidden instantly by grey clouds. Men threw themselves down in panic, hiding their ears against the thump of sound that pressed against their skin and deafened them. Some who had been close to the guns and yet escaped rushed forward in a sort of madness, shrieking with weapons high and their eyes wild with death.

After the cannon had fired, the line was overwhelmed. One last single shot cracked out, behind the queen's ranks, perhaps on a longer fuse or damp powder. That ball smashed through running men. All the rest had fallen silent. Warwick clenched his fists as his hand-gunners were butchered, their weapons no more use than sticks. Some thirty of them tried to rally the retreat, and Warwick watched in despair as they stood in a line and brought their weapons up to aim. His spirits sank as they peered along the barrels, pulling the curved fuses into place and seeing only a damp puff of smoke or nothing at all.

The rain had ruined the moment and the queen's forces knew one thing – archers or crossbowmen had to be rushed. It was an old balance between the power of a spear or an arrow or a bolt – and the ancestral knowledge that if you could just get close, a chopping billhook was the best answer.

The queen's ranks gave a howl and the sound was terrible to all the hand-gunners still struggling with damp powder, scraping it out with their bare fingers and fumbling for a dry quantity in a purse or horn. Those who came at them carried axes and seax knives that would not fail in the rain. A few more guns cracked to send soldiers tumbling, but the rest of the hand-gunners were slashed and stabbed aside, run down.

Montagu's entire battle of men had been rolled up, the broken rags of it running back to interfere with the stronger centre. Those were Warwick's best-armoured knights, his Kentish veterans and captains.

Warwick was surrounded by bannermen and a dozen guards whose sole task was to protect him. He looked round as angry voices sounded over on his right, then he called on his men to let the Duke of Norfolk through.

Norfolk brought his own close group of riders, all in his colours. Their master wore no helmet once again. He stared at Warwick from under heavy brows, his head a block on a wide neck.

With a gesture, Warwick called the man closer. As a man in his forties, Norfolk was still in his prime, though oddly pale. Warwick wished again that he could trust the duke as he needed to. There had been betrayals before, between the houses of York and Lancaster. With all the stars lining up for Queen Margaret, Warwick could not afford another misjudgement.

'My lord Norfolk,' Warwick called as he approached, acknowledging his own lesser rank by speaking first. 'Despite this poor start, I believe we can hold them.'

To his irritation, Norfolk did not reply immediately, appearing to make his own assessment as his gaze swept over the broken rear, the abandoned cannon and the massed ranks still coming down out of the town. Norfolk shook his head, looking up into the rain so that it sheeted down his bare crown and face.

'I'd agree with you if the rain hadn't ruined all the guns. My lord, has the king been recaptured?'

It was Warwick's turn to look back over his shoulder to where the oak tree stood, far back in the ranks of queen's soldiers.

'The devil's own luck put Henry right in their path,' he said. 'I thought him safe at the rear, where no man could reach him.'

Norfolk shrugged, coughing into his hand.

'They have all they wanted, then. This battle is over. The best we can do now is to withdraw. We have lost only a few souls – fewer than six hundred, of a certainty.'

'My brother John among them,' Warwick said.

His own estimate of the dead was much higher, but Norfolk was trying to salve the news of the disaster. Warwick could not bring himself to feel the righteous indignation he might have felt at receiving such advice. The rain poured down and they were all wet and cold, shivering as they sat their horses and stared at one another. Norfolk spoke the truth, that King Henry's capture in the first moments meant the battle had been lost before it had properly begun. Warwick cursed the rain aloud, making Norfolk smile.

'If you choose to withdraw, my lord Warwick, it will be with the army largely intact and with little loss of honour. Edward of York will reach us soon and then . . . well, then we will see.'

Norfolk was a persuasive man, but Warwick felt a fresh spike of irritation intrude on his rueful mood. Edward of

York would be a roaring, stubborn, chaotic part of any campaign, he was certain. Yet like his father before him, there was the blood of kings in York, a stronger claim than any other except King Henry himself. The bloodline had power, that was the simple truth of it. Warwick hid his annoyance. If Lancaster was brought down, only York could take the throne, deserving or not.

At that moment, Warwick had more pressing concerns. He took a long look across the battlefield, wincing at the thought that any withdrawal to the north would take him past every yard of the useless defences he had prepared.

His gaze settled on where he had seen his brother fall. If he still lived, John would be held for ransom. He could hope for that. Warwick filled his lungs with frozen air, knowing it was the right decision from the sudden rush of relief he felt.

'Withdraw in good order!' he bellowed, waiting until his captains took up the cry. He groaned aloud at the thought of leaving his marvellous cannon behind, but that part of the field had already been overrun. There was no going back, even to hammer spikes down the barrels to ruin them for anyone else. Warwick knew he'd have to cast others in northern foundries, bigger guns, with weather-proof covers over the touch-holes.

His order was echoed a hundred times across the field. On another day, perhaps the enemy ranks might have pressed forward in response, delighted at the scent of victory. Under that downpour and in the sucking mud, they stopped as soon as a gap appeared, standing to wipe rain from their eyes and hair while Warwick's army turned its back on them and marched away.

*

Margaret sat in a pleasant tavern room, warmed by a fire of very dry wood. The owner had set an entire pig's head to simmer for the queen. In a cauldron, it bobbed in a dark liquor with vegetables and beans. As she watched, some part of the pale snout or face would surface to peer at her, before tumbling away and vanishing. It was oddly fascinating and Margaret stared at it as the inn bustled with her people all around. Her son Edward was sitting silently in a temper, having been prevented from poking the pig's face with a stick.

The usual patrons had been turfed out for her guards and her son. Margaret had heard some sort of scuffle in the street as some local lads objected. Her personal guard of Scots and English had been happy to run them off, helping along anyone too slow with their boots. The town had fallen quiet around the tavern and all she could hear was the drumming of rain on the roof, the murmur of voices and the steady hiss and flutter of the fire. She wound her hands in and out together, using the nails of one to clean the other.

Margaret had seen battle before, enough not to want to see it again. She found herself shuddering at the memories of crying men, their voices raised as high as women or slaughtered animals, shrieking. In all other walks of life, a sound of agony would cause some effort to stop it. A wife would run to her husband if he cut himself with an axe. Parents would run to a child keening in fever or with a broken bone. Yet on the field of battle, the ugliest of sobs and shrieks went unanswered, or worse, they revealed weakness in the wounded, drawing in predators. Margaret stared at the bobbing head of the pig as it faced her and she looked away, pimples standing up on her arms.

Outside, she heard horses draw up and men's voices calling out the watchword of the day to her guards. Derry Brewer had insisted on such things, saying he would look a right fool if he let the queen be captured for want of a few childish passwords and rituals. Margaret frowned as she heard the voice to match the name, wondering why her spymaster had returned from St Albans. Surely the battle could not have been won so early in the day?

Her son rose and ran to the open door, waving and calling a greeting. Margaret looked up sharply when he fell suddenly silent, his eyes grown wide. She was half out of her chair and rising as she heard a clatter of armoured men dropping to kneel on the cobblestones of the street. Derry's voice rang out, louder.

'Gentlemen, I give you His Grace, King Henry of England, Lord of Ireland, King of France and Duke of Lancaster,' he said.

Margaret could hear the satisfaction in his voice. She strode to the door and pressed past her son, still standing with his mouth hanging open like any village dolt. As her dress swept across the boy, Edward seemed to come awake and he rushed out with her into the rain and wind.

Margaret had not seen her husband in eight months, since she had saved her son and herself, leaving Henry alone in his tent at Northampton. She felt herself flush at the prospect of a rebuke, but raised her head even so, a fraction higher. Warwick and York had been triumphant then, carrying all before them to capture the Lancaster king. From that low point, Margaret had turned their victories right over. York and Salisbury were dead and Warwick was at bay. Her husband had *lived* through his ordeal. That was all that mattered.

Henry turned from dismounting and staggered under the impact of his son embracing him.

'Edward,' he said. '*Boy!* How you have grown. Is your mother here? Ah, Margaret, I see you there. Have you no embrace for me? It has been a long time.'

Margaret stepped out, feeling the wind like a slap. She bowed her head and Henry reached out almost wonderingly to her damp cheek. He was very thin, she saw, his skin as pale as the pig's face in the pot behind her. She knew he rarely ate unless pressed to do so, and those who had kept him would not have cared overmuch. Henry did not look strong and his eyes were as empty and guileless as they had always been.

'You are a Madonna, Margaret,' he said softly. 'A mother of great beauty.'

Margaret felt her colour deepen as she breathed. She was thirty years old and there were matrons of her age with a dozen brats and hips wide enough to have birthed them in litters. She knew she had her vanity, but that was a small sin in comparison to some others.

'My heart is full to see you, Henry,' she said. 'Now you are safe, we can pursue the traitors to their destruction.'

She knew better than to expect praise, but she felt herself curl with the need of it even so.

'I brought an army south, Henry,' she went on, unable to stop herself. 'All the way from Scotland, some of them.'

Her husband tilted his head, his eyes faintly quizzical, like a dog trying to discern the wishes of its mistress. Was it too much to ask that her husband might speak in love and praise to her, after a battle won and a rescue? Her heart seemed to shrink as he gazed back, blank as a man asked questions he did not understand. Margaret felt tears prickle into her eyes and she raised her head further so they would not spill.

'Come, my husband,' she said, reaching out to take him gently by the arm. 'You must be hungry and cold. There is a fire within and some broth. You'll enjoy both, Henry.'

'Thank you. If you say so, Margaret. I would like to see Abbot Whethamstede, for my confession. Is he close by?'

Margaret made a small, choked sound, almost a laugh, as they reached the warm interior of the inn.

'Oh, Henry, what sins could you possibly have managed in your captivity?'

To her surprise, his arm stiffened in her grip. He turned to her with a frown on his pale face.

'We are *creatures* of sin, Margaret, capable of lies and foul weakness even in our innermost thoughts. And we are weak in *mind*, so that sin creeps in. And we are frail in *body*, so that we can be swept from the world in a moment, choking – and gone! With sins untold and a soul damned for ever! You'd have me sit unshriven, while on my shoulder lies eternity? For what? A warm room? A bowl of soup?'

Her husband had grown red in his passion. Margaret drew him into her shoulder, comforting and shushing him as she might have with their son, until his breathing steadied.

'I will have the abbot summoned, Henry. If the battle means he cannot come, I will have a priest brought to your side. Do you understand?'

He nodded, visibly relieved.

'Until then, Henry, it would please me if you would eat and rest.'

'I will, as you say,' Henry replied.

Margaret could see that Derry Brewer was stepping from foot to foot, waiting to speak. She passed her husband into the care of her steward and one of the English guards, making sure that both men had some idea of how to address and speak to the king. As soon as Henry was seated with a blanket over his legs, she hurried back across the room to her spymaster.

'Thank you for my husband, Derry. What news of the battle?'

'Not yet won, my lady, though we had a fine start. It was the merest luck that they put the king at the rear. Half our lads walked right past him. Mind you, I've found good luck comes after hard work, not quite as the mysterious gift some would call it.'

'I have found my prayers are answered more often if I chivvy them along with coins and plans and the right men, yes. "Try first thyself, and *after* call on God", Derry. He does not love a lazy man.'

Margaret pressed the knuckle of a thumb into her eye socket, holding it there over her closed eyes. Derry waited patiently enough, preferring the warmth and the smell of broth to anything he might find outside.

'I am reeling, Derry, to have all this come so fast upon me. My husband safe, unharmed and whole – or no worse than he ever was. My son with me, my lords Somerset and Percy bringing retribution on those who would still stand against us. We are *restored*, Master Brewer! The king is, what, a dozen miles from London? We'll be there tomorrow and the whole country will learn that Lancaster has survived. They'll see my son and know there is a fine heir. I cannot take it in, Derry! We've come so far.'

'My lady, I'll know more by tonight. Until then, you can

keep your husband safe and warm and comfortable. He always was the key to the lock, my lady. He still is. I think . . .'

The clatter of horses could be heard long before they reached the tavern – at least sixty mounts on iron shoes striking the stone road. Derry frowned to himself as the sound grew louder. Dunstable was barely ten miles from the battlefield and he had ridden slowly to get King Henry to safety. It was not beyond possibility that some enemy had seen him go and sent out a troop of violent knights or men-at-arms to bring him back.

'My lady, be prepared to move the king away if those are not our men,' he said.

Derry moved swiftly to the door and left it swinging behind him. In the rain and mist, he could not make out the shields of the approaching riders. Each was spattered in thick mud, thrown up by the hooves of their mounts. Around Derry, thirty armoured knights prepared to defend the royal family to the death.

'Peace! Hold there! Somerset!' came from the lead rider.

He was as caked with mud as anyone, but he wiped his breastplate clear with one hand and levered up his visor, reining in a few feet from those who raised swords and axes against him in the road.

'Somerset! I've said it. My name is my own password and I'll have the head of any man who bares a blade at me. Is that clear? Where is the queen?'

'It is him, lads,' Derry called. 'Let my lord Somerset through.'

'Brewer? Lend a hand here, would you?'

Derry had no choice but to obey, approaching the duke and taking hold of the spurred boot pressed into his hand.

The duke swung his leg out and down with great speed, so that Derry staggered and almost fell. As the younger man stood before him, Derry could see that Somerset recalled being heaved off the same horse once before. The duke looked coldly at him, very aware of his own power in that moment.

'Take me to Queen Margaret, Brewer,' he said.

'And her husband, King Henry,' Brewer replied.

The duke hitched in his step as he passed the reins to a servant, hesitating for just the tiniest of instants. Having the king back would be an adjustment for them all, Derry thought.

8

Edward of York dismounted as quietly as he could, tying his reins to a low branch. He could not help the creaking of his armour, nor the snap and flutter of the great wolf-skin cloak he had taken to wearing. Some of the sounds would be hidden by the wind and swallowed by the forest and crags around him. He did not give it too much thought, but he knew the pack of wolves would not be fooled. As predators themselves, even intent on their own hunt, they would know he was there.

Edward could hear snarling as he stalked between the granite outcrops. It was rough country around Northampton, with rocks as old as time and covered in dark-green moss. He had not seen another soul for two days of his hunt and he had no fear of being ambushed, though the path narrowed until the sky was just a strip of grey over-head. In that cramped space, his shoulders rubbed the walls and the growling and barking intensified ahead, that primal combination of rage and fear that was the signature of a pack. The thought crossed his mind that it was not a wise thing to walk in unannounced on so many wild wolves, at least until he knew there was another path out. If he blocked their escape, they would surely attack him as savagely as any other prey.

He smiled at the thought, certain in his own strength and speed. Risk was a clean thing, he'd discovered, one part of the world that could still give him joy, where all else was sickness and grief. In danger, he was all white bone, without the weight of flesh. He welcomed it.

It was dark between the walls of stone, so that the light ahead was almost painfully bright. Edward strode as fast as he could, until the sound of fighting and yelping grew as loud as a battle. He broke into a run as the path widened and then skidded to a halt as it opened into a bowl, no more than forty yards across. He risked a brief look upwards, seeing no spot where he might climb out. Just a few paces from him was a huge, rolling pack of wolves, howling and snapping at the hound they had brought to bay. It barked in turn at them, the sound lost in their cacophony. The wolves had backed the animal up against the far wall and left no gap for it to escape.

They knew a man stood behind them. Edward could see that in the glances they threw at him. Lesser members of the pack ducked their heads in fear at his odour of unwashed sweat. Three young males turned to face him, driven to barking, jerking frenzy as they lunged toward and away, stiff-legged and huge-eyed.

Edward felt beads of fresh perspiration running down his face. He had expected a small pack, six or perhaps a dozen. Instead, more than thirty wolves ranged about, all thin-waisted, yellow-toothed killers. He had been standing there in the cold for just a few heartbeats and they were still reacting to him.

The dog they had run down was a black-and-white brute, Edward saw that much; some sort of hunter's mastiff, with the sense to stay close to the wall. It was trapped in that place and the pack would surely have killed it if he had not come. He knew they still might.

Edward looked up as something flickered above him,

on the edge of the canyon walls. The bowl in the ground was no more than six or seven yards deep at his first guess, twenty feet or so. It had a regular look that made him think of the work of men rather than some ancient river's course. There were still Roman rings and stones left to be found in the forests; he'd seen them. The bowl had that feel.

Edward thought he might see a shepherd boy and feared the sight of a soldier. He did not expect a young woman to rear up amidst the bracken and ivy. He stood open-mouthed as she clung to the root of a stunted rowan bush, peering into the bowl. She raised her right arm and Edward saw she carried a stone as large as an apple. She seemed to sense his gaze and looked across, apparently astonished to see a bearded warrior standing there in wolfskins and armour.

'Get away there!' she shouted, throwing the stone hard into the midst of the pack. It struck one of the smaller bitches, so that she gave a great jerk and squeal, snapping at herself in confusion.

Edward's heart sank as he saw the woman raise her arm again. He could see she was intent on saving her dog, but the result . . . He felt the acid of anger rising. He was in armour and he had his cloak and a sword his father had given him. He drew the long blade as more stones smacked and skipped amongst the wolves. They yelped and darted away under that torment, forgetting their prey. In an instant, all they wanted was to escape.

There was a man in their way. Edward sensed the mood change as the biggest ones turned and glared. A big male loped towards him to challenge, thick-furred and wide at the shoulder. Edward swallowed, but he was eighteen years old and his own senses kindled to heat. His sword had been made especially for him, with a tapering spine of steel that ran the three-foot length of the blade. It was too heavy for most men to use well, but it could withstand the force of his blows. He held it as if the weight was nothing.

'Come on then, boy,' he said aloud, growling the words. 'See what I'll give you.'

Edward had hunted wolves many times but never seen the action of a pack when they were faced with a clear choice. With no beat of hesitation, every one of the animals launched themselves at him in lunging, frothing rage. Despite his size, Edward was slammed back against the wall of the cleft, almost brought to his knees with the sheer weight of them. His armour saved him then, the scarred metal proof against claws and teeth. The wolves grabbed and savaged his cloak, tearing holes in it as they jerked their heads back and forth, pulling him around and off balance. Edward made his own battle cry. He swung his sword in scything blows, though he did as much damage with his gauntlets.

It was over in heartbeats, just as soon as the pack leaders had drawn or yanked him away from their only path to freedom. Edward panted, resting his hands on his knees. Four wolves lay on the ground near him, two alive and two clearly dead.

The rest of the pack were long gone and there was no sign of the woman who had set them all off. Slowly, wincing from the bruises and scratches he had taken, Edward sank down to a crouch, reaching out to one of the wounded animals. He could see her back was broken and her haunches dragged as she tried to stand. Her lips curled and her eyes widened as his hand came closer, until he smacked her hard on the muzzle. She barked once, then crawled away from him, whimpering all the while.

Edward straightened up carefully as the enormous mastiff padded over, growling deep in its throat whenever one of the wolves moved. They were no threat and the black-and-white dog was not afraid. Scuffed and dusty, it walked right up to Edward, limping on a paw that ran with blood. As Edward looked down, the dog pushed at him with its head, rubbing its muzzle into the folds of his cloak. He did not think he had ever seen a larger hound.

'You *are* a big lad, aren't you, boy?' Edward said. 'Like me. Was that your mistress, up there? The one who set the whole pack on me? Yes, it was. Was that your mistress, boy?'

The dog wagged a tail like a leather whip. To Edward's amusement, the huge-headed animal smiled visibly as he rubbed it between its shoulders. For all the scratches and cuts it had taken, the dog was simply pleased to be patted by someone friendly.

Edward looked up as small stones and leaves rained around him. The woman he'd seen was climbing down through the rocks and undergrowth, hanging on to roots and stones while her dress snagged and showed her legs to the thigh. He was bruised and hot and irritated, so he went on to one knee and rubbed harder at the dog until it rolled suddenly and presented an almost hairless belly to him, beaming stupidly, its tongue lolling.

Edward could hear the woman's breathing, louder in that cleft than it might have sounded above. He waited for her, content to pat and fuss over the dog while his own breathing returned to normal. The injured wolves around him were whining and he considered using a knife to end their suffering, then thought better of it. They had attacked him and the experience had been frightening, though he would not have admitted it to anyone. Despite his mail and plate, adult wolves were both heavy and blindingly quick. If he'd gone over on to his back, he knew they'd have ripped his throat out. He still had a memory of yellow teeth snapping shut so close to his eyes that he'd expected searing pain to follow.

For what seemed an age, he waited, aware of the woman's presence above but not reacting to it. She had climbed halfway down, but then stopped on a steep bit of moss-covered granite, about a dozen feet from the ground. It was still too high to jump and he could hear her crabbing back and forth in frustration, looking for another step or handhold and not finding one.

He heard her slip, looking up as she cursed. Whatever she had been holding in both hands had given up its grip on the ground with no warning. She flailed and in the last instant kicked away from the wall, so that she was falling towards him, a dark shape against the pale sky. He had only to rise and take a step to catch her.

Edward watched, idly scratching the dog's ribs as the woman crashed to the ground beside him, to lie gasping up at the sky. He did not know if she had been badly hurt. The dog rolled to its feet and ran over to her with its tail a blur, whining and yelping as it licked her face and pressed its nose into her open hands. Edward unwrapped a piece of twine from a loop around his waist and began to knot a collar for the dog.

'You will need a name, old son,' Edward said. A thought struck him and he looked over at the woman. She was still gasping, lying where she had fallen despite the dog's slobber and nuzzling. 'What did you call him?'

She groaned suddenly as she sat up, her face and hands badly scratched and stained in green and brown. There were leaves in her long hair, he noticed. On another day, perhaps a day when she had not fallen and scraped her way down a cleft in the ground, she would have been called beautiful. Even then, glaring at him, her eyes were arresting, over-large and bright with anger.

'He is mine, whoever you are,' she said. 'And my brothers are coming down that path, if you've a mind to hurt me.'

Edward waved a careless arm back at the path.

'I have an army around here somewhere – and a hunting party of forty men. I'm not worried about your brothers, or your father. Or you. But the dog is mine, so what did you call him?'

'You're *stealing* him?' she said, shaking her head in amazement. 'You didn't catch me and now you're *stealing* my dog? Why didn't you catch me?'

Edward looked at her. Her hair was a reddish blonde, dragged back and held in a knot behind. Half of it had come loose and stood out like a brush. There was something about the heavy-lidded eyes that made him wish he had caught her, but he could not retreat from the position he had chosen. He shrugged.

'You caused me pain, with your wolves.'

'Not *my* wolves! I was trying to save Bede from them.'

The mastiff pricked up its ears at hearing its own name. Still at her side, it leaned against her until she scratched its back. The dog groaned and huffed in pleasure. Edward felt a pang of loss.

'Bede the scholar? That is a poor name for a dog. I shall call him Brutus, perhaps.'

'You are a poor excuse for a man, for all your size. You

did not catch me and you cannot name a dog better than a child. *"Brutus"!*

Edward coloured, his cheeks deepening as his mouth tightened.

'Or Moses, perhaps. Or Brindle, for his colours. Is that your name, boy? Brin? Is that it? I think it could be.'

Something colder had come upon him as he talked to the dog. His eyes seemed to darken and he hunched slightly, radiating a threat where before he had seemed gentle. The woman closed her mouth on any further protest. His great size had misled her at first. She realized he was years younger than she had guessed, with a fine black beard to cover most of his face. His cloak had been torn and tattered by the wolves, but it still swirled around him, adding to the sense of his bulk in that small place. She stood, not yet sure if he would be a danger. It was clear enough that her dog would be no use at all. She frowned, feeling her aches and pains begin to throb.

'You shouldn't steal a dog, above all other things. If you would like him, you should buy him from me – and you should pay a fair price.'

Edward rose with her and seemed to blot out the sky above. It was not just his height but the huge breadth of him, the shoulders and arms built by years of working with a sword and shield. His beard was unkempt and his hair was long and matted with dust, but his eyes were steady. She felt a fluttering in her stomach and womb as he shook his head.

'I imagine you are persuasive, woman. But I won't bite. Here, Brin. To me.'

The enormous mastiff came back to his legs and stood panting, its head split almost in two by its grin. Edward looped his twine around the animal's neck, making a leash of the rest and winding it around his left hand.

'You should climb back out, if you can,' he said over his shoulder. 'My men will be looking for me and you don't want to be found by them. The dog is payment for my wounds, my lady. Good day to you.'

Elizabeth Grey watched him leave. She could sense the glassy darkness in the young giant, as well as the physical power in him. The combination was enough to bring an odd weakness when he had gone. She reminded herself that she was a married woman, with two strong boys and a husband in Lord Somerset's ranks. She decided not to mention such a strange meeting to Sir John Grey. Her husband could be a suspicious fellow. She sighed to herself. She would just have to tell him the dog had died.

St Albans was barely twenty miles from London, not even a day on the road. Every man marching with the king and queen knew they could set off with the sun still climbing and see the Thames before dark. The prospect raised all their moods. London meant inns and ale. It meant being paid – and all the good things that came after. In preparation for the last march, Margaret's army smartened themselves up as best they could, laughing and joking as they packed up the equipment and loaded carts.

Almost as soon as Warwick and Norfolk had withdrawn to the north, the news of the king's rescue had spread. The importance of it was not lost on those who had been fighting. They were jubilant, wild with relief. Cheering had sounded across the open plain and into the town itself, gathering force in waves until they were hoarse, then beginning all over again as the royal family rode in to join them that evening.

Some of those men had marched or fought all the way from Scotland to the south. The very least of them had trudged through forest and valley to fight twice for the king against his most powerful enemies – and they had triumphed, at both Sandal and St Albans. Now the sun was rising once again. London lay ahead – and in the capital city, all the trappings of power and reward, from the courts and the sheriffs to the Palace of Westminster and the Tower. It was the heartland. London meant not only power but safety, and above all, good food and rest.

For once, Margaret did not make a show of consulting Somerset. As soon as dawn lit the camp, she passed on the order to march south. With her husband and son at her side, her lords bowed, deeply and with respect, smiling all the while.

King Henry's presence was a talisman, Margaret could see. Those who had grown surly or resentful under her orders were once again careful and blank-faced. Others who had become too familiar in her presence kept a new, respectful distance. Drummers thumped out martial rhythms and the men sang marching songs with one hand on their hearts. The mood was both joyous and brittle, a mélange of having survived and having suffered, with the prospect of reward still ahead.

It did not matter that Henry understood nothing. The king and queen of England rode with the Prince of Wales to their capital city. The heavy cannon they had captured at St Albans fell behind as the army spread for miles down the city road.

The royal family rode abreast, with Somerset and Earl Percy slightly ahead. For all the sense of victory, the senior officers were aware of Warwick's army somewhere close.

It could not be a triumphal march in those circumstances, and neither could they allow Margaret and King Henry to ride in the first ranks, where an ambush of archers might bring them down in a heartbeat. Somerset had his best-armoured soldiers in rows all around the king and queen. He made no plans for the marching Scots, but they were there too, loping on bare-legged, with various weapons. Those bearded men stared with unabashed interest at the pale king they had rescued, commenting to each other in their own strange tongue. The mood was light as a summer fair, and the men strolled along with laughter and occasional song as they ate the miles and the road to London.

9

The army that approached London along the raised road had become almost a parade or a Royal Progress. Merchants and travellers were forced to drag their carts off the road and on to marshy ground as armoured knights rode past them four abreast, with banners fluttering on pikes above their heads. Farmers and traders stood with bowed heads and their caps pressed into their chests when they heard it was the king and queen returning at last. Some of them cheered in the wind and cold, while they all gazed on Henry and Margaret as if to fix them in their memories for ever.

It was true the royal banners were worn and mud-spattered. They had been kept folded in chests for the best part of a year and denied a decent airing. The men who bore them were ragged enough themselves, after so long on the road, but they raised their heads at the sight of the massive London walls ahead, with a blare of warning horns sounding over the city to signal their approach. London had seen riots and invasion over the previous year, with the Tower breached and cannon used in the streets against its own people. For over a decade, the house of York had threatened and schemed against the rightful king.

All that was behind. Margaret could feel it in the clean winter air. The city might smell of rot and open sewers in the warm months, but the wind blowing into her face brought scents of wood and plaster, brick and smoke and salted meat. She could not help recalling her first sight of the city, when she had been fresh from France. They had carried her on a litter then, made to halt on London Bridge while the city cheered and hollered and the aldermen bowed in colourful robes. It had overwhelmed her, that girl of fifteen who had not known there could be so many people in the world.

Margaret felt her pulse quicken as Somerset eased his horse beside her so that they rode together. They had not spoken since Henry's return, though the young duke was always close, ready to advise or receive orders. Henry Percy, Earl of Northumberland, rode in the rank behind the queen, with Edward, Prince of Wales. Margaret wondered if Lord Percy would be thinking of his father and brother, lost to the years of battles and bloodshed. Perhaps it was a chance for them all to put such family tragedies behind them. After all, she had won. For all the trials and travails, her husband was yet the anointed king of England, true and alive and once more in her grasp. Margaret had learned a great deal since her first sight of London.

The road from St Albans led directly to the Bishop's Gate, in parallel with another road to Moorgate, just a few hundred yards along the wall. It had been King Henry's only contribution during the ride. When Somerset had asked the queen which approach he should choose to enter the city, some spark of memory had made the king look up, just for a moment.

'I would enter through my father's gate,' he had said, shyly.

That was Moorgate, cut into the massive Roman wall

before Henry had even been born, as the roads north became congested with carts and crowds, worse every year. Without a word, Somerset had sent fresh orders ahead and the front ranks had crossed to the Moorgate road, which rose six feet above ground so soft in places it could trap a horse and rider. That road had been built with London taxes and it was well maintained and dry underfoot, even in winter. They made good time as Moorgate loomed ahead.

The London wall was manned with soldiers from the city garrison. Margaret could see their darker outlines from half a mile away. She had left and returned to London many times over the years, to and from Kenilworth Castle, her private refuge in the bleakest times. She could not remember a single occasion when the gates had been shut before sunset, as they clearly were on that day. A frown appeared on her brow and she looked aside to the lords riding around her, waiting for one of them to react or remark.

It was Somerset who took responsibility, sending men forward up the line and easing back the pace for the rest. Those he sent ahead went with his stinging orders in their ears, furious that some fool had closed the city gates against the king. Margaret craned in the saddle, seeing the messengers gesticulate in the shadow of the wall. Men above leaned down to them and she blinked in confusion as the huge mass of iron and oak remained closed. The royal army could not slow much more. Margaret watched in growing anger as Somerset's messengers returned and blurted out their surprise. They were bright red in the face, the queen could see that much. Something of the same colour came to Somerset as he listened and guided his horse over to her. Before he reached the queen, the duke ordered all ranks to halt.

Barely a hundred yards of road lay between the front rank and the London wall, but the massive gates remained closed.

Edward of York pulled his cloak tighter around him, already irritated. He was being called back to his responsibilities; he could sense it like a noose around his throat. He'd felt the first touch of the thing when his father's chief steward had tracked him down in Wales, waiting patiently for three days while Edward roared and cursed him to hell. Hugh Poucher was a white-haired Lincolnshire man who must have been the wrong side of sixty, though it was impossible to be certain. The wiry steward maintained an expression of deep irritation, almost pain, as if he were working a wasp along his gums and would one day spit the foul thing out. Poucher had weathered the storms of Edward's rages in contemptuous silence until the young giant had finally agreed to listen to him.

His father's title meant dozens of estates had come to Edward, with staff and tenants numbering many hundreds, or even thousands. His father had kept a close eye on those holdings, and the men who ran them understood perfectly the limits of their own authority – and would not move one step beyond for fear of losing their livelihoods. It was work Edward did not desire or care for, though he appreciated the bag of gold noble coins Poucher had brought with him.

With his father's man came duty, squeezing his chest and wrapping him up in all the smothering laws and rules and reasons to be sober. Edward could have sent Poucher away, of course. He'd come close to it when he realized the man had assembled a staff of clerks from the nearest estates to assist and educate their young master. That coterie of scribes now accompanied Edward wherever he rode, all ink-fingers and scrolls bound in leather and wax. There was always more for Edward to read, no matter how often he stormed off with his mastiff and some of the rougher knights to hunt for a few days. When he did agree, without fail his thoughts would wander as he read, most often to his father and his brother Edmund.

Edward had seen spiked heads before, many times. It was no great stretch of the imagination to picture his father soft and rotting on the walls of York. Edward had almost three thousand men with him, and York was in reach. There were times, out hunting, when he found he had drifted into range of that city and he would wonder whether he could just lunge for the wall, or whether it would be a trap and they would catch him. In his private thoughts, he sometimes wished Richard Neville were there. He too had lost his father to the queen's vengeance. Warwick would know what to do.

On some mornings, Edward woke filled with determination to storm York and take back his father's head. By the time he had emptied his bladder and broken his fast and sworn at Hugh Poucher for bringing him fresh accounts to look through, the dread had returned. Richard of York had been both clever and powerful, but it was his head that gaped down from stone walls. His father's death had stolen a great deal of Edward's brash confidence, for all he struggled to hide the loss with rudeness and bad temper. He knew the men walked warily around him and it was his own fear that drove him, yet he only made it worse with every forced attempt at friendship, followed by kicking over tables or drunkenly knocking out one fellow with a single blow.

The path to the manor house was long, so that Edward's knights made a solid column three abreast. The grounds were well kept and had been trimmed right back for winter, every tree and bush still showing the white marks of ruthless pruning. His father's voice returned to him then, murmuring the ancient garden lore that 'Growth follows the knife'. Edward wondered if she would even be there, or whether she might have moved to another house and shuttered this one.

Elizabeth was another regular object of his wandering thoughts, most often when he was warm and his senses were pleasantly blurred in drink. He would remember those heavy-lidded eyes then, watching him. When he recalled their first meeting, he always caught her when she fell, until he almost believed he had. It was surprising how often he thought of it.

The house was wood-beamed and solid-looking, the home of a knight with a good family name but perhaps no great fortune. It had taken long enough to find the place, even with the pretence of returning a dog to its master. Edward dismounted as long-dead leaves spun around the stone courtyard before the main door. His men either dropped down with him or trotted out around to check their surroundings. They had not been given orders to do so, but they knew his rages well enough by then and worked hard to avoid them.

The main door led to an inner courtyard, visible through a grille. Edward had to bash his mailed glove on the wood before a servant came running to answer him, the first sign of life he had seen in that place. The old man took one glance at the white-rose crests and shields of York and could not do enough, calling for his mistress and struggling with great iron bolts to open the door.

By the time the quivering ancient had them all worked free, the woman was there. Her hair was no longer tangled and torn, nor trailing leaves and skeins of spiderweb. The change suited her, and Edward realized there truly was a touch of red in her dark-gold hair. It seemed to have more colours than he could possibly name and her eyes too were almost a red-brown. Her figure was full and her waist . . .

'Have you brought my dog back?' she said, tiring of this silent scrutiny. 'The one you stole?'

The door had swung open, so that there was no longer anything between them. Edward stepped forward and wrapped his hand around her waist. He had planned for such a moment, in his dreams and daylight fantasies. He drew her in and pressed his second hand behind her shoulder blades, bending her back as he leaned. She was rigid as he kissed her, clashing their teeth together, so that they both winced. In the courtyard behind, a child began to cry. Edward released her and Elizabeth Grey stood in blushing shock, touching her hand to her lips as if she expected a smear of blood.

'You are . . . the most *boorish* man I have ever known,' she said.

He could see there was a brightness to her eyes, despite the shocked tone. He had sensed a softness in her mouth and, with some smug satisfaction, he noted a spreading flush on her skin. It was something weak men, shorter men, would never know, he thought cheerfully. They would never truly understand a beautiful woman without that knowledge. Those dogs might whinge and complain, or ape his manner, or even call him a rogue or a devil, but Edward saw her interest in him and he knew it was real. He stood and drank her in for a long moment.

When he did not reply, Elizabeth looked past him to where her dog was being held lightly on a rope. She whistled and the animal almost dragged its handler to her side. Certainly the man had no choice in the matter. Edward turned to watch the bounding, lunging mastiff and narrowed his eyes.

'If he comes so easily, why did you let me leave with him before?'

'I was dazed from a fall. There was a great rude oaf who did not catch me, if you recall.'

'You hoped to see me again,' he said, smiling wickedly.

Elizabeth rolled her eyes.

'I did not. I thought you might become as violent as you look if I called him back.'

Edward snorted. He made no attempt to hide his emotions, letting them play across his face with the disarming honesty of a child.

'I *am* a violent man, my lady. I have been so and will be again. Not to you, though. When I think of you, I am softer.'

'No good to me, then, Edward of York.'

He blinked at that, his mouth working in confusion as his colour deepened.

'No good . . . sorry, you . . . what?'

The baby wailed again and she lost the wry smile that had widened her mouth on one side.

'I am called away, Edward.'

'My name is in my banners,' he said. 'I know yours too, Elizabeth Grey.'

'Yes, that is my name now. Grey wife and mother.'

She stared up at him for a long time, her eyes calm as she made a decision without hurry. Her husband was a decent man, but he had never made her shudder with desire the way the ox had done with just one clumsy embrace. She blushed hard at her own flirting.

'Come and see me again, Edward. Without your men, perhaps.'

Before he could do more than stare at her, she had turned in a swirl of skirts and was gone. The old man who had opened the door looked in reverent admiration at Edward, then found his boots equally fascinating for a time.

'Shall I, um . . . take the dog in, my lord? My mistress did not say, in the end.'

'What? Oh.'

Edward looked down at the black-and-white mastiff, who had chosen to lie on its back and kick at the air with one back leg, showing no sign of worry whatsoever. The dog was watching him, he noticed.

Edward sighed. When the door had closed on Elizabeth, he'd felt something alter inside himself, something drawing tight that he had not known was still flapping loose. His father's responsibilities had been a burden at first. Now something had been sealed or tied down within and that was no longer true. There were things he had to do, that no one else could do for him. They were *his* responsibility, and he realized he felt not the weight but the strength needed to bear them. He understood suddenly that the strength came *from* the burden. It was a revelation.

For the first time he could remember, he felt a prickling of guilt at something he had done. It did not matter that Elizabeth had given every sign she accepted him. Pressing his suit on a married woman was in the same camp as drinking himself blind, or fighting bare-fisted with the blacksmiths until they were all too wounded to stand. Edward groaned almost inaudibly, raising his head and breathing hard. He saw himself as a child running from what he needed to do, and he was ashamed.

He glanced to the south, past the house and the trees, imagining Queen Margaret and all her noble lords raising wine cups and congratulating themselves on their victories. He was still tugged in two, called south to demand a reckoning and yet held in the north by the thought of his father's humiliation. Spring was on the way. How could he leave the north, with his father's head? How could he *not*, with his enemies still alive?

'Yes, take him,' he said to the old man, standing wide-eyed and unnerved by the big man's silences. 'I'll be gone for a time and he should be with his mistress. Give him a bone of cold pink mutton. He likes that.'

'I hope we will see you again, my lord?'

Edward looked down and smiled. It was not that his grief had gone. It was just that it could no longer unman and ruin him in the space of a single breath. He knew his father watched him and that there was a debt to be paid. His thoughts were clear and he breathed slowly and calmly.

'Perhaps, if I live. If you live, too. For one who has seen as many winters as you, I suppose every day is a blessing.'

The old man blinked, unsure how to respond as Edward turned and stalked back to where his horse was held for him. His captains had watched and heard all and they seemed to sense some change, so that the horses moved restlessly, wanting to be off.

'My lord?' one of them called.

'Have the men break camp,' Edward replied. 'I am ready now. I will speak for York. And I will be heard.'

One of the men near Edward crossed himself in reflex, while another shuddered, his skin tightening down his back. They were heading to war once again. All those men had witnessed the battle of Mortimer's Cross, where the sun had risen in three places, casting impossible shadows. They had seen Edward stalk with his sword across a field of the dead, bare-headed in red armour, gone mad with grief. All his captains and knights knew what he could do and they looked upon him with a sense of awe.

10

There was no food in the queen's camp, not even a morsel of eel or dog to feed fifteen thousand men – and only seeping, brackish water to wet their throats. The last of anything edible had been consumed either before the clash at St Albans or with the walls of London in sight. As they gazed upon the capital city, stomachs rumbled and groaned at the thought of thick winter stews, soups, puddings and roast haunches turning slowly on inn-house spits, basting in their own clear juices.

For hours, the men Margaret had brought south either stood or sat their mounts in confused and whispering still-ness, overawed by the thought of the king being kept waiting like a beggar. Margaret had given no orders for them to rest or make themselves comfortable, so no tents were unpacked from the baggage train at the rear, nor were any of the men allowed to sit. Those few who made the choice on their own were bawled at and dragged to their feet by red-faced serjeants.

As the sun touched the horizon and washed the walls in gold, Margaret accepted the requests of captains to allow men out to hunt, or even to take food from villages around the city, as far as a day's ride away. She made a point of sending small parties only, just half a dozen horsemen at a time, but the truth was that the situation was utterly des-perate. If the gates remained closed, her army would starve and be forced to move. She did not know what would happen after that, with all the power and wealth of London denied to the king's party. Such a thing had never happened before.

Derry Brewer had been busy from the first moment of arrival, working closely with Somerset as both men put aside their dislike in the face of a greater need. Together, they had sent a formal deputation to the gates to demand entry for the king. The Royal Seal had not been found, but Somerset wrote a dozen letters under his own wax, his frustration showing clearly. Derry sent messages of a different kind, written and spoken. He relied on less well-known routes, carried by urchin boys around the walled city, where the guards might not be quite so full of their own importance.

It was not as if London remained unaware of the army camped outside its walls. Neither Margaret nor her lords could understand it. They were the *victors* against York. They were Lancaster restored. Yet they could not take one step into London while nervous soldiers watched them with crossbows on their shoulders, as if they were some foreign force of invasion or more of Jack Cade's rebels.

The formal demand for entry was carried up on ropes to disappear into the city. Somerset had remounted to wait in the front rank, still certain the gates would be opened. On his right shoulder, the winter sun began to sink. His horse scraped at the road with a hoof, but he stayed in that spot. The capital city of King Henry's realm could not possibly leave the king and queen to freeze in the open. The young duke waited with his bannermen clearly visible on the road, ready to dig in their heels and ride through the gates as the vanguard, the moment they were opened.

The light faded swiftly and the cold was bitter as darkness came and the moon appeared low in the sky.

Somerset found he was shivering in his armour. He moved, shaking his head with a creak of metal and slumping just a fraction as he eased aching muscles.

'Find a place to sleep,' he snapped to his men. 'They won't open the gates at night. That's it until tomorrow, may they all be *poxed*.'

He turned his horse and trotted back to where an ad hoc camp had sprung up on the road itself. It was no help to the royal party that the ground alongside was soft and wet. A man standing there could watch green water seep over his boots in just a few minutes. They could certainly not sleep on such a marsh and instead were forced to cram themselves into every dry spot on the road, stretching back for miles. It was a misery of inconvenience, but none of them had imagined they might be held outside the city.

As Derry had expected, he was summoned to King Henry's presence as soon as Somerset gave up his furious vigil at the gates. Derry was not at all sure the king knew why they had halted, but Margaret was alive with anger, pacing up and down a narrow strip between two carts brought up to shelter her. An awning had been drawn tight between them and raised on poles in case it began to rain. Torches had been dragged up, along with a brazier from the gun teams, so that there was a dim golden light. Derry ducked under a flap of cloth and waited until a guard recognized him before going further in. They were all a little jumpy that night and it would not do to take a knife in the ribs for pushing past a guard. Derry spotted a boy he knew looking for him and he clicked in his cheek to catch the lad's attention. One of the guards was quick enough to snag the lad as he darted towards Derry. The spymaster stepped over quickly.

'Mine,' he muttered. 'One of mine. Hands off.'

'Like boys, do you?' the guard replied, ruffled.

Twenty years before, Derry would have battered the guard to his knees. He was weary and more than fifty years old, with a long campaign and the fury of being blocked at the last point to make his anger simmer. All of a sudden, he didn't care. He grabbed the guard and sent the man reeling in a flurry of short, clubbing blows, to the shocked audience of the queen's tent. For a brief time, Derry was unaware of all of them as he whipped crosses against the man's lolling head and alternated between throttling him and thumping his fist into the guard's nose and lips. No one stopped him, and when Derry finally released his grip and let the guard fall, he turned to see both Clifford and Somerset regarding him. Lord Clifford looked distinctly unsettled, while Somerset chuckled and shook his head, amused.

The messenger boy was taking a breath to crow when he became aware of the silent scrutiny of Queen Margaret. Her husband sat to one side in that makeshift tent between carts, his head lowered either in sleep or in prayer. The London urchin snapped his own mouth closed, standing mute and staring at the stone floor.

'Outside, lad,' Derry said, panting, cuffing his employee with an aching hand. His knuckles would be swollen and black by the following morning, he was certain. By God, it had felt good, though. He did not look down at the guard as he stepped over him and half dragged the boy into the darkness.

'I hope you have something good for me after that,' Derry said, bending lower. 'Well? What did you find out?'

The boy was still thrilled to have witnessed a proper beating and grinned in admiration at the queen's spymaster.

'I spoke to Jemmy. He 'elped me in.'

Derry reached out and smacked the boy across the back of the head in one fast movement. He was not in the mood for stories and he knew well enough that there were a hundred places where an agile crawler might gain entrance to the city. He'd used one or two of the spots himself when he'd been younger and his knees hadn't been quite so insistent in their complaints.

'Why are the gates shut?'

The boy rubbed the back of his head sullenly, his good mood gone as quickly as it had come.

'They're all afraid of northern dogs and servages what eats children.'

'Savages,' Derry said.

'Thassit. The mayor and 'is old men.'

'Aldermen,' Derry murmured as the boy went on.

'Thass 'em. There was a mob or summing, full of merchants and rich folk. Told the mayor they'd 'ave 'is gizzard if 'e even fort about openin' the gates. So 'e sits tight and does nuffin'.'

'Have you *seen* the mayor?' Derry asked. 'Can I tap him on the shoulder?'

The boy knew the phrase for having a man killed, but he shrugged, his skinny shoulders moving sharply.

'Maybe, but the 'ole city's frightened of your rough dogs. They aint 'eard nothing but stories of rape and killin' for a month. Look . . .' The boy knew Derry would not want to hear what he had to say. Derry saw the lad rub his nose and sniff, steeling himself to go on. 'Look . . . they're all afraid. Anyone who goes near a gate to open it will get a knife in 'is back.'

'The king of England . . .' Derry said, raising a hand in disbelief.

The boy flinched.

'It doesn't matter if God and all 'is Saints are out 'ere. No one's getting in. *No one*. Not till spring.'

The boy noticed the spymaster was staring off into space and held out his hand. Derry reached into a pocket and counted out tiny silver farthings and full pennies. He passed a few of them into the boy's grasping fingers, oblivious to the growing smile as he overpaid.

'This one's odd-lookin',' the messenger said, holding it up. 'Funny picture on it.'

Derry focused, seeing a Scottish penny. The boy's instincts were good, as the thing was only two-thirds silver. He wondered which of Margaret's Scottish companions had slipped it into someone else's winnings.

'Here's a better one,' he said, holding up an English penny. 'Now go on with you. I hope you get to spend it in the city.'

'I will if I want. Not your fancy lords, though. They ain't movin' from this spot.'

'Go on,' Derry said, ducking back into the fug of smoke and sweat and too many bodies pressed into too small a space.

The guard had been replaced by another, staring coldly at him. The murmur of conversation dropped away as those inside looked up and recalled that Derry Brewer might have some information. Somerset raised his eyebrows and even Clifford kept his thoughts to himself.

'Well, Brewer?' Somerset said. 'What news? Are they all traitors, then, beyond that gate? Shall I have the cannon I took from Warwick brought up to break the walls of our beloved capital?'

Responding to the acid tone, Derry smiled just as mirthlessly and shook his head. He'd spoken to half a dozen lads and read two letters smuggled out to him. They all said the same thing. There was no joy in being proved right, not if it meant London was barred to them.

'Your Majesty, Queen Margaret, my lords. It's my belief we're seeing fear more than the actions of traitors or those in league with York. The Londoners are afraid of this army, let loose on their streets. They have heard all the tales, and seen the *columna nubis* – the pillars of smoke, my lord Somerset.' Derry paused for emphasis and Somerset dropped his gaze for a moment. 'The mayor sees only another army howling to come in – and he's heard too many ragged families talk of barking northerners and bare-legged Scots. He is a faint-heart, of a certainty, but I think not a traitor throwing in with Warwick.'

'This mayor, he can be reassured, then?' Margaret said suddenly. Somerset dipped his head over whatever he had been going to say, allowing the queen to have the floor. 'What do you suggest, Master Brewer?'

'The city is fearful of our soldiers, my lady. I would march the army away for a mile or two, leaving only a small force of guards and lords with King Henry. There is a chance the mayor might open his gates for those . . .'

'That fat *grocer*?' Lord Clifford interrupted. 'The mayor has already had the gall to refuse the orders and authority of King Henry. He saw the royal banners! I would rather have cannon brought to the front. Let him see the consequences of his betrayal!'

There was a growl of support in that small space. The simple fact of the king being refused entry was still shocking to all of them. There was at least something satisfying about the image of blowing Moorgate into pieces. They had the guns to do it, left on the field by Warwick's forces. It would be almost poetic.

Derry cleared his throat to speak again. He eyed King Henry for a fraction of time, assuring himself that the king would not play a part in the discussion. Henry remained still and silent, though his fingers twitched on his thighs.

'My lady, it is possible Lord Clifford has not fully considered how using cannon on the walls of London would be seen around the country,' Derry said, his expression tight and his gaze fastened on the queen. 'With a little more reflection, my lord Clifford may realize that it would weaken King Henry's authority as almost nothing else could. Perhaps as a last resort, but those walls are twelve feet thick and the gates are reinforced with iron.'

Clifford snorted and Derry went on quickly before the man could speak over him.

'I do not say they *will* not fall. Only that it will take time. If an iron gun is brought up, the team will be vulnerable to archers on the wall – and whatever cannon they can raise to the walkway and the mountings up there. All those long guns are from London foundries, after all. With the height, they can match our range – and much further.'

Derry let that thought seep into those gathered around. It seemed to have stolen some of the rising anger.

'So, before we stand out here pounding on the gate like a drunk, we should consider other ways in. The mayor will fear some sort of treachery from us – a trick or a trap, or simply some fearful punishment once he opens the gate and allows us to pass through. He will delay and discuss and send letters back and forth.' Derry bowed his head in Margaret's direction. 'I suspect he will accept your assurances as to his safety, my lady. From what I remember of the man, my lord Clifford has the right of it. Mayor Richard Lee is not a warrior. He will surely be sweating in terror at this moment. We must simply show him a path through the thicket – and he will take it.'

Derry did not need to remind those present of the shadows hanging over them. They had defeated Warwick in one battle, but his army had not been broken, merely bloodied and sent running. The man was somewhere out in the forests and valleys, licking his wounds like any other wild dog. Derry rubbed a spot between his eyes, wishing he could sleep. Warwick would have expected them to march straight into London. How long would it be before the earl discovered they were still on the road, the entire royal family vulnerable to attack?

Beyond that sobering prospect, there was another army and another angry son out in the darkness. Derry had hoped to have the king and queen safely behind London's walls by the time Edward of York joined with Warwick. The spymaster had not allowed himself any false sense of victory, not while two such powerful sons were still unaccounted. There were a couple of spikes empty on the Micklegate Bar of York. Until they were filled, Derry suspected he would never know true rest.

*

The sun rose on new exchanges of letters and furious demands, all ignored by the mayor and his aldermen. As chief magistrate of the city, the mayor was well versed in law and tradition. Yet he had no right at all to refuse the king entry and Derry suspected the man regretted allowing an impossible position to develop. As things stood, even if the nervous crowds inside the walls stood back for the gates to be opened, the mayor's next and final destination would certainly be the Tower, his life measured in days. The people of London would have a fair idea of the anger they had caused the army and the lords waiting outside. Every hour of waiting made the retribution worse in their imaginations – and kept the gates shut.

In the afternoon, royal heralds rode right up to the massive gates and hammered on the iron with staffs, only to turn away when there was no response. There had been a little food gleaned from local villages like Chelsea, too far from London to have heard of the army before the soldiers turned up to strip their winter stores. Yet even those meagre rations were only enough to feed a few hundred at a time. The vast majority of the fifteen thousand were on a second day without food – and they had been skin and bone before that. By the time the sun set again, the situation had become completely desperate. They were all starving.

On the second night, the gathering around the queen was not so full of energy and bluster as it had been. Hunger was taking a toll on all of them, though Clifford seemed to have eaten well enough, from some private supply he had chosen not to share. Derry swore he could see a smear of grease on the man's jowls and wanted to strangle him. Tempers were short for them all.

Margaret stood, pacing back and forth three steps at a time as she weighed her choices. Her hair brushed the awning above, so that it sounded like a whispering voice. It was dry at least. That had been their only blessing, though in England, the winter rain would surely come again before long.

'Gentlemen, my lords. Those who starve have few choices,' Margaret said.

Derry could see she was clenching one fist in the long sleeve of her dress. The cloth was as marked and dusty as any soldier's jacket, and the queen was shivering, whether from cold or lack of food, he did not know.

Margaret stopped suddenly to face them all. Her husband was present as the visible symbol of her power, but the truth was that Henry made no difference to her hold on those present. From the bearded glower of Laird Andrew Douglas of the Scots, with his leine and brat wrapped around him, to Somerset, Earl Percy, Clifford, Derry Brewer and all those clustered out in the darkness – *she* had brought them to that field and to that narrow strip of road. It would be Margaret's decision, and Derry was interested to see how they looked to her like men warming their hands at a fire. Her beauty had something to do with it, of course. Men have always been fools for a fair face. Yet some of those present had known Margaret for half her life – and not one year of that time had been spent in peace. She had been held to a millstone as it spun – and left her blood on it. The struggle had surely hardened her, but that was true for all of them over the years of war.

'Those who cower behind the city gates are either traitors or fools,' Margaret said. Her voice was soft and low in that small place. The lords craned in to hear her.

'Whichever it is, we cannot remain here. The men are falling ill, reduced to bones after such exertions, with no food to keep them hale. It will not be long before we see them begin to die around us. Either that, or Warwick and York will find us, trapped before the walls – and they will come with fire and iron. So. My husband's orders are for us to march away to the north, to Kenilworth and better lands, but first to towns where we can find food and regain our strength.'

No one argued with the king's will, as delivered by his queen. Margaret's eyes were unnaturally bright, as if she burned with a fever or tears. Derry's heart went out to her in her frustration, even as he felt it himself. They had won! They had come so *close* to safety, only to be left out in the cold and dark.

The days were still short in February. The awning fluttered above their heads and a spattering of rain could be heard, making them all look up. Derry could sense the light fading all around them. It suited the mood of humiliation and weary despair. The orders went out to break camp ready to march at dawn, once more without food to begin the day.

11

Warwick found it difficult to reconcile the image of Edward in his memory with the bearded giant facing him in a bronze-studded tunic, thick woollen hose and armoured boots. With gruff pleasure, Edward reached out between them. He clapped Warwick's shoulder with massive gloves, every inch of him thick with dirt and reeking of horse and nights spent on the road.

There was little sign of civilization in the young Duke of York as he reined in, dismounting with an ease and grace that made Warwick feel old at thirty-two. On the ground, they embraced in a brief clasp, preferring to be reserved rather than risk opening a door on grief. The awareness was there, in both of them. The last time they had met, their fathers had been alive.

Around them, York's smaller army made a camp for their noble captain, a role Edward seemed to relish as he whistled and signalled orders. Warwick could see the black beard and deep-set eyes were well suited to a brigand or the leader of a war band. He did not doubt the young duke was capable of ferocity. The stories of the warrior son of York had already begun to spread, told and retold around a thousand village hearths. No doubt the tales were embellished as they went, but still Warwick found his gaze drawn to the sword Edward kept at his side. Rumour was that it had snapped halfway along its length from the sheer strength of a blow. Some of the stories had it breaking with a note like a struck bell when the news of his father's death came in.

'It does me good to see you,' Warwick said with dark satisfaction. 'I give thanks for your deliverance from the Tudors.'

Warwick had to look up as they stood together. It was oddly grating and yet he had not lied. The disastrous rout at St Albans had cost Warwick part of his confidence. His army of eight thousand men had suddenly not seemed enough for the tasks ahead, not with that behind. He knew he had been outfought, but far worse, that he had been outmanoeuvred and made to look a fool. Warwick still burned with it and it did his heart good to see Edward's three thousand added to his own.

Warwick decided in that instant not to stand on his dignity. It was true Edward was a younger and less experienced man, for all he owned a more senior rank. The young duke would not expect to lead the greater force. By rights, Edward stood in line behind the Duke of Norfolk for any such honour, but Warwick vowed not to humiliate him. There were a hundred ways to do so, but Warwick was determined to include the son of York in all the plans ahead, to honour Edward's father, but also to train the young man.

The fact that that Edward's men had won their battle played some part in his decision. It showed in their bearing and the scornful glances they shot to the men of Kent. More than a few scuffles had begun as insults were called back and forth and voices were raised in indignation and surprise. Warwick showed no reaction as his captains jogged over with cudgels to bring a little peace and quiet back to the standing ranks. Sensing scrutiny, he turned his head to find Edward of York watching him.

'I give you no blame for what happened at Sandal,' Edward said. His voice was oddly loud, so that Warwick blinked. 'You could not give your men wings to get there in support – and I know you share my loss. I know your father died with mine, for the same cause and on the same field. Were my father's words reported to you?'

'He told the queen she had won no victory,' Warwick replied, almost in a whisper. He had known Edward first as a thirteen-year-old boy, learning to drink and fight with the English garrison in Calais. There was a disturbing intensity in the hugely muscled warrior facing him with such blue eyes. 'He said she had only unleashed the sons.'

'He did,' York said. 'He *did* say that, as I've heard it from a dozen men who came to tell me of his last moments. And he would have known I'd *hear* him, long past the day of his death. He knew I would hear what he said to me.' Edward filled his chest in a great gulp of air, blowing it out through his nose. 'Let us be all unleashed, then, Richard. Before these men who follow us. Let us admit to no rein nor bridle, no curb, nor hand on our arm – until we have taken all we are owed, from all those that owe us.'

As he spoke, Edward felt himself waver between soaring confidence and trembling nerves. His rage at least was clean and could be understood to the edges of it. In the quiet hours, though, he did not know what to say, what to order. At those times, he felt his men must know they followed a painted soldier, a man who felt like a boy, dressed more as an outlaw than a duke. Lost in his own fears, Edward did not see the way they looked to him, the shining pride they took in their own giant.

Under that piercing gaze, Warwick nodded slowly. Edward breathed in relief.

'We have . . . what? Twelve thousand between us?' Warwick said, rubbing the bristles on his jaw. 'The queen and Somerset and Percy command more, but perhaps it is not too many.'

'I am the Duke of York,' Edward said, his brow furrowing at the still-strange sound of the title. 'As you are Earl Salisbury now. The country towns teem with brawny great smiths and farriers, or grocer boys wanting to hold their heads up in pride. They'll join us, Richard – if I ask them in my father's name. If you ask for yours. They'll come to avenge them. They'll come for the damned spikes on the walls of York.'

Warwick saw the young man shudder, Edward's eyes closing over an unpleasant vision before opening again with even more fire and fierceness.

'The queen will be in London,' Warwick said.

His neck began to grow pink as he skirted the subject of his lost battle. Edward did not notice, cutting the air with his hand like a cleaver.

'Then that is where I want to go. You see? It is all simple. Wherever our enemies stand or sleep, there we'll be. How far to London?'

'Forty miles, no more. Two days' march, perhaps, if the men are fed and fit.'

Edward chuckled.

'Mine won't fall behind. They've walked or run all the way from Wales with me and they've brought herds of sheep that were hundreds strong when we set out. We've eaten so much pink mutton I don't think I'll ever love it again. Your men are welcome to the few dozen we have left, though the animals have grown thin as we grew fat.'

'My men will be grateful for the gift. More than you

know,' Warwick said. He felt his mouth fill with warm saliva at the thought.

Edward shook his head, uncaring. His voice was as cold as the day as he went on.

'I need them strong, Richard. I saw my father treat King Henry and his allies with respect. The result was his head on an iron point. Do you remember how you stayed my hand in the king's tent last year, with Henry unarmed and helpless? If I could go back to that morning, I would cut his throat and perhaps . . .' His voice had been rising as his throat tightened over grief, strangling his words. Warwick waited as Edward's eyes squeezed closed, leaking tears that vanished into the black bristles on his cheeks. 'Perhaps I would have saved him then, my father. Perhaps he would live now if I had cut that mewling child when I had . . . Ah, hell and poxed damnation. There is no going back now, Richard. I can't recall a single day, or any one of the mistakes I have made. I saw three suns rise, did I tell you that? As true as I am standing here before you, I swear it. In Wales. I could not make even *one* of them go back and return on its course. Not even for my father. God keep his soul. Christ save his soul.'

Warwick held his breath at the rage he saw in York then. The man brimmed over with it, like an oven door half shut.

'You might find a little comfort in talking to my brother George,' Warwick said.

He understood that Edward had not had his family around him in Wales, only those who followed his orders, hard and violent men who would have scorned weakness if he'd allowed them to see any. Edward of York had lost a younger brother he'd loved, as well as a father he'd thought was too strong to fall. Warwick could see the shock in him still.

'No, I don't need to talk,' Edward replied. 'I need to see Queen Margaret die. I will not turn my other cheek to that white-faced harpy, Richard. Perhaps that means I am not a good man; I don't know. But I will be a good *son* – and I will be unleashed.'

The queen's army was a far more subdued force heading north than it had been with London in sight. Men who had laughed and talked now trudged along with their heads down, lean as greyhounds, watching their boots as seams flapped free and had to be bound and rebound in green twine.

On the advice of her lords, the army had swung west, well away from the burned houses and stripped towns on their previous route. Almost from the start, it was extraordinary what a difference it made to have the king with them – that single, visible symbol of the rightness of their cause. They had gone south to rescue God's anointed sovereign and there he was on a mare's back, nodding and smiling as crowds gathered to see him.

Even without the king's Great Seal, prosperous market towns no longer hid their supplies or fought back or barred their gates against them. Moneylenders fell over themselves to lend coins by weight rather than number, wiping sweat from their brows as they watched their entire fortunes depart with the king and queen. With those funds and the craftsmen of the midland cities, the army could be fed and resupplied. Money flowed once again and if there would be a reckoning when the interest came due, it did not seem to trouble Margaret. She had sent Derry out with a hundred others to negotiate for supplies. The results came in bleating sheep and hissing flocks of geese, far more than she could have believed. For one with silver coins, England was a larder, able to feed them all and a hundred times their number. For the first time in months, her men could bite into thick slices of meat from the spit, feeling their strength return as their stomachs swelled and groaned. They were still too thin, but their eyes were no longer dull. After just a few days of roasts and stews and fish, they had put on weight and muscle. It was a heady feeling to lead such men.

At her own castle of Kenilworth, Margaret halted the army and gave instructions to have the best of meat and equipment brought, whatever they needed. Straggling lines of men filed along to collect some part of the pay they were owed, counted out by serjeants from new cedar chests. Women from the local villages wandered up to earn a few of the coins in a variety of ways. Some of them sewed and mended.

Sunset seemed to come as quickly as it had for months, with the icy ground never softening under the few, precious hours of weak light. Winter was hard and there was no sign of spring on the way. If anything, it was getting colder. The grasses sparkled with dull grey frost each morning and there were days when it did not lift at all.

Margaret stood and watched from a high window, seeing her own little city around Kenilworth in the hundreds of cooking fires. Some of the men were singing, despite the cold. She could not make out the words, but the tune rose and fell almost like the sound of bees. She wondered if she would feel the vibration of their voices if she reached out to the pane of glass.

'I am almost a mother to them, sometimes,' she said.

She could sense Somerset's presence like a weight. He was some years younger than Margaret, lithe and strong and forceful in a way her husband had never been. She wondered if older men and women found one another's wrinkled flesh attractive, or whether she would always look on firm young muscle and straight shoulders and healthy colour as something fine. One lock of her hair had escaped her clasps and Margaret toyed with it, tilting her head and thinking of a hundred things.

Somerset wasn't sure how to respond to the idea that Margaret maintained a maternal instinct to kilted Scots and rough, swearing soldiers, so he cleared his throat and untied a leather wrap on a batch of letters.

'I'm sure they . . . appreciate your concern, Margaret. How could they not? Now, I have here a demand for indentured men. We do not yet have the Great Seal, which is an obstacle and a nuisance. I imagine it is still in London, or perhaps in the personal baggage of Earl Warwick. Without it, needs must I continue to use my own family crest in wax, with King Henry's ring and the assurances of the king's support written into the levy. Even then, the absence of the seal will be noted by some. Margaret, are you certain King Henry will . . .' Somerset paused, rubbing a hand from his forehead to his chin in weariness and embarrassment. He hated discussing the king's thoughts and actions with the queen, as if the man was a wooden doll. 'Are you certain he will sign the documents? Without his seal, his name will suffice, if he is gracious enough to provide it.'

'I think so. Henry agreed when I asked him, of course.' She exchanged the briefest of glances with Somerset at that. Both of them knew that Henry would agree to

127

anything at all. It was the very heart of his weakness. 'If I have to, I will sign his name myself.'

Somerset looked shocked and Margaret stepped closer to him, waving a hand.

'Oh, do not look so appalled, milord! I would not do that – though only because some of his bishops or noblemen might have other papers with his name, much loved and often read. I would not be found out in a lie; otherwise, I would sign my husband's name and use his seal to do anything.' She saw Somerset's discomfort and shook her head in frustration. 'I would do only what Henry would do – if he were able. Do you understand? My son is the Prince of Wales and will come to rule. The only *obstacle* is the fact that my husband's capital city closed its gates on him and refused entry to the rightful king! The only *nuisance* is the action of Warwick and York and an army that will not submit to the rightful authority of the king of England!'

She reached out and touched Somerset along the cheek and jaw with her open palm. He did not flinch or look away as her eyes searched him for the strength she needed.

'I would do *anything*, my lord, to keep this throne now. Do you understand? I have not walked so far along this path only to fall at the last step. I need more men than the souls gathered around this castle. I need twenty thousand, *fifty* thousand, whatever it takes to rid this country of those who pose a threat to my husband and my son – and to me. That is all that matters now. Whatever you ask, I will do.'

Somerset coloured, aware of her touch as she pulled her hand away, leaving a sense of fading heat on his skin.

*

The gates of London stood open for the army that had approached under the banners of York. Edward and Warwick rode together at the head of a column and as they passed through Moorgate, there was no fear evident in the people gathering to see them. It was true the capital city came to a halt as the news spread right across it, even to the rookeries. Men and women put down their tools or stood from table, taking up shawls and cloaks against a cold that seemed to be growing more bitter with every passing day.

The sky was a dark blue, clear and frozen above the city. There was said to be ice on the Thames as Edward and Warwick rode through packed streets, trotting their mounts in a clanking line with banners before and behind. Both of the young men were in full armour for such a formal entrance, carrying the crests of their houses on their shields so that everyone who saw them would know who passed. Warwick's men had done their best with grease and paint, but after months of wear, the metal parts were scuffed and cracked, while the leather inserts had grown hard and moulded themselves to the forms they held.

Warwick's men dipped his banner as they rode past the aldermen of the city, resplendent in robes of blue and scarlet. With the mayor, they had all come out of their Guildhall to acknowledge the army entering London. Those men were flushed as if they had been running, but they bowed deeply to the bear-and-staff of Warwick, with the white rose of York held high above them all.

Warwick smiled and shook his head as he looked over the small group. They had refused entry to the house of Lancaster, to the king and queen of England. They had made their choice then and there was no going back after it. It was no surprise that they would interrupt the breaking of their fast to come out and bless Edward Plantagenet. They had entwined their fates and their lives with the house of York.

Warwick looked back over his shoulder as he passed. The mayor really was a great hog of a man, with big pink hands and features hidden in bulging rolls of fat. Warwick felt irritation simmer that such a one should eat so very well while soldiers stayed thin. He grunted to himself, knowing that the two things did not coincide. Unless he fed the mayor to his army, of course. In that way, the fellow's excesses would all be paid back. The thought was strangely cheering.

The roads around their path towards the river were filling, bringing back memories of Jack Cade's invasion of the city. Warwick had seen mobs then, as well as horrors unspeakable. He shuddered and told himself it was the cold. He only hoped he had persuaded Edward on to the right path. The young Duke of York had been intent on making a second attack on the queen's army. They'd gone south with that in mind, but other news had come back along the road. The king and queen had been turned away from their own walls, denied entrance to the capital city of England. It changed everything, and Warwick and York had talked long into the night.

Warwick prayed he had made the right choice. The queen's army would have had their confidence knocked, the rightness of their cause brought into question. It all added up to a chance to drive a sword into the flank of Lancaster at last.

Yet instead of chasing hard upon their heels, Warwick had argued that he and Edward should enter the very city that had refused King Henry. The young duke had been furious at first, bellowing his disagreement, caring nothing that all their men could hear. In a great storm of temper, he recalled Warwick holding him back once before, when King Henry had been at their mercy. Edward referred to that battle by Northampton again and again, his pain and grief writ clear on his face. Yet he was not a child. Though the eighteen-year-old made his Herculean effort at control all too visible, he had listened. He'd allowed Warwick to talk, to explain what London could do for them.

When Edward had understood and accepted Warwick's quiet argument, he'd leaped from surly refusals to becoming enthusiastic and full of wild laughter, as if the idea had been his own. Warwick was left wiping sweat from his brow after the blasts and storms he'd endured. It had not augured well for the future between them. Edward had allowed himself to be persuaded, it was true, but there was no question of his being *made* to do anything. He had agreed and so they would follow one path and not another.

With some misgivings, Warwick had recalled that Edward had shown respect only to his father. Now that Richard of York was gone, who else was there who could hold the son in check? After suffering hours of rage and rudeness just to convince Edward of his own best interests, it was not a prospect Warwick relished, if the task ever fell to him.

As big as London was, there had not been any question of bringing their entire army inside the walls. Eight or nine thousand of them were still a mile away from the city, on dry ground. They waited for the three thousand accompanying Warwick and York to settle in and bring out stores and food. The usual number of captains had mysteriously doubled for the ranks entering the city, so that some eighty veteran officers were there to oversee the men. Under their command, soldiers spread out along the streets, keeping the populace quiet as the tramp of marching feet passed every house and stopped at every shop or tavern. Ale was one thing they could not often get on the march. Some of the men had not drunk a drop of anything but water for months. The captains licked cracked lips and thirsted for it. On York's orders, they had been given their pay, so that many of them had fat purses to empty. Between them, they would drink the city dry by the morning. It would be a wild and drunken rabble by dawn, but they had been stern and sombre for an age, always in fear of an attack. It would not hurt for them to drown their cares for a night.

Only a hundred or so accompanied Richard of Warwick and Edward of York right across the city. Warwick did not know if those men were honoured at the role they had been given, or just sour at the loss of a night's debauchery. They rode with heads high, heading always south to the river and the great house of York in London that was known as Baynard's Castle. Built of red brick, it stood tall and square against the river, sheathed in ivy that reached to the top of the towers there. The news had gone ahead of them and the gates stood open for the mounted troop. Edward saw the courtyard and dug in his heels, wrenching them all with him so that they rode in at a perilous speed, the horses skidding on the slick stones.

They came to a halt, panting and smiling at the exertion. Warwick watched the younger man, still unsure. The bets were all made, he knew. They could not be called back. Every hour they spent in London was one more for the queen to plan or gather soldiers, or simply march further away. Yet they dismounted in a York stronghold, with the River Thames passing by the walls. It was strange to be safe in such a place, in a city that had refused Lancaster. Warwick felt some of his muscles unclench as Edward called for wine and ale and a good fire. They had spread three thousand men through the city, billeting them in every inn and major household. Those who had come with Warwick and Edward included the Duke of Norfolk and his most experienced advisers, as well as Bishop George Neville and his coterie of servants. For just one night, all the senior men were under one roof. Warwick crossed himself at the thought of what would come before they saw the sun rise again.

'I am the heir to the throne,' Edward said, addressing them all. 'By act of this London Parliament, my father was made heir to King Henry, not a year past.' A slight tremble and tightness in his voice betrayed his nervousness as he cleared his throat and went on. 'I am the first son of York. That honour falls to me.'

The hall was packed and not just with those Warwick and Edward had brought into the city. As the night deepened, Warwick had noted senior gentlemen sidling in from the cold to hear Edward speak. The large head of the mayor could be seen over to one side, with three of his aldermen. Members of Parliament too had come, to judge and report back to their fellows. Perhaps even more importantly, Warwick recognized the heads of two merchant guilds and the master of Holy Trinity Priory. Those men could provide vital loans, if they liked what they heard.

Beyond Edward's voice, the only sound came from the fire. The great hall of Baynard's Castle could well have been the warmest spot in London that night. Scores of small logs were still being fed to the flames, tipped in by red-faced servants who then hurried away for another armful. Kitchen boys added lumps of coal from iron scuttles. The flames grew with a crackle of sap, an exhalation of heat that loosened men's jackets and made them wipe perspiration from their faces. It was not too much to bear, not after months of winter and numb feet. For all its fierceness, the fire was a welcome blessing and the men clustered around it, leaving only a few away from the light and the warmth.

Warwick remained outside the shifting core by the fireplace, saying nothing. It was no small thing to have the massive wealth and authority of London stand with them. The men of power in the city had little choice but to support York after refusing the king and queen. There was no third party, no middle ground. He pursed his mouth, feeling his lips thin and his jaw clench. It was true Henry of Lancaster and a dozen powerful lords still stood in the path of that ambition. The reality of that seemed not to trouble Edward. The young man had not hidden his intentions, nor tried to be subtle. It was Edward's desire to meet Lancaster on the field and settle it there, once and for all.

The son of York leaned against a massive buttress of brick, part of the chimney stretching into eaves overhead. The fire huffed and breathed behind him, so that he was shadowed and lit gold, catching glints of light as he turned. Warwick observed the men as closely as he watched the young duke, seeing how they stood, how they reacted. Blood had power. The house of York was a direct male line from kings. That simple fact gave Edward authority over all those who allowed it. Men like the block of bone that was Norfolk, over twice York's age and experience, yet still standing with his head slightly bowed, looking up from under his brows. That was to the good. They needed the man's soldiers and his strength of arms.

It did not hurt the cause that Edward was such a massive figure. It was not just the height; though Warwick had known only two men as tall in his lifetime. Both had been lopsided and odd-looking, twisted imitations of a warrior. In comparison, Edward had a thickness of limb and a sheer breadth of shoulder that made him a force in any room. In armour, he would be a terrifying figure. Warwick shuddered at the thought. Alongside his training and massive strength was Edward's youth, with all its speed and limitless stamina. It would be like facing an armoured bull. If Edward had been born to a smith, say, or a guild mason, his size might have made him a knight or more likely a captain of great fame. With his blood and his name, there was no limit to what he could become.

'I watched my father struggle with terrible forces,' Edward went on, his voice ringing. 'I saw him wrestle with the respect he felt for the king of England – and the *despair* he felt at the man who *was* king. On the one hand, my father gave honour and bent his knee to the throne. As he should have done! As he was was bound by oath to do!'

A murmur of agreement went through the men, tinged with nervousness. Edward swept his gaze over them all, resting at last on Warwick and nodding to him.

'On the other hand, he found a beardless innocent sitting on that throne, dishonouring England by his unworthy rule. Losing France. Splintering the noble houses. Seeing London raided by mobs and the Tower breached. Allowing discord and armed forces to roam the country without check. In his weakness, King Henry brought England and Wales to the brink of lawless chaos. I do not believe there has ever been a head so unworthy to wear that crown.'

Edward paused to sip at a cup of mulled wine, allowing those in the crowd to take quick, shallow breaths. There was no doubt now that they were listening to treason. The knowledge shook them all.

Warwick recalled a time the young man would have knocked back a dozen big mugs of ale and still called for more. With the roaring fire warming one side of him and the other cold and dark, Edward gulped once and placed the goblet on the bricks to warm. He did not seem nervous then, at least to Warwick's eye. The young duke standing with a furnace at his back spoke to those men as if he planned a day's hunting. They waited for him, held in stillness by the silence and the importance of the words being spoken.

'The house of Lancaster stood above the house of York,' Edward said. 'By the distance of one son – John of Gaunt, that great counsellor, over Edmund of York, my ancestor. The house of Lancaster gave us two great kings and then a weak one, a strong line spoiled. How often have we seen a run of good wine followed by years of bad grapes? It happens with blood as well as wine – and that is why the men of Parliament saw fit to make my father heir to the throne. Like any careful gardener, they reached back to the good green branch, to the spot before the vine failed – and they cut away the poor growth.'

Some of those around Edward chuckled at that, others muttered 'Yes' into their beards or dipped their heads, or even knocked goblets against metal, so that odd clanks and bell tones sounded in the hall, rising to the rafters overhead.

'I am of the same vine,' Edward said.

Warwick was among those who cried 'Yes!' in response.

'I am the Duke of York. I am the heir to the throne.'

'Yes!' they cried out again, laughing along.

'I will be king,' Edward said, his voice rising in volume and strength. 'And I will be king *tonight*.'

The laughter and noise fell away as if a door had been closed. The crowd stood still, though some twitched as sweat made them itch or a shiver ran down their backs. Warwick had known what Edward would say, but he was one of very few who had. As a result, he was able to watch all the rest and see where there might be resistance. His eyes were on the most powerful, but as they swept across the gathering, he realized to his surprise that no one turned their head away from the giant standing by the great fire. They looked to Edward as if he were the source of the light.

The moment of stunned shock passed. They began to stamp and cheer, louder and louder as Edward pushed away from the wall and stood upright before them. With one sweep, he reached down and fetched his cup for a toast. Though Warwick saw that the heat stung his hand, Edward ignored the pain and drank deeply. The men around him did the same, calling for the servants to refill their goblets.

'A cup or two, no more, my lords and gentlemen!' Edward went on, laughing.

His beard had crisped brown from the heat of the cup at his lips. Over his smile, his eyes were strained. He searched the crowd for Warwick, waiting for him. They had agreed he would speak then, and yet Warwick rested a beat. He could feel the moment pressing on him, the sense that once he opened his mouth, the future would rush down upon them like a devouring flame. He filled his chest, the colder air shuddering in to cool his blood.

'My lord York!' Warwick called across them all. 'If you would be king *tonight*, you'll need a crown and an oath – and a bishop to represent the Holy Church. Would that we had such a man of God, my lord.'

At Warwick's shoulder stood his brother in robes, hands clasped as if in prayer. Bishop George Neville knew what was expected of him and he raised his head and spoke up immediately, exactly as they had practised. In that huge space, with the fire crackling, his voice rang out with more force than they had known he possessed.

'My lord York, yours is a royal line. By law, you are the heir to the throne; no man can deny that. Yet there is a man who sits in that throne. What say you, my lord?'

More than a hundred heads turned back, delighted at the question and the tension of it. They turned to see if Edward would be undone, as if they witnessed the climax of a mummers' play. Yet Edward was ready for it, standing tall and confident. He had asked the same, appalled question the night before. How could he be king when Henry lived? He was willing enough to face Henry on the field of battle, but he could hardly deny the man his own throne while Henry still sat on it.

'For a time, there must be two kings of England,' Warwick had said on the dark road. 'As King Edward, you'll be able to raise the men we need. Knights and lords will come flocking to a Plantagenet king – with their men-at-arms. No matter what else occurs, you must not leave London without a crown on your head. With it, you will truly come to rule. Without it, Edward, your ambition and your vengeance will be trampled with your banners. You must speak aloud and *make* it true. Or remain silent, for want of daring.'

'I have no such want,' Edward had said. 'I would dare anything. Find me a crown. Let your brother touch it to my head. I will wear it. I will show you how it should be worn!'

In the great hall of Baynard's Castle in London, with the Thames rushing past outside, Edward spoke again, his voice cracking out with no softness in it.

'It is my thought, Your Grace, that the throne of England lies empty, even with Henry of Lancaster in it.' A chuckle ran around the hall. 'I claim the throne, by law, by right of blood, by my sword and my right of vengeance against the house of Lancaster. I claim it tonight and I will be crowned tonight, in Westminster, as so many others before me. I will join a brotherhood of kings before dawn, gentlemen. Which of you will ride with me to that place and see me declare for the throne? I will not dawdle here in London. I have business to be about and it will be a rough-hewn ceremony. Which of you will be my witnesses? I will not ask again.'

Warwick crossed himself and saw that he was not the only one to do it. To a man, they skirted blasphemy and dishonour, but Edward *had* a claim, if they did not examine it to death in the details. He was the heir and he did have the support of an army outside the city. Warwick imagined William of Normandy had no better claim than that – and he had been crowned in Westminster Abbey on Christmas Day in the year of our Lord 1066. It had been done before. It could be done again. All laws could be remade on strength of arms, if the need was great enough.

The crowd of men felt the gale and they bent like long grass. If they knew indecision or distrust, or even fear at challenging a divinely chosen king, they did not show it. Instead, they waved their cups and then cast them amongst the flaming logs and coals. The goblets blackened, seams opening so that flames shone through.

Some of the men chanted prayers; some recited family

oaths of fealty, or remembrances of childhood honour. When Edward moved, they went with him.

The night was dark and frost lay white on every surface. They crashed out into the yard in life and noise, with Edward at the very heart. It did not last beyond a few wild shouts. The numbing cold they drew in helped to sober them as much as the empty streets. Servants scurried and brought horses, but the mood had dampened and the true scope of what they were about had come home. In the silence, more servants brought out the banners of York, great swathes of dark cloth marked with a white rose, others with a falcon and fetterlock. As they were flung open, the banners crackled and blew dust under the moon, like a trail of light. Edward looked back at dozens of them, hanging pale. They were the symbols of his noble house and he bowed his head, whispering a prayer for the soul of his father before he raised his voice once more.

'Some of you were with me in Wales,' Edward said. 'Before the battle of Mortimer's Cross, we saw the sun rise in three places, casting such strange shadows as I have never seen. Three suns, shining on the house of York. I will bless the white rose until my dying day, but I will have a sun on my own shield. It warms those it loves, but it burns as well. Life and destruction, whichever I choose.'

Edward smiled then, enjoying the authority, though Warwick swallowed at the depth of anger glittering in the younger man.

There could not *be* two kings of England. If they made another in Westminster Hall that night, it would mean war, without pause or rest, until there was just one king once more. Like raging bees from different hives, the followers could not suffer each other to live. That was their course, their compass. That was the path he had proposed and York had chosen to follow. The banners of white roses and white falcons snapped and fluttered as the men rode out of Baynard's Castle to the Palace of Westminster, looming against the river flowing dark.

Margaret watched indulgently from a corner of a fine, warm room, enjoying the scent of polished wood and dried flowers. Her lords stood and talked in murmuring voices, abashed in the presence of King Henry. It was pitiable how they still looked to him, she thought, expecting some glance or spark of life, when all he could do was nod and smile and demonstrate the emptiness that had brought them to the edge of ruin. She could not remember the last time she had felt any compassion for him. His weakness endangered their son, Prince Edward. For that sweet boy, her heart could break with just a glance – and in that soaring dedication, she would feel again the thorns that were Henry's blank eyes and foolish smile.

If he had been a carpenter who'd lost his wits, perhaps it would not have mattered. When his lack of will endangered his son and wife and all the good men and women who had devoted themselves to his cause, it was a source of bitter anger whenever she dwelled on it.

Lords Somerset and Percy talked together, perfectly audible from where Margaret sat and worked the threads of a tapestry square. She had no eye for the work, and the result would probably have to be unpicked, but it allowed her to sit and listen, until she was forgotten and could learn all she desired to hear. With her husband's return, such subtleties had become necessary as her lords remembered her role once again.

Margaret smiled at the thought. Men worried about their place, more than she had ever known as a child. They needed to know who stood above them and who they could safely tread on below. She did not think women gave so much time to calculations of that sort. She smirked for a moment. Women trod on all their sisters, without special favour. It was safest that way. Each one sensed the dangerous potential in all the others, as men rarely could.

The walls of the Mercer guildhall of York were hung, predictably enough, with fine tapestries, each one surely representing the work of years. Looking at them, Margaret understood the desire to plan for the future, to begin an enterprise that could not be finished in a season. It was the very essence of civilization and order, she thought with a trace of smugness. Through her efforts and her patience, her most puissant enemies had been brought low. It had taken years, but then the fine strong cloth she had made would hold its colour for a thousand more, long after they were all dust.

She had raged at first, when London turned away her husband. She had not known then how such an event would sow dragon's teeth of *outrage* the length and breadth of the country. The city of York's gates had been held open for her lords, with men riding out to the king hours before their arrival to make it clear the royal party would not be refused.

In part, that had been Derry Brewer's doing, Margaret knew. Derry understood the story that needed to be told and he'd had it whispered in every inn and every guildhouse, from Portsmouth to Carlisle. The queen had found a valiant few, risking her life to bring Scots down from their mountain fastnesses. From rough northern towns, she had gathered a band of brave men to save the king – and she had brought Henry out of the clutches of traitors, tearing him from their grasp while sending their enemies running. At the last, she had been betrayed by London itself, a rogue city of merchants and whores, a city of madness, burning with fever. A city that needed a hot iron laid against its flesh.

The days of despair had changed to wonder as the numbers of her ragged army began to swell and grow. Each town they passed brought marching men to join them, responding to a king dishonoured. The news spread to every hamlet and village and town and city, driven by Derry Brewer's messengers and the king's purse. A thousand taverns had all their ale bought by the king's coin while some young serjeant told the tale and then led them out the following morning, ready to defend King Henry.

Margaret watched the men, seeing how those with authority stayed still, while others moved from cluster to cluster. As she drank in their movements, she began to wonder if it was not the other way around, especially as Derry Brewer was like a bee dipping his beak into a dozen blossoms, then starting again at the beginning. She did not know if bees had beaks. If they had, they would have resembled Earl Percy, she thought. His great nose was so prominent that it was hard to recall anything else about him once he had turned away. She saw the Percy earl with a fellow from Ireland whose name she did not know and . . . Courtenay, Earl of Devon. There were so many new captains and knights and senior lords, as if they had awaited only the right cause, or the chance to win.

She shook her head, touched by a heat of irritation. They had not come to her aid when the house of York had her husband in chains, when her cause had been hopeless. No, these were practical men. She understood that even as she despised them. She could still be grateful that, in their cold assessment, her side had become the place to stand.

Her hands ached from working the threads and she let them lie on her lap, drawn tight from the fiddly work, so that she had to use one to smooth out the palm of the other. The Mercer guildhall was a grand place, but there must have been three hundred there, swirling from group to group, eating and drinking and laughing their fill. Lords Dacre, Welles, Clifford, Roos, Courtenay; their captains, who threw back their heads to laugh but were still wolves, with names like Moleyns, Hungerford, Willoughby. She shook her head, closing her eyes. She could not learn them all; it was impossible. What mattered was that they had come to her cause. What mattered was that they had brought thousands of men, more than she had ever seen before. Her fifteen thousand had been engulfed by a great sea of retainers and knights and shields and war bands and archers and . . . She smiled dreamily to herself. York was a new London. No, a new Rome, if Warwick and Edward Plantagenet were to be broken on the armies around it.

She thought then of the blackened faces she had gone to see at Micklegate Bar. The heads of Salisbury and York had not cured well in the rain and bitter cold. Some local guard had pasted tar on to them to make them proof against the elements. Margaret could see them clearly in her mind's eye. Richard of York, Richard of Salisbury. York's paper crown was long gone, though some dribbles of tar still held scraps of it. She rubbed a spot on her temple, feeling an ache develop and groaning softly as flashing lights appeared on the edges of her vision. Such an ache had become more common in recent years. There was no cure for the pain but darkness and sleep. She rose to her feet and was instantly the focus of the room as servants scurried to aid her and all the men turned to see what had caught the attention of the rest.

Margaret blushed under that scrutiny, pleased that she still could, though she looked at them with one eye half closed against the pain. Her husband was watching her with something like affection, she saw. She curtsied to him and left them behind to their plans, knowing she would hear it all in time. It did not matter if they had come out of loyalty to her or to her husband. It did not matter if they saw her as a French nuisance who hardly understood how things were meant to work. She cared nothing for that. They had not come when she had needed them most – and she had won even so, saving her husband and taking the heads of two powerful enemies. She smiled at that thought. It was a never-ending source of delight to think of it.

There was work still to be done, of a certainty. Edward of York and all the Nevilles would have to be burned out. The wounds ran deep across the country, with resentments and hatreds for the years of war. Yet the blame was firmly on York and Warwick – and no matter how many men followed them, or the wealth they had gathered, they could not stand against the entire country. Once those houses had been broken and attainted, once their castles had been burned and their lines cut for ever, Margaret would be free to watch her son grow and her husband rest at prayer. Perhaps she would even be blessed with other children, before it was too late for her.

The servants closed the door as she left and behind it

she heard the conversations begin again. Margaret reached down and picked up the hem of her dress just enough to walk without fear of catching a foot in the cloth. She raised her head at the same time, though one eye seemed fastened shut, too sensitive to the winter light.

Outside, the clouds were rolling across the city of York, the sky a faded grey, like a sheet of lead, or a pale horse.

13

Dawn was hours off in the darkness of a winter's morning. Candles had been lit by scurrying servants, reaching up with long poles. Those gathered in Westminster Hall could see their own breath on the frozen air.

Edward of York stood in a belted robe of dark blue and gold over his armour, his long sword on his hip in its scabbard and tied with its own wide belt. As Warwick watched, the young man scratched vigorously at something biting him in his beard. There was mud still on his boots, Warwick noted. He wondered if Edward had seen the stone chantry of King Henry V in the Abbey across the road. The battle king, the 'Hammer of the Gauls', as it said on his tomb, had his likeness carved in robes – the effigy of a saint, not the leader of a war band.

Edward loomed tall above Bishop George Neville, his hair standing up wild without a helmet to press it down. The young Duke of York could see all the way across the vast hall, lit by so many hundreds of candles that the entire echoing space gleamed gold.

The King's Bench was a simple marble seat, dragged into place at the High Table, as wide as two men lying down. Edward stood behind the massive wooden surface, leaning slightly forward so that his gauntlets rested on black oak and his shoulders hunched like a raptor's wings.

The news was spreading fast. Members of Parliament had already taken their accustomed places along the walls, but lawyers and sheriffs and merchants and every man of authority who had been woken in those small hours were pressing in through the great doors. Shivering crowds could be glimpsed beyond them, all jostling for a view. Westminster Hall was able to take thousands before it was full, and men and women from the city entered in shuffling steps, seeking out any spot where they could stand in silence to wait and watch. The whisper was already running the length of London, carried on racing feet and in the throats of bakers and children and monks and anyone else awake at that hour.

Edward lowered himself on to the bench, resting his hands on the table. Bishop George Neville passed him a golden sceptre, taken from the Tower treasury. A sigh sounded in that cold from all the people gathered. It had not been a lie. The house of York was claiming the crown while King Henry of Lancaster was still alive.

The table was made for a man of Edward's size, Warwick realized. It had been the High Table for hundreds of years, second only in importance to the Coronation Chair in the Abbey. That would come later. The Hall of Westminster was for the declaration. Edward's smile showed that he was satisfied. Warwick could not deny he looked the part on the dais above them all, the man lit gold under a ceiling lost in shadows.

Standing in full robes, with a crosier in his right hand, Bishop Neville rested his left hand on Edward's shoulder. The message was clear: the Church would stand with York. As the young duke and heir bowed his head, the bishop spoke his blessing, calling on the saints to guide them all to wisdom. When it was done, everyone present made the sign of the cross and looked up.

The night before, the bishop had explained the oath that needed to be made. Edward had been impatient with the details, though he understood well enough. He needed men to fight for him, in huge numbers. Only a king of England could summon the country. Only a king could empty every shire village of its archers and young men.

'My lords, gentlemen,' Edward began. 'I am Edward Plantagenet, Earl of March, Duke of York. By the Grace of God, I am the vray and just heir to England, Wales, France and Ireland, all. I claim my right, in this place, at this High Table. I claim it through blood, from my father, Richard, Duke of York, who was descended from King Edward the First and through him to William of Normandy. And from my mother's line, who was herself descended from Lionel, Duke of Clarence, second son of King Edward the Third and senior to John of Gaunt. I hold these two strands as golden – and together, higher than any other claim on this seat and this throne and this land. I deny the right of Henry of Lancaster to my inheritance. Therefore, by God's Grace, I claim the realm. I am King Edward the Fourth of that name. There is no greater line – and I acknowledge no other man before me.'

He paused and Warwick saw sweat trickling down his face. With his size, and that great dark beard, it was all too easy to forget that Edward had lost his father barely two months before and was still eighteen years old. Yet his voice had rung out with force and confidence, astonishingly loud in the empty spaces of Westminster Hall.

Warwick glanced over his shoulder to see the source of the whispering and shuffling he had ignored all the time Edward had been speaking. He froze then, aware that a sea of faces stared back, thousand upon thousand, filling every row and space, standing in every window alcove, on every ledge. Men and women held children above their heads to see, or sat sleepy boys and girls on their shoulders, yawning. Most of them were smiling and their eyes reflected candle flames as they strained to hear every word and see it all.

Next to Warwick stood the slight figure of Edward's steward, Hugh Poucher. Warwick grinned to see the man's mouth hanging open at what he had witnessed. He leaned in a little closer.

'I take it your master did not share his plans with you, Poucher?'

The Lincolnshire man shook his head slowly, his mouth closing as he gathered himself. To Warwick's surprise, Poucher knuckled a tear with one hand and sniffed, shaking his head.

'No, but I will *not* let him down, my lord.'

Warwick blinked, more aware than ever of the responsibility he had undertaken by helping to raise Edward to the crown. There would still have to be a formal coronation in Westminster Abbey, of course, an event too important to throw away in the small hours of a winter morning. When that day came, the city would come to a halt and Edward would be toasted in every room, on every street, on the deck of every ship passing along the Thames and out to sea. Bells would ring in each church across the land.

'I am King Edward Plantagenet,' Warwick heard again. His gaze snapped up, suddenly afraid that everything they had planned would be ruined by the huge oaf who could not keep his tongue still.

'You will ask how there can be two kings in England,'

Edward said, as the crowd fell silent once again, hanging on his words. 'I tell you there cannot. There is only one. I summon all men of honour, as your king, to tear *down* the banners of the usurper, Lancaster. To stand with me as I make war on my enemy.'

Warwick's eyes widened as Edward stood and threw back his cloak. He reached out and one of his men passed over a jingling steel helmet with sweeping curtains of mail rings and a gold circlet cut into the brow. Warwick raised his hand and took a quick breath, suddenly afraid that Edward would crown himself and make a mockery of the Church. Such a thing could lead to them all being cast out and damned.

Whatever Edward intended, Bishop Neville was quicker. He took the helmet from Edward's outstretched fingers. The young man barely had time to look back before it was jammed on to his head, with the cloth of metal rings draping his shoulders.

The audience roared its approval as he turned once more to face them, understanding that they were witnessing an event they would always remember. With the birth of a child and the day they were wed, it would be with them until it was just a gleam of gold, as the weakness of death pressed them down. They had seen a man made king and they had seen a war begun.

They cheered Edward to the rafters of the hammerbeam roof, their voices echoing back and forth, multiplied until they were legion. In response, the ancient bronze bell of Westminster began to peal, the sound taken up and echoed by the Abbey and then by other churches, until the whole city echoed with the clashing sounds, over and over and over, as people woke for the day and the sun showed at last on the horizon.

Warwick watched King Edward being congratulated by a dozen powerful men, his own dear uncle Fauconberg among them. He recalled a tale he had heard of William the Conqueror's coronation. The Conqueror's men were viking by blood, but they spoke French and Norse and knew no English. The English spoke no word of French. Both sides had roared out their congratulations, growing louder and angrier with every passing moment as they strove to outdo one another. The king's guards outside the Abbey had thought fighting had begun and set fire to local houses. Apparently, they had believed a bank of smoke would interrupt whatever plan was afoot. In terror and confusion, riots had broken out all over London.

Warwick sniffed the air. No smoke, though he knew there would be bloodshed soon. Edward wanted it, more than any other man. The young warrior had no fear of taking the field. All he needed was enough men to walk with him.

Warwick saw his brother George making his way through the laughing, cheering crowd.

'Well done, Brother,' he called over the noise, having to shout.

The bishop nodded, applauding with the rest.

'I hope we have judged this right, Richard. I believe I have broken my oath in blessing another man as king.'

Warwick studied his younger brother's face, recognizing the real pain in him. As a bishop of the Church, it was no small concern. For him to have spoken it aloud hinted at an ocean of grief hidden beneath his twisted smile and distant gaze.

'George, I *made* you do this,' Warwick said, leaning in so close that his lips touched the bishop's ear. 'The responsibility, the error, is mine not yours.'

His brother leaned back and shook his head.

'You cannot take my sins on your shoulders. I have broken my word and I will confess and do penance.' He saw the concern in Warwick and sought to ease it, forcing himself to smile. 'It is true I am a bishop, but you know, I was a Neville first.' Even as Warwick chuckled, his brother's face grew cold. 'And, Brother, I am our father's son, just as you are. I would see his murderers shown a quick road to their death and damnation.'

York was the second city of England, with high walls and thriving trade that had created a class of merchants all vying to build bigger houses and employ more armed men to protect their fortunes. Every day that passed increased the size of the army around the city, though the leper hospital outside the walls was given a wide berth, with ropes and stakes keeping a path clear and the softly rotting inhabitants well away from healthy soldiers.

Derry Brewer sank the last of a pint of ale, gasping and wiping his lips up and down a bit of a beard he was growing. It was coming in grey, which bothered him. On the other hand, he admitted to being fifty-three years old, give or take a year. His knees hurt and his arms were too short to hold whatever he wanted to read, but he was still in a very good mood.

The only other man in the room was chained to a wall, though but lightly. The manacles were not spiked or tongued in iron to chafe him or tear his flesh. As brother to Warwick and a noblemen in his own right, Lord John Neville of Montagu was too valuable to bruise. Derry cleaned his nails with a tiny knife, kept especially sharp. He could feel Warwick's younger brother eyeing him whenever he thought the spymaster had his attention elsewhere. Not that there was much to stare at in the little cell below the guildhall in York. The only light came from a slot at street level, opening on to some private yard where passers-by could not look in. It was a quiet place, where no one could hear or see.

Derry peered into the jug of ale, seeing the best part of a pint still in it. John Neville's lips were cracked and sore from licking at them, his whole mouth a shade of raw pink. The ale had been meant for him, but Derry had been feeling thirsty. Ale drunk was never ale wasted, everyone knew that.

'Are you awake, my lord? The guards said you were shouting again, demanding your right to a priest or some such. The ransom has not been paid, John, not yet. Until it has been, we'll keep you alive and in reasonable comfort, as might be expected for a man of your station. Or I could hand this knife to our queen and leave her alone to tickle your parts with it, what do you think? She'd take that wrinkled purse of yours to keep her pins in, quick as you like. I don't think she'd refuse, do you?'

The prisoner straightened in his chains and gazed at Derry Brewer with all the confidence of one whose body had never betrayed him. Faced with that noble scorn, Derry briefly considered hobbling him. One tendon in the ankle – just one, sawn through – and the Neville family would remember the name of Derry Brewer until the Day of Judgement.

'Or would you like to declare for King Henry, perhaps?' he asked the young Neville lord. 'God is with *Lancaster*, son; that much is obvious! Why, I remember when we cut your dear father's head off. Now, I said then . . .'

He paused as Montagu lunged at him, his lips cracking as he snarled and heaved at his chains. The young man strained as if he thought he could rip them right out of the wall, but under Derry's cool gaze, he gave up and took a step back, flicking the chains like a snake coiling.

'Your father *was* a fool, John,' Derry said. 'He cared so much about his feud with Earl Percy that he very nearly brought down the king.'

'If he had, York would be on the throne,' Montagu said suddenly. 'You're a *paid* man, Brewer, for all your airs. You don't truly understand honour, or care. I wonder if you even know loyalty to those who press coins into your hand. Who are you, Brewer? A servant?'

'No more,' Brewer said, his eyes strangely bright.

'What? Are you saying "No, I am more than a servant"? Or that you are not more than a servant? Or . . . no longer a servant? Are these the sort of foolish games you play? If I had spit, I'd spit on them and you.'

The lord turned away and Derry stepped into the range of his chains. Montagu spun round, but Derry brought a cudgel down on his head, finding the right spot so that the young man slumped into the filthy straw. Derry looked down on him, panting and then surprised that he was breathing hard after so little exertion. He missed being young and strong and certain in everything he did.

His problem that frozen morning was that Warwick had sent the ransom for his brother without a word or a delay. The chest of gold coins had arrived in York on a cart, guarded by a dozen armed men. With the vast army around York, they had almost sparked off a minor slaughter as they came into range. Those guards had none of Lord Montagu's protections, so Derry knew they were being questioned with iron and flame about their masters. Either way, it meant he would be losing John Neville. It was a simple matter of self-protection for the lords around King Henry and Queen Margaret. If they did not release their noble enemies, they could not expect to be released themselves, if fate went the other way. Before sunset, Montagu would be given a horse and put on the road south. By tradition, he would be given three full days before he could be captured once again.

As Derry had observed before, the king's spymaster could not be a noble man. There was a well of spite in him that had no sounding, at least when he had the chance. For fifteen years, he had been made to run, to hide, to sweat by York, Salisbury and the Nevilles. It was true he was on the winning side, but that eased his brooding anger not at all.

'Master Brewer?'

A voice from above interrupted his thoughts, calling down the steps. It was one of the York sheriff's men, downy-cheeked and stiff with his new responsibilities.

'Have you freed Lord Montagu? There is a mount for him here . . . I have . . .'

The voice trailed away and, without looking up, Derry guessed he was staring into the room and at the sprawled prisoner.

'Has he fallen ill?' the officer said.

'No, he'll be fine,' Derry said, still thinking. 'Give me a few minutes alone, without you breathing down my neck, would you? I'd like to speak to him.'

To his surprise, the young man hesitated.

'He does not look aware, Master Brewer. Did you strike him?'

'Is that milk on your mouth, boy?' Derry snapped. 'Did

I *strike* him? Go and wait with the horse. Lord Montagu may need a hand to mount. Jesus *Christ*.'

The young man's face flamed with either anger or humiliation, Derry couldn't tell. He could almost feel the heat of it recede as he retreated up the stairs. With a sigh, Derry knew the boy would be trotting off to find a senior man. He had only moments and no time for invention.

He took hold of Montagu's outstretched hand and turned it palm down, folding the fingers into a fist. With quick, deep slashes, he cut a 'T' for 'traitor' into the flesh. Dark blood rushed to fill the lines, spilling over. Montagu opened his eyes as Derry finished, jerking the hand away from him. The Neville lord was still groggy and clearly no threat as he unlocked the chains. Derry struck him again with the cudgel, so that he fell face-first.

'Master Brewer?' came a growling voice from the stairs. 'You will release the prisoner to me now.'

The sheriff of York was not a young man. Derry imagined the white-haired old stick had seen about everything one fellow could do to another over the years. He certainly didn't seem surprised by the blood dripping from Montagu's fist or nose as Derry removed the manacles and dragged the young lord over the flags and straw. He saw the sheriff examining the letter he'd carved.

'Nice work,' the old man said with a sniff. 'Did you addle his brains?'

'Probably not,' Derry said, pleased at his calm.

To his astonishment, the old sheriff lunged suddenly at the man in Derry's arms, chopping a punch into his lower rib. Montagu groaned, his head lolling.

'He stood against the king. He deserves to have his balls taken,' the sheriff said.

'I'm game if you are,' Derry replied immediately.

He watched the old man consider and sensed Montagu struggling to regain his wits, dimly aware of what they were discussing. Derry readied his cudgel to silence John Neville once again.

'No, perhaps not,' the sheriff said reluctantly. 'It'd be my own if I allowed it. I'll have him tied to his horse so he don't fall off. You'll need to wake him a bit more to sign his name, or I can't let him go.'

Derry clapped the old man on the back with one hand, sensing a kindred spirit. Together, they heaved Montagu up the stairs, towards the fading light and his freedom restored. The blood from the nobleman's swinging hand left a trail, as the wounds would leave a scar.

Margaret shivered as the band of Scots regarded her. It was not from fear. Those bearded lads had been loyal – if not to her, then to their own queen. Yet the cold seemed to grow more fierce every day, though Margaret wore cloaks and layers of wool and linen under them, proof against the wind. March had begun and there was still no sign of spring, with the ploughed fields hard as stone. The city of York huddled around fires and ate stews made from the sort of beans that lasted decades and were only brought out when all else had gone. Winter meant death, and she could hardly believe these young men would walk bare-legged into the north once again. A slight shudder crossed her shoulders at the thought of losing four thousand of her army, but she had offered them everything she had. There was nothing left to keep them there.

'My lady, it has been an *honour* for these boys,' Laird Andrew Douglas said, through his hedge of black beard, 'to see how another great lady conducts herself. I will take back the news to our queen – of the destruction of your most powerful enemies and bringing your husband King Henry out of the fell clutches of those who might have hurt him.'

The Douglas nodded to himself in satisfaction and many of the young men on horses or on foot echoed the movement and smiled, proud of what they had achieved.

'No man could say we have not fulfilled our bargain, my lady. My lads have bled into this land – and in return, you promised Berwick and your wee boy Edward in a union.'

'Do not lecture me, Andrew,' Margaret said suddenly. 'I know what I have done.' She waited a beat to let the Scottish laird colour in embarrassment, then went on. 'And I will honour all my promises. I would promise more, my lord, if I thought you would stay. Your men have shown their strength and their loyalty.'

She might have bitten her tongue then, given that the loyalty was all for their own queen, but it was true they had kept their side of the agreements between them – and helped to win back all she had lost.

'My men have farms to plant in spring, my lady, though it is good to know we are held in high esteem so far to the south.'

Margaret blinked at the idea that York could be considered a southern city to a Scot.

'And yet we would not leave if you had not half of England coming to take arms for you.'

The Douglas gestured around him to the vast camp by the city, lords and warriors who had streamed in from north, west, south, even the coastal villages, where ships landed and disgorged more men. There had been little sign of so much support while Henry was a prisoner and Margaret was chased like a spring hare. Now, everything had changed. She dipped her head, showing respect to the laird, who coloured even more deeply. Margaret reached out and took his hand.

'You have my letters for Queen Mary. They contain my thanks – and I will not forget the part you played, Andrew Douglas. You came when I was lost and in darkness, with not a single lamp to show the path. God's blessings go with you and keep you safe on the road.'

The laird raised his hand and the captains he took with him cheered, waving caps and spears. Margaret turned slightly as Derry Brewer came to her shoulder to watch them march away.

'It brings a tear to my eye to see this . . .' Derry said. Margaret looked at him in surprise and he raised his eyebrows. 'When I think of all the things they have stolen, my lady, just walking away with them now, wrapped in their breech-cloths.'

In surprise, Margaret clapped a hand over her mouth as Derry went on, showing his teeth at the pleasure of making her eyes round.

'They clank as they walk, my lady. I think that bearded laird has Somerset's dagger and Lord Clifford's boots, though I would not begrudge him those.'

'You are a bad man, Derry Brewer. They came to my aid when I had need.'

'They did, but look at us now,' he said, raising his head.

Around them, their fifteen thousand men had doubled in number and still more came in. She could afford to dismiss the Scots at last – and if she had not, they would have gone anyway, serving another queen.

In amiable silence, Derry and Margaret watched the marching ranks dwindle into the distance, before the fading light and deepening cold made them both shiver too hard to stand out any longer.

Buffeted by the sound of bells and roaring voices, Edward beamed. Outside, Londoners were surging like bees between the Abbey and the great Palace of Westminster, filling every inch of open ground until they were up on the feet of the columns to catch a glimpse of the new king. He knew they had refused King Henry and his French wife. Perhaps they had been afraid of the city being sacked, but the result was that they had declared for York. He had not been certain the people of London fully understood the new reality. Their cheering reassured him.

Edward strode down the central aisle, thin ranks of his men holding back the mob. The path narrowed behind him as the soldiers were pushed inward. Everyone who could reached out and tried to touch Edward's coat or armour.

Warwick and his bishop brother were shoved aside in the mass of men and women pressing to see Edward and wanting to follow him out. Bells rang above and the echoes filled the open spaces, becoming discordant as they refused to die away. Warwick swore as a great, pink-cheeked merchant raked a boot down his shin and trampled one of his feet, straining to see over the heads of the others. With a shove, Warwick watched the man go down hard and stepped over him, bawling for them to make way, to clear a path. Norfolk and his guards were not gentle in their handling of the crowd, and cries of pain showed their progress to the open air.

They could still see the head and shoulders of Edward, taller than anyone else. The sun had risen and Warwick stood still for an instant as Edward reached the even colder air outside and the light caught the ring of gold set into the harder metal. Even then, with the uncomfortable sense of too many pressing around him and a thousand things needing to be done, Warwick froze for a heartbeat, then blinked as an even greater roar went up from outside. He pushed and shoved more roughly, forcing his way through and ignoring both the apologies and the shouts of anger from those he wronged or knocked flat.

By the time Warwick reached the outside air, he was panting and red-faced, with sweat drying instantly on his skin. Edward noticed his arrival and laughed at his ruffled state.

'See them, Richard!' Edward shouted over the noise. 'It is as if they have been waiting for this moment as long as I have!'

With a flourish, Edward drew his sword, held bare in his hand. Smiling wryly to himself, Warwick noted the blade was unbroken.

The crowd raised their hands and voices, seeing a king of England standing before them – and not a slight and pious figure, but a warrior of such physical power and height that he carried majesty in him. Some of them knelt, on stones so cold they numbed flesh in moments. It started with just a few monks, but the rest followed and the action spread along the square, revealing the members of Parliament, where they still stood and watched.

Edward met the stares of the Parliament men and he was not abashed, standing calmly until they too knelt in turn. They had made his father the heir and they held something like power, but there was not a man there who misunderstood the reality. In that moment, all Edward had to do was point his sword and they would have been torn apart by the crowds, desperate to prove themselves to the new king.

'London is a great fortress on a great river,' Edward said suddenly. He made his voice hard and very clear, so that it rang back from the walls around him. He spoke like a Caesar. Watching the young man, Warwick felt his heart leap with hope for the first time since he had heard of his father's death.

'I have become King Edward the Fourth on this day, King of England, Wales and France and Lord of Ireland by the Grace of God, in the presence of His Holy Church, in the name of Jesus Christ, Amen.'

The kneeling masses echoed his final words, crossing themselves. Not one rose, though they shivered in a freezing wind. Edward looked down on them all.

'I call you now, as your liege lord. Noble or commons, I call you to my side. Bring sword, axe, dagger, staff or bow. I am Edward Plantagenet, King of England. Send word. I call you out. Walk with me.'

14

Edward held up one half of a round silver seal, weighing it in his hand. With his thumbnail, he scraped away a trace of red wax, flicking it through the air. Around him stood a dozen long tables, all laid out with Writs of Array summoning knights and lords. Thirty-two counties and a dozen cities would receive the vellum scripts demanding the best armed men in the country to answer the new king's call.

Edward smiled as the four bearers of the Great Seal scurried about their business. The braziers created enough heat to make them all sweat. One man stirred a great vat of wax the colour of blood, while two others tended smaller pots of hot water bubbling around clay jugs. When the wax was liquid, they picked up the jugs with rags around the handles, bowing their heads to signal they were ready.

Edward gestured to them, tapping air.

'Go on,' he said.

'Your Highness does not need to ... We have, er ...' One of the men blushed and stared at his feet.

'No, I'll do it. My first Royal Seal deserves my own hand.'

The official swallowed and he and his companion approached the ring of tables. Edward laid the seal down and both men stepped in quickly. One poured exactly the right amount of wax into the silver mould, while the other placed a gold ribbon and smeared a disc of wax on to the vellum to prepare the surface. It was the work of expert hands and eyes, and Edward was fascinated as he turned the setting seal over before the wax could harden too far. He waited then, for what seemed an age, as the seal-bearers fussed around the substance that ruled their lives.

One of them removed the silver halves, revealing a perfect image of Edward enthroned and bearing the royal sceptre. It had been cast for him the night before by the Tower mint's silver master and he could only marvel at it as the Chaff-wax cleaned the seal and dropped it into a bucket of freezing water to aid the process.

'Again, then,' Edward said, looking around the ring of white cloth.

'I will take that finished one, Your Highness, with your permission,' came Warwick's voice behind him.

Edward turned with a smile, gesturing to the Chaff-wax to hand it over.

'It is a strange thing to see my face in wax,' Edward said. 'I can still hardly believe it. We have moved so fast.'

'And we still move,' Warwick replied. 'I have eighty horsemen waiting, ready to carry your call as far as we can. Norfolk is out gathering knights, proclaiming a new king and the house of York on the throne.'

Edward nodded, moving with the seal-bearers and upturning the silver mould once again. He stared at the image left in the wax, shaking his head in wonder.

'Good. That is enough for now I think, gentlemen. You may continue without me, until they are all sealed. My lord Warwick will bear them away then.'

The four officials bowed deeply, clutching their jugs and silver pieces to their chests. Edward pushed one table aside to leave the ring, moving the massive piece of oak with just one hand.

'The night before last,' he said, 'I was declared king. The result seems to be that everyone else has a thousand things to do, while I sit here and play with wax. Will you deny it?'

Warwick chuckled, though he ceased to make the sound when Edward's eyes became dangerous. Away from the torches and the tables, the new king seemed to grow taller.

'Should you concern yourself with nails and billhooks and salt fish?' Warwick said. 'The men are coming in, but we need weapons, food – a host of items to put them in the field. In your name, I have borrowed four *thousand* pounds today, with more to come from the Holy Houses.'

Edward whistled softly to himself, then shrugged.

'Will even that be enough? I want the best archers, of course, but I must have townsmen as well. Those who cannot use a bow will need good pollaxes, bills, shields, mail, daggers.'

'We have the Royal Mint,' Warwick said. 'I thought to borrow what we needed, but if it comes to it and consequences mean nothing, we could take the bars.'

Edward held up a hand, already tired of the details.

'Not till the end, for that. I won't be a thief. Do whatever else you have to do, my lord Warwick. Put my name to the life's savings of all the Jews in London if you wish. I would be on the road into the north today if I had the men I needed. Yet you say I must delay and *delay*. You hold us back.'

Warwick closed his eyes in anger and Edward frowned, understanding before he could reply.

'Ah, yes. I must wait – because my father rushed north with yours. Those two friends were too determined to bring their enemies down. Yes, I understand.'

For just an instant, Edward raised his head, struggling against the grief that made breath shudder in his chest. Unable to trust his voice, he clapped Warwick on the shoulder, staggering him.

'These Writs of Array are the sparks, Edward,' Warwick said softly. 'We send them out to begin a great conflagration across the land – a bonfire on every hill, calling them in. Thirty-two counties, from the south coast to the River Trent.'

'No further?'

'Beyond Lincolnshire? I have not troubled. The queen has her North Lords. All her support is there. They have already chosen their side.'

Edward shook his head, thinking.

'Send one more Writ then, just one, to Northumberland, like all the others going out. Send it to the sheriffs there, as if the Percy family had not chosen to defend a mindless, weakling king and his French wife.'

'The Percy family will never join us,' Warwick said.

'No, but they will have had their warning. They began this war. I will win it on the field, I swear it on the Holy Cross. Let them know I am coming and that I fear them not.' Edward put his hands behind his back, one fist holding the other as he leaned down to Warwick's height. 'You have one week more to assemble an army. After that, I will ride. On my own if I have to. But better with thirty or forty thousand, eh? Yes. Better we have enough men to finish the she-wolf once and for all. I will have those heads back, Warwick, from the Micklegate of York. I will take them down – and yes, I will find others to put in their place.'

Margaret rode a grey mare, with her son trotting beside her on a sleepy old warhorse. The vast numbers supporting King Henry had spread around the city of York in all directions, taking billets in every local town and village. The official camp was just to the south, where the London road crossed the village of Tadcaster. That was their gathering place, where men walked or rode across ploughed fields to join the house of Lancaster in war. Clerks and scribes checked names for pay and handed out pollaxes and savage billhooks to any man without one.

As Margaret guided her son through a landscape of banners and tents, of archers and axemen, hundreds knelt until they had passed. Six knights trotted armoured geldings alongside mother and son. The banners streaming out behind them showed three royal lions, as well as Henry's antelope and the red rose of Lancaster. Margaret wanted the symbols to be seen, wanted to show them all.

Every one of her lords was busy with a hundred tasks, or so it seemed. It would have made sense for her husband to ride with her, to show himself to the ranks assembling. His father would certainly have done that, cantering into every camp and speaking to all the captains and the men he would ask to stand and die for him. That was what they said. Instead, her husband had retreated into his own peaceful world of prayer and contemplation, far from the dangers she faced on his behalf. On a good day, Henry would rouse himself enough to discuss some thorny moral issue with the Bishop of Bath and Wells. At times, Henry could even fluster that poor old man with his learning. Yet he could not ride out to oversee an army setting tents and sharpening weapons, ready to put their lives to hazard in his name.

In King Henry's place, Margaret showed them her son, Edward. At seven years old, he was a tiny figure to be perched on the wide back of a warhorse. Yet he rode proudly, with his spine straight and a cool gaze looking out over the camps.

'How many there are, Mother!' he called to her, showing a pride that squeezed her heart.

Somerset and Derry Brewer both said he had the blood of his grandfather in him, without a doubt, the warrior king and victor of Agincourt. Margaret still watched the boy for his father's weakness, but there was no sign. She crossed herself and muttered a prayer to the Virgin Mary, as a mother who would understand her fears only too well.

'They have come to stand against traitors, Edward – to punish the evil men in London.'

'The ones who closed the gates?' he asked, pursing his mouth in recollection.

'Yes, those very men. They will come with great fierceness and anger, but we have here such a host as I have never seen – perhaps the largest army ever to march.'

She reined in with gentle pressure, halting her mare and turning to her son.

'Learn the banners, Edward. These men will stand with you when you are grown. If you ask them. When you are king, by God's Grace.'

Her son beamed at the idea and, for just a moment, she laughed with unaffected pleasure, reaching out to his head and rubbing his blond hair. Edward scowled at that and pushed her hand away.

'Not in front of my lords, Mother,' he growled at her, red-faced.

Margaret was caught between outrage and delight at his spirit, with one hand held near her mouth, where she had pulled it back.

'Very well, Edward,' she said, a little sadly.

'I will ask them to follow me, when I am grown,' he went on, trying to ease the sudden stiffness in the way she held herself. 'They must not see me as a boy.'

'But you *are* a boy. And my delight, my sweet jelly, whom I could squeeze to death whenever I see you frown. I could bite those ears of yours, Édouard.' He was in the middle of mock-groaning, half delighted at her quicksilver moods, until he heard the French pronunciation of his name and shook his head.

'Mama, that is not my name. I am Edward of Westminster, Prince of Wales. I will be king of England – and of France. But I am an *English* boy, with the dust of green hills . . . and ale in my veins.'

Margaret looked coldly at him in turn.

'I hear your voice, Edward, but I hear the words of Derry Brewer. Is that not so?'

Her son blushed furiously, glancing away. She saw his expression change and looked in the same direction. Margaret was not sure if she was relieved or annoyed to see Derry Brewer's spavined old mount jogging along towards them, all hooves and elbows. The man was a rotten horseman.

'Master Brewer! My son was just telling me how the dust of English hills runs in his veins.'

Derry beamed at the Prince of Wales, pleased.

'And so they *do*, my lady. With the water of English

streams in his blood as well. He will make us all proud, I do not doubt . . .' His voice trailed away as he realized Margaret was not smiling along with the idea. Derry shrugged rather than argue. 'His father is the king, my lady. His grandfather was the greatest battle king we have ever known, just about. Some would say Edward the Third, but no, for those of us who know true value, Henry of Agincourt was the man to follow.'

'I see. And there is no French blood in my son, then?' Margaret said.

Derry scratched a bit of mud off his horse's ear before replying.

'My lady, I have seen enough children born to know the mother is more than just a vessel, or a garden for a seed, as some say. I have seen mothers with red hair and every child they bear has the same ginger locks. The womb must scorch the child within, I can't deny it. Yet Edward here *is* a prince of England. God willing, he will be king one day. He has grown on English meat and learned English manners. He has drunk ale and water and wine from grapes in this soil. There are some who see the value in that. There are some who might say that makes him blessed above all other tribes, my lady. And some who don't, of course. Mainly the French.'

He grinned at her and Margaret tutted aloud, looking away to the vast camp.

'You did not seek me out to discuss being English, Master Brewer.'

He dipped his head, pleased that she would let the subject rest.

'Lads, would you take the prince here to see the cannon? I heard Captain Howard was test-firing two wheeled

guns today, with balls as big as my hand. Not Captain
Howard . . .'

He stopped himself, aware that Margaret was already
irritated with him. She waved a hand to give permission
and her son rode away with two of the banner-bearers,
proclaiming his name and blood with the quartered English lions and French fleurs-de-lis.

Derry watched him go with affection on his flushed face.

'He is a fine lad, my lady. You should not fear for him. I
only wish he had a dozen brothers and sisters to secure
your line.'

It was Margaret's turn to blush and she changed the
subject.

'What news, Master Brewer?'

'I did not want your son to hear, my lady. But you should
know. Edward of York has declared himself king in London. I had a man half kill himself to bring the news to us.'

Margaret turned fully to face him, her mouth opening
in shock.

'What do you mean, Derry? How can he call himself . . .
My *husband* is the king!'

Derry winced, but he forced himself on.

'His father was made the official heir to the throne, my
lady. In time, we would have put that right, but it seems the
son has taken that and bargained it into something greater.
He has . . . well, it seems he has a fair gathering of support,
my lady. London made a choice when they kept the gates
shut. They must support him now – and that means gold
and men and authority, come from Westminster Hall, the
Abbey – the thrones and sceptres, the Royal Mint.'

'But . . . Derry, he is *not* the king. He is a traitor and a
usurper, a mere boy!'

'My man said he is a giant, my lady, who now wears a crown and summons soldiers and levies of men in the king's name.'

He saw that the blood had drained from Margaret's face as she sat with her back slumping. His heart went out to her, fearing it was one blow too many.

'The only good news, my lady, is that all pretence is thrown aside now. There will be no more lies. Many men who might have stood by and waited will come to you. The army is already the largest I have ever seen. It will grow further, as the men of the north come to preserve the true king from traitors.'

'And we will crush him then?' Margaret said faintly.

Derry nodded, reaching out to her and letting his hand fall away without touching.

'We are not far from forty thousand men, my lady, with a fine solid core of warriors and archers.'

'I have seen armies torn apart, Master Brewer,' Margaret said faintly. 'There is nothing certain once the horns are blown.'

Derry swallowed, growing irritated with her. He had a dozen important things to do and comforting Margaret was not one of them. At the same time, he was aware that he felt some trace of arousal. There was just something about a beautiful woman in tears that perked up his spirits. He considered what it might feel like to press his mouth hard on hers, and then shook himself, forcing his mind back on to a safer path.

'My lady, I must be about my business. There cannot be two kings. What Edward has done is lock us together until there is only one.'

15

Fourteen days after he had declared himself king in Westminster Hall, Edward rode north with a vast host. The Ides of March, the midpoint of the month, was three days behind. He thought of Caesars as he walked his horse along the London road, away from the city. The winter was still strong on the land and there would be no foraging in the path Margaret had taken with her northerners and Scots. Edward and his captains passed burned manors by the dozen, with villagers running into woods as soon as they sighted his marching ranks.

For such an army, there was no question of using the paved road, more was the pity. Edward had suffered through meetings with Warwick and Fauconberg, who explained that staying on the road would create a line *days* long, so that any vanguard met by the queen's army would be cut off from support. Rather than become too long a thread, they had to stay in wide formation. The men marched in ranks a mile across, in three squares. The advancing lines clambered through forests and over hills and through streams, slogging through thick clay and mud so glutinous it seemed alive. The city of York was two hundred miles into the cold north and Edward was resigned to losing nine or ten days to the march. His men were well supplied at least, thanks to the favour and wealth of London. Merchant ships had brought the food they needed up the Thames, while the city's moneylenders seemed to have understood that their futures lay with his.

Edward rode proudly in the front ranks of the centre, surrounded by banners bearing a sun in flames, his father's falcon and the white rose of York. He had given command of the right wing to the Duke of Norfolk, as the most senior lord present. Warwick and Fauconberg had been given the left, and if the two Nevilles saw any insult in that, they had not shown it. In truth, Edward had not meant it as a criticism of the forces who had been overrun and routed at St Albans, though they made up the bulk of that square. If half the reports coming into the south were correct, the queen's army was at least the equal of his own. Scouts and merchants were given to exaggeration, but Edward had the sense that he could not delay. Battles could be lost but wars still won. Every day on the road was another for the queen and her lackwit husband to bring in more soldiers and more lords.

Having his lords out in command of their own vast squares also meant that Edward did not have to speak to them, which suited him well enough. He was not even in sight of their portions of his army and he spent his days with the Welsh captains and archers, once again feeling as if he were better suited to being a clan chief than a king. Yet his nineteenth birthday was still a month away and he revelled in his strength and surety of purpose. The army around him was a mass of coloured surcoats over armour and mail, a thousand different family crests woven or painted on to cloth and shields. Beyond the professional soldiers in the employ of knights and barons, the common men had come to his side, sick of the failures of Lancaster and driven by memories such as Lord Scales using wildfire on a London crowd, all in the name of King Henry. They carried their pollaxes and billhooks like bristles on a hog, beech handles resting on their shoulders or used as a staff – all overmounted by an iron head. The pollaxes were part axe, part spike and part hammer, while the billhooks tended to have a heavier blade. In unskilled hands, they were still solid cutting tools. In the grip of those who knew them well, they could pierce armour and allow a common man to stand against a knight in plate.

Edward had been astonished at how many of the surly lads marching along with him seemed to nurse a personal grudge against the house of Lancaster. Half of his Kentish and Sussex contingent used the name of Jack Cade as a blessing – and would tell anyone prepared to listen how the queen had broken an old promise of amnesty. They had given their oaths to York out of anger and betrayal. In return, Edward could only bless every mistake Margaret had made.

The cold tightened its grip as they pushed north. At first it was a relief to men who had grown exhausted plunging through sucking mud. They shivered and blew on numb hands and the hard earth was unforgiving when they slipped and fell, yet they made a better pace on the frost. The carts of food and equipment kept up with the marching men on the London road and Edward read tallies of boots and injuries in the evenings, when his servants set up a tent and a meal. He spent hours before sleep overseeing weapons work with his knights. At first, the common soldiers had clustered around the flickering torch square to watch the giant who led them. Something in their stares had irritated Edward and he'd sent them away to their own sword practice. Every night after that had been filled with the shouts of captains and the clash of metal.

Edward could sense the power of a king in the way

others looked to him. He saw it in the knights so eager to spar, to show their worth. It was more than just the favours or even the titles he could bestow. The young knights saw a new England in him, after years of ruin and confusion.

At times, it felt like magic. Edward had asked Warwick about it only once, after a perplexing introduction to a squire too red-faced and choked to speak at all in his presence. Edward frowned whenever he thought of that. He felt some of the same awe, but not so much as to render him speechless. Perhaps it was in him from birth, or because his father had shown him the truth of power.

'They'll hang on your every word,' Warwick had said in London. 'They'll flatter you, but they'll fight for you, long after they should have run – because you are king. They will cherish the memory of just a few words with you as perhaps the most precious moment of their lives. If you are a man to follow, the crown will gild you further and make you . . . heh, a true giant, a King Arthur in silver armour. On the other hand, if you rape or strike a woman, say . . . if you show cowardice, if you kill a barking dog even, or show some petty temper, it will be as a mirror breaking.'

The words had gone deep. Edward had only shrugged at the time, though he had committed them to memory and had decided to live by them, with a certainty he could feel in his bones. He had even refused drink each evening, letting the men see him sober and pouring with sweat as he trained. He drank water and ate mutton and salt fish, revelling in his health and youth as he slept like a rock and rose again before dawn.

Four days out from London, they met John Neville coming south. He had made his way down the London road, following the Roman flagstones and healing as best he could, though some fever still laid him low. Warwick had greeted his brother with riotous delight until he saw the fading bruises and the pus-filled cut on the back of his right hand. Warwick had grown cold then and pushed the men on, turning his brother in his own tracks back to the north.

For his part, John Neville was delighted and awed at the sight of so many thousands. On a fresh horse and fed on meat for the first time in weeks, he recovered enough over the days that followed to ride the bounds of them, trotting his mount for miles to the east and west. He passed on all he had learned, but Derry Brewer had kept him blind-folded whenever there had been something to see. Even so, Warwick gave thanks for his brother's deliverance. For all he shared a common cause with Edward, there was something disturbing about the unleashed wolf of the new king, simmering with anger at the slightest provoca-tion. Edward was not easy company and Warwick had missed the easy trust he'd shared with his younger brother, where he did not have to watch every word.

King Edward's host had been nine days on the road when the furthest scouts came across the first sign of a hostile enemy. The London road ran through the village of Ferrybridge, where a fine construction of oak and pine planking had always stretched across the River Aire. The waters now raced past broken and splintered beams, the bridge cut down. Edward's ranks were a mile east of the crossing and he gave orders for Fauconberg and Warwick's square to move up and repair the bridge – to build a new one from felled trees so that the army could funnel through and continue its progress north. The city of York lay not twenty miles further on and Edward was determined to enter those walls and retrieve the relics of his father and brother. Every day lost was one more of humiliation and he would not be denied.

Warwick watched the carpenters work. Overseen by a couple of serjeants who knew their way around peg joints, they had set to with a will. Replacing a bridge was meat and drink to such men, good solid work with the satisfaction of a craft and a task completed. They smiled as they hammered axe-head wedges into birch logs to split them, while others took over with adze, billhook and plane.

The bridge piles were still there, of course, too deeply set to pull out and too wet to burn. They would sit in the water for a century; all his men had to do was put beams and planks over them. They anchored ropes around their waists and risked falling in to carry the planking across the piles, hammering in spikes with massive blows. It was crude work, but it did not have to last for a generation, just a few weeks.

Fauconberg wandered over, eating a wizened apple. Warwick heard him crunch through the core of it and turned.

'Uncle William,' Warwick said. 'It will not be long now. There's half of it in place already. We'll be back on the road by tomorrow morning.'

'I was not checking on you, lad. No, this is land I know well enough. I hunted not ten miles from here with your father when we were young fellows together.'

Warwick's smile became slightly strained. His uncle's stories could catch him unawares, so that he felt his eyes prickle and his breath become short. He resented it, as if it was weakness dragged out of him.

'Perhaps you could tell me another time, Uncle. I have some papers I must read and letters to finish.'

He looked at the sun and saw it was a smear of light behind grey clouds. There would be lamps lit in his tent and the cold was already bitter.

'I see,' Fauconberg said. 'Go to your work then, Richard. I will not hold you. Your brother John was standing here not an hour back, just chafing to cross the flood. I take pride in you both, you know. You would make your father proud.'

Warwick felt his chest tighten and a surge of anger in response. He inclined his head.

'Thank you, Uncle. I hope so.' He gestured to the river, so swollen that the banks were crumbling in swirls of brown clay. 'The work goes well enough. We'll move when the sun rises again.'

Lord Clifford was not in the best of moods. He had not appreciated being given the task of cutting the London road to the south and he was near certain that Derry Brewer was behind his being singled out in such a way. It was surely the sort of work better suited to a lowly serjeant or a band of common labourers. There was no need at all for a man of high birth to oversee two hundred archers and as many with axe-handle billhooks, all trudging along and casting resentful glances in his direction. Somerset and Earl Percy of Northumberland would not have agreed to such a task, he was certain. Still, it was done. The bridge had been hacked apart and the pieces thrown into the torrent, to vanish downstream as if it had never existed.

Clifford had asked a senior captain about removing the bridge piles. The man had shown clear insolence on his grinning face – an expression that had earned him a dozen lashes. The man had been popular amongst his fellows, it seemed. Certainly they thought his treatment entitled them to glare at Lord Clifford as they marched back to the main army. He refused to respond to such rudeness, staring always ahead.

'My lord! Lord Clifford!' came a voice.

Clifford turned with a sinking feeling, knowing that the strain in the young scout's voice would be an unlikely herald of good news.

'Report,' he commanded, waiting while the scout dismounted and bowed, as he had trained them to do.

'There is a force of soldiers at the bridge, my lord. Already cutting new wood and nailing on.'

Clifford felt his heart leap in anticipation. The bridge was still down and he had archers. If this was the first sighting of the Yorkist army, he had a chance to wreak havoc in their lines. With the advantage of surprise, he might even manage to thump an arrow through the chest of Warwick or Edward of York himself, the false king whose very existence made heaven rage. He would return to King Henry and Queen Margaret as a hero . . .

'My lord Clifford?' The scout had the temerity to interrupt the bright-coloured visions parading across his eyes. 'Begging your pardon, my lord, but do you have orders? They were using the old piles across the river and it will not be long before they are on the road behind us.'

Clifford put aside his irritation at the younger man's questions. He'd known those damned piles would be a problem. If the captain hadn't burst his heart during the flogging, he would have dragged him back to the river to have him shown the point.

The sun was setting and Clifford knew he had ridden only a few miles from the broken bridge. He looked at the archers halted around him, suddenly seeing why Somerset had insisted he take such a force for so very ordinary a task.

'Back to the river, gentlemen! Let us surprise these traitors. We'll show them what good archers can do.'

The men around him turned where they stood. Without a word, they began a loping trot that ate the miles, racing the fading light of the sun.

As darkness came, Warwick had finished the last morsels of a fine brown trout, caught in the very river he had stared at all day. The temperature had dropped even further and he was weighed down by thick blankets over his jerkin and underclothes. Well wrapped, he was content and beginning to drowse when he heard the jingle of armed men moving. In the black tent, Warwick sat up on his elbows, staring into nothing.

Outside, across the river, he heard voices call for archers to draw. Warwick threw back his coverings and sprang across the tent, yelling for shields as he scrambled into the night.

The camp was not dark, he realized in horror. He had given orders for the work to continue during the night, lit by dim yellow lamps. It meant that the workers out on the river gleamed gold, all oblivious to the sound of men approaching as they hammered and sawed.

'Shields! 'Ware archers!' Warwick bellowed.

He could see spots of light all over the ground

thereabouts, each one the embers of a cooking fire for thirty or forty men.

'Douse those *fires*!' Warwick yelled. 'Water there!'

He was answered by shouts of confusion and surprise, while over the river a single order rang out. Warwick took in a frozen breath, hearing arrows whine into the air, loud even over the rushing of the torrent. Out of instinct, Warwick raised a hand over his face, then forced it back by his side. Without armour, it would not save him, and he did not want his men to see him cower. All around, he could hear shafts strike, thumping into wood and metal and flesh, tearing tents and ripping choked screams from sleeping soldiers. More and more punched the ground on his side of the river, white feathers visible.

There was almost no light, the moon but a crescent. Warwick caught glimpses of men in shirts or jackets grabbing shields, sacks, anything. Some even swept up planks of birch, carrying them in front of their faces, though arrows thumped through and pierced their hands. Warwick was sweating, expecting an arrow in his flesh at any instant. When his steward took his arm, he swore in shock, accepting a shield held out to protect him with embarrassed thanks.

The cooking fires were smothered, dropping darkness on to the camp. The torches on the river had vanished as the carpenters threw them into the water. Warwick knew he was panicking. He had been caught by surprise and horrible confusion. Yet the enemy archers could not move past the opposite bank, some two hundred feet away. The answer struggled slowly through his addled mind.

'Fall back three hundred yards – fall *back*! Move!' he roared.

The shout was taken up by others, over the sounds of screeching pain and dying men. He had the sense of arrows arcing in towards him, but he had his own shield up by then and he did not dare to stop moving. The light on the river was gone, making the water a stretch of impenetrable darkness. Beyond it, there was not a single lamp, just the sounds of moving men, taunting and jeering at a camp in disarray.

Warwick turned away, feeling a surge of terror at showing his back to archers, with shafts still whirring in all around them. Some of his men had draped shields or planks on their backs, but the only true protection was in getting out of range. There was no sense of decorum in that dark flight. Warwick felt himself buffeted by men who did not know him. He fell, but staggered up and pushed his way past others, struggling against the fear of sudden death that was upon him.

He saw Edward coming towards him, lit by flaming torches. Even in the darkness, the banners gleamed silver, catching the moonlight. The presence of the king was like cold water thrown across the faces of the fleeing men. They lost their wild look and wide eyes, suddenly ashamed and stumbling to a halt.

'Someone report!' Edward shouted at them. He had found his army running away into the darkness and he was consumed with rage. Not one of them would meet his stare. 'Well? Warwick? Where are you?'

'Here, Your Grace. It was my order to take the men out of range of archers. They sit across the river and they cannot drive us further away.'

'Yet I would cross that river,' Edward snapped. 'And how can I do that if there is no fucking bridge?'

Warwick swallowed his irritation at being lectured in such a way by the young man. His uncle Fauconberg spoke before he could.

'There is another crossing place, Your Grace, some three miles west of here.'

'Castleford?' Edward replied. 'I know it. I hunted all these lands as a boy and . . . more recently.'

He had an image in his mind of a woman then, in a house not too far from that spot. Elizabeth, her name had been. He wondered if she thought of him at all, then smiled to himself. Well, of course she did.

'Very well. Lord Fauconberg,' he said, putting aside more pleasant thoughts. 'Take three thousand fit lads and *run* to that ford. Be sure some of them are archers as well. Understand? Some small part of the night remains – you should be back on the other bank before dawn or thereabouts. Let's see if we can surprise our brave attackers.' Edward waved Fauconberg away and turned to the man's nephew. 'Warwick, get the damned bridge finished. Have shields held over the carpenters, as you should have done before, whatever you need to do – but make me a crossing.'

Warwick bowed his head stiffly.

'Yes, Your Grace,' he said.

Turning on his heel, Warwick was pleased the darkness hid his seething anger. He had helped to make Edward a king, an eighteen-year-old giant, who it seemed would order him about like a bootboy. At the same time, Warwick reminded himself that it did not matter if the young man was brash or thoughtless. What mattered was that King Henry and Queen Margaret were brought down – the queen far more than her pitiful husband. There were heads on the Micklegate Bar in York, and Warwick knew he would swallow any humiliation or unfairness to see them removed.

The dawn's dim light revealed everything Lord Clifford had hoped to see. Careful not to stray into bow range, he rode as close as he dared, as soon as he could make out the opposite bank. He shook his head then, in disbelief and delight. Four of his captains rode with him and they thumped each other on the backs and laughed in awe at the carnage and destruction they had created.

'You see, gentlemen, what good planning and foresight will bring!' Clifford declared. 'For the price of one bridge, for a morning of hard effort, we have torn the heart out of a traitor's army.'

What had been hidden from view the night before was the sheer numbers of men killed in their beds. They had lain close-packed on the ground, wrapped in blankets like cocoons against the chill of the night. As the fires had died, they'd shuffled closer and closer, risking scorched hair and cloth to keep from freezing. Into that packed mass had come some three thousand shafts – two hundred men with a dozen or eighteen arrows each, shooting blind until even their long-accustomed shoulders burned. There had been no answer to the rain of death they had laid down across the waters. Under the pale sky, Clifford was only sorry it had not been more.

Hundreds of corpses were still being collected and laid out in rows, even as Clifford rode up to observe. Most of the bodies remained where they had been struck, sprawled around the bridgehead, dark in a field of white shafts. Boys ran to collect the arrows, at least where they had struck into marshy ground and could be salvaged. They hurried around with armfuls of them, barbs snagging on their woollen jerkins, so that they hung like bee stings.

Beyond those scurrying boys and the dead, a dark line of horsemen rode up in silence, wider and wider, with Edward at the centre of them. Clifford's smile grew sickly as the banners of York were raised on either side of the man who claimed the throne of England, who dared to call himself a king. There was no mistaking the son of York. The horse he sat was a huge stallion, uncut and aggressive enough to snap at any other horse near him. The rider made no acknowledgement of Clifford or his captains. Edward simply held his reins loose in one gauntlet and waited, staring. Above them, the sky was full and pearl-white, the wind dropping to nothing as the cold only deepened.

16

Lord Clifford's four captains rode up to his side, each wearing his crest of a red wyvern on white surcoats over their armour. Despite that proud symbol, somehow Clifford sensed they made a pitiful group compared with the false king and his knights on the other bank. He could make out the banners of York as well as those of Warwick. There was no sign of Fauconberg or the colours of the Duke of Norfolk. Clifford felt his much smaller force was under similar scrutiny. He sat as tall as he could in his saddle.

The oldest of his captains cleared his throat thoughtfully, leaning over to spit on the muddy ground. Corben was a wry, dark man, with deep lines cut into his cheeks and right around a mouth that some might have called sour. He was a veteran of twenty years' service to the Clifford family and had known the baron's father.

'My lord, we might try a last handful of shafts dipped in oil and set afire. Now that the sun has risen. It will slow the work once again.'

Lord Clifford looked at him in pity, recalling why he had never considered putting the man forward to be knighted.

'We do not *want* them delayed further, Captain Corben. I'm certain His Majesty King Henry has not assembled an army of so great a size just to wait for spring. No, I have achieved my purpose – and much more! I believe I have struck the very first blow in this "war of two kings" – as it may come to be known, in time.'

Clifford smiled to himself, still imagining the praise due to him. Staring off along the river into his own future, the baron was one of the first among his men to see what was coming. Captain Corben looked in confusion at his master as Clifford went wax-pale.

'My lord?' Corben asked, before looking back over his own shoulder and swearing.

In the dawn's light, the fields along the river seemed to have come alive with running soldiers and cantering horses.

'Archers!' Clifford called immediately. 'Archers to the front there!'

'They have no shafts, my lord,' Corben retorted instantly, even as Clifford caught himself and was drawing breath to countermand the order. The baron shot a furious glance at his captain as he shouted across the ranks of men.

'Disregard that order! Withdraw north – all ranks in good order. *Withdraaaw!*'

The captains and serjeants echoed the final command, grabbing milling archers and shoving them roughly round, away from those rushing up behind. It seemed to take an age under the constant pressure of the approaching enemy. Clifford's voice cracked and rose as he yelled across them all once again.

'Captains, can you not get the men moving faster? Withdraw to the main army!'

As if to make his point, the outlying archers racing along the river bank had stopped at the most extreme range to bend their bows. Arrows leaped up from them, falling short but clearly visible to those who had turned their backs and were jogging away. Though there were no wounds, it caused panic in those retreating ranks, so that the men pushed and shoved, forgetting their discipline.

Clifford's archers were fastest, without armour or mail to slow them. They began to slip through the other ranks, pulling away from those following. With Clifford, not more than a dozen of the men were ahorse and they had been up all night. It was a miserable group that trotted and jingled away from the river and broken bridge. Behind them, an eerie hooting went up from three thousand throats on the chase, howling in mimicry of owls or wolves as they closed the gap.

Lord Clifford forced down his rising fear, summoning Corben to his side.

'Send a rider to summon our support, someone quick. You should have had scouts out to give me more warning, Corben.'

'Yes, my lord,' Corben said, accepting the rebuke with no change of expression beyond his usual hawkish glare. 'I have already sent young Anson, my lord. He's small and his mount is the fastest we have.'

For a moment, Clifford considered taking Corben with him. The man had served his family for twenty years. Then again, it had been with no particular distinction.

Clifford looked past his captain once again, shaking his head in fear at the closeness of the enemy. 'It may be that I . . .' His mouth worked, seeking the right words. 'I can go further and faster than these men on foot, Corben. It may be . . .'

'I understand, my lord. My oath was to you – and to your father. I do not hold such things lightly. If you ride north after Anson, we may be able to hold them for a time here.'

'You understand,' Clifford said, nodding firmly. 'Good. I am . . . valuable . . . to the king.' Sensing that the words were not quite enough when leaving a man to his death, he chewed the inside of his lower lip for a few more precious instants.

Corben shifted in his saddle, his horse prancing to the side.

'My lord, they are almost upon us. I must see to the men.'

'Yes, yes, of course. I merely wanted to say . . . I could not have asked more from a servant, Corben.'

'Well, *no*, my lord!' Corben snapped.

Clifford stared in confusion as the grim-faced captain wheeled his horse and cantered away, the hooves kicking up thick wet sods. The baron waited long enough to see the first arrows come soaring in earnest, dropping the rear ranks of his retreating force as if claws had been laid into their flesh. They could not protect themselves as they withdrew, and he realized very few would survive. Clifford looked past his own lines to the horsemen cantering easily up on both flanks. He swallowed, suddenly feeling his stomach and bladder clench as fear made his heart race. The howling ranks were men who had seen their friends and captains killed the night before, torn from life in a darkness of whirring shafts. There would be no mercy from them and every man retreating knew it.

Clifford looked up as something cold touched his face. Snow was falling, softly, the first drifting flakes followed by more and more, so that whiteness seemed to come down with them, drawing in the world until he could hardly see the dark riders over the river, or the ranks racing towards him on this side. He wiped his eye and dug in his spurs, forcing his startled horse to gallop away.

*

Edward of York glowered at what he could see happening, just a quarter-mile across the river. His warhorse sensed his surging emotions. The animal snorted, throwing up its head to make the armoured scales at its chest rattle and clash. Horses along the line responded, calling and blowing until Edward reached down and patted dust from the animal's neck, settling its nerves.

He leaned forward in the saddle, the better to glare across the water to where Warwick's carpenters were finishing their work. A last load of wood had been wheeled out on to the rickety line of planking, wide enough only for one horse or two men at a time. The entire front rank of Edward's army waited to funnel through that pinch point. Senior men set about it as a tactical problem, preparing pike teams to rush across first and establish a safe spot on the other side, then knights on horseback to pursue the fleeing enemy. It would be difficult and dangerous work, and all the while, snow fell from the white sky, vanishing into the River Aire with a sound like a breath.

Everyone with the king could feel the rising excitement, the strain building in the air. Fauconberg was blowing hunting horns on the opposite bank, his men hooting like gangs of ruffians as they chased down an enemy left with no arrows to keep them at bay. There was a righteous slaughter in the offing – and those with Edward wanted to be a part of it, every last man of them.

Warwick's attention was on his men hammering and thumping pegs into holes to hold the planks, then iron crucifixion nails to secure them to the bridge piles. The river was already running fast and deep – if they rushed the labour and the bridge broke, it would mean the lives of whoever fell in. Yet they could all see Clifford's red wyvern retreating, with its curved tail like a snake. Edward had certainly seen it. The big man quivered at recognizing the very lord who had murdered his brother at the field of Sandal Castle. He wanted Clifford and he was almost at the point of risking his horse in the flood to get across.

Warwick jerked from his reverie as Edward spoke. At first his voice was just for those around him, but the young man paused and then repeated his words at the top of his voice, carrying to them all.

'You know the custom of the battlefield is to kill all common men and spare those nobles who surrender or ask to be ransomed.' He shook his head, an expression of great bitterness twisting his mouth. 'My father was not given such a chance. His great friend Earl Salisbury was not. My brother Edmund was not. So, I have this to say to you. This is my order: kill the nobles. Obey me in this.' He took a slow breath, making his armour creak. 'Allow no ransoms. Accept no surrender. I desire to keep my people alive. But not the poisoned houses which stand against me. Not Northumberland, not Somerset, nor Clifford, though he is mine or he is fate's victim. Unless he breaks his neck, I will put him in the grave this very day.' Edward paused again, pleased that not a man spoke or even seemed to breathe as the air thickened with snow. 'There will be blood shed this morning, a torrent like unto the river you will cross. It must be so, to wash old wounds clean, before they kill us all. We have been hot with fever, but it will be cut and drained here, in this snow.'

Ahead, on the river, Warwick's men raised hands to signal the completion of their work, hurrying onward to stand alertly on the other side. Neither Clifford's forces nor those of Lord Fauconberg were still in sight, though in part it was because the world had come in close around them, the swirling snow stealing away the long view. Edward looked across the river, watching flakes hiss into the waters. There was no one left to threaten his men and he lost patience.

'To the devil with standing still,' he snapped. 'If you would honour me, follow me now!'

He put on his helmet and dug in his heels, so that his horse lunged. The great destrier clattered across the make-shift bridge, setting all the new pins and pegs to rattling under the combined weight. His bannermen and knights went hard after him, trying to keep Edward in sight as he dimmed in the white air.

The rest came across in urgent file, without gaps, moving nose to tail or pressing against the next man in line, while those ahead streamed away immediately, creating more room. Thousands crossed and formed squares while the snow settled on the ground, turning the fields white.

Lord Clifford knew he had lost the main road when the sound of his horse's hooves changed from a bright clop to a dull thumping on ploughed and frozen earth. He dared not stop and try to find it again. The entire world had been reduced to barely a hundred yards in any direction.

He rode at great speed alongside a valley, looking across it and seeing nothing more than the sweep of land dropping away, all the rest hidden in the curtain of thick falling flakes, spinning and floating but incessant, filling the air to choking. His one comfort was that the messenger boy Anson would be far ahead, perhaps even already at the royal camp. If Anson was as fast as Corben had claimed, perhaps he had already delivered his news and there would be an armed force racing back along the road, ready to spring on those who pursued him. The biter bit! He chuckled at the thought of it.

Clifford felt himself shivering as he rode, wiping cold-tears from his eyes and looking back over his shoulder every few moments for some sign of pursuit. Captain Corben and the four hundred he had brought to cut the bridge were long behind, of course, doing their duty in holding back their pursuers. With a clench of his jaw, Clifford accepted they would be run down and killed.

That would not be well received in the king's camp. He shook his head at the unfairness of it. If he had only left the river while it had still been dark! There had been no snow then and he would have stayed ahead of any pursuit, making it safely back to the main lines with a grand story to tell. He cursed his luck. All Somerset and Percy would hear now would be that Clifford had lost four hundred men, with two hundred precious archers amongst them. It was dispiriting – and all for the sake of seeing the destruction they had wrought in the night.

His horse stumbled violently in a great lurch. Clifford cursed the animal, wrenching at the reins and settling himself once again, panting from fear of falling on such hard ground. He reined in for a moment, listening to shouts and sounds of fighting far behind. It was near impossible to judge distance in the snowfall, but there was at least no one in line of sight. If his horse went down, he knew he would be as helpless and vulnerable as the meanest foot soldier. He squeezed his knees and the horse snorted uncertainly, jerking into a trot. Clifford's face and hands were bare and quickly going numb. He dipped his chin and blinked against the flakes, just enduring.

The main camp was just a dozen miles north of Ferry-bridge, though it seemed a world away at that moment. Surely Somerset would have scouts out? It could not be long before Clifford was warm once again, describing the vital part he had played in bloodying the army with Edward of York, delaying them from joining battle. Clifford had heard there was an Earldom of Kent with no man to claim it. One of his captains had gone drinking with Derry Brewer and the spymaster had let such a delicious titbit slip while deep in his cups. It was not beyond reason to imagine the title finding its way to the lord who had held Ferrybridge against the entire army of York. Clifford's minor losses of men would surely be forgotten in the face of such momentous news.

Derry Brewer reined in on his horse, Retribution, watching closely as a stripling youth struggled with two impassive sentries, completely failing to dislodge the grip that those men had on him.

'Let me go, you fools!' Anson screeched, growing utterly frantic, like a fox caught in a snare. 'I have vital news of Lord Clifford!'

His face had grown red and Derry saw he was little more than a blond boy, fourteen or fifteen at the very most and not even well grown.

Derry dismounted with a grunt, passing his reins to one of the guards and standing over the lad with the other. He saw a grey horse resting nearby, its reins loose as it cropped the snow for grass underneath. The boy was still flushed and one side of his face was swelling from whatever blow he had received for his cheek.

'What's your name, lad?' Derry called to him.

'Nathaniel Anson, sir. If you'll have these ... *men* unhand me, I am a messenger and herald for my lord John Clifford.'

'What's that? Clifford? He's down at Ferrybridge on some make-work. You'll find him there.'

'*No.* I've come *from* there, sir! I have news to report to Lord Somerset.'

'Somerset is a busy man, son,' Derry replied, his interest prickling. 'Tell me what you have been instructed to say. I will pass it on to the right ears.'

The boy Anson sagged in the hands holding him upright. He was bursting to tell and it was clear he would not be allowed to go beyond the sentries without giving at least some part of his information.

'The vanguard of York's army has reached the River Aire, sir. Some of his men have crossed further down and are threatening the small force with my master. Do you comprehend my urgency now, sir?'

'I do,' Derry said. 'Though we don't let wild young men ride to the heart of an armed camp just because they shout to let them pass, do we, son? We follows the rules, or such young men might find themselves with an arrow through the chest, say, or one in that swollen eye. Is that understood?'

The young man mumbled agreement, his face flaming.

Derry jerked his head to the closer of the two sentries.

'Get on then, Walton. Take the boy's horse and pass the news of York to Somerset and the captains, Lord Percy if you see him. They are to make ready to defend camp, or march out, that's not my concern.'

The sentry jumped up on to Anson's grey, causing the animal's head to jerk up and a gasp of outrage to issue from the lad. Derry took his own grip on the boy's jerkin in case he tried to run for it.

'Now then,' he said, when the sentry had vanished into the falling mists of snow. He saw Anson was shivering violently, his sweat turning to ice after the exertion of his wild ride. Derry found himself impressed by the lad's determination, though it did not sway him from his chief interest.

'You say Lord Clifford is threatened?' he demanded. 'Tell me about that.'

'When I left, I saw two, even three thousand men coming along our bank. They must have found a fording point . . .'

'Aye, there is one at Castleford, not three miles west,' Derry replied. 'How many fine fellows did Lord Clifford have with him?'

'A few hundred, sir. Not one for a dozen of the enemy! They had the soldiers running like . . . in great number. Now, please, let me go. If you can spare another horse, though that fine mount was my own, a gift. I would return to my master's side, to fall with him if I must.'

'Oh, good lord,' Derry said. 'You sound an educated boy. Are you perhaps his bastard? No? Not his catamite? I cannot say I like the man, but I have never heard that he found his interest in . . .'

He was surprised by the slap, from such a source. Anson had reached high and delivered it with as much force as he could muster. Derry turned back in surprise, a smile spreading across his features.

'How *dare* you, sir,' Anson began.

Derry laughed at him. He raised a fist and saw the boy repress a flinch, steeling himself in contempt for whatever beating would come. Derry opened his hand on the jerkin and let Anson fall and scramble back.

'Son, if I am to save your master from his own stupidity, I must gather a great number of hard and violent men – and ride out. Go back now, along the road, before you freeze to death in this snow. Go! You have passed word. I am Master Brewer, steward to King Henry. I will not fail you.'

He added the last in a flourish. The boy struggled up and ran away into the whiteness.

Derry waited for a time, until he was certain the boy had gone. When the world had grown quiet, he turned to the sentry, still standing and watching him, ready for orders.

'Well?' Derry said.

The man shrugged and said nothing. The lack of response was not enough for Derry and he leaned in closer to the taller man.

'How is your wife? It was . . . Ethel, wasn't it? Fine hand with a shirt. Fine woman, built strong.'

The man flushed and looked away.

'Her name's not Ethel, no. But you don't need to threaten me, Master Brewer. I ain't seen nothing. I ain't heard nothing either.'

'That's the way. You might find a purse in it for you as well, son. I don't like to threaten good men, though some need to be told. Would you like to ask me about Lord Clifford?'

'No, Master Brewer. I 'ave no interest at all.'

'That's the spirit, son. God giveth and God taketh away. Just be sure you're present when he giveth – and somewhere else when he taketh it all back.'

The spymaster chuckled and rubbed his face, still

feeling the sting of the boy's blow. Winter cold made fighting into an agony, weakening men so that wounds hurt worse and legs grew stiff and numb. Not for nothing were wars fought in spring and summer, anything rather than the bleeding snow.

Derry put his misgivings aside. He'd made his decision. It was to do absolutely nothing. Some miles to the south, Lord Clifford would be plunging on in growing desperation, seeking the royal camp in a world where everything had vanished into whiteness. Derry laughed out loud at the thought. He just could not think of a man who deserved it more.

17

Clifford reined in once again, to listen. It was extraordinary how the falling snow soaked up sound. All he could hear was his own breath in his helmet, until he took it off to turn his head back and forth, straining for any sound at all. Snow brought an exaggerated stillness, with even the small noises of his horse and armour magnified. He might as well have been riding a featureless plain, some vast and empty valley with no other sign of man. He knew there were armies surging forward to clash and die, but he could not perceive a single sign of them. The sick sense stole over him that he could well have been turned around. The road was long behind and his own hoof-prints filled as he went. There were perhaps three inches of snow lying on the ground, or three times as much, he did not know or care. He had a vision of riding in lost circles until he stumbled into his enemies, or more likely froze to death. It was infuriating and yet all he could do was go on, searching for some sign of the royal camp. A dozen miles had never seemed so far as it had that morning. The very air was smothered in the silence.

A dark spot appeared over on his left-hand side, drawing his attention. It was no more than a smudge, but it stood out in the world of whiteness. Even the trees had lost their dark shapes in so heavy a fall. Clifford craned his neck, wiping the flakes from his face in a rough gesture to squint across the field.

There, he saw movement and more than one shape. He could hear his heart and felt his throat dry. If those men were sentries from the royal camp, he was home and safe. If they were not, he was in mortal danger. He fretted, curling his hands into the reins. After a moment's thought, he drew his sword and held it across his chest to obscure the red wyvern. Better to prepare to fight, though his instinct was to run.

'Hello, the line!' he called. 'What banner?'

Whoever the men were, they were trudging through the snow. Recruits then, common men with billhooks of iron and beech, like forest huntsmen. In the snow, they would not dare attack a mounted lord, in case he was one of their own. Clifford gave thanks that his red wyvern surcoat was painted on white cloth. He could get close before they identified him, and if they were of York, he would be off, galloping away. He placed his helmet on the saddle horn as he walked his horse across the line, angling in closer with every step, his panting breath coming hard.

He heard them shout in reply, though their words could not be made out. Clifford cursed at the lack of banners in the marching line. They were forming out of the white by then, dark ranks appearing at the edges of his vision. He heard hoofbeats somewhere not far off and began to panic, suddenly aware that his mount was as weary as he was himself and could be overtaken. Yet it would be madness to run from the safety of the royal lines and he hung on, teeth chattering in the cold.

'Ho, there! What banner?' he called again, tightening his grip on the reins and his sword. He could see a pole in view and he blanched as he made out the same quarters of red diamonds and blue rearing lions that had driven him away from the River Aire. Fauconberg. As Clifford gaped in horror, he understood he had been turned around, that he had approached the men on his own trail. In a heartbeat, he saw the marching men were archers, hundreds of them. They had seen him, heard him calling in the muffling snow.

Clifford began to wheel his horse, too late and too slow. A few dozen men had heard that lone voice and been searching for some sight of him. When they saw a rider in armour, they reacted as archers, fetching out arrows from the long quivers bumping on their hips, nocking and drawing as easily as they breathed, sending flat shots instinctively aimed, lost into the white, invisible the moment they left the bow.

Clifford was struck hard in the side and back, rocked with his horse as it screamed and reared. Another shaft took the baron across the throat as he flailed away in blind panic, straining to get clear of the animal before it crushed him in the fall. He was dead before he struck the ground, his armour crumpling with metallic protests as the horse rolled over him, legs kicking.

Those who had made the shots could not leave their position in the marching ranks, though they cheered and held up their bows, calling for others among their number to note the skill. A different part of the line reached Clifford's broken corpse and identified the red wyvern on white with satisfaction. A serjeant halted three men around it and runners raced to take the news to Edward. Another was dispatched to Warwick and Fauconberg, so that they too trotted across to see.

It did not take long for the leaders of the York army to reach that spot. Fauconberg was there first, looking down on Clifford's broken figure with a grim expression. The news had already spread that Edward would not allow prize ransoms to be taken, causing some resentment. A common man could make a fortune on the battlefield with the right prisoner. Still, the billhook men waited in awe for Edward to arrive, dropping to one knee in the snow when he stood before them. Warwick and Fauconberg completed the same movement, giving Edward honour with the eyes of thousands on them.

Edward's gaze was on the corpse. He reached down and took a grip in Clifford's hair, turning the head to get a good look at the stiffening face, already distorted from where it had lain.

'This is the coward who killed Edmund?'

Warwick nodded and Edward sighed to himself, letting the head fall back with a thump.

'I wish it had been by my hand, but it matters more that he is dead. My brother can rest and this one can no longer crow like a cock on a dunghill. Very well. We go on, my lords, though I cannot see much further than I can spit. Has anyone laid eyes on Norfolk? I have not seen his banners for an age. No? This snow is poor stuff for a battle. Call out when you reach our enemy, or if you sight our missing wing.' He breathed hard through his nose, controlling his irritation and nervousness. 'The captured men say Tadcaster is the main camp. It will not be so far away now. March on and blow horns when you see them shaking and dropping their weapons in terror before you.'

The gathered men chuckled as they turned away.

'Your Highness,' Fauconberg called. 'I am still ahead of your centre square. I know it is the Duke of Norfolk's wing that should brace them first, but I had a . . . thought about the snow. I have a thousand archers with me, Your Highness. I would use them to surprise and break the heads of those waiting for us, with your permission. Unless the Duke of Norfolk would take a slight by my so doing.'

Edward turned back, hiding his worry under a grin. It had pleased him to have Warwick's uncle use his royal title with ease, as if it had always been so.

'Perhaps if my lord Norfolk were here, he would, but it seems my strongest wing has wandered further than I would like. Yes, you have my permission, Lord Fauconberg. I will send another thousand archers over to you, if you take a slow mile.'

Seeing that Warwick remained, Edward smiled.

'Will you hold the centre with me, Richard?' he called.

'I will, Your Highness,' Warwick said, pleased. At such a moment, he could only shake his head in awe at the young king, formed from clay.

Edward turned to the ranks watching him intently, their eyes bright with excitement. He sensed it and put aside his worries about Norfolk and eight thousand men vanishing into the snow when he needed them most.

'Onward, lads. We'll bring a king down today. This was just his dog.'

They cheered him and resumed their march, stamping hard to bring back feeling to frozen feet. Around them all, the perfect stillness faded, replaced by a rushing wind that stung their bare faces and hands. The eerie silence had gone, but the cold was worse. The gale seemed to drive them forward, spitting fragments of ice against already numb skin. Many of the men looked left and right along their own line as they marched, always disappointed at how few of their ranks were revealed. The air was thick with flakes, whipping across them and driven into every fold and seam of their clothing. Made blind in the snow, shaking as they walked, all they could do was go on, with their heads bowed.

William Neville, Lord Fauconberg, urged his great left square ahead of the king's centre, pushing his captains hard over white fields. His scouts had vanished into the snow ahead and all he wanted was to close on the Lancaster formations as fast as possible. He and his men had already seen fighting that day, though it had been more in the nature of a slaughter, as three thousand fell upon Clifford's four hundred – and half of those armed with nothing more than bowstaves and knives. The odds had not troubled his soldiers. If anything, the easy killing of exhausted enemies had settled and delighted them. A dozen times, Fauconberg had seen one of his lads battering away at a fallen man, landing four or six blows with a pollaxe to shatter bone and spread red drops on the snow. They were both savage and skilful with the tools they had been given. They were good fellows, he thought. They would do.

For the moment, though, his mind was on his archers, still slogging along with full quivers of two dozen shafts to a man. Fauconberg looked up as he rode alongside them, feeling the wind increase and break across from the south-west, funnelled through snow into an icy blast. It gusted even harder and he could see darker patches in the whiteness, as bushes and lonely trees gave up their weight of snow and shook free, only to be touched once again by whispering flakes.

Not far ahead lay the lines of King Henry and Queen

Margaret, he was quietly certain. The few men he had captured that morning had told all they knew, babbling anything to save their lives. Fauconberg did not know if they had been spared or killed after that. What concerned him was the closeness of the Lancaster camp. His men had marched for half the morning, though their pace was necessarily slow as the drifts built. The land was never flat and they had passed isolated farms and darting, bleating sheep as they went. Without complaint, his men had trudged down hills and up escarpments, crossing entire valleys. He did not know if they marched for him or perhaps for some new-forged loyalty to King Edward of York. It did not matter, as Fauconberg saw it. He gave orders for his ranks of archers to move to a wide front, their precious bows wrapped in oiled leather to protect them. Without the long shafts of pikes, they would be vulnerable to horsemen, but Fauconberg accepted the risk on their behalf, as their commander. The wind was growing in strength behind them, pushing into the teeth of the enemy. It too could be of use.

It was on a downward slope that two of his scouts finally found him. One of their horses had gone lame, limping visibly from being forced over rough ground. Yet risks had to be taken if they were to survive, that was simply the be-all and end-all of it. Fauconberg acknowledged the young man who dismounted before him, then his companion as he raced up and reined in, leaping down and staggering in his excitement. Both were pink-faced and freezing, pointing back along the route they had come. The simple gestures were made with good reason, as the snow had thickened, tossed and swirled in the wind, so that the entire world vanished into dancing mists of flakes.

'Four or six hundred yards, my lord,' one of them panted. 'Flags of Lancaster. There they have chose to stand. And wait.'

'I saw pikes, my lord,' the other scout chipped in, not wanting to be overlooked. 'Standing in a host, like a . . . like hog bristles. The snow hid many, though I went right close on my belly and crept up until I could hear them breathing, just waiting on us all.'

Fauconberg shuddered. No one fought in winter, which meant no one knew what to expect or how best to use the extraordinary circumstance of two armies practically sitting on each other's cloaks without knowing it. He had two thousand archers, with those Edward had marched up to aid him. He felt the young king's trust as a weight on his shoulders, but not as a burden. He made the sign of the cross and kissed the family crest of his signet ring.

'Now then, lads. Everything I would like to bring about depends on your skill. Finely judged distance will be the key to it. While I pass the orders, I'd like you to pace it out, separately, then bring me your tally. Get as close as you dare, but do *not* let them see you, or we will all be lost. We have a chance to spill their guts on this snow, if we do it right. Go!'

The scouts raced off, leaving their mounts. Fauconberg whistled for his captains. The snow swallowed the sounds of them approaching, so that he had a sense of how the enemy must still be waiting, straining to hear, never knowing how deaf and blind they had become.

Fauconberg passed on his orders and waited for the scouts to return, desperately afraid of the sudden shout and call to arms that would mean their presence had been discovered and reported.

The two young men came back within moments, of each other.

'Five hundred and twenty,' said the first.

His colleague looked scornful.

'Five hundred sixty,' he said.

'Very well, gentlemen,' Fauconberg replied. 'That will serve well enough. Rejoin your horses now and make ready.'

He passed the word and the waiting captains and serjeants dropped pikes across the waists of their own men. It was impossible to halt so many with no sound at all, but the voices were muffled and dim, passed on and on until they were all standing still. Fauconberg's archers moved slowly and quietly forward, away from the rest of his men. The gap widened until the entire force of two thousand had vanished into the white.

The Duke of Somerset cantered along the lines, passing waiting men stretching off into the distance, snow settling on them. It was an impressive array. As well as pikes and bowmen, there were huge numbers with billhooks, pollaxes and swords. They waited on foot or in mud-spattered troops of mounted knights on either wing. With drummers and water-carriers, the camp followers of a dozen other trades moved between the ranks while the soldiers checked their weapons and equipment, touching and patting pouches and blades.

The king and queen were safe in the city of York, eight or nine miles away. Somerset had command of the army, with Earl Percy in the centre, a dozen barons and scores of veteran captains. With news of a vast force approaching, Somerset had marched them out of camp and some way between the villages of Towton and Saxton, on bleak and frozen earth. On his order, they had drawn up on a featureless bit of scrubland, with the ground falling away before them to the south. Somerset shook his head in awe at the scale of it all. Just six years before, Warwick and Salisbury and York had challenged the king with a mere three thousand men at St Albans – and come close to winning. Somerset looked over three squares of at least twelve thousand each. He had found a good spot for them, with flanks protected on his left by marshes and on his right by the Cock Beck, the river running thick and fast with all the snow that had melted into its waters. It filled Somerset's heart to see the fervour and stoic acceptance in the men. They would stand for King Henry. They were loyal.

The weather was the one aspect that infuriated the young duke. Somerset wore polished plate armour, lined in leather and thick cloth, designed to soak up impacts that would otherwise kill a man. It was also proof against the freezing cold, much more so than the layers of wool and greasy linen his pikemen wore, with bagging hose and just a jerkin to protect them. None of them had experience of fighting in winter, that was the problem. Even his most senior captains were unsure if the soldiers were better off crouched or lying, whether they were more likely to freeze to death on the ground or standing still. It made sense to keep them moving around, though it wore at their strength and interfered with ranks and stations. Some of the old hands said sweat was a subtle enemy, that if a man grew too hot in the plunging cold, his sweat could freeze on the skin and whip the life right out of him. While they waited, the wind had risen in strength, doubling in gusts until it whipped stinging crystals of ice into their faces. Many of them stood with arms raised against it, eyes narrowed down to the thinnest of lines.

Somerset shook his head like a twitch. He waited with the greatest army he had ever known – close on forty thousand men, with billhooks, bows and axes. More, he had the favour of the king and queen, especially Queen Margaret. Yet the frozen air and the snow made him doubt it all. The cold scratched at his confidence, as if he breathed it out in the plumes of mist that made drops run down the inside of his helmet. In truth, he knew he suffered less than older men. Some of his standing lines were red-faced townsmen in their forties or fifties. Men who had volunteered in hot blood had not expected to have it chilled in a vast silence, with just the wind's whistle for company.

'Come to halt!' Somerset heard, somewhere out in the white. He looked up in sudden alarm. Somerset's fear communicated itself to his horse, so that it skittered and danced. He could see his front ranks looking at each other, asking if they too had heard the voice.

'Archers, *nock and draw*!' came the same voice, almost on top of them. 'Loose! Loose! And nock and draw! *And nock and draw!*'

Somerset wrenched his horse back to face the shouts. He squinted into the snow, but there was nothing to be seen.

'Cover!' he shouted to his stupefied captains. 'Shields and cover! Archers to the fore, here! Archers! Archers to answer!'

None of his pikemen carried shields. The huge poles that worked so well against cavalry needed both hands to balance the weight of the iron head. The billhook and axemen controlled their blades with two hands, like woodsmen hacking at saplings. They stood, dumbstruck, still. Then the terror of the archer surged across them, driving them to a frenzy as the whining, shrieking sound grew. The rushing breath of arrows in the air had men throwing themselves down with their hands over their heads, or crouching to make themselves small. Somerset's captains bullied them back to their feet, bawling for them to stand like men.

Somerset looked up into the whiteness, blind, though he could hear the shafts coming. It was the most terrifying moment of his life.

When they struck, the arrows were moving too fast to see. They appeared out of the snow as a blur, then were suddenly visible in flesh and hard ground, quivering, or wrenched around by the agony of whoever had been hit. Somerset hunched as they battered at him, rattling off his shoulders. Every surface of his armour was rounded and polished to give arrows no purchase. He thanked God for it even as pain bloomed in his thigh and he looked down with a gasp to see white goose feathers. One shaft had struck him cleanly through the iron, pinning his leg to the thick leather and wood of his saddle. With a curse, he took a grip and just pulled, growling, until the red gave way to a black head, appearing in a spatter of blood. A bodkin tip, smooth and piercing. He breathed in relief that it had not been barbed. No one had heard his cries of pain, not over the screams and shouts and wails of hundreds more who died as he watched, their twitching bodies and jerking limbs slowing and becoming utterly still.

'Fall back there!' Somerset bellowed. 'Archers to reply! Archers here!'

The only answer to the arrow storm was for his own bowmen to force them to break it off. Even as his archers pushed their way forward, shafts kept falling in incredible numbers, as unceasing as the snow itself. The ground was littered with stripped feathers, stained in blood or shattered on metal. The front ranks stumbled raggedly away from the death they could not see or find cover from. They fell back in fear, dazed and terrified by the sudden assault.

Somerset knew only minutes had passed since the first arrows had hit. In that time, the air had been thick with them, every heartbeat. It could not go on; that was the hope to which they clung. The enemy's quivers would empty, fingers would reach for shafts that were not there. When that happened, the answer could be brought down on their heads.

The arrows died away like the last rattle of a summer storm, leaving hundreds and hundreds weeping and groaning in pain, with God knew how many bleeding out their lives and falling still. Swearing archers pushed past dying men, bending their bows and loosening shoulders. Somerset exulted at the number of them, enough to reply in turn. He only prayed that York and Warwick would be caught as he had been, staring into nothingness as iron tips came spinning down at them.

Somerset waited until the first volley was shot, thousands of shafts, then again and again. It was a rain of destruction, easily the equal of the numbers that had fallen on his camp. It would do. Though his leg had gone numb and blood dripped from his iron boot, Somerset raised his hands for messengers to carry new orders, watching his archers bend their bows to the sky over and over, sending great looping shots to spear down on an enemy.

Fauconberg stood in silence, listening to distant screams. A smile tugged at his mouth, though he was shivering and grim with lack of sleep. His archers had brought the most powerful weapons of the field to bear, then darted back, exactly as he had ordered, jogging three hundred yards away from the enemy lines. They had no arrows by then and the carts with fresh quivers were somewhere far behind, or lost with Norfolk's vanished right wing. Fauconberg would let them fall back until they were furnished once again with the arrows they needed.

He had waited for just a short time when the Lancaster archers responded. Fauconberg's smile increased, his eyes glittering. Those men shot into the wind rather than with it, as his archers had done. Better still, the thick snow meant they had no idea his men had fallen back. Thousands upon thousands of arrows fell where his ranks had been standing just before, a rippling, hissing edge of death that reached almost to where they stood, but landed still and silent, with not a single life taken. The archers grinned at their immunity and Fauconberg laughed at the audacity of another thought. He waited until the rattling sounds stopped. They were not finished then, not quite yet.

'Archers to collect shafts,' he called across them.

Men who felt secure only when their quivers were full raced forward, yanking out arrows from where they had sunk into the earth. Some had shattered or cracked, but others were whole. They compared the quality of each other's finds and seemed pleased, laughing at the way Fauconberg had out-thought the enemy.

When they had full quivers, Fauconberg gave fresh orders to his captains and the archers bent their bows once more, sending the arrows of Lancaster back down the throats of those who had shot them.

18

Edward of York let out a growl of satisfaction as he saw marching lines coming towards him. They were indistinct in the snow, just a blur of darkness and raised pikes at that distance. Horns blew on both sides as the forces of King Henry trudged down the sloping ground to meet him. Looking up at the pale sky, Edward thought the visibility was improving. He could see a little further, though there were still thick flakes in the air and every step crunched through a sparkling surface, left churned and brown behind by the ranks plodding over it. Still, he had not brought twenty thousand men two hundred miles to act the bashful suitor. His aim was to make an ending.

'I have made confession for my sins and I have offered my soul to God. I believe I am ready, my lord Warwick,' he called. 'Now, will you stand with me?'

'Yes. Yes, I will,' Warwick replied.

Edward grinned and both of them dismounted. They could see the banners of Somerset and Percy ahead, the tramping lines growing closer, accompanied by drums and pipes and wailing horns to stir the blood.

As Warwick and King Edward touched the ground, a shout from nearby captains halted the centre square with impressive discipline. Thousands of eyes flickered between the young king and the approaching ranks intent on their destruction. There seemed to be no end to them.

Warwick patted the neck of his horse and then took a

pollaxe from a surprised soldier, whipping the hammer side of the weapon through a circle and bringing it down with a terrible crack on the mount's broad forehead. The animal collapsed instantly, already dead. The men around them cheered and Edward swore in surprise, chuckling.

'A fine gesture, Richard,' he shouted, for their benefit. 'You will not run, then. Yet if I did the same, I could not find another horse big enough to carry me!'

To his pleasure, the men around him laughed, repeating the words to those who had not heard. Edward's massive destrier was taken back through the ranks by proud boys. Others raced to the front to give out drinks of water to anyone who needed them. All the time, the dark lines came closer, more and more men appearing on the wings out of the swirling snow.

On foot, Edward and Warwick took their position in the third rank. Banners were held high around them, declaring their presence on the field to ally and enemy alike. Both men hid their nervousness as they rolled their shoulders and whistled to the captains. The entire central square lurched into movement once again, this time with a king walking with them. The dead horse vanished into the marching ranks.

Edward's helmet left his eyes and nose uncovered, though metal wrapped his chin and jaw. He had refused the helms that reduced the world to a slit, despite the threat of an arrow through the face. Better to see, he'd said. His eyes were pale and cruel as they stared across the lines facing him. There was no doubt in them.

'Let us put an end to these weak men!' he called. 'No pax! No surrender! No ransoms!' His voice was like a blow for those standing near him.

'For King Edward!' Warwick roared.

Thousands of men yelled it even louder, stripping their throats raw as they clashed axes and long knives together. Edward laughed in simple pleasure, raising his sword in salute to them. The sound crashed out, so that some of those approaching flinched or missed a step. Edward's soldiers did not let the sound die away, though for a time it became an incoherent growl of angry men, forced to that cold place with iron in their hands.

Warwick could feel his bladder squeeze and his breath grow lighter in his chest, as if his lungs would not draw well. He wore the crest of his family on a surcoat over his armour and he carried a sword and shield with the same Neville colours. He had played his part in making Edward a king, in daring that blasphemy in the face of King Henry and the Lancaster throne.

'Your uncle did amazing well before, Richard,' Edward said into his ear, breaking in on Warwick's thoughts. 'He understood the snow better than us, I think. Better than anyone.'

'He is a good man,' Warwick yelled back with a shrug.

The noise around them had reached the level of thunder cracking overhead or lions roaring. The ground seemed to shake and Warwick felt borne along on a great wave, pressed in with such force that he could not resist. His focus was on those Edward affected not to notice, solid pikemen and axemen striding along, their faces burning with delight at the thought of engaging the usurper king. They could see the white rose banners and they would be angling towards that spot.

'Have you any news of Norfolk? I have had no word of him since daylight.' Edward grabbed Warwick's shoulder, their helmets tapping together and scraping. 'I fear the worst from him.'

Warwick risked a sidelong glance, realizing again that Edward was very young. The king was fresh from his declaration for the throne, marching towards a huge army, barely three months after the death of his father and brother. Yet it seemed to be more than just the nervous desire to speak. Every step brought more and more of the Lancaster ranks into view. Without Norfolk, Edward knew how badly they were outmatched. His gaze was worried.

'You may trust Norfolk, *Your Highness*,' Warwick shouted over the tumult. He gave York his title deliberately, wanting Edward to hear it and be reminded. The army they had gathered needed him brash and wild, not suffering doubts. 'I am certain he lost his bearings in the snow and last night's darkness. Yet Norfolk is a man of these parts. He will not be far behind. He will come in fury, the more so for falling back.'

Edward dipped his head, though Warwick could see that the shadows across his eyes had darkened, his expression grown even colder. They were well within arrow range and Warwick understood how many lives Fauconberg had saved by pulling the teeth of the Lancaster archers earlier that morning. As one who had suffered the particular terror of arrow fire, Warwick gave desperate thanks for that. There was no sound in the world as frightening as the bird-screech of arrows coming in.

Not a hundred yards separated the two armies by then. Many of the men had laughed and joked at first, or called out thoughts and remembrances of old debts as they closed. Voice by voice, they had felt their mouths dry. The drums still rattled and captains and serjeants exhorted their men to strike first and strike hard, but the laughter and the light words had come to an end. The great squares stretched beyond the limits of sight and the snow still fell.

Warwick readied himself for the hardest physical task he had ever faced. He had trained his entire life for it, from childhood striking posts to dozens of tourneys. He was as strong and as fit as he had ever been. He breathed shallowly, panting in his helmet. He wished the wind would cease and the snow come to an end. No one fought in winter, because it was a misery even to reach the field, before the archers and ranks had met.

On both sides, captains drew in great draughts of frozen air and called on their lads to charge. Horns blew, up and down the lines, a brassy, ugly blare that jerked the men into a stumbling run. The ranks raced at each other, holding back the swing of blades, ready for that first, strong blow into whichever traitorous whoreson stood against them.

They struck on snow that lay untouched and perfect, only to be trampled into brown mush in an instant and then stained dark red as the first blood sprayed or poured or seeped from the cut and dying.

Derry Brewer stepped out of the tent, deep in thought. The wind was freezing, howling across the camp behind the fighting lines. The loss of Clifford's small force was nothing, but Derry could still hardly believe how many men had fallen to the barrage of arrows coming at them in the snow. English commanders had known the dangers of archery since before Crécy, for at least a century. Armies simply could not march without a contingent of archers, not if they expected to survive. Yet Somerset's clash had left some six thousand men dead or too badly injured to fight again. Derry had never seen so many cut down, all in a few bare minutes of the archers' duel. The damned snow had done for them as much as anything. Many of the survivors would die over the course of the day, bleeding to death for want of someone to wrap a wound. The king's physicians had instructed a few boys and servants, but it was rough work and there were too many injured, with the fighting just begun.

Derry shuddered as he thought of the weeping, groaning men he'd seen in the tent, screwing up their faces in pain, all with terrible wounds. He'd survived battles before – and gone on to eat a hearty meal that evening, but there was something disturbing about watching the king's surgeon scoop out a gashed eyeball. It was that particular horror that had forced him back out into the fresher air.

He'd have to send a messenger to the queen, of course. She'd be desperate for news. At least she was safe in the city with her husband and son. With more than thirty thousand men to fight for her, she would expect a great victory and an end to the wars.

As he walked away from the tent with all its horrors, Derry was stopped by a hand on his chest. He gripped it from instinct, looking up at a hard-faced, unshaven fellow, standing in a belted, studded tunic and hose, with the gamey odour of unwashed flesh. Derry gave the hand a twist, even as he sensed others stepping in behind him. There were four in all, each watching him closely as the one in front glared and rubbed his wrist.

Derry felt a calm steal over him, a great weariness and an understanding.

'Ah, lads,' he said, almost reprovingly. 'Who was it, then? Who gave the order?'

'My lord Clifford,' one of them replied proudly. 'A price on your head – on reports of his death. We'll be claiming that bag of coin, Master Brewer, from the paymaster. You'd do well to go quiet, but it's the same either way.'

Derry saw them tensing for sudden violence. He looked over their shoulders for someone, anyone, who might come to his aid. The trouble was that the camp was filled only with whores and the wounded. There should have been servants and tradesmen, wives and seamstresses, but they would all be at the edge, straining their eyes for some sign of the fighting. The captains and serjeants were all away at the battle.

Derry was alone. He closed his eyes for a moment, surprised at the strength of his acceptance. He was no longer a young man, that was the truth of it. He could not fight his way out of the grasp of four brawny soldiers, all ready to slip a knife into his ribs at the first sign of a struggle. No. He was done. The best he could do was go out with dignity.

'Very well, lads,' he said softly, looking around at them all. 'Though there will be a man who comes to find you, after. He'll make a point of seeking you out and showing you why you should have disobeyed a dead lord's order, why you should have run when you could.'

'You're full of piss and wind, aren't you, son?' one of them said with a hard chuckle, giving him a shove along the muddy track. 'Walk on now.' The man jerked his head to the other three. 'We'll do it in the woods, in the quiet, like.' He gave Derry another push, making him stumble on the slush. 'If you don't make a fuss, I'll do it clean, like a Christmas goose.'

Derry shook his head as he was marched away. Snow

still fell. It was hard even to make out faces over any dis-tance. He knew if he called for help, they'd just knife him on the spot and walk off. There was no one who would come. Clifford's men had picked their moment well. Derry almost smiled at that, though he felt acid surge, making him belch. He hadn't thought Clifford had it in him, the spiteful old sod.

The worst of it was that he had work undone, work that needed Derry Brewer's particular collection of skills. Or so he told himself. His shoulders slumped and he let it all go, feeling lighter at having made the decision, so that he raised his head. Derry Brewer walked west with the men, out of the camp, while everyone looked south, to the bloody meadow close by the village of Towton.

Warwick wondered if he would burst his heart. Perhaps he would suffer an apoplexy, a fit on the field that would leave him unable to speak and with his face like melted wax. His breath had gone beyond mere panting, to a hard 'Huh' with each exhalation, as if he spat flame through the lips of a wound. It hurt to breathe. It hurt to walk. He knew there was no action or labour that stole more strength than fighting. Only felling trees came close, and it was for that reason that every knight wielded axe and sword for hours of training every day if they hoped to fight on a battlefield. Native skill counted for nothing when your arms were shocked into weakness. A warrior made his bones thick, his muscles like oak boards to protect those bones. That way, he might live.

Edward was just a prowling lion. It was not his height but the fact that he was born to the work. He moved with grace and husbandry, so that he tired more slowly than the men around him. No stroke was wasted, no swing taken too far. He had killed at least a dozen men and his armour was already battered and dimpled and gashed. The bill-hooks in the hands of those they faced were ten inches of hard iron that came to a point designed to cut armour, at least with a strong man's weight behind it. Edward's chest plates showed three of the triangle cuts, one of which dribbled blood. The three who had reached beyond his guard were long behind, trampled and cold.

Warwick could only watch as the king stalked forward, in balance, untiring. No one wanted to face the king any longer. There was something savage about him, leonine or lupine. Warwick shuddered as he struggled just to breathe and keep up. He no longer had any doubts that Edward was fit to be king. He had the bloodline and he was a Goliath on the battlefield. Empires had been built on less. Even as Warwick watched and breathed pain, Edward was gliding across churned ground, seeking out anyone who would stand against him. In response to the huge warrior in shining armour, they leaned away from his direct path, as if he burned too hot. He laughed at them as they slipped and fell, clashing his sword on his shield and making them scramble back.

Warwick jerked at warning horns blown on his left. Sound was capricious in armour and he turned his head back and forth even as he walked forward with Edward, guarding the man's flank from anyone who might dart in. As he had the thought, some young farmer in leather and wool stepped across with a billhook swinging, trying to take Edward unawares. Warwick brought his own blade down on the man's arm, shattering the bone and leaving the limb flopping on a thread of sinew. The farmer fell screaming, clutching himself. A thrust ended his cries, but the horns were still sounding.

Warwick looked for the source, squinting into the distance. Edward's central square had pushed deeply into the forces of Lancaster, becoming a wide, shallow spearpoint. Every step had been hard-won, but Warwick thought they had gained at least a few hundred yards over the bodies of enemies. It was impossible to know how well his uncle was holding the left wing, but Edward's heart and violent action was driving on the centre, some eight thousand men taking their stance and their confidence from the armoured king roaring out defiance.

Somewhere on Warwick's left, he could hear horsemen where horses had no right to be. He swallowed drily, his throat so thick and raw he could barely croak a call.

'Your Highness . . . *Edward*. The left wing!'

His uncle Fauconberg would be somewhere over on that side with his brother John, though Warwick had seen nothing of either man since the arrows and alarms of that morning. He had learned to hate the snow for the blindness it brought, more even than the cold that made bruises worse and hands too numb to hold a hilt.

He saw Edward turn and follow his pointing gauntlet over to their left. The young king's mouth firmed and he looked around in cold assessment, judging what quality of men he could call.

'Some sort of horsemen there, out of the woods,' he shouted to Warwick.

The noise that followed was brutal, a great crash of metal and cries of pain that echoed like a clap of thunder across the battlefield. Hundreds turned to see what was happening, losing their lives for the moment of inattention.

'How many?' Warwick shouted back. He wished then that he had not killed his horse, for all the goodwill it had brought him.

'Too many,' Edward replied. He cupped his hand around his mouth. 'My *horse* here. Bring him up.'

He allowed the front two ranks to march past him, swallowed in their number as he joined the third rank once again and waited for the great stallion that could bear his armoured weight. As Warwick understood what Edward was about, he sent his own runners to four nearby captains, telling them the king required their immediate aid and presence at his side. They began to close on Edward's position.

'You must press on with my centre, Warwick,' Edward shouted. 'These are my best men. They will not falter.'

To Warwick's surprise, Edward was grinning, lifted by some dark delight. His armour was spattered with mud and blood, his surcoat stained red over the royal lions. Yet in that moment, in his youth and grief and anger, Warwick knew Edward had never experienced such untrammelled joy. He was drunk on violence. The battlefield could break a man; Warwick knew that well enough. It also made a few, as they discovered a place where their strength and skill and fast hands mattered, with no other worries to distract them.

Edward's delight showed in his glare and his wildness. He shoved his knee into the hands of the knight who brought up his mount, finding the saddle with quick ease and then becoming a mounted warrior in a heartbeat, joining the animal so that his own strength and reach seemed to treble. The destrier kicked out suddenly, just missing a marching man behind.

'Press the centre!' Edward cried, for the benefit of those around, though he focused on Warwick. 'These Lancaster men are just boys. They cannot stand.'

The king trotted his mount across the square, interrupting ranks that stopped and cheered. His knights formed a phalanx around him, holding his banner poles high. With the four captains, hundreds pressed through with him, grinning like madmen to jog along in the wake of the king on his warhorse. They headed towards the tumult of fighting on the left wing, to answer whatever force had come out of the trees.

Fauconberg swore as he fended off a spear with his sword's hilt. The copse on his left shoulder had seemed too small to conceal all the horsemen who had come charging out of it. His leftmost ranks had been caught standing, their attention on the maw of the fighting ahead. Just forty yards from where he stood, Fauconberg's foremost soldiers were still grinding bone and iron and shedding blood as captains and serjeants on both sides roared at each surge, each step gained. The lines swayed back and forth like bloody lips. Sudden lurches and a steady pressing force had gained Fauconberg some ground, but the cost had been high. The left wing was normally the weakest – the last to engage. Yet along with the snow, the sheer scale of the battle was rewriting the rules. If Norfolk's right wing had been there, he should have gone in first, supported by Edward and Warwick in the centre, and then finally, perhaps not at all, Fauconberg's left wing. Instead, the battle lines had been so wide that the centre and the left crashed in at the same time – and Norfolk had vanished into the snow.

More and more were fed through to the front, where they stood until they were exhausted – and then fell, to be replaced once again. Fauconberg marched in the second or third rank, pulling men forward or back with two serjeants, trying to allow the mortally weary some respite, before their lives were torn out of them. He faced the strongest wing of Lancaster, with the banners of Somerset visible just a hundred yards away.

Into that stalemate had come the ambush from the copse, two hundred heavy horse left hidden to attack his flank. They'd carried long lances or spears and they were already at full gallop when Fauconberg saw them appear out of the snow, just a blur and growing thunder, until entire ranks were shuffling back as a boy might step sharply out of the path of a wild dog.

They had smashed right through the stolid marching men, waiting their turn at the battle mouth with patience and courage. Instead, they had been smacked down, broken on the instant by the armoured weight crashing into them or spitted through by iron and splintered wood. Shards exploded across the left wing as it bowed in, cringing away from the charge. The entire left square faltered, compressing marching lines so that they came to a stop, while others continued to push around the outskirts almost mindlessly. Some of them put up pikes in rows, as they had been taught to do against horsemen. They were too few and Fauconberg swallowed as he snapped orders, shoring up the lines, pulling the men clear to re-form. They left shrieking wounded and cooling dead behind.

Fauconberg pulled off a gauntlet to wipe sweat from his face. The true enemy was panic, as it always was. Two hundred riders could not destroy an army or even one wing of it, not when that wing was eight thousand strong. But while the riders rode unchallenged and killed without answer, the ranks pulled back from them, waiting for someone else to respond to the threat. Fauconberg saw one of his men launch his pike like a spear and send one of the attackers tumbling right off his horse. The man darted then at the prone figure, but he was sent skidding back to the ranks by the rider's companions as they galloped up. They had drawn swords, content to cut at the marching ranks. In fury and frustration, Fauconberg sent a boy racing to the rear, where his archers trudged along. Just a few hundred arrows would end the threat. They'd used the last of them hours before, but perhaps a few shafts yet remained. It was a vain hope, he knew it.

A dozen of the riders rushed his flank yet again. Some of his serjeants called for pikes and the line bristled with them, though not before the horsemen wheeled out with new blood on their swords. They roared and jeered as they rode up and down, delighting in their power over the miserable lines marching past them.

Fauconberg glanced to his right, looking for help. His heart seemed to swell in his chest as he saw Edward's banners coming closer.

'Yes!' Fauconberg muttered. 'Good lad. Good *king*.'

He chuckled at his own words as Edward came in a rush. The great squares slowed as he crossed their path. Some men simply stopped to stare at him, while their officers yelled blue murder to get them moving again. For just a moment in the hours of struggle, soldiers on both sides watched Edward ride to shore up a broken wing.

'Clear a path there!' Fauconberg shouted to those around him. 'Let the king through!' He was beaming like a fool, he knew it, yet the banners raised his heart: the white rose, the falcon of York, the sun in flames, the royal lions.

Those riders who had attacked the wing saw Edward coming just as clearly. A few of them pointed back to the woods behind, choosing to preserve themselves. Others clearly indicated the king pressing through his own ranks to reach them. It was not hard to imagine the argument between them. If they brought Edward down, they could well turn the day for King Henry.

Fauconberg felt his chest tighten, his skin seeming to grip his bones. King Edward passed him at no more than twenty yards, his huge warhorse trotting with easy grace. With him went a core of banners and, around them, billhook and pollaxe men, burly and fit, loping along at the king's side.

Edward and his knights sprang out of the flank at those horsemen who waited for them. In just moments, the king had downed the first two who stood against him. He was struck twice by spears skidding off his armour. A third was thrown by a man solidly in Edward's path, with all his strength. It missed as Edward cantered into him, smashing him off his smaller horse with a thump of his shoulder. Fauconberg winced at the impact. It was like seeing a falcon strike a pigeon, leaving it crushed. Speed and weight mattered, but he could only imagine how hard it was to keep your nerve with Edward bearing down on you. The king did not swerve or hold back. He rode straight at anyone in his path and broke them, cutting with his sword or sending them tumbling with a blow. The king was more skilful and much faster than older men, feinting and sending them one way only to smash them from their seats as they turned. In the flower of his youth, he made some of them look like flailing children.

Around the king, Edward's billhook men were in their element. As the enemy horsemen milled and swarmed, holding the ground, hard men would step up and cut a horse's leg right through or spear the riders from beneath so that they fell, blowing blood. Those who used billhooks with the most skill were butchers and smiths and tanners and brickmakers, well used to the work.

It did not last long. Edward looked around at the corpses of men and the shrieking horses dying around him. It had been brutal work, but he found himself exulting, to the point where he wondered if he should hide the emotion as somehow obscene. He could not. Instead, he raised his sword and yelled his victory. Around him, hundreds smiled and cheered, the sound spreading to the entire left wing and beyond it to the centre, where Warwick was laughing as he fought on. It was one small action, but Edward had proven himself. His ride across the face of the army had been seen by almost all of them. If there had been doubts before, there were none then. They fought for a king of England, and in that knowledge, they found new strength.

19

The snow continued to fall, the wind gusting so that the fighting men had to squint against flecks of ice. Their skin and hair and the creases of cloth were all rimed with it, crackling and falling away with every step or swing of a blade. The day wore on with the two vast armies locked together, neither giving way unless it was over the dead bodies of their own. Pikes jabbed forward as captains charged into a gap, tearing holes in lines. All the while, pollaxes and billhooks rose and fell, with short falchion cleavers doing brutal work.

Behind the fighting lines, ranks compressed themselves together for warmth, to get away from the wind whistling through them and stealing away their strength. They stamped their feet and blew on hands as they were drawn inexorably forward. They could not retreat, could barely even manoeuvre, as the dim light began to fade and shadows fell across tens of thousands standing on frozen earth, with wood and iron in their hands.

There were moments when the snow was blown back and the battlefield was revealed. For those lords and men-at-arms who had come north with Edward, the sight was not one to inspire. The army of Lancaster was yet a host, a dark flock swarming like starlings on the white ground. Exhausted men from the south looked at each other and shook their heads. With the light leaving, it was hard to see such a sight and not quail, not feel some touch of despair, with bodies aching and stiff with cold.

Boys still ran through the lines, carrying leather water bags with a pipe that could be sucked like a mother's teat. The urchins allowed parched men to snatch a desperate mouthful, cursing and prodding them when they took too much or spilled the precious stuff down their beards. All the time, the fighting went on, lines heaving together, men crying out for friends and loved ones as they understood they would die in the dark, shrieking at the last or slipping down amidst the legs of those trudging past.

When the sun went down, it took something vital. Seasoned fighters hunched their shoulders and dropped their heads, settling in for grim endurance in the darkness. No one called a halt, not the lords or their captains. They seemed to understand that they had come to that place in the service of two kings; they would leave serving only one. Horns and drums fell silent, no longer smothering a roar of men that built and sobbed away like waves crashing on shingle, nor the voices of the dying, calling like gulls.

Men-at-arms who had fought for hours had reached a point of leaden weariness and confusion that only grew worse in the dark. They stumbled along with their mates and if they were caught by fresher enemies, they were cut down like wheat. The number of deaths grew and grew as the strong fell savagely on weakened men – and then became weak, to be cut down in turn.

There was a sullen desperation growing in the York ranks. Even at the centre, where Edward stood and fought as if he could not tire, they had seen the extent of the Lancaster lines. The young king had not returned his horse to the rear. With a salute to Fauconberg, he had ridden over to Warwick, accepting the cheers of the centre as they welcomed him. There were no arrows or crossbow bolts flying by then, seeking out the fine target that he made. Without cannon on the field, Edward was near untouchable, as long as his strength remained. Knights who grew too weary could be knocked down and stabbed between plates, or have their helmets hammered in. Yet if a man of Edward's size could keep fighting, it was hard to see how he could ever be stopped. It took a near perfect blow to pierce his armour – and as it was aimed, there he was, looking at the wielder with a wild grin, striking back before the blow reached him. He had finally lost count of all those who had fallen to him.

The darkness was upon them when Edward saw movement on the right. Without the snow, he would not have noticed, but on white ground he saw a dark mass charging, appearing as the snow still swirled. From the height of his destrier, Edward had more warning than anyone else, though he only stared. Runners were already scrambling towards him, boys racing each other to take his orders, whatever they might be. Edward held up his hand to them, the fingers outstretched. He told them to wait as he waited, his heart thumping hard, so that he felt dizzy and sick. If the queen's army had brought fresh reinforcements, he was looking at his death and the final dishonour of York. His men had been outnumbered from the first. The ranks coming in would break him.

The hammer crashed against Lancaster's left flank. Norfolk had found them, in the snow and the darkness, bringing Edward's entire right wing against the weakest ranks of Lancaster. They struck at a run and they sent up a roar that echoed over the entire field. Norfolk's banners flew to lead the way, and at the sight of them, Edward and

Warwick found each other's gaze and howled with the rest. It could not have been better judged – and if two hundred horsemen had almost broken Fauconberg's wing earlier in the day, nine thousand fresh warriors shattered the Lancastrian wing, sundering the army and leaving thousands cut down. Norfolk's men were surely weary from half a day spent pressing on in the snow, seeking out the battlefield. Yet they were fresh and full of life compared with the poor, half-dead wights who had fought for all that time.

In the darkness, there was utter confusion in the Lancaster lines. A great attack had come, and men turned away from it in blind terror, trusting in the dark to hide any dishonour. As Norfolk pressed in, Edward and Warwick and Fauconberg felt the lines suddenly give way before them.

Men who would have held for ever in daylight broke in the dark. They turned and ran, assailed on all sides by screaming men and clashing iron. They slipped and fell and got up, spreading panic as they pushed through lines of men who still knew nothing of what was happening, who grabbed at them and shouted questions as they jerked away and staggered on. Hundreds broke, then thousands, letting fear close their throats and send them wild. They raced away down the sloping ground to the river, falling in armour and crashing over and over.

Behind them, the ranks of Edward and Warwick had met those of Norfolk surging across their front. Together, they sent up a bellow of savage glee, chasing running men. Just moments before, they had been looking at an army at least their equal in size. That knowledge stayed with the army of York as they surged over the field. Two or three men would catch some unlucky knight, knocking him down with a sweep at his legs, or crashing a pollaxe against his back so that he stumbled and fell. Once down, some-one would swing the axe-handles in a swift circle, bringing it on to a head or a neck. They would not stop then, made savage in their own fear. Blow after blow fell, until bones had been broken into pieces and bodies pierced a hundred times.

Knights and noble lords called 'Pax! Ransom!' as they were brought down in the darkness, yelling at the top of their voices to men who could not see them well against the snow. No mercy was granted to them, and the bill-hooks thumped down.

The butchery went on until the rising sun cast a dim light from a clear sky, with the snow all spent and covering humped bodies in all directions. Thousands of armoured men had drowned in the Cock Beck, held under or chopped by those chasing them as they struggled to cross. Scattered corpses spread for miles in all directions, cut down and set upon by men who had been lost for a time. As the dawn came, they would not meet each other's eyes. The darkness had hidden horrors that would stir them from sweating dreams for years afterwards. York's men had triumphed, but they were drained by it, exhausted without sleep, stained in blood and filth, their lips blue, their eyes tired.

Under a paling sky, they formed in the squares once more, with Fauconberg riding over to check that his nephew and his king had survived. Norfolk had offered up his life for his failures, but Edward had waved it off. The man was visibly exhausted and ill, with blood crusting along his lips and a cough that seemed to overpower him in pain. It was true his late arrival had almost cost them the battle, but at the end, Norfolk had come when they needed him. He had redeemed himself, and both Edward and Warwick understood the power of it.

As the sun cleared the horizon, men emptied bladders, shivered and stamped. They were just about hungry enough to eat the dead by then, sharp-set and aching with it after the day before. King Henry's camp lay just two miles north, at Tadcaster. It gave Edward some satisfaction to tell his captains that they would eat there. He imagined the camp followers waiting for their people to return and he laughed. They would see banners of York on the road instead, held high and proud.

He had taken not one prisoner, not one lord held for ransom. He would not play the games those men knew, not then nor ever again. As well as Lord Clifford, Henry Percy, Earl of Northumberland, had been killed on the field, along with a number of lesser lords and hundreds if not thousands of knights and wealthy followers. It meant there were rich pickings amongst the dead. Edward's captains had no difficulty finding volunteers to remain at the field, collecting anything valuable. It was vital work and food would be sent back to them. They would count the fallen. Great pits would take the corpses of unknown soldiers, though the labour would be hard on frozen ground. The captains would have servants make lists of names as best they could, from ring crests and surcoats and letters kept close to the skin. Others would roam the battlefield with hatchets, seeking out those who had been knocked unconscious or had hidden themselves in the hope of creeping away. A group of bearers would carry their own wounded to nearby manor houses to be tended, or more likely to bleed and die. It would be the work of many days, though Edward would not see any of it. He had other tasks ahead and he turned north with the blood-stained survivors, facing into a wind that had veered to blow even colder. King Henry and Queen Margaret would discover that the world had changed around them in the night.

Warwick had been found an unclaimed gelding. It was skittish and forced him to turn it in a tight circle every few steps before he could make it move on. He understood the animal's wide eyes. Though the wind cleaned the air of the smell of bowels and blood, there was still a sense of death around them, like a man sensing the slow movement of insects beneath a floor. The snow hid some of it, but wherever he allowed his eyes to rest, they would slowly make out some shape that would become a horror.

He reined the horse in, dipping his head as he approached Edward and Norfolk, Fauconberg and his brother John. Warwick was the last of them to gather there, four men with Neville blood and a Plantagenet. They were all battered, though even as Warwick looked them over, he could see Edward was recovering, his face set and determined.

The moment of silence stretched all around them. Some of the men had vomited weakly as they'd gathered back into ranks. They had not been mocked for it as they hawked and spat yellow streams. There was no food in them to lose, at least. They were grim with all they had done, all they had seen. They cheered the king, of course, when their captains called for it. The sound and the action brought a little life back to pale cheeks and glazed eyes.

Leaving a thousand or so behind to tend and tally, the ragged army of King Edward marched north.

*

Margaret watched the sun rise from behind the glass of a high room in the guildhouse of York, her back warmed by a fine fire. She could see her breath mist on the glass and wiped at it, her hand looking pale and thin. Beyond those panes, the south gate of the city could be seen. She could not rest, not with an army fighting for her. Every moment passing was a strain as her imagination supplied endless horrors.

At such a time, she would have liked to ask Derry Brewer for his opinion. She knew her spymaster had ridden out on his old nag to the camp. Yet he had been absent the entire day, while she sat and waited, winding one hand into another until the knuckles were pink and sore. She had shivered at the snow falling, making the world beautiful but deadly, so that she stayed close to the fire.

Her son had spent the morning clattering about with toy soldiers and a ball, unaware of the stakes of that day. Margaret had finally lost her temper and slapped the seven-year-old, leaving a pink mark on his cheek. He had looked up at her in fury, and her response had been to gather him into an embrace while he squirmed and complained. When she'd released him, he'd scrambled away out of the room and silence had returned. Her husband nodded by the fire, not asleep, or reading, but simply staring peaceably into the flames as they twisted and flickered before him.

Margaret took a sudden breath when she heard hooves clattering in the street. There was snow on the outer panes and it did not shift when she rubbed a palm across the inner surface. She could see very little outside, just a few horsemen dismounting below. She turned to the door as loud voices sounded and her servants replied.

The door crashed open and Somerset stood there, his chest heaving as he brought cold and snow and fear into that warm room.

'My lady, I am sorry,' he said. 'The battle is lost.'

Margaret went to him with a low wail, taking his hands and shuddering at the exhaustion she saw. As he moved, she saw it was with a limp, one of his legs barely bending. Droplets of melting snow flickered across her skin, making her shiver.

'How is it *possible*?' she whispered.

Somerset's eyes seemed bruised, darkened all around and still showing the red lines of a helmet pressed against his flesh.

'Where will the men rally?' she demanded. 'Here, by this city? Is that why you have returned to this place?'

Somerset's shoulders slumped as he forced himself to speak.

'There are ... many dead, Margaret.' It hurt him to break her, but he had the sense of time against him and he snapped the words. 'All dead. The army was broken, slaughtered. It is the end and they will be coming here with the sun. By noon, I expect to see King Edward walk his horse through the Micklegate Bar of York.'

'*King* Edward? How can you say such a thing to me?' Margaret cried out in grief.

Somerset shook his head.

'It is the merest truth now. I watched him on the field, my lady. I give him that honour, though it scorch me.'

Margaret's face hardened. Men were too given to grand gestures. It was true it sometimes led to dreams of heroes and round tables. It also meant that when they found a wolf to follow, they could have their heads turned like a young girl. She reached out and touched her hand to Somerset's cheek, shivering again at the deep coldness in the young man.

'Have you come to kill me, then?'

Life returned to his eyes, though the duke swayed. His hand came up and gripped her wrist.

'What? *No*, my lady. I have come to bear you away from this place, with your husband and son. I would spare you whatever ending York has in mind. On my honour, you must think of a safe place now, if there still is one.'

Margaret thought swiftly, trying to concentrate as fear and anger screeched within. The day before, a vast army had stood for her, an army that dwarfed the forces at Agincourt or at Hastings, or any other time the English had fought. Yet they had failed and fallen, and she was *lost . . .*

'Margaret? My lady?' Somerset said, worried at how long she had stared into nothing.

'Yes. It will be Scotland,' she said. 'If there is nothing left in England, I must ride for the border there. Mary of Guelders holds the throne for her son and she will keep me safe, I think. I think she will.'

Somerset turned to shout orders down the stairs to his men waiting below. He stopped at the touch of her hand on his arm.

'Where is Derry Brewer?' Margaret asked. 'Have you seen or heard of him? I need him to come with me.'

The young duke shook his head, showing a flash of irritation.

'I do not know, my lady,' he said in rebuke. 'Lord Percy and Baron Clifford were killed. If your Derry Brewer lives, I'm sure he will find us in time. Now, you should have your servants pack whatever you will need.' He bit his lips, his eyes suddenly bright with a sheen of grief. 'My lady, you should not expect to return. Take gold and . . . clothes, whatever you cannot bear to leave. I have spare horses here. We can carry it all.'

Margaret looked sternly at him.

'Very well. Now pull yourself together, my lord Somerset. I need you sharp and I doubt you've slept at all.'

He smiled ruefully, blinking.

'Just dust, my lady. I must apologize.'

'I should *think* so. Now fetch your men up here to help gather the things I shall need for the journey. I want you to remain at my side, my lord. To help me with my husband and to tell me everything that happened.' She paused for an instant, raising her head against the urge to despair. 'I cannot believe it. How is it *possible*?'

Somerset looked away, calling down the stairs to his men. When he returned, she was still waiting for an answer. He could only shrug.

'Snow, my lady. Snow and luck were enough. I do not know if God or the devil was on their side, but . . . surely one of them. They had King Edward fighting at the centre, leading men who fought like fiends to impress him. Even so, they should not have won, *could* not have won against the numbers we brought. God or the devil, or both. I don't know.'

20

With long banners flying on either side, Edward entered the Lancaster camp. The king's mood forbade conversation, though it was not a cold thing, just the numbed awareness of so many events having happened quickly.

There was no armed resistance as they rode to the centre. What few guards remained had run as soon as they saw the banners of York coming up the road. Drawn by the smell of cooking, Edward dismounted to accept a bowl of mutton stew, a glorious steaming warmth that smothered the hunger cramps.

The eighteen-year-old king sipped broth with Warwick and Montagu, Norfolk and Fauconberg, all staring across the camp. The only sound then had been Norfolk coughing into a cloth, a wet hack that went on and on until he grimaced at blood and spat more on to the ground.

After a time, Edward's captains brought him some tally blocks marked in fine lines, but he waved them away. He had no interest in the work of clerks, nor yet the business of ruling. He had no doubt his father's man Poucher would track him down eventually, but there were far more important things to do first.

Lancaster servants scurried to bring food and water, appalled and in shock, but already sensing a new world forming out of the bloody fields behind. They still needed to eat and to be paid to labour when their masters had been killed. Some of them wept as they worked, understanding that the head of their house would not return. Haunches of cured ham were discovered in a storehouse and hacked apart with blades that had cut living flesh not too long before.

As exhausted men settled down to eat and rest, Edward mounted once again, wincing at the bruises that ran from his right arm and shoulder right down to both legs. His armour had soaked up dozens of blows but spread them, so that he would be mottled blue for weeks. The iron plates showed neat holes where some weapon had cut through. Edward counted four billhook triangles. They were all on his chest, which suited his pride. Each was rimmed with blood, though the wounds beneath had caked and set into the layers of leather and thick, stitched linen. He groaned as he stretched to mount, turning it into an angry shout as every joint protested. He left his helmet in the hands of a servant and closed his eyes as sweat dried and the breeze touched him. He did not need the spiked gold band set into the iron to show he was king. The truth of it was in the battle he had won. No fluttering banner or house colours mattered half as much as that.

It was a little before noon when his six hundred horsemen were sighted from the walls of the city of York. Edward had wondered whether he would find the gates closed against him, just as Margaret and Henry had been barred from entering London. He had already decided to gather cannon and reduce the city to rubble if they refused him entrance. His glower eased as he saw Micklegate Bar open ahead of him. There were no guards visible, nor anyone else on the road into the city. He squeezed his reins, slowing the destrier to a walk, suddenly dreading what he would see there.

Warwick glanced curiously at the king, then dug in his heels, calling knights and captains to match his pace. They went in fast, hooves clattering as they swept under the stone tower, with the guardhouse and walls looming on both sides.

Edward followed, walking his horse, with his gauntlets clenched into fists. He reined in, coming to a halt, looking out over the muddy streets spreading away from that point, the jumble of packed houses and the spires of churches. Cooking fires had stained that same air for ten thousand years, longer. It was an old town, with old stones.

When he was ready, Edward turned his mount to face the Micklegate Bar and looked up. His eyes narrowed and his chest shuddered with something close to sobs as he stared at the heads of his father and his brother Edmund. The third head had twisted on its spike so that it leaned awkwardly. Edward glanced round as Warwick dismounted and strode towards the iron ladders set on both sides of the gate tower.

Jumping down, Edward was but a pace or two behind the earl as they began to climb together. The snowstorm had spent its strength the day before, so that there was no more than a breeze at that height. The king of England shuffled out on to a ledge and reached to his brother Edmund's head, quailing in horror at the black tar stuck to the skin. He could hardly recognize the features he had known and he was grateful for that.

The heads had rotted in the months since Sandal Castle. They were lightly held by the iron and, almost without looking, Edward removed and dropped the first down to Fauconberg to hold and wrap. A Christian burial would follow; the agony of his brother's humiliation had been repaid in the best of coin. Edward saw that Warwick had lifted his father's head and, with a slow exhalation through pursed lips, he did the same, muttering prayers as he held the tarred jaw and felt the hair touch the back of his hand with a shiver.

Fauconberg and Montagu stood below with outstretched arms. They received the heads with solemnity, passing them to be wrapped in clean cloth. Above, Edward Plantagenet and Richard Neville rested for a moment, their backs against the cold stone.

'You played your part, Richard,' Edward said. 'You and your Nevilles. I can make your uncle the new Earl of Kent, a fine title with sweet land and great wealth. He played his part and more. Did you see how many had been struck down by arrows, when we passed them by? Thousands, Richard. He may have won it for us.' The king's expression grew stern and thoughtful then as he contemplated the older earl. 'You, though, Warwick? You have as many castles and towns as I have, or a few more. What can I offer you, who did so much to make me king?'

'I want for nothing,' Warwick said, his voice low and hoarse. 'And you held the left wing, when another man would have seen it crushed. You inspired the men, so that even now, I can see you in my mind's eye. I will not forget it. Without you, I would not have my father's head to bury in consecrated ground. That is no small thing, not to me.'

'You must take *something* from my hand, Warwick. I will not be denied in this, nor will I let you retire to your estates. I need you at my side as we restore peace to the realm.'

'Then call me King's Counsellor, or King's Companion. For such an honour, I will remain for ever at your side. Like the last King Edward, you'll rule fifty years.' Warwick forced himself to smile, though his eyes shone. 'You'll win back France, perhaps.'

He saw Edward's brows rise in interest at the thought and he laughed.

'Will you find some reward for Norfolk?' Warwick asked suddenly.

The man himself was not a hundred yards off, visible as he waited for the younger men to climb back down to the world. He seemed reduced by the cold. As Warwick watched, Norfolk doubled over to cough and heave for breath.

Edward's mood dampened and he shrugged.

'I know he made the ending, with God's aid. Perhaps in time I will find it in me to praise him. Yet I have not slept one night since I was cursing Norfolk to hell for the gap he left in my army. Your brother John fought well, I think. I am of a mind to honour the Nevilles, Richard. Your father's place in the Order of the Garter is still vacant.'

Warwick considered what his father might have said to such an offer. He rubbed a ball of sticky tar between two fingers.

'Earl Percy was among the dead, Your Highness. If you wish to honour my father's family and mine . . .'

Northumberland was a vast earldom, millions of wild acres and a title of real power. Yet Edward needed no more unrest from that bastion of the north. Warwick saw him chew the inside of his cheek.

'My brother will always be loyal, Edward.'

The king dipped his head, his expression lightening now that the decision was made.

'Very well. I'll give him a writ under my seal and see how quickly he brings order back to the north. I am content to have a Neville in Northumberland. After all, Richard, I will need loyal fellows around me now. Those with wits and courage, both! I find I have a kingdom to rule.'

Both men climbed down, becoming reverent once again as they observed the heads being wrapped in cloth and leather, belted and tied to the saddles. It was Norfolk who approached Edward, dropping to one knee on the stones as he waited with his head bowed.

'Rise, my lord,' Edward said softly.

'My lads have been asked in the tavern, Your Highness. The people of the city are all afraid that you will bring some punishment upon them for sheltering King Henry and Queen Margaret.'

'And so I might, still,' Edward replied, though his heart was not truly in the words. Faced with an army the size of the one that had camped at Tadcaster, the city of York had been hostage. He decided on the spot to hold them innocent and seek no penalty, either in gold or bloody executions. His father had said that a man was revealed by how he conducted himself when he held power. It mattered to the young king.

Norfolk dipped his head further, well aware that he was still blamed for his late arrival, hated and praised in the same breath by some. He had chosen to make no excuses, though the hours lost and desperate in the snow had been perhaps the hardest of his entire life. He had thought he would trudge through white nothingness for ever and see a kingdom lost as a result. He had thought he might choke to death on the blood that surged into his throat.

'Your Highness, they say also that Queen Margaret and her husband rode out of the city with the sunrise.'

'With carts, carriages?' Edward snapped, his gaze sharpening. It was only an hour or two past noon. If Margaret had taken a trundling cart, he might overtake them yet.

'Left behind, Your Highness. They took only horses, with saddlebags for kit and coin. I could send a dozen men out after them, even so, my lord. They went east, perhaps to the coast. They all agree on that in the tavern.'

'Send your dozen,' Edward said, happy to make a quick choice. 'Bring them back.'

'Yes, Your Highness,' the duke said, bowing low.

Edward watched Norfolk as he strode back down the street to the waiting riders. The young king was enjoying the way men came to him for favours and answers. It was a heady feeling, and the best of it was that he knew his father's spirit would be roaring out his delight. The house of York had come to rule all England. Wherever Margaret ran, it would not change what she and her husband had lost on the killing field between Saxton and Towton – or what Edward had won. It was as if they had dropped a crown and seen it roll through blood to his hand.

21

Margaret hid her bitterness, keeping her head high and the faintest of smiles on her lips. She understood by then what it was like to see a precious alliance torn up and tossed on the fire. All she had left was her pride, and she clung to that.

At first, crossing into Scotland had felt like a weight lifted away. The hard ride north had taken her family out of King Edward's reach, bringing such a surge of relief that she had been dazed by it, almost falling from the saddle. Yet from their first meeting, Queen Mary of Guelders had made no secret of her disappointment and anger. It showed in the scowls and scornful glances of the Scottish lairds, in the very tone of their voices when they deigned to speak to Margaret at all.

Margaret had been a woman to flatter before. After the slaughter at Towton, she had nothing left to offer. Worse, she was hunted and weary, holding on to her dignity by her fingernails and little else. Crossing the port in moonlight, she tried not to let them see how much they had hurt her.

With a curse, she felt her foot twist on the cobbles, as if even the stones wanted her away. Biting her lip, she put out an arm that Somerset held until she was steady. Dawn was still some way off and Laird Douglas had decided to use the dark to bustle her small party out to the ship waiting for them.

King Henry and her son walked at the heart of them,

the boy fallen silent for once in that tight group of warriors, all ready to defend or attack. Margaret could not see
her husband's expression, but she ground her teeth at the
sound of his humming, the man utterly untroubled by any
sense of danger. It was not beyond possibility that they
would encounter armed men waiting on the docks, either
hunters sent by Edward or just some local bullies who had
not been properly bought.

Margaret had heard the orders Mary of Guelders had
given to Laird Andrew Douglas and his soldiers. If they
were stopped or challenged, their response was to be fresh
blood on those cobbles. One way or another, the ship
would sail before dawn. Margaret suspected the Scottish
queen mother wished only to be rid of her little family. It
had not been said aloud, but it was clear that there would
be no gift of Berwick to the Scottish court for the army
Margaret had taken south. Nor would her son be expected
to marry a Scottish princess. Margaret had lost everything
it had been in her power to promise, and Mary of Guelders
would have to make peace with a new king in England.

Margaret prayed in the darkness that she would not be
betrayed. She knew she depended upon a woman's sense
of pity – and that thought was not a pleasing one. It was
all too easy to imagine the ship sailing round the coast and
up the Thames, to be greeted by a delighted crowd of
Edward's lords. She shuddered at the thought.

Margaret could see the merchant cog in the moonlight.
The vessel rocked on the stone dock, snubbing the lines
that held it to the shore. Dark figures scurried in the rigging and across the yards, loosening gaskets on the sails so
that they fluttered white in the darkness.

As they came to the very edge of the wharf, Margaret

saw that a gangway led up to the waist of the ship, wide enough for a horse. Laird Douglas cleared his throat and halted the little party while six of his men went on board and searched the holds and tiny cabins. They returned with a low whistle and the Douglas relaxed, making a crackling sound in his lungs as he wheezed. He was not a well man, Margaret realized, but the Scot had completed the duty given to him. He had not been one of those who frowned too hard at her for all she had lost, and she was grateful to him. It was all part of the world she was leaving behind – a world of loyal men. She had five servants with her, two guards and three maids to help with her husband. One of them was a strong Scottish girl provided by Mary of Guelders. Bessamy had forearms like legs of ham, and though she spoke little English, she had been enormously helpful in entertaining the Prince of Wales.

Margaret felt her smile grow strained and false at the thought. Her son would be just Edward of Westminster, or Edward Lancaster, when they left the coast. His title had been stolen from him along with his inheritance, though he did not fully understand the loss, not then.

The Scottish guards had taken up positions along the dock. The servants had gone on board with the bags and chests, with Bessamy taking Edward by the hand and telling him he was a dote and a plum. Margaret remained with Laird Douglas and Somerset and her husband, who had stopped his humming to look at the ship and the sea beyond.

'My lord Douglas, you have my thanks for all you have done,' Margaret said. 'Will you allow me a moment now to speak to my lord Somerset alone? There are things I must say.'

'Of course, my lady,' the Douglas replied, bowing low, though it set his lungs to wheezing once again. He strode away and drew the closest of his men with him along the docks, for all the world like a father out strolling with his warlike sons.

Margaret turned to Somerset, taking his hand in both of hers and not caring who saw the gesture. Weeks had passed since Towton. The spring had reached even so far north as the east coast of Scotland. They could not have sailed if it had not, but even in spring the little merchant cog would hug the shore until they crossed to France. She had been told it could take just three or four days with good winds. Beyond that, she had written letters to run before her, calling on names and places in France she had not considered for half her life.

She breathed out slowly, aware that her mind was running wild on trivial details, just to avoid speaking aloud the decision she had made. She did not want to see Somerset disappointed in her.

'Margaret, what is it?' he asked. 'Did you leave something behind? Once you are safely in France, I can have anything sent to you.'

'I want you to keep my husband,' Margaret said. Her voice cracked with nerves as she rushed on before he could reply. 'You have friends and supporters still, men who would hide the true king of England. I have only a few servants and I cannot look after Henry where I am going. Please. He knows nothing of France now, his life as it is now. He would suffer away from the things he knows.'

She stole a glance at Henry, but he still stared out to sea, lost in the glitter of moonlight on the deep waters.

Somerset gently removed her hands from his own.

'Margaret, he would surely be safer in France, where he can be hidden away. King Edward would not invade to seek him out, at least I do not think he would. But if you leave him here, there will always be a chance of him being found or betrayed. I do not think you have considered it all, my lady.'

Margaret set her jaw, clenching the muscles there so that her teeth creaked. She had endured a great deal in fifteen years. England had given her much but stolen away more than she dared to examine. She thought of her sister's happy marriage and her mother's less happy one. Margaret's father still lived, she knew. She would visit the old man in Saumur Castle. The thought of it brought a pang of homesickness she had not experienced for years. She glanced again at her husband, more child than man, more fool than king. Her father would scorn him and humiliate him. If she took Henry to France, he was most likely to be used and sold to the French court. They'd wipe their knives on him and hang their cloaks on his shoulders. Somerset was perhaps too decent a man to know how poorly Henry would be treated. She raised her head, in control of herself.

'It is my order to you, my lord Somerset. Keep my husband safe, in manors far from the roads. Let him be given what books he asks for – and have a trusted priest hear his sins each day. He will be happy then. That is all I ask.'

'Very well, my lady,' Somerset replied.

He was stiff and hurt, as she had known he would be. The young man wore the same look of suffering as when she had told him he would not accompany her. Though Somerset would surely be hunted and attainted, the young duke was a man of good reputation and high estate. Others would still rally behind him, perhaps. Either way, he would not suit her new life in France.

One by one, she had cast off the coins weighing down the seams of her cloak. She had her son, and if she had lost the rest, at least it had been lost well. She had given half her life to England. It was enough.

'Message here! Hie! Message!' came a voice from the wharf buildings, where the merchants stored their cargoes.

The laird and his men bristled immediately, drawing swords and daggers and striding back over the cobbles to put themselves between Margaret and any possible threat. Until the ship had left the dock, she was their responsibility.

The messenger was a young man, wearing a fine cloak over what could have been bright colours in better light; Margaret could not tell. The Douglas had oil lamps brought over from the ship while the stranger remained silent, under guard. In the gleams they cast, Margaret watched as the man shrugged and stripped to the waist at a barked order. He revealed a physique as ridged and marked as that of any pit-fighter in London. Though the Scottish soldiers removed a single and obvious dagger with its scabbard, the appearance and number of scars troubled the Douglas and Somerset in equal measure.

'I don't like this, my lady,' Somerset murmured. 'The fellow is dressed as a herald, but I would not trust him into arm's reach.'

Margaret nodded, knowing only too well that King Edward could have sent a dozen killers after her. Such men were more common in France and Italy, but they existed right to Cathay and spent their lives training for a perfect kill. She shuddered.

'Speak your message aloud, sir,' she called to him. 'These

are trusted men around me and they will kill you if you mean me harm.'

The young man bowed elaborately, though his face remained stern.

'My lady, I am told to say this to you: "I am the smiler, the knife beneath the cloak." Though I have no beer, I would serve you on my honour. My name is Garrick Dyer.'

Margaret felt herself grow pale, even as Somerset and the Douglas both erupted in anger and confusion.

'I believe I do know Master Dyer, gentlemen,' she said. 'I am just sorry I did not . . . recognize him before.'

It was a moment of bitter-sweetness, perfectly suited to her mood in leaving a country she had grown to love – and to hate. Margaret turned away, gathering her skirts and cloak to walk on to the waiting ship. By then, all movement had ceased and the sailors were still in the shrouds and rigging.

She heard the snap of a crossbow behind, but she did not see Garrick Dyer struck, so that he raised his hand in confusion to the inch of iron showing through his ribs. He dropped to sprawl on the cobbles. Margaret was still turning as the Douglas roared orders and Somerset grabbed the queen and bustled her to the gangway.

'Get on board, Margaret!' the young duke shouted in her ear.

The lamps had gone flying as men dropped them to reach for swords. Yet the moonlight was enough. In that pale whiteness, from between the cargo houses came a shuffling figure, bent over, with an oddly twisting gait. Somerset would have rushed Margaret right across the deck and down to the hold, but she struggled in his grasp, wanting to see.

'It's just one man,' she said, panting. 'One assassin who has shot his bolt and will not live to reach me now.'

She watched as the Scots surrounded the shadowy figure. He was speaking to them, she could see, his hands gesturing. She was ready to turn away once they went in to kill him. She had seen too many deaths in her thirty-one years. Yet they did not. One of them called back to the laird and Margaret's brow creased as the Douglas went stomping over to hear whatever the man was saying. To her surprise, the elderly Scot took the fellow firmly by the arm and walked him over the quay towards her. Some of his followers gathered the fallen lamps once more, lighting one from another until they could cast light on the assassin.

Margaret gasped, raising her hand to her mouth. Derry Brewer's face was wrapped in filthy strips of cloth, so thick with dried blood that it changed the entire shape of his head. He regarded her with one gleaming eye, though she could see he was bent over some deeper wound, unable to stand straight. He limped with every step, and yet she knew she had left him at the camp in Tadcaster, some two hundred miles to the south. In that moment, she had a glimpse of his determination. She felt a rush of shame at the fine welcome and aid she had been given, all while a wounded man came after her.

'Evening, my lady,' Derry Brewer said. '*I* am the smiler, the knife beneath the cloak. I don't know who that other cunt was.'

'*Derry!*' Margaret said, in shock as much at his appearance as at his words.

'I'm sorry, my lady.' Derry looked back at the body on the cobbles and shook his head. 'He was one of mine. I'll claim him in death, my lady. I can do that much for him.'

'If he was your man, why did you . . . ?' Margaret broke off as her spymaster raised his head, peering at her from under brown cloth. He held one hand into his stomach and every inch of him was grimed with dirt or blood.

'He would have welcomed my return, right enough, then finished me with a dose, or a knife, or a fall over the side. Or I misjudged him. Either way, I've learned not to regret what I can't change. I am returned to you, my lady.'

Derry staggered slightly and would have gone down on to one knee if the Douglas hadn't held him up.

'You'll be allowing this fellow on board, then, my lady?' the Scot asked, his expression sceptical.

'Of course, my lord Douglas. Whatever else he has done, Derry Brewer is my loyal servant still. Have him taken below, please, to be washed and fed and tended in the warm.' She could see Derry's head was lolling, at the ragged end of exhaustion and unhealed wounds.

Margaret waited until the Scots had passed Derry into the care of her servants and stepped down to the quayside. She faced the Douglas and Somerset squarely, accepting their bows before she turned to her husband and stood between him and the sea.

'Lord Somerset will keep you safe, Henry,' she said.

The king looked down at her, smiling gently.

'As you say, Margaret,' he murmured.

There was nothing in Henry's eyes beyond a perfect peace. Margaret had wondered if she would feel the sting of tears in her own, but she did not. All the battles were lost. The hand had written 'Mene, Mene, Tekel, Upharsin' on the wall, those ancient words in a language no one knew. Not a letter could be taken back and all her decisions were made.

Without another word, she walked up on to the ship, grasping a rail as the sailors cast off and leaped aboard behind her, agile as apes. The wind and tide bore Margaret away: to France, to her childhood estate of Saumur and to her father. She had no doubt the old slug would scorn her for her failures, yet she had come so close. She had been a queen of England and tens of thousands had fought and died in her name, for her honour. She raised her head in pride again at that thought, banishing despair as the wind picked up.

Her son Edward clattered out on deck as soon as he felt movement, leaning out to watch the dark water sliced into foam and calling to his mother in excitement to come and see. Spring was on the way and Margaret took heart from that. She did not look back at the men standing on the shore, left behind.

PART
TWO

1464

Three years after Towton

PART

TWO

22

'Who *is* this woman?' demanded King Louis of France, fanning himself against the still, heated air of his palace. 'To write so often, to beleaguer me in such a way?'

'Margaret of Anjou is your first cousin, Your Majesty,' his chancellor whispered, leaning forward to speak into the king's ear. Louis turned to him with an expression of scorn.

'I know very *well* who she is, Lalonde! I exclaimed aloud as a question *théorique*, or *de rhétorique*, given that none of you seem able to explain my best course.'

The rumour at court was that Chancellor Albert Lalonde was at least eighty or even ninety; no one knew for certain. Lalonde moved and spoke slowly, but his skin was surprisingly smooth, with lines so fine they remained invisible until he frowned or suffered pangs from his two remaining molars. He admitted only to being in his sixth decade, though his childhood companions were all long dead. There were some in the court who said the chancellor's earliest memories included a sighting of the ark. King Louis tolerated him for the stories Lalonde could recall of his father as a boy and young man. It was certainly not for the chancellor's intelligence.

The French king watched in fascination as the old man chewed at his loose mouth, made restless in the heat. The upper and lower lips slid over each other with extraordinary slackness. With some reluctance, Louis pulled his gaze away. Half a dozen lords waited on him, marshalling between them both fortunes and a huge number of armed soldiers, if he had need. He rubbed the length of his long nose, polishing the bulb of the tip between forefinger and thumb as he thought.

'Her father, Duke René, is not a fool, for all the failed claims he has made on Jerusalem and Naples. Still, I will not criticize a man for ambition. In turn, it means I must not assume his daughter lacks wits. She knows I would rather not find a match for her son, a boy without lands, without title, without coin! No, my concern is more with *King* Edward in England. Why would I choose to support a beggar prince of Lancaster? Why would I antagonize Edward Plantagenet, at the beginning of his reign? He fills the years ahead, Lalonde. He sends his friend Warwick to my court to ask for a princess, offering gifts and islands and flattering me with talk of a hundred years of peace to follow a hundred years of war. All lies, of course, but such pretty, *pretty* lies.'

The king rose from his throne and began to pace, with his fan fluttering once again. His lords and servants scurried back so they would not touch him by accident and perhaps lose a hand.

'Should I send such a king into the arms of my enemies, Lalonde? I do not doubt the Duke of Burgundy would welcome his interest, or milord of Brittany. All my rebellious dukes have daughters or sisters unwed. And there is Edward, king of England and without an heir.'

His fan stirred the air only sluggishly and he dabbed at fresh sweat on his forehead with a silk cloth.

'Cousin Margaret will surely know all this, but still, Lalonde . . . *still* she asks! As if . . .' He touched a finger to his lips, pressing in the centre. 'As if she knows Edward will never be a friend to this court. As if I *must* support her and that I will know there is no other choice. It is all very odd. She does not beg, though she has no favours owed to her, nor funds beyond a few small rents from her father. All she has to offer is her son.' Louis brightened suddenly, a smile crossing his face. 'It is like a wager, Lalonde. She is saying, "My little Edward is the son of King Henry of England. Find a wife for him, Louis – and perhaps one day you will be repaid." Poor odds of that, Lalonde, eh?'

The elderly chancellor looked at him from half-closed eyes. Before he could respond, Louis waved a hand in the air to show his frustration.

'She gambles her future on my dislike of English kings. Yes, if I had a dozen sisters still unwed, I might consider one of them to give to her son, but I have seen so many die, Lalonde. *You* know. The twins, poor Isabella. And I have seen three dead children of my own, Lalonde! I have reached out to shake the shoulders of more little bodies than any father should ever see.'

The king stopped talking for a time, staring across the great empty hall of his palace. Every man and woman present held still so as not to break his chain of thought. After what seemed an age, he cleared his throat and shuddered.

'Enough of such things. My mind pricks me with old sorrows. It is too hot. No. Lady Margaret will be disappointed, Lalonde. Draft a reply, expressing my eternal regrets. Offer her a small pension. Perhaps then she will cease to trouble me.'

His chancellor bowed over his cane in response.

'As for King Edward Plantagenet, who stole his crown

from another of my cousins . . . *mon Dieu*, Lalonde. Should I give my daughter Anne to such a wolf when she is grown? Should I throw my dear lamb to a rough English giant? When my father gave a sister to the English, their King Henry decided he was king of France! I remember when the English still strutted through French towns and cities, Lalonde – and claimed them. If I honour this King Edward with my little girl, how long before the horns blow again? If I do not, how long before Burgundy and Brittany blow their horns for war? It is most vexing.'

To his surprise, Chancellor Lalonde responded.

'The English have bled themselves white, Your Majesty, at the battle they call York Field, or Towton. They will not threaten France again, not as long as I live.'

Louis regarded the old man dubiously.

'Yes, though we will be lucky if you survive another winter, Lalonde. And this Edward is a son of York. I remember his father, before this enormous pup was even born. Duke Richard was . . . impressive – cruel and clever. My father liked him, as much as he liked anyone. I cannot make an enemy of his giant son, who triumphed against thirty thousand on the field of war! No, I have made my decision. None of my sisters remain unwed. My daughter is three, and of course the newborn, God grant she lives. I could betroth Anne to marry him when she is fourteen, eleven years from now. Let him cool his ardour for a decade! Let him prove himself as a king first before I send another daughter of France over the sea.'

'Your Majesty . . .' Lalonde began. Louis held up a hand.

'*Yes.* I am *aware* he will not wait. Do you not understand a flight of fancy, Chancellor Lalonde? Do you comprehend humour at all? Or is it the deafness? I will send a delegation of lords and pretty birds to meet King Edward, with spies and scribes and pigeons ready to bring news back to my hand. They will suggest my daughter, perhaps, but he will demur, refuse! Impossible to wait for so long, without heirs! Then we will offer him my widowed sister-in-law, Bona, or one of the nieces who cluster so at Christmas and beg for gifts from my hand. He will accept and perhaps we will have prevented the giant from bringing an army across that sleeve of tears they call the English Channel. Do you understand now, Lalonde? Must I explain myself again?'

'Once . . . is enough in this heat,' the old man said, his eyes cold.

King Louis chuckled.

'Spirit! In one so very ancient! *Incroyable*, monsieur. Bravo! Perhaps you should be part of that delegation, yes? To meet the king in London. No, don't thank me, Lalonde. Merely go from here and make ready. Immediately.'

The summer seemed to have lasted a lifetime, as if there had never been a winter before it. The entire country baked, wilting listlessly as every day broke with a new promise of heat. The inner walls of Windsor Castle remained somewhat cooler, so many feet of stone proof against even the hottest days. As Warwick watched, King Edward pressed his forehead against smooth limestone and closed his eyes.

'Edward, until you have an *heir*, nothing is written in stone!' Warwick said, exasperated. 'If you suffered an apoplexy after one of your feasts, or if a cut spoiled and made your blood sour . . .' He summoned the nerve to say the words to the enormous man who glowered through the window. 'If you *died*, Edward, with things as they are, what do you think would be the result? You have no son, but your brothers are too young to inherit. George is, what, fourteen? Richard is only eleven. There would have to be a regent. How long then before Margaret and Henry and their *son* set foot in England once more? It is not so long ago that every family in the country lost someone at Towton, Edward. Do you want to see chaos return?'

'This is all madness. I *won't* die,' the king said, turning away. 'Unless, of course, a man can be lashed to death by your tongue,' he went on, half to himself. 'How is Richard now? Has he settled at Middleham?'

'You see, this is why I never know what you will *say*!' Warwick replied, throwing up his hands in exasperation. 'In one fell swoop, you can refuse all good advice and then remind me you have placed a brother into my care! Yet if you trust me, you should listen!'

'I *do* listen,' Edward replied. 'Though you worry too much, I think. The worst will not happen! As for my brother Richard, he is about the age I was when I went to Calais with you. You were a good teacher to me then – and I have not forgotten how I looked up to you. I had some thought of sending him to the garrison there, but he is . . . well, more delicate than I was at his age. My mother coddled him, I am sure. He needs sword work and hours with an axe each day. You'll know what to do, just as you did with me.'

Warwick sighed, fed up with the role he was forced to play, some combination of older brother, stepfather and chancellor that meant he had no real power whatsoever over the headstrong young king. He had thought it a great honour at first when Edward had passed his youngest brother into Warwick's care. It was common enough to allow young men to grow to manhood away from their families. It toughened them and allowed them to make their last childish mistakes away from those they would disappoint. It built alliances as well, and Warwick was pleased Edward thought it worth his while. None of that obscured the utter emptiness of Warwick's role as king's companion.

It had not mattered much for the first two or three years, while he and Edward tore through Lancaster rebellions in the north. That had been a heady time, with small-action battles and racing across the land to catch spies and traitors. Hundreds of great houses and titles lay unfilled as a result, with their owners either still hiding from justice, or dangling from trees or spiked on London Bridge. Edward had taken immense satisfaction from attainting the noble houses which had supported Lancaster, removing both the titles and the wealth of their lands. He and Warwick had been ruthless, of a certainty, but they had been given cause.

It had been exciting, dangerous work while it went on, but then the country had fallen quiet and there were no more rebellions for an entire summer, not even a manor burned or news of a rising in King Henry's name. It was those airless, sweat-soaked months that had Edward scratching at any door, wanting to be out hunting. He had always been happier in the cold, where he could wrap himself in fur. There was no relief from summer heat and it stole even his great strength, leaving him as weak as Samson shorn of hair.

Warwick watched him, wondering at the cause of his restlessness. One suspicion came to his mind and he gave it voice.

'You know, Edward, since Towton, we are not yet strong enough to consider crossing the Channel, no matter how much you might want it. We don't have the army for it.'

'They were just six thousand at Agincourt,' Edward snapped, stung to anger at having his thoughts read. 'Five thousand of them were archers.'

'And that army was led by a king who had *already* fathered his son and heir,' Warwick exclaimed. 'Edward, you are twenty-two and a king of England. There is time for any campaign you wish in the years ahead, but please secure your heirs first. There is not a princess alive who would not consider your suit.'

Warwick paused for a moment, aware that Edward was staring out over Windsor grounds. Warwick had no doubt the young man was considering throwing off duty and vanishing for a week or a fortnight, turning up reeking of sweat and blood, as if he had no other responsibilities. It didn't take much more than a rumour of some wild animal menacing a flock or a village for Edward to be gathering his knights and sounding a hunting horn.

Warwick sensed he was losing the king's interest and attention as Edward's gaze sharpened and he leaned close to the glass panes, his breath misting them. The Thames was visible from the tower. No doubt Edward had seen ducks skimming down to land. If it wasn't hunting with dogs, it was falconry that obsessed the young king. He seemed to have a touch for it, or so they said in the royal mews. Something in the savage birds of prey put Edward in a joyous mood and he was never happier than riding out with his great speckled gyrfalcon on his arm, or coming back with a few brace of pigeon or ducks over his shoulder.

'Your Highness?' Warwick said softly.

Edward turned from the glass at his title. They had fallen into the use of first names from long association. Edward knew Warwick only used one of the royal forms of address when he thought something was truly important. He nodded, standing with his hands clenched at his back, wondering if he should give voice to what was truly troubling him. For once in his life, Edward was embarrassed.

'This French king Louis is Margaret's first cousin,' Warwick went on, unaware of the inner struggle in the man he faced. 'In her exile, she might have asked for land or a title, but instead she calls on him to arrange a marriage for her son. King Louis is said to be clever, Edward. I cannot say I felt any especial warmth from him as he considered our request. I do know any union of Margaret's boy and the French throne would be a dangerous thing.'

'None of that would matter if Margaret's simple husband hadn't lost France!' Edward retorted.

Warwick shrugged.

'That is in the past. Yet if we allow her son to marry a French princess, he could one day be king of France – and then claim England as his birthright. Do you see the danger now? Do you see why I have spent two years flattering King Louis and the French court and sending gifts in your name? Do you see why I have feasted a dozen of their ambassadors and entertained them at my estates?'

'Yes, I see it. But you will tell me anyway,' Edward replied, turning back to the window once more with a sullen expression.

Warwick's mouth tightened, feeling an old surge of impotent anger. He was absolutely certain of the best path, yet completely unable to force it on a man who was his superior in arms and status. Edward was not stupid, Warwick reminded himself. He was merely as bull-headed, ruthless and self-regarding as the falcons he flew.

Earl Sir John Neville had reason to be satisfied with his life. After Towton, King Edward had included him in the Order of the Garter, making him one of a select band of knights who could always reach the king and be heard. It had been his father's own place in the order and John had felt immense pride to be able to add the Garter legend to his crest: 'HONI SOIT QUI MAL Y PENSE' – 'Evil be to him who evil thinks'. That had been a great honour, but it paled to nothing compared with being made lord of Alnwick Castle.

The earls of Northumberland had been one of seven kings once, before Athelstan united them all into England. It was one of the largest landholdings in the country – and it had fallen to the Neville family over the Percy line. There was no other title that could possibly have meant so much to a man who had fought against the Percy father and sons. John Neville had survived a Percy attack on his own wedding. He had watched the elder Percy earl die at St Albans. One by one, the lords of the north had fallen. It was a constant joy to know that the last heir languished in the Tower of London, while a Neville strode the battlements at Alnwick and used their maids for sport.

He had been cruel to the retainers, it was true, weeding out the ones he did not trust and leaving them to starve without work. It was always hard when a new lord replaced an old line. Hard, but the victory of better blood, in his humble opinion.

In return for that generosity, the new Earl of Northumberland had ridden and worked for three years to winkle out every last hiding place of Lancastrian support. He was directly responsible for the execution of more than a hundred men and found he enjoyed the work. With his troop of sixty veteran men-at-arms, John Neville followed rumours and paid informers, much as he imagined Derry Brewer had done before him.

That was one man he would have liked to see again. The letter 'T' that Brewer had carved had scarred thick and pink on the back of his hand. The cut had been so deep that John Neville found it hard to hold an eating knife and his fingers could be shocked open at the lightest blow. Still, for all that had been taken from him, he had been given more. He did not count the cost of his good fortune.

Lord Somerset had lost his head stretched on a tree stump, pulled out from the basement where he had hidden from loyal Yorkist men. John Neville smiled in memory of the man's spitting fury. It was extraordinary how those Lancaster lords and knights would creep into the earth to hide from their just fates. Sir William Tailboys had been caught in a coal pit and dragged out coughing and black with dust. Dozens more had been tracked and found, or betrayed for coin or vengeance. His work consumed him and he knew that he would rue the day it came to an end. Peace had never brought John Neville the satisfactions and rewards of war.

His only regret was coming so close to taking King Henry himself. He was certain the king was still in England. There were rumours of a dozen sightings in the north, particularly round Lancashire. John Neville and his men had found a cap with a Lancaster crest in an abandoned castle just two weeks before. He could almost feel the tracks getting fresher and the men hiding the king growing more desperate as he drew closer, following every scent and whisper. He might have left that last task to others, but he wanted to be there at the end. The truth was that he enjoyed hunting men more than deer, wolves or boar. There was more sport in those who understood the stakes and would fight as easily as run.

The earl kept a tight rein on his excitement as he followed the broken road through Clitheroe Woods. It made sense that King Henry would be safest in Lancashire. His family name came from the ancient Lancaster fortress in the north-west, one of the largest castles in England. Lancashire was Henry's heartland, perhaps more than anywhere. Yet the Tempest family had still betrayed him, whether out of loyalty to York or promise of later reward, John Neville neither knew nor cared.

When he had arrived at the Tempest manor house, King Henry had been spirited away from his rooms. Three of the king's attendants had escaped with him: two chaplains and a squire. How far could they have travelled in just a day, if the Tempest sons had told the truth? John Neville had men who could follow a man's steps well enough, sheriff's men well used to tracking down felons who ran. Even on rough roads baked hard in that summer heat, it had not taken them long to pick up one trail over all the others. A group of four, with just one on horseback. There could not have been too many groups of that kind.

The Earl of Northumberland looked up as green shadows moved in bars across his face. He did not like deep forest, where brigands and traitors hid. He was a man who preferred open spaces, where the wind could howl. He was well suited to Northumberland, with its wilderness and valleys and raw hills that stirred his soul. Yet he had to follow where the tracks led; that was his duty.

He murmured low orders, bringing eight crossbowmen to the fore and half a dozen more in good armour close around him, though it was hard to go faster than a walking pace in the brambles and the bracken. As the light faded into shadowed gloom, John Neville sent his two best trackers ranging far ahead, a pair of Suffolk brothers who could not read or write and rarely spoke, even to each other. They sniffed the air like hounds as they went and seemed to know all the tricks of prey, dark and brutish as they were. At night, they slept curled up in each other's arms, and in truth, their master suspected some foul intimacy between them. Flogging them had no effect, as they merely endured and stared with dull resentment, useless for work for days after.

The brothers vanished into the green ahead, while his hunters hacked and slashed through foliage. There were animal paths in places, formed by deer or foxes over years. They were too narrow for armoured horsemen and the going was slow and infuriating, as if the forest itself was trying to prevent his progress. John Neville set his jaw in anger. If that were the case, if the trees themselves wished him to leave, he would *still* press on and do his duty to King Edward, who had raised him beyond his wildest dreams and answered all his prayers.

His foot had tangled in some thorny vine. With a muttered oath, he yanked at it. Ahead, he heard an owl hoot and his head came up with a jerk. The Suffolk lads made that call when they had seen something and did not want to send it racing away. John Neville used his dagger to saw his boot free. He could not help the crackle of dead leaves, though they were not hunting deer, who would surely have vanished by then. His men cut aside the worst of the bushes and he made his way up until he could see the two grubby young men lying flat and looking over falling ground.

The Neville lord could hear a river beyond and he dismounted, creeping forward as quietly as he could manage. Both the Suffolk lads turned to grin at him, though they had only a few teeth between them, and those rotten. He ignored them, peering through the leaves of a birch clinging to the bank with its roots half exposed. The trunk shuddered as he leaned on it, weak enough to fall at any moment.

Not forty yards away, King Henry of England was crossing the river, stepping from one stone to another with a man before and behind him, holding their arms outstretched in case he fell. The king was smiling, delighted by the sunlight on the water and the wide river itself, with brown trout showing between the stones and darting away. As John Neville watched in astonishment, King Henry pointed delightedly at one of them passing beneath him.

John Neville stood up and walked out of the foliage. He reached the water and did not hesitate, stepping into the flow and striding across it, sending up sheets of spray. The flowing river reached barely to his knees and he kept his eyes on the king and his helpers.

One of them dropped a hand to a dagger at his belt. The Neville lord glanced over at him, touching the sword on his hip with unmistakable meaning. The squire let his hand fall and stood like a beaten dog, miserable and afraid. John Neville grabbed King Henry by his upper arm, making him cry out in surprise and pain.

'I lay hands on you, Henry of Lancaster. You will come with me now.'

For an instant, John Neville glared at the two chaplains. They could see armed men spreading out along the river banks and they were a long way from the road and the law. They knew very well that their lives were not worth a straw at that moment. Both men crossed themselves and prayed in a stream of whispered Latin. They stood with heads bowed, not daring to look up.

John Neville made a disgusted sound and pulled Henry through the shallows with him, half dragging the king back to the bank.

'This is the third time you have been captured,' the Neville lord said, as he pulled Henry up the muddy slope.

The king looked utterly confused, to the point of tears. With a sudden growl, his captor slapped his face hard. The king looked at him in wonder and dismay, his wits sharpening so that life came back to his eyes.

'Why would you strike me? Criminal! How can you dare . . . ? Where is Squire Evenson? Father Geoffrey? Father Elias?'

No one answered him, though he repeated the names over and over in his fear. One of the Neville men-at-arms helped him to mount, then tied Henry's feet to stirrups so that he could not fall. They led his horse back along the path they had cut into the green forest, until they reached the end of the trees and saw the road ahead.

23

Warwick frowned, shaking his head at the two servants trying to catch his attention. Either one had the potential to embarrass him, which was why he had been so stern with his instructions before bringing them to London. Both were dressed in livery of dark red and white, the colours of his house. The older of the two was Henry Percy, last son of the line of Northumberland earls. The boy had lost his father, his grandfather and his uncle in the wars, before his entire family was attainted and the title he might have inherited given away. The truth was that on his return from Towton, Richard Neville had not found it in him to abandon a sobbing fourteen-year-old in the Tower of London. The Percy lad had been pathetically grateful and served him ever since as a squire, ready at his call.

It had been the obvious thing to have the boy train with Richard, Duke of Gloucester, still too young for his title. Warwick found himself sweating as he tried not to see the smaller lad leaning in to catch his attention. Both of them were stifling laughter, their eyes bright. Warwick swung between irritation and indulgence at their antics. The two noisy youths had caused extraordinary bouts of chaos in Middleham Castle. They woke the household regularly with their yelling. On one occasion, they had to be coaxed down from the highest part of the roof, where they had tried to stage a sword fight and almost fallen to their deaths. They ate a prodigious amount and tormented the maids with captured foxes and stag beetles smuggled in from the woods. Even so, Warwick had not come to regret the impulse to tutor either one of them. He had no sons of his own. When he was at home and the peace of Middleham was interrupted by them crashing about, it made him wistful and a little sad. His mother or his wife would catch his eye then and take him into a misty embrace, laughing all the while. Then they would interrogate the boys and take a stick to whichever one had brought about that day's destruction.

Surrounded by the delegation from the French court, Warwick ignored both lads bobbing away like sparrows on the outskirts. Whatever it was could surely wait and it was time they learned a little patience. He turned his back.

Feeling other eyes on him, he bowed over his wine cup to the head of the group, Ambassador Lalonde. The man was ancient, leaning on a silver cane with his shoulders humped over, though that was not what held Warwick rapt in fascination. At intervals, the old man would pass his wine to a personal servant, then take out a pot of some unguent from a pouch at his waist, dipping a finger before smearing it across a line of pale yellow teeth that sat too prominently in his mouth. Warwick could not decide if they were made from the real teeth of dead men, as he had once heard described, or carved in ivory, with some dark wood shaped and drilled and set with wire to hold them. The results were extraordinary, slipping and chuckling through the ambassador's speech, so that already old-fashioned French became completely incomprehensible.

Warwick could only wait and stare as the old man greased his false teeth to his complete satisfaction, so that his lips slid smoothly across the surface once again. As the ambassador's serving man handed back his drink, Warwick was astonished to feel a touch on his arm. He turned to see Henry Percy standing there, his face bright pink. With the French party watching every move he made, Warwick could only smile, as if he had asked to be interrupted.

'This is important? Yes?'

The young man ducked his head, clearly nervous in the company of such strangers. Warwick relaxed a fraction. It occurred to him that his French guests would not expect a common servant to speak their tongue. Yet the Percy heir had been raised with a French tutor and spoke the language with perfect fluency. He considered leaving the lad near the ambassador to overhear their private conversation. For the moment, though, he could see something had the young man bursting to speak. Warwick took Percy by the arm and began to guide him to the edge of the room. As he moved, he saw two of the French party bending to speak to their own breathless servants, with yet a third rushing in to bow before his master.

Something was happening. Warwick had never doubted some of the French servants were spies or informers, along with those who could make sketches of faces and the lie of a river. Every delegation from France was the same, just as it was when England sent men across the Channel for formal events.

Ambassador Lalonde turned his teeth away to watch the progress of the French servants. Warwick took a firmer grip on the boy's arm, steering him to where Richard of Gloucester waited by the open doors of the hall, away from the closest French ears.

'What is it?' Warwick hissed. 'Come on, *one* of you. Quickly now!'

'Your brother, my lord,' Henry Percy said. 'Earl Sir John. He has the king in his custody by St Paul's, at the Ludgate.'

'What madness is this? Why would my brother . . . ? Wait . . . King Henry?'

'As a prisoner,' Gloucester said, his voice breaking high. 'Your brother's man came running and we said we'd carry the word to you. He's waiting outside.'

'I see. Then you have both done well,' Warwick said.

He had to struggle to keep his expression blank under the scrutiny of all those trying to pretend they were not watching him. He looked back at the French ambassador and the thirty-six men who had landed just two mornings before. King Edward was due to arrive amongst them at noon, to greet them all and show them what a fine, healthy young male he was, unmarked, unscarred and looking forward to reigning England for half a century. It would all find its way back to the pink and shell-like ears of the French king.

'Tell my brother's man I am coming now,' Warwick said, sending Edward's younger brother away with a push. The Percy boy followed as Warwick shooed him out in turn, distracted. He could see the news spreading through the group. There was nothing he could do about that, except keep them in that hall.

'My lords, *gentlemen*,' Warwick announced, using his best parade voice. Silence fell and they turned to him, some with suspicion, others in carefully blank interest. 'With regret, I am summoned. I must attend His Majesty, King Edward, for an hour, perhaps less.'

Warwick snapped his fingers to three servants and

muttered quick instructions to them before raising his voice once more.

'Please continue to enjoy this fine claret and the cold meats. More will be brought. These servants would be honoured to show you the chamber where our Parliament sits, and perhaps . . . the river . . .'

He had run out of further inspiration, so bowed deeply to Ambassador Lalonde and turned to go. Warwick stopped once more at the door to warn the master-at-arms not to let anyone leave. As he raced away, he heard a furious argument begin as the French servants discovered they would not be allowed to follow.

Warwick's horse was still in the finery his staff had arranged for greeting the French, with a red-and-gold headpiece that stretched right down its neck, leaving only the horse's eyes uncovered. The animal didn't like the garment and snorted constantly, shaking its head in irritation as he rode along the river path to the city proper. In response, he kicked his mount to a gallop, throwing up clods of muck and scattering children and mothers as he went, so that they either screeched in anger or whooped in joy behind him.

By the time he reached the stone bridge over the Fleet and saw Ludgate open before him, Warwick was spattered with mud, from his boots to his cheeks. He was pleased to see that his brother's troop of hunters had not yet entered the city, seemingly content to wait for him.

From some way off, Warwick had recognized the dark cloak his brother John wore over silver armour, as well as the slight, slumped figure within his arm's reach. Warwick observed his brother's pride as well, unmistakable in the set of his chest and shoulders.

Walking his horse the final few paces, Warwick approached the troop, John Neville's hard-bitten men parting before him. Warwick knew their reputation was deserved, though if they hoped to make him nervous with cold stares, he had eyes only for the king.

Henry had not been well treated, that was clear enough. The king's feet were tied to his stirrups and the leather saddle was dark with urine. Henry swayed slightly, his eyes blank as Warwick approached. One of the men had a hand on the horse's reins, but the miserable king was in no state to escape, Warwick could see that much. Henry was barely aware, very thin and bedraggled.

It was hard to hate such a man, Warwick realized. In one sense, Henry's weakness had led to the death of Warwick's father, but if he had expected anger, all trace of that had seeped away in the years since Towton. The king had suffered as much as anyone else, if he could even understand suffering. Warwick sighed, feeling hollow. His brother John was waiting to be congratulated, and yet he felt no joy of it. Henry was an innocent, in his way. There was little satisfaction in capturing such a man, for all he was the heart of the Lancastrian cause.

'Pass him into my custody, Brother,' Warwick said. 'He will not run from me. I will take him to the Tower.'

To his surprise, his brother frowned. John Neville drew his reins tight, moving his horse a step back and forth as the animal shifted and whickered under him.

'He is my prisoner, Richard. Not yours. Would you have for yourself the praise I earned?' He saw Warwick's flush of anger and spoke again. 'You have not hunted him across moors and heaths, Richard! Paid bribes and listened to dozens of common men earning a few pennies to inform on him. He is mine. For our father's memory.'

Warwick was aware that his younger brother had dozens of veterans around him to carry out his orders. There was no question of taking Henry by force, though Warwick was stung to fury by the lack of gratitude and the assumption of some low trickery. He had done more than anyone to raise John Neville from the ranks of knighthood to the nobility. His brother owed him for his estates and his titles. Warwick had assumed that was understood and appreciated. Instead, the younger Neville acted as if there were no debts at all between them. Still, Henry could not be torn from his grasp, not with so many brigands in armour around them.

'Brother, I will not impose my rank on you . . .' Warwick began.

'You *could* not! Are you a duke, then? Or are we both earls? *Brother*, I had not thought to see this arrogance in you! I called you first because this is a Neville cause, and . . .'

'And I am the *head* of the Neville house and clan,' Warwick replied. 'Like our father before me. And I am the man who asked for you to be made Earl of Northumberland, when King Edward inquired of me how he could reward my family. Do not test my goodwill in this, John. I seek no gain, but I will take Henry to the Tower, as I did with the fourteen-year-old heir of the Percy family, to remain in a cell there while you enjoy the lands he owned.'

It was not, perhaps, the time to reveal that he had renamed the lad and kept him in service. Warwick was not above manipulating his brother when the need was great. As with King Edward, if those around him could not see the best choices, it was Warwick's task to bend them to his will in some fashion. He did not care if it was by flattery or force or persuasion, as long as they followed his path.

Earl Sir John Neville felt a muscle twitch at the side of his mouth as he stared in frustration at his older brother. He had adored Warwick in their childhood, when neither of them had known titles or estates. As a young man, John had nursed a jealous resentment for the extraordinary marriage Warwick had made. In one grand gesture, Richard Neville had inherited honour and land enough to sit at the highest tables in England. From that, Warwick had become their father's close companion and York's vital supporter, setting the course of the war between them. All the while, John Neville had been a mere knight, not even a member of a grand order like the Garter. Their father's death had made him Lord Montagu; Towton and the king's generosity had made him an earl. He could see his brother Richard had grown into his titles, wearing power like a comfortable old cloak. The Earl of Warwick was intimidating in his confidence, even then, even surrounded by John's own men.

The younger Neville wondered if he would ever wear authority so lightly. He grimaced, shaking his head. He was the Earl of Northumberland and a king's companion. He would grow into that cloak in time, with nothing to prove to any man and certainly not to his brother. Even so, he felt a pang at the thought of giving up Henry. For all John Neville told himself the man was no longer a king, it was hard not to look on him with awe. John could still feel the place on his hand where he had slapped Henry's cheek. The thought of that deepened his colour, knowing how Warwick would react if he knew.

Warwick waited for an age while his brother stared at him in silence. Richard Neville knew when to refrain from pressing his arguments. He let his younger brother remember the debts he owed. Warwick could see anger flickering there and he did not understand that, with all he had done for John. He supposed a constant sense of gratitude would be wearisome, but that did not mean it wasn't deserved. The simple truth was that his brother was not half the man he was. Warwick expected John Neville to know it.

'Very well,' John said hoarsely. 'I give Henry of Lancaster into your custody. I will leave you a dozen of my men to ensure safe passage through the city to the Tower. The crowds will gather as you pass, once he is seen.'

Warwick inclined his head, touched and pleased at the way John Neville had matured. He was still a very angry young man, but then he had been present for the execution of dozens of Lancaster knights, captains and lords. Perhaps all that blood had cooled John's desire for vengeance, just a little. Warwick hoped so.

Henry did not resist as Warwick took his reins from the man who held them and led the horse through Ludgate and into the city of London. St Paul's Cathedral loomed over the streets there, massive and solid, with the voices of a choir singing softly within.

In the darkness, the Tower of London was a frightening place. The main gate was lit with just two small braziers on iron poles. They cast light in yellow eyes around the gatehouse, fading to blackness along the inside of the walls. Individuals of high estate were allowed candles or lamps in their rooms, whatever their families were willing to afford while they were confined. Yet most of the ancient fortress was without light, the stones invisible against the black river running by.

Warwick could hear Edward's arrival long before he saw him. He swallowed nervously, unsure what he would witness that night. The king had sent word he was coming, and for the hours of waiting, the Tower guards had bustled around at a run, checking everything and reporting to the Constable of the Tower, whose responsibility began and ended with the king's presence. The sprawling complex of towers and buildings and cells and moats was all the property of the king, including the Royal Mint and the menagerie within the walls. In his absence, the Constable ran the Tower, overseeing every movement of the guards and keys.

The gate was opened to admit Edward and a group of three armoured figures on horseback, clattering in fast as the king preferred. They dismounted, falling in behind Edward and the Constable as he led them to the rooms where Henry was held.

Warwick heard the ring of metal coming closer until Edward appeared, bareheaded and stern. Warwick went down on one knee and bowed his head. The young king preferred the displays of honour, though he was usually good-natured and raised men quickly back to their feet.

'Up, Richard. Your knees must be complaining on these old stones.'

Warwick smiled stiffly at that, though at thirty-six, it was true that his right knee sent a spike of pain when he put his full weight on it.

'You know my brother George,' Edward said casually, looking past Warwick to the corridor of stone beyond.

Warwick smiled and bowed deeply.

'I do, of course. Good evening, Your Grace.'

The fifteen-year-old had been made Duke of Clarence

three years before at Edward's formal coronation, lifted out of obscurity to wealth and power by his older brother. Just three sons of York had survived the perils of childhood and the violence of war. Warwick thought it a fine testament to Edward that he had raised both his brothers to the highest rank of the nobility. He wondered if the lavish grants and titles were in recompense for the loss of their beloved father. In silence, walking the gloomy path to Henry's room, Warwick considered his brother John again, made Earl of Northumberland. It had not brought their father back to life, but if the old man could see, Warwick knew he would be proud. That mattered. Since his father's death, he had kept a sense of being watched, of his most intimate moments perhaps being seen and judged by his father. For all he had loved the old man, it was not a pleasant feeling.

Warwick could certainly not fault the young king for such acts of generosity. Edward was a creature of grand gestures, able to grant an earldom in the same breath as he ordered a man's imprisonment or execution. He was utterly mercurial, Warwick thought, a quicksilver king. It paid best to show him honour and respect. Edward did not seem to notice the elaborate courtesies, yet he was very aware when they were not offered.

Edward guided his brother George forward, to the outer door to Henry's rooms. The hand on his brother's arm was paternal and Warwick smiled, understanding that the entire visit was perhaps just to show a younger brother the face of a fallen king.

Edward thumped his fist into the oak. They waited as the peephole slid back and forth and the door was unlocked by one of the guards who always sat with Henry of Lancaster, as both a servant and a jailer. Edward did not acknowledge the man as he caught sight of his old enemy through another door, kneeling on stone with his face raised to a window of iron and coloured glass. There was no light outside, but a small oil lamp in an alcove lit some part of Henry's face. His eyes were closed; his hands clasped together. He appeared at peace and Edward frowned at the sight, unconsciously irritated.

Warwick fretted, recalling a time before when he and Edward had found King Henry in a tent and captured him without a struggle. More than once, Edward had mused on how they might have changed the years ahead if they had killed Henry then.

Henry was completely in Edward's power and without one friend or supporter. Warwick's gaze was on Edward and he sensed it, turning suddenly and smiling. With one arm, he pushed his dumbstruck brother George forward to observe the kneeling king. At the same time, Edward stepped over to whisper in Warwick's ear.

'Have no fear, Richard. I have not come here for violence, not tonight. After all, I am king now, blessed by the Church, proven in battle. This poor fellow cannot take that from me.'

Warwick nodded. To his intense embarrassment, Edward reached out and clasped the back of his head, almost as if he would draw him into an awkward embrace. It might have been intended as a gesture of reassurance, but Warwick was thirty-six and a married father of two daughters. He did not enjoy being patted like a favourite hound. He held himself stiff until Edward clapped him twice on the same spot and drew back his arm. Edward stared at him, seeing something like resistance and misunderstanding it.

The king took Warwick by the arm and walked him to the outer rooms, away from the kneeling king in torchlight.

'I feel only pity when I look on him,' Edward said softly. 'I swear to you, Richard, he is in no danger.' He chuckled, the sound touched with bitterness. 'After all, while Henry lives, his son cannot claim my throne. Believe me, I wish that simpleton forty years of good health, so that they can never have a king over the water. Fear not for Henry of Lancaster in my care.'

Warwick was reassured, though he almost made the mistake of pulling away as Edward took his arm again to lead him back in. The king was vastly more tactile than Warwick, especially in his oblivious youth. Warwick sighed in silence to himself, passing through the knights gawking at Henry.

The kneeling king was at least clean, though Henry was painfully thin, with his skull showing under stretched skin. He had not opened his eyes once while Warwick had been watching, with the king's hands shaking just a fraction from the pressure of being held together. It was not a peaceful pose, Warwick realized, but one of desperation and grief. He shook his head, sorry for the broken man and all he had lost.

George, Duke of Clarence, knelt for a time at Henry's side, his head bowed in prayer. The knights and King Edward joined him, making their own peace and asking for forgiveness of their sins. One by one, they made the sign of the cross and left the room, with its guard and single permanent occupant. At the doorway, Warwick looked further to the narrow bed on the far side of the room. Books lay on a table there, with a flask of wine and two small apples. It was not much for a man who had ruled

England. At the same time, it was more than he might have had.

Outside, the Constable of the Tower was practically falling over himself to thank Edward for his presence. Warwick rode with the small party out of the main gatehouse, taking a huge breath when they were through. It was a small pleasure, but they could breathe free air as those within the walls could not. It eased some slight constriction in Warwick's chest to fill his lungs to their utmost, leaving the stillness of that place behind.

Warwick walked his mount closer to the king, seeing that a contemplative mood had crept upon them all.

'Your Highness, you have not told me how the meeting went with the French ambassador,' Warwick said. 'I am to see him at dawn tomorrow, to discuss which one of the charming French princesses will be yours.'

Weeks or months of negotiations lay ahead, and he said the last with a chuckle, but Edward did not respond, seeming, if anything, gloomier. The young king blew out his cheeks, looking away across the Thames running past.

'Edward?' Warwick asked. 'What is it? Is there something I should be told?'

He had known the young man for most of Edward's life, and yet the embarrassed grimace was not something he had seen before. Warwick saw Edward's brother George look away, staring deliberately at the river. The young duke's face was flaming. He knew something.

'Your Highness, if I am to serve you in this, I must . . .'

'I'm married, Richard,' Edward said suddenly. He took an enormous breath and blew it out. 'There. I have said it. Oh, it is a relief! I could not think how to tell my council of lords, while all the time you were negotiating with the

French. Then they came to London and I thought I *have* to tell you the truth; it's already gone too far . . .'

The king was babbling while Warwick simply stared in shock, utterly still. He realized his mouth had opened in amazement and he shut it carefully as it dried in the night air.

'I can't . . . Edward, who *is* she? You're married? How? *When*, for Christ's sake? No, *who* – that is what matters most.'

'Elizabeth Grey, Richard. Or Elizabeth Woodville before she was married.' Edward waited for that to sink in, but Warwick could only stare at him and he went on. 'Her husband died on the field at the second battle around St Albans. A knight, Sir John Grey, fighting for Queen Margaret and King Henry.' Edward risked a sheepish smile then. 'Your defence meant the death of the one man who could deny me happiness. Is that not passing strange to think on? Our lives intertwine, like . . .'

'Her family are not of royal blood?' Warwick asked in amazement. He saw Edward's colour deepen, touched by the anger that was always close to the surface. He would not accept being interrupted.

'No, that is true, though her father is Baron Rivers. She has two sons by her first husband. Good lads, both of them.'

'Of course. Two sons. And now I must go to the French delegation and tell them to put themselves back on a ship and return empty-handed to King Louis, as if we have made mock of them all for our amusement.'

'I am sorry for that, Richard, truly. I wanted to tell you before, but I knew it would be difficult.'

'*Difficult?*' Warwick demanded. 'There has never been a

king of England who married outside the royal families. Since Athelstan. Never. I mean, I would have to see the archivists in the White Tower, but I do not think it has ever been done – and never to one who has married before, with two babies of her own.'

Edward nodded, then caught himself.

'Not babies, not really. The oldest is ten.'

'What? How old is the mother?' Warwick asked.

'Twenty-eight, I think. Perhaps thirty. She will not tell me.'

'Of course. Older than you. I suppose I should have expected it. Married before, not royal, a mother, older than you. Is there anything else? I imagine the ambassador will ask me, when I try to explain how the king of England can make a secret marriage without telling a soul! Who were your witnesses, Edward? Where did the service take place?'

'It was at her family chapel, in Northamptonshire – and I grow weary of these questions, Richard. I am not a school-boy summoned before you. I have said it all. Now, as my counsellor, you may tell the French to go home. I have had about enough of your astonishment! George, with me.'

Edward dug in his heels and his warhorse surged into a canter along the cobbled street. His two knights fell in around him without a backwards look. George, Duke of Clarence, glanced delightedly at Warwick, grinning at everything he had heard, then rode after his older brother with his reins flicking back and forth for more speed.

Warwick was left alone in the darkness, quite unable to imagine what he was going to say to the French delegation when the sun rose once again.

24

The musicians trooped away with their instruments held high, flushed with pride at the cheers of the assembled company. It had not hurt the appreciation of their performance that wine and ale had flowed in a river all evening, with no cup left empty. Beyond the candles at table, dozens of dark figures moved in and out, refilling jugs and replacing empty platters with full ones. The forty guests at King Edward's great table were in a fine and raucous mood. They listened in delight as each man present told a story about a moment when he had been brave – and another when he had run away. The first brought solemn toasts and murmured thanks for great virtue; the second was amusing. Most of the men present had fought in battles or jousts. Between them, they had a thousand such tales to tell, until the drunken guests were roaring and wiping their eyes.

King Edward removed a gobbet of clear chicken grease from his lips with a cloth, smiling contentedly at them all from the head of the table. His wife sat on his right and she reached out to touch his hand as he laid it down, a moment of intimacy that showed she was thinking of him in the midst of the ribaldry and laughter.

'Is it my turn, then?' her father demanded of the table, waving his cup of wine so that red drops sloshed out of it. 'Ah, well, you have me at a loss. I have *run* from no man, by my oath!' Baron Rivers rose to his feet as he declaimed, his voice becoming a bellow, answered by crashing cheers.

Elizabeth hid her head in her arm, caught in equal parts by laughter and embarrassment. Her father's capacity for drink was reaching even his limit. He swayed as he stood, blinking as he tried to remember what he had planned to say.

'Oh yes! No man! But I did once run from the wife of a fisherman, a wench with forearms as broad as mine own. She had found me with her daughter, swiving like knives, I tell you, under a boat on the beach. Oh, to be young. I tell you, the smell of fish was such . . .'

'Father!' Elizabeth said.

Baron Rivers stopped to peer at her, his face swollen and his eyes swimming.

'Too far? My daughter is delicate, for a mother of two fine sons. A cup to my grandsons. May they know women as lise . . . as *lithe* as eels.'

A great shout of laughter went up and Elizabeth buried her head once again in the crook of her arm. Her two boys were delighted to be mentioned by their grandfather and they accepted the flagons of ale pressed into their hands. They looked ruefully at each other then, having already been out once before to vomit in the garden. Still, they sat with the king of England and could not refuse as he raised a cup in their direction.

Warwick did his best to smile along with the rest, though the occasional brief moment of silent communication with his brother John was of some help. The new queen had brought almost an entire court of her own family to London the moment the news of the marriage had become public. Within a month, no fewer than fourteen

Woodvilles had moved in to the rooms and great houses of the capital, from Baynard's Castle to the Tower and the Palace of Westminster itself. They had arrived like starving rats discovering a dead dog, as far as Warwick could see, though he would never have said such a thing, even to his own brother.

Warwick let his gaze pass over the brothers and sisters of the new queen. Half of them were already filling roles in the royal houses, all of which carried a decent amount of coin. Elizabeth's own sister had become her maid, at forty pounds a year.

They were, at Warwick's best estimate, country folk, with rough manners and no particular subtlety. Yet as that year's summer had produced great surpluses of fruit and crops, so it had shone on the Woodville line, even as a pale reflection of Edward. The king withheld nothing from Elizabeth, granting her every wish, no matter how transparently it served her family. It had not hurt her cause to have fallen pregnant so quickly. The curve of it showed well under new dresses cut for her. Edward, of course, was as proud as a cockerel, doting on her. Warwick could only smile and keep silent as valuable titles were granted, one by one, to men and women who had been mere tenant farmers before, of no particular estate.

Edward was resting his great head on his arms, laughing at something Elizabeth had muttered to him. Her hair spilled over the table, red run through with gold, a most extraordinary colour. As Warwick watched, the young king reached out and toyed with a lock of it, murmuring some endearment that made his queen blush and slap at his hand. Warwick had thought they were oblivious to his scrutiny, but Elizabeth had noticed his attention. When

Edward turned to a servant to demand more wine, War-wick found himself the object of her calm and steady gaze.

He blushed as if he had been caught doing something wrong, instead of simply staring. Slowly, he raised his cup to her. He thought her expression grew cold at that, but then she smiled and he was reminded what an extraordinary beauty she was. Her skin was pale and lightly marked, the tiny circles of old pox scars on her cheek. Her mouth was a little thin, though her lips were as red as if she'd bitten them. It was her eyes that held his attention, however, heavy-lidded and sleepy, on the verge of yawning. There was something wicked in such eyes, and Warwick could not help thinking of the bedchamber as she raised her cup and tilted her head in return, as if to an opponent before a joust. He drank deeply and saw that she matched him, so that the red wine stained her lips further.

Warwick glanced at Edward almost nervously, so intimate had this exchange felt with Elizabeth. The king had put his head right back and was trying to throw some part of the meal so that it landed in his open mouth. Warwick chuckled at the silliness of it. For all his roaring and drunken games, Edward had chosen a woman who brought him no advantage at all. In an older man, it might have been something to admire, a measured choice of love over alliance or wealth. Yet Warwick did not trust Edward's youth.

Just as Edward had rushed to the battle of Towton – and yes, triumphed there – so he had hurled himself into a marriage with a woman he hardly knew. The sheer number of Woodvilles infesting the royal palaces seemed to have surprised Edward as much as anyone, though he only shook his head indulgently and retired to his private chambers for his more experienced wife to keep him amused.

Warwick lurched, spilling his wine as a young man gestured, singing or shouting with wild movements that overset a ham and sent it spinning with a crash of crockery. He swore under his breath, sensing that Elizabeth was still watching him. She had appeared puzzled by his role in her husband's life, seeing no reason for Edward to have private meetings with Warwick and a few other men. The Privy Council had not been disbanded, but in the previous three months of her influence, Edward had attended only once. If some matter of law or custom needed his attention, it had to be brought to him in person, with Elizabeth often present at those times, to cast an eye over the papers and have her husband explain them to her.

Warwick settled down to wrestling a dark clove from where it had become stuck between two of his teeth. Of course, Edward had no fine understanding of Parliament or bills of law, so it fell to lawyers and lords to reduce them for the queen, while she listened with wide eyes and her bosom artfully displayed. Much older men grew flustered and pink under that complete and perfect attention.

Warwick sank his cup of wine and watched it refilled. He realized he disliked the woman intensely – and unfortunately lusted after her at one and the same time. It was a frustrating position and he sensed he would have no satisfaction on either count. Elizabeth had been crowned queen consort. She was clearly of the opinion that her great lumbering husband needed no other counsel but her own, at least where the Woodvilles were concerned.

'Of course you must sing for us, Richard!' Warwick heard Elizabeth cry out. He choked on a draught of wine and coughed wildly as the table cheered and stamped. Yet it was Edward's brother who stood and bowed, smiling shyly at his sister-in-law and sipping from a goblet of wine to clear his throat.

Warwick only hoped Richard of Gloucester would not be made a fool of in that place. He knew him well enough by then to take pride in his accomplishments. Stranger still, to think Warwick could recall the father's pleasure at his birth. It was just twelve years and perhaps half a dozen lifetimes before, when the world had been better, when his own father had been still alive and he had wanted somehow to force Henry to be a good king . . . Warwick felt his brother John's gaze and raised his eyes in bitter self-mockery. There was never a way back. There was never a chance to undo old mistakes. A man simply had to go on, or let it break him.

The king's brother had a sweet enough voice, clear and calm as he sang of courtly love. Warwick let the tune wash over him, remembering a gardener at the Middleham estate he had once known. The man had worked for his father for thirty years, his skin as brown as leather from a life outside. Looking back, Warwick realized Charlie had been a little simple. The woman he lived with in their cottage on the estate had been his mother, not his wife, as the boy Warwick had believed. Certainly, Charlie had never recalled his name, greeting him as 'Curly' each time they met, though his hair was straight. Warwick looked blearily into his wine cup, wondering why the man's memory should have intruded upon him in that place. He remembered Charlie's leg had been crushed by a cart when he was a boy, leaving it twisted and the leg always, *always* in pain.

'I have known cuts and fevers,' the younger Warwick had said to him, in all his youthful innocence. 'And a rotten tooth that had me weeping like a child until it was pulled. How is it that you can bear your biting leg, as you have described it, beyond bearing, waking and sleeping, never coming to an end? Charlie, how does it not break you in two?'

'Did you think it doesn't?' Charlie had murmured, staring into the darkness. 'Why, I would say I have been broken a thousand times, reduced to a helpless, weeping boy. Yet I do not die, Curly! The sun comes up and I must rise and be about my work once again. But never say I am unbroken, sunshine. I break every day.'

Warwick shook his head, rubbing his palm into an eye socket. The damned wine was making him maudlin – and in a company of sideways glances and cruel smiles that made him feel he had fallen in with wolves.

The song ended, the young singer blushing as praise was called from one end of the table to the other. As Duke of Gloucester, Richard Plantagenet had been given vast estates, all managed by stewards and just waiting for him to take them up. From King Edward's hand, generosity flowed without stinting, without thought of consequence.

Perhaps Edward sensed the intensity of Warwick's gaze on him. He met Warwick's eyes and rose to his feet, swaying slightly, so that he leaned forward and braced one arm straight amongst the jugs. His brother Richard sat down and the laughter and conversations fell away as they waited for the king of England to speak.

'I give you all honour tonight, but I will raise a cup with one who saw me as a king before I did myself. Earl Warwick, Richard Neville, whose father stood with mine – and died with mine. Whose uncle and brother fought with me at Towton, when the snow fell and we could not see . . . I tell you, I would not stand here today without his aid. I give you the toast then. To Warwick.'

The rest of them rose to their feet with much scraping and squeaking of chairs, quickly echoing the words. As the only one still seated, Warwick tried to ignore one of Elizabeth's brothers, whispering and laughing. They were small men and women, of a cheap and vulgar line. He bowed his head to Edward in thanks.

As the drunken king collapsed back into his chair, Warwick heard Elizabeth's question to him. She had half hidden her mouth behind her hand, but the timing and the volume were perfectly judged to carry to his ears.

'Yet he could not win without you, my love. Is that not what you said?'

Edward did not seem to realize the words had reached anyone else. The king merely chuckled and shook his head. A servant placed a platter of sizzling kidneys on the broad table by Edward and his eyes widened with fresh interest, reaching out with a knife to spear a few before he could be served. The young king was too drunk to realize the volume of talk and laughter at the table had fallen to whispers and murmurs. Half the Woodvilles there were waiting in delight to see how he would answer, taking their confidence from Elizabeth as they hid their mouths with cloths and darted glances at one another.

'At St Albans, Edward?' Elizabeth went on, pressing. 'You said he could not win without you there. You had to lead at Towton. My brother Anthony fought on the other side – oh, you have forgiven him already, my love! Anthony said you were a colossus, a lion, a Hercules on the field.'

Elizabeth sought out her brother along the table's length, a great ox of a man, with hairy forearms resting unnoticed in a slop of beer and gravy. 'Did you see my lord Warwick on the field at Towton, Anthony? They say he fought the centre.'

'I did not see him,' her brother replied, grinning in Warwick's direction.

The man had seemed sharp enough before. Perhaps he thought his sister was jesting, enjoying a little rough sport or mockery at Warwick's expense. To Warwick's own eye, the little queen was deadly serious, seeking out some weakness in him. He smiled at her, raising his cup and dipping his head in her honour.

To Warwick's pleasure, Richard of Gloucester responded at the other end of the table, raising his cup in turn and beaming back at him. Warwick found genuine amusement and wondered if the boy understood he had taken the sting from an unpleasant moment, or whether it had just been good fortune and an error made from kindness. The boy was clever enough, all his tutors agreed on that, but he was still very young. To his surprise, Richard winked at him then, without warning, leaving Warwick staring in delight. It was hard not to like the little devil.

Windsor Castle was both an ancient fortress and a family home, but warmth had never been among the castle's attributes. When the country turned to short and frozen days, memories of Towton returned for those who had been there, as they did every winter, in dreams of snow and blood.

Warwick shivered as he leaned against a bare stone wall with his brother George. The Archbishop of York had grown a sight heavier over the previous year or so, though he still worked up a sweat in sparring with his brothers when they had the chance. Such idle hours had grown somewhat fewer since the arrival of the Woodvilles at court.

'It is passing strange,' George said. 'In the summer, I complained about the heat. I remember it was unbearable, but the memory no longer seems truly real. With the white ground and frost in the air, I convince myself I would give anything to sweat once more – and if I did, I do not doubt I would yearn to return to this cold. Man is a fickle creature, Richard. If not the entire class of man, at least the bishops.'

Warwick chuckled, regarding his younger brother with affection. As an archbishop, George was a man of power and influence. Only cardinals in Rome truly outranked him, yet George was still youthful and smiled back at his brother with impish humour. The truth of their shivering was that no fire had been lit in the halls outside the king's audience chamber.

Warwick had been kept waiting for an hour, though it had seemed like six. As his brother looked back with longing on the summer, Warwick recalled the days when he had been able to approach Edward without announcement, without being left to kick his heels in waiting chambers like a common servant.

The reason for the change was not a mystery. It had taken a little time, but Warwick had accepted at last that his fears were not misplaced. Elizabeth Woodville had taken a measure of the Neville influence over her husband and decided to ease them out. There was no other explanation for the way she had arranged her family like pieces on a board. Less than a full year after her arrival at court, her father had become Earl Rivers and the royal treasurer. Two of her sisters had been married off to families of power, selected with care. Warwick could only imagine that the queen spent her time in the archives at the Tower, seeking out families who might bestow yet another title on her line. Her sisters would inherit houses and lands that other-wise would have reverted to the Crown or, in one case, to a Neville cousin. Warwick grimaced at the thought, though he knew it was no more than he would have done himself. Elizabeth had the ear of her husband – and Edward was a little free with his rewards for bedplay. Warwick and the Nevilles would have to endure; there was no help for it.

'How fare your wards?' his brother said, breaking into his thoughts. 'Still making their fortune?'

Warwick groaned in memory of the day Richard of Gloucester and Henry Percy had been discovered in the market of Middleham, selling a selection of hams and bottles of wine from Warwick's own cellars. One of the other stallholders had sent a runner to the castle and the boys had been captured and brought back. The memory still made Warwick flush in embarrassment.

'I am sorry to say they have discovered betting now. Some lads from the village are perfectly happy to take their coins, of course – and then they fight and Mother or my wife is called to rule on an entirely new set of injustices.'

Warwick's brother leaned closer, amused by the affec-tion he saw.

'I'm sorry you didn't have sons,' he said. 'I can see you would have found joy in it.'

Warwick nodded, his eyes crinkling.

'I have so *many* memories of you and John and me, with

the cousins, with those boats we made that sank, remember those? Or the horse we caught that dragged John half a mile, but he would not let go. Do you remember that? God knows I love my two girls, but it is not quite the same. Middleham was too quiet for a while, without us.'

'My lord Warwick?' a servant said.

Warwick winked at his brother and pushed off the wall. The archbishop patted him on the shoulder, passing him on to the great doors that led to Edward's royal presence. They opened before him.

Gone were the days of empty rooms and silent, scurrying servants. Dozens of scribes sat at small tables along the edges of the long hall, copying documents. Others stood in small groups, discussing their business like merchants haggling a price. The court felt busy, full of bustle and serious intent.

Warwick had a sudden memory of finding the king alone in that same hall a year or so before. Edward had been in full armour, missing only his helmet and, for some reason, one metal boot, so that his bare foot showed. The king had been wandering through the castle with a huge jug of wine in one hand and a cooked chicken clutched in the other. Those days were in the past, it seemed, under Elizabeth's influence. For the first time, Edward had a working staff to bear the weight of ruling the kingdom. His factor, Hugh Poucher, had been a man Warwick had come to like, one who could be approached and who would always listen. He looked for some sight of him, but the man was nowhere in evidence.

Warwick found himself following the servant through an antechamber and over to a long gallery of pale limestone. As they drew close, he heard the sound of an arrow shot. Warwick flinched instinctively, as one who had faced such things in battle. The sound echoed strangely indoors, even in that great hall. The servant had caught his shocked reaction, Warwick realized with a touch of irritation. As they reached the gallery, the man introduced him and vanished, trotting away as if he had a dozen other things to do.

Edward stood with a drawn bow and a huge basket of arrows. A target of straw and cloth about as tall as a man had been wedged at the far end of the cloistered gallery, at least a hundred yards away. It would have been an easy distance for a true archer, but as far as Warwick knew, Edward had never shot a bow before. Most men could not even have drawn one, but the king seemed to have the strength in his sword arm. Edward had not glanced round, utterly absorbed in holding his bow steady. The target rested against oak panelling and two arrows had missed the straw circle completely. With the tip of a pink tongue showing in the corner of his mouth, Edward was the picture of concentration. He opened his hand and the arrow flew too fast to see, sinking to the feathers into the outer edge of the target. Edward smiled happily.

'Ah, Richard,' the king said. 'I have a hundred marks resting on my skill with Sir Anthony here. Would you like to take a shot?'

Warwick glanced at the thick-armed knight who was watching him closely. Four of the Woodville men had been added to the ranks of the Garter order, giving them the right to enter the king's presence as his most loyal companions. Warwick had known there would surely be one or two in attendance. He wondered if Edward was even aware that he spent very few waking hours without one of the Woodvilles in his presence – and of course, his nights were spent with Elizabeth. It disturbed Warwick how completely the family had ensnared the young king. He had considered offering advice more than once, but criticizing a man's wife was incredibly perilous. With an effort, he had kept his silence through every barb and thorn under his skin.

Anthony was perhaps Edward's favourite of the Woodville males. Ten years older than the king, the big knight seemed to enjoy their sparring – and was perhaps the only one of the Woodvilles who could last more than a few moments in a tournament mêlée. There was a certain amount of bristling from him when Warwick had him in sight, as if the man wanted to be a threat, or had already decided Warwick was his enemy.

'Your Highness, if you would allow Sir Anthony to return to his duties, I will try a shot or two with you. I do have some Privy Council business to discuss.'

Edward scratched one side of his face, understanding but unwilling.

'Oh very well. Anthony, perhaps you would collect the arrows. I'll have that hundred marks off you yet. I'm sure my lord Warwick will not take too much of my time.'

Warwick hid his dismay and bowed his head. He felt Anthony Woodville watching him and ignored the man until he was out of earshot.

'How is my brother?' Edward said before he could speak.

'Happy enough now,' Warwick replied. Some of the affection he had shown outside was still there to be seen. Edward looked closely at him.

'Good. Axe and sword, though – perhaps the bow as

well, to build his shoulders. He was too weak before. Let me know if he gives you any trouble at all.'

'Of course. His tutors say he is very quick in his lessons.'

'Which will do him no good at all if he is too soft to stand in plate while another man tries to smash his face in,' Edward said. 'I was about as soft as wet leather when I went with you to Calais. Three years with the garrison made me the man I am today – under your command. Do the same with him, if you please. He is the youngest of us and he has been a child too long.'

Warwick eyed Anthony Woodville at the other end of the hall, trying to judge how much time he had. The man was wrenching and grunting at an arrow sunk into the wooden panelling. Edward saw him looking and grumbled in his throat.

'Oh very well. Say what you have come to say to me.'

'It is about this latest marriage, Edward,' Warwick said in relief. 'John Woodville is just nineteen. Norfolk's mother is almost seventy. If Mowbray were still alive, he would petition for justice, you know that. Your Highness, I understand the Woodvilles wish for titles, but a marriage with such a gulf in age is a step too far.'

Edward had grown very still as he spoke, all his lightness gone. Warwick knew he was in exactly the dangerous position he had tried to avoid for a year. Norfolk had barely survived the battle of Towton, dying of some pestilence of the lungs just a few months later, which surprised no one who had seen him that day. It was a miracle he had lived to see spring.

'Mowbray was a decent man, Your Highness – loyal to you when the world said he should have marched with

Lancaster. Norfolk's mother is a Neville, Edward, so I take pride in his loyalty. Yet you would allow a beardless Woodville to sit at his hearth, kissing that mother's wrinkled cheek? I think you and I owe his family a little more dignity than that.'

'Have a care . . .' Edward said softly.

He held the bow like an axe-handle, almost as wide as one at the centre point. Warwick had the sudden sense that Edward was imagining lashing out with it, some almost imperceptible play of the muscles which made him want to duck out of danger. He had seen Edward on the battlefield and knew very well what he could do. Yet he held himself still, and stared back calmly.

'I do not dispute your wife's right to find a good match for any one of her sisters or brothers, or her sons. Yet this one . . . this is a travesty, with half a century between them. When the old woman dies, the title will be his. How will she weep to have a stranger call her "wife" and take everything that was her son's? This Woodville pup would be better off buying the title, Edward! To steal it in this way . . . it is diabolical.'

'Your own marriage brought you great estates, Richard, did it not?' Edward replied.

'A marriage to a *young* woman, to produce my two beautiful daughters. As *you* have done, Edward. This loveless joining of Norfolk and Woodville is too obvious, too cruel. It will cause only unrest.'

In less than a year at court, the new queen had given birth to a daughter, Elizabeth of York as she was known. Edward's wife was already pregnant again, as fertile as a young mare. Warwick had agreed to be the first child's godfather, believing the offer to be an olive branch between them. Yet at the baptism, the queen had leaned over to him and murmured that she longed for a dozen fine boys with the king. Her amusement at his expression had soured the day and troubled him ever since.

The worst of it was that the Nevilles had done much the same during his grandfather's time, placing a dozen brothers and sisters into the noble families of England. Warwick had thought the marriage to the Dowager Duchess of Norfolk might be a point of weakness, but the expression on Edward's face showed he was mistaken. Warwick realized the young king was utterly smitten, made blind and deaf by his wife's skirts. There was true anger on Edward's face as he sensed criticism of Elizabeth. Warwick had not seen him so enraged since Edward had stood in other men's blood at Towton, five years before. He could not help shuddering at the sense of violence in the giant staring at him.

'You have brought me your concerns, Richard,' Edward said. 'You are my counsellor and it was no more than your duty. I will consider them, but you should know I believe John Woodville is a fine man. He wears a hair shirt under his silks, did you know that? I saw it when he stripped to bathe in a river while we were hunting. His skin is like raw meat and he makes no complaint. He is a fine hand with a pack of dogs – and he is my wife's brother. She wishes to raise him up. It pleases me to please her.'

Anthony Woodville was returning at last, having cut the last of the arrows from the woodwork with his knife. He was striding up the gallery, straining to hear the end of the conversation. Warwick took a step back and bowed rather than give the man the satisfaction. That said, he supposed his words would be repeated from Edward's lips to Elizabeth that evening. He could hardly ask that they be kept private from the king's own wife. He waited for Edward to release him and walked away, feeling Woodville eyes on his back as he went.

25

Thirty horses had to be walked out one by one from their stalls in the foetid hold. It took time, and as he waited, Warwick stood frowning on the docks at Calais. The quays themselves were of dressed stone and iron blocks, but the walkways were of planking, stretching away to the warehouses and taverns along the front, all crushed together with never enough space. He had memories both good and bad of the port fortress. It had once been the gateway to English Normandy, the place where anything could be bought and sold, from apes and ivory to lavender and rubies and wool. King Henry's weakness had put paid to all that.

The port was about as noisy and stank just as strongly as he remembered. A dozen ships rocked at anchor outside the sheltered waters, all waiting for the harbourmaster's skiff to row across, their captains shouting insults to one another. No one could enter Calais without that permission, not with the cannon pointed out to sea to smash them to flinders. Gulls called in high voices overhead, swooping down to squabble over any smear of scales or fish guts.

On the long quays, eight merchant crews were heaving bales and barrels out of their holds as fast as they could, doing their best to distract and confound the English port tallymen who tried to keep track of taxes owed and a bewildering array of custom stamps, forged or real. Fishing boats bobbed in between and around them, the French boatmasters holding up good examples of their catch. Warwick remembered the life and the cackle of the place, though it had taken on a twitching, feverish energy since his younger years. It had been just one port in thirty then, with all the coasts and two-thirds of France thriving under English control. He shook his head in sadness.

Calais was still worth thousands a year to the Crown, in taxes and profits both – and not one cloth yard, not one iron nail or haddock passing through, was strictly legal, not between two countries that had never declared a formal peace. Men on both sides had thrived in the uncertainty, using Calais as the entry point to all of France and Burgundy, even down to Sicily and North Africa, with enough bribes paid.

Warwick watched a wooden crate of oranges being yanked open, his gaze drawn to the splash of colour on the whitened wooden docks. The English merchant peering at them suddenly speared his thumb deep into the core of one, then licked the grease, nodding. Fruit in winter, from lands much further to the south where lemons and oranges still grew. Sugar from Cyprus or the Levant, even suits of armour from Italy, where a master smith might demand fortunes for his work. Warwick owned such a set himself, measured to his frame so that it fitted him perfectly and had saved his life more than once.

Warwick whistled and the merchant looked up, his suspicion clearing when he saw the earl's surcoat crest. Warwick waited while the man's servant ran up with three large oranges, for which Warwick tossed him a silver penny. Calais was still a place where fortunes were made, for those who had the eye to see it. Yet she was not what she had been.

The last of the horses were unloaded and saddled, and his men formed into a neat phalanx of armour and horse-flesh to pass through the port. Warwick waved an arm and turned his mount away from the sea, heading along the main street to the walls that enclosed everything in the port town. They loomed over everyone alive inside, a constant reminder that this was a port in a hostile land, with walls twelve feet thick, to withstand a siege. King Edward paid for hundreds of men to keep those walls, often with wives and children who had never seen England. Calais was its own little world, with alleys and shops and smiths and thieves and fallen women whose husbands had died of disease or been drowned.

Warwick rode to the inner gate and presented his papers with the seal of King Edward to the captain there. At his back, thirty men in armour kept their talk small, sensing the earl was in a darkening mood. The only one who could not stop gazing around in amazement and happiness was George, Duke of Clarence. For the young man, the docks were spiced with exotic flavours and smells, entrancing every sense. As the gate opened, Warwick tossed him an orange and he caught it with a grin, pressing the strange fruit to his nose and breathing in.

The sight of George of Clarence so full of life went some way to ease Warwick's gloom. Calais was the stepping stone across the Channel to a continent, he knew that. It was also a poor place to land if your destination was Paris, as his was. Far better to take a ship to Honfleur, even though it was no longer an English-held port.

As Warwick felt his horse stretch out into a canter, he let the animal have its head, after being confined and blink-ered in a stinking hold. Horses could not vomit and a sea crossing sometimes meant they suffered terribly, growing sicker and sicker but unable to empty their stomachs. It did them good to have a run, and the road ahead cleared quickly at the sight of horsemen thundering down it.

He heard Clarence give a whoop as the king's brother came abreast of him. Warwick leaned forward over his horse's neck, easing into a gallop, caught up in the pleasure of speed and danger. A fall might kill them, but the air was cold and sweet, filled with the promise of spring in the green verges.

Warwick found he was chuckling as he rode, almost gasping. He had been confined for too long as well, with two, almost three years of watching Woodvilles promoted to every position and post that carried a salary in England and Wales. It was pleasant to leave that behind him, in all senses.

He was old enough to remember when an English lord sailed to Honfleur and upriver to Rouen, then took a smaller boat along the Seine to the heart of Paris. Yet their fine warhorses could not be taken in fragile riverboats. It was true he would arrive with dust and sweat and grime clinging to every inch of him. He and his men would need another day to find rooms and bathe. Yet perhaps he would feel refreshed even so. He heard Clarence laughing as they clattered along a good road at a reckless speed.

Warwick looked back at the young man. Clarence resembled his older brother in some ways, though he had not grown as tall and was infinitely more amiable. As one who had watched Edward become a man, Warwick had been wary of another son of York at first, accepting his presence reluctantly. He supposed Edward's brother was always likely to report the most interesting events back to the king and queen. With the young Richard at Middleham, Warwick could never completely escape the sense of their eyes on him. Yet George of Clarence had an open face, without any guile or suspicious looks. It was with a twinge of sadness that Warwick realized he liked all the York sons. If it had not been for Elizabeth Woodville, he thought the Plantagenets and the Nevilles could have made an unbreakable bond.

On lesser mounts, they might have exchanged them at post-houses on the Paris road, one hundred and sixty miles from the coast. Like the most ancient roads in England, it was a clear, wide surface in good, Roman stone, running across what had once been the edge of Caesar's Gaul. Merchants thronged its length, but dragged their carts and families sharply off the road when they saw Warwick's knights flying.

Before the first morning ended, Warwick had twice been stopped by French captains, each time sent on his way as soon as he had presented his papers, all countersealed by King Louis's Master of the Household in Paris. The soldiers had become remarkably polite and helpful after that, recommending the best places to rest on their route to the capital. Warwick and his men found taverns before sunset and if most of them had to sleep among the horses in the stables, or wedged under the eaves of an attic, it was not such a hardship.

On the fourth night, Warwick and Clarence had taken a table set with olives, bread and a flask of wine strong enough to make their heads swim. The owners appeared delighted to have English lords in their house, though Warwick had still sent one of his men to watch the food being prepared. He had the excuse of avoiding poison, but the truth was his man was a skilled cook and loved to learn new flavours, asking about every spice and powder and insisting on a taste. By the time he returned to England, Warwick knew he would have a dozen new dishes of French country fare to enjoy.

They sat by a fire in an iron grate, enjoying an evening without the clank of armour as both men had come down from their rooms in simple jerkin and hose. As the first course came to an end and they wiped their fingers, Warwick raised a cup to the young man, wishing him good fortune in everything he did. He found Clarence surprisingly good company, not at all garrulous for one so young, but given to comfortable silences. Warwick's toast prompted another and Clarence obliged, his face already bright with drink.

'And to you, my brother's great friend. And to my brother Edward, first man in England!' he said.

The strong wine was affecting the younger man and he slurred the words. Warwick chuckled and sank his cup, refilling it from the flask before the tavern maid could do more than take a step in his direction. She stood back, blushing, with her hands clasped at her waist. She was not used to English appetites or manners. The first platter of two small chickens in fennel and mushrooms had been reduced to bones in no time at all, barely interrupting the two men's conversation.

'Edward has made a fine match, of course,' George said suddenly. He was staring into the fire and did not see the way Warwick's expression tightened. 'With two daughters born, though I do not doubt there will be a boy or two to come! Elizabeth is pregnant for a third time, so I will pray it is a son and heir. Yet, I . . . well, I am . . .'

Warwick looked sharply at him and the young man

flickered a glance in his direction. Such a deep colour appeared on his cheeks that it looked as if he was choking. The young duke was clearly nervous and sweating more than the heat of the small fire might have justified.

'I . . . ah . . . I asked to accompany you to Paris in part because I have not seen the city itself and I thought it would be a fine journey, with new sights, and perhaps I might discover a book or two to offer as a g-gift . . .'

Warwick looked at him in alarm. The peaceful silence of their past few days had vanished. He began to wonder if George of Clarence would have an apoplexy, so much was he shaking and spluttering.

'Have a drink, George. Here, the joint has arrived! Allow me to slice it for you. Perhaps you will broach whatever it is that has you in such a fine froth.'

Warwick set about carving the pork haunch delivered to the table, placing slices on the wooden platters in front of them. He took his own knife and cut pieces he could spear as he talked, then refilled both cups of wine yet again. No doubt it would be a late start the following day, but the thought did not disturb him unduly. Some nights could not be better spent than in wine and good company.

George, Duke of Clarence, chewed miserably, his mouth stuffed too full even to attempt to talk. He wrestled with a strip of the finest crackling he had ever tasted, wrenching it back and forth until he thought it would never give way, then swallowing manfully. The meat seemed to settle his swimming senses enough to speak again, forcing himself to rush through the words before his heart exploded in his chest.

'I had thought to ask you, sir, my lord, for the hand of your daughter Isabel, in marriage.'

It had been said. The young man sagged in his chair and upended his cup of wine while Warwick gaped at him, his mind working. It was a better match than he could have hoped for – especially with Woodville men and women claiming every title in the country as soon as they came free.

'Have you mentioned your desire to my daughter?' he asked.

George spluttered through his wine and stammered his reply.

'I have not told her of desire, sir! I would not presume, until I had spoken to her father. Until our wedding night, my lord, sir!'

'Take a *breath*,' Warwick said. 'And now another. There. I meant your desire to marry, nothing more. Have you . . . I don't know, talked of love with Isabel? If so, I am a little surprised you could get more than a word past that babbling stream.'

'I have spoken three times to her, my lord, in chaste company. Twice in London and once at your estate in Middleham, last summer.'

'Yes, I remember,' Warwick said, summoning some vague recollection of seeing his then sixteen-year-old daughter talking to a sweating boy. He wondered if George, Duke of Clarence, was interested in his daughter for her beauty or for the lands she would inherit. Warwick had no sons and whoever married Isabel would eventually become the richest man in England, inheriting the vast estates of Warwick and Salisbury both. Isabel might have been married already if not for the extraordinary dominance of the Woodvilles as she reached marriageable age.

Warwick frowned, looking with fresh eyes at an

eighteen-year-old duke who might become his son-in-law. It was one thing to consider George as a half-decent brother of the king, quite another to think of him as the father of Warwick's grandchildren. He saw a deep nervousness, but also some courage as the young man met his gaze and held it, instinctively understanding the scrutiny.

'I know you will want to think about my offer, sir. I will not mention it again, now that I have brought it to you. Only this, my lord. I do love her, on my honour. Isabel is a wonderful girl. When I have made her smile, I want to laugh or weep for the joy of it.'

Warwick held up his hand.

'Let me digest the news, with this fine meal. I think I would like another flask of this red wine, to settle my stomach.' He saw the young man swallow and look pale and decided not to press him. Instead, he yawned. 'Or perhaps I will sleep and rise early. We have a long day on the road ahead – and Paris the day after. We'll need to be sharp.'

'Will I have your answer by then, my lord?' George asked, his eyes desperate.

'Yes, you will,' Warwick replied. He had no desire to torture the young man. His instincts were all in favour, not least because his wife would not have dreamed of their daughter marrying a duke. It was no small thing that the marriage would infuriate Elizabeth Woodville as well, though that would remain a private pleasure.

The thought stopped him as he rose from table.

'You know, even if I am willing to entertain your suit, the king will still have to grant his permission, as he must for all marriages between noble families.'

'How fortunate, then, that King Edward is my brother,'

George said, smiling, 'who would grant me anything in his power.'

The young man's enthusiasm was infectious and Warwick smiled along with him. George of Clarence was still a man unmade, on the path to what he would be. Even so, Warwick found himself hoping the king's brother would be successful.

Charing Cross was a rough crossroads lying between the houses of Parliament and the walls of the city of London, further along the river. On the bend of the Thames, it was best known for the huge cross erected by the first King Edward, on the death of his wife. Though it had been a hundred and eighty years, the cross remained as a landmark to one man's sorrow and loss.

Edward bowed his head and raised his hand to touch the polished marble. He could see the mark where a thousand others had patted it for luck, and he said a prayer for a long-dead queen. Perhaps it had more weight coming from one who shared old Longshanks's height and name and blood. Edward felt close to the king men had called the Hammer of the Scots.

Beyond the cross and the turning circle, the wide road stretched away west to Chelsea, the great coach stop and stables, where travellers could bathe and eat before heading out into the wilds. The river was close by and Edward could smell the bitter green taint of it, opening up his lungs. He cleared his throat, settling his dislike of thick mud and all the damp and desolation around him – as well as the task ahead.

It had to be done. Elizabeth had opened his eyes to the influence of the Neville family on the English court, how they had insinuated themselves into every nook and cranny. It was astonishing how often lucrative posts were held by unremarkable men and women, who just happened to have Neville parents or grandparents. Elizabeth described it as 'the rot', though she had been intrigued by how it had been accomplished.

Edward chuckled suddenly, making the men with him look up from their patient stances. His wife was a wonder, a private joy that came from her adoration of him, her delight in his every part. They laughed easily, and if his lords thought she had caught him by her thighs, well, he could not completely disagree. Yet all the while he understood Elizabeth would do anything to protect him – there was no one else in the world whose interests were so completely his own. She had said so a thousand times. No one else could deserve his complete trust, for they had motives and loves and friendships apart from him. Elizabeth was devoted to her king, her lover and her husband, for the children and the crown.

He looked up at the open door of the Charing Cross inn, which occupied a fine position on the coach road west and was well known for its food. The innkeeper had been warned he would receive the king. He stood bowed over, unable to rise.

Edward dismounted slowly, his thoughts still on his wife. She was right, of course. If a gardener discovered a vine had grown all around his borders, through every hedge and bush and bloom, he would not ignore it. He would cut the root and tear it out, curl by writhing curl, to be thrown on the fire. That was what she wanted.

To have so many Nevilles in the great offices of the realm meant that Edward ruled only with their support. He had discussed it endlessly with Elizabeth, until he saw the vine clinging to every estate and noble family from the south coast to the border of Scotland.

Poor King Henry had never seen how far they had grown, how coiled and strong the vine had become. Of course he had not. Edward, too, had been blind to the extent of the influence of men like Warwick and Earl Sir John Neville of Northumberland; of Fauconberg, Earl of Kent; of the Duke of Norfolk, with his Neville mother; of George Neville, the Archbishop of York. King Edward clenched his jaw as he looked up at the windows of the inn on the crossroads. Elizabeth had painted an appalling picture for him. Was he to rule only as long as he did not cross Neville interests? He would not allow such a thing, now he had become aware of it. Even if he held back from the bonfire Elizabeth wanted to see, it would do no harm to trim some part of that dark growth.

Archbishop George Neville walked out of the tavern door, drawn down by the news echoing round the rooms that the king himself stood outside. All movement had ceased around them for hundreds of yards as passers-by froze to watch the young man who ruled England.

The archbishop had knelt before to the king, at Edward's coronation. He wore a fine cloak and robes beneath, but when he saw the king had truly come, he did not hesitate, approaching Edward and dropping to one knee. There was the look of wolves on the knights around the king. More than one had touched a hand to his sword hilt as the archbishop came close. George Neville kept his head bowed until Edward murmured for him to rise.

'So many men and horses,' the archbishop said softly. 'I am your servant, Your Highness. What would you have of me?'

Although George Neville was a head shorter than the king and was a man of the church, he was as broad-shouldered as any of the knights present. Standing straight, he gave them no sign of guilt or fear, but merely returned their stares with steady calm.

'I have come to retrieve the Great Seal, Your Grace,' Edward said. 'You may hand it to Robert Kirkham here, the Master of the Rolls. He will keep it safe.'

George Neville paled, his eyes growing large in his shock.

'Am I then to be dismissed as your chancellor, Your Highness? Have I offended? Have I failed in my duties?'

He could see Edward was growing uncomfortable, a mottled stain of anger spreading across his face and neck.

'You have not, Your Grace. I have merely decided to pass the Great Seal to another.'

'Who, then, will assign judges and courts to the cases already brought before me? Whom shall I tell the penitents to approach, Your Highness? I . . . I cannot understand . . .' George Neville looked around at the knights watching him balefully. '*Armed* men? Did His Highness think I would resist? I gave an oath of fealty at your coronation!'

Edward flushed further. He had imagined fury and manipulation, not the raw hurt he saw in the archbishop. The king set his jaw and said nothing, watching as the outrage faded and George Neville's shoulders dipped.

'Marren!' the archbishop called. 'Fetch the king's seal to me. You will find it in the leather satchel marked with a gold crest. No, bring the satchel as well, if it is to be taken away.'

His servant raced back into the inn, clattering up the stairs and vanishing into his suite of rooms. In the street,

George Neville had recovered his dignity. The king still stood in sullen silence, waiting. Around them had gathered a crowd of staring faces, men and women and children, all delighted or in awe.

'I do not dispute your right to have any chancellor you please,' the archbishop said in a murmur. 'Yet I suspect you have been misinformed.' He waved a hand at the armed knights standing with cold menace all around. 'I am a man of God and a loyal subject. Until this moment, I was also the chancellor of England. I remain loyal – and a man of God. That is unchanged.'

Edward inclined his head, accepting the point, though he did not reply to it. The archbishop's servant came skidding back across the muddy road, bearing a satchel on a wide strap over his shoulder. Edward passed it to the Master of the Rolls, a man too embarrassed to do more than grunt an affirmative as he checked the contents.

With sharp and jerky movements, the king and his knights remounted. The crowd parted in haste as they realized Edward was leaving. The archbishop was left staring as they turned their mounts and cantered east, towards Ludgate and the city of London, taking the Great Seal with them.

26

The Palace of the Louvre was about as impressive as it was intended to be, three times the size of the Tower of London even before the vast gardens were taken into account. When Paris had been under English occupation, the Louvre had been left almost empty, with just a small part used as stables and a residence for the king's lieutenant and governor.

All that was past, Warwick thought ruefully – and he would surely not live to see such days return. It had been almost heartbreaking to ride through countryside that could so easily have been Kent or Sussex or Cornwall. Normandy and Picardy looked so very much like southern England, it was surely no surprise that English kings had taken it for themselves once or twice. Warwick smiled at his own reflection in the window, looking out at ornate hedges stretching for what looked like miles along the banks of the Seine. Such thoughts were out of place, with so much expected of him.

The presence of the young Duke of Clarence had not hurt his cause at all, Warwick was prepared to admit. From the moment their arrival in the French capital had been formally announced, King Louis and his most senior courtiers had spared neither expense nor flattery of King Edward's representatives. The mere presence of King Edward's own brother was greeted with flushed pleasure, as if sending Clarence was proof of a new English will to seek peace and legal trade. It helped that the young duke spoke excellent French, though at Warwick's urging, Clarence limited himself to compliments on the palace and the city.

King Louis was an early riser, it seemed. To do him the courtesy of waiting on his royal presence, Warwick had to get up long before dawn, trotting through the misty streets of Paris, just as that ancient city was coming alive. He had fallen into the habit of stopping at a bakery in a street not far from his lodging house, tearing pieces of hot bread from a loaf while he rode. The majority of his knights were lodged around the city, leaving Warwick with just two veterans, the Duke of Clarence and two servants to accompany him into the royal palace each morning. In other years, Warwick knew he might have been forced to wait entire days, but miraculously he had grown used to just a little delay as the king broke his fast and was bathed and perfumed, appearing with his hair oiled and his velvets brushed. Warwick had been flattered by the king's genial attention, greeting him each morning almost as if they were friends.

The doors at the end of the hall crashed back, a signal for all guards and servants to stand straight. The herald began the recitation of King Louis's many titles and honours and Warwick and Clarence went down on one knee, a perfect pair of English courtiers in all their finery.

Through the heralds the French king strolled, his great red robe of state carried by a host of tiny boys in matched costumes of blue and white. Around him came a dozen of his thin-faced scribes, who recorded every word he uttered, scratching with their quills in a language all their own to match the speed of his speech. Warwick had been present when one of them had fainted two days before. That fellow was nowhere to be seen, replaced no doubt by one who could keep up with the torrent. King Louis loved to talk, though it was never empty chatter. Warwick found he spilled words like a fisherman with a lure, watching all the time to see if anything would rise from the depths.

'Up, my fine English lords who rose before the sun to greet me this morning! Have your appetites been sated, gentlemen? Your thirsts allayed?'

A true answer was not expected and Warwick and Clarence only nodded and bowed as the king swept past them. They stood in absolute silence as the court assembled around its heart, appearing out of side doors while Louis settled himself at the head of his black marble table. It had some significance, Warwick had learned, though he did not know what it was. He had noticed it was rare for anyone to pass the thing without reaching out to touch the stone, whether for luck or as a relic, he had not asked.

Fruit was brought and more chairs, with eight or nine strangers appearing to whisper into the king's ear. It might have been a dumbshow to impress the guests, though Warwick sensed there were serious matters being discussed in front of him, information brought to the king and his responses delivered behind guarding hands.

A full hour passed, possibly two, without Warwick or Clarence showing the least sign of fatigue or boredom. Once Warwick had turned it into a private challenge, it had become a game between them, so that they were able to meet each other's eyes with only mild interest and hidden humour, no matter how long the delay.

'Gentlemen! Approach me, please. Here, here. Come, come. Oh, I am desolate to have kept you waiting for such an age. Chancellor Lalonde will be present to advise me, of course.' The king eyed the old man as if daring him to respond. The chancellor stared back, hunched over his cane. 'You know, gentlemen, I rise each morning with the knowledge that one day Lalonde will be absent, missing from the rolls. I grieve in advance, if you follow me, imagining the sorrow I will surely feel, as if I can somehow reduce the pain of it by experiencing it early.'

'I suspect you will grieve for him even so, Your Majesty,' Warwick said. 'I have learned that time can steal away the sting of the cut, but it does little for the deeper wound.'

King Louis looked from Warwick to Clarence for what seemed a long time, for once oddly silent. He raised a single finger and wagged it back and forth before pressing it to his lips.

'Ah. Your father. Earl Salisbury. And of course, milord, that great man and friend to this house, the Duke of York. You have both been tempered by pain, by loss. That is the English word? Made stronger, like metal in a forge. You know, when my father passed from the world, he and I were not . . . reconciled, if you understand. He appeared to see me as a threat, a misjudgement of character that was most unlike him. He thought I was wasting my talents. Still, I miss him.'

With no warning, the king's eyes grew bright with tears and he choked, tended instantly by servants bringing him water, silk cloths and wine. In another moment, the signs of grief had vanished, his gaze cold and as sharp as a spur.

Warwick could only bow his head in response, once more struck by the odd sensation of being watched by a man who was actually looking at him, as if the eyes were opaque coloured glass and the flood of thoughts and words were all to conceal the true king within, peering out.

'I saw in you, my lord Warwick, a man of sensibility, from the first moment. A man, if you will forgive my flattery, who would be worth my time and who might repay my trust. You came to me without guile or games, to state your desires for trade and peace in that wonderfully frank English way, all laid out like beans on a drumhead, to be counted and swept up, or refused. My father detested you all, as I am sure you will understand, given that English clods and farmers strolled along his streets as if they owned them.'

Warwick smiled, waiting for the question or the point that he knew by then would surely follow.

'I am now faced with a choice, milord Warwick, as to *your* character, a choice that brings me pain. I must decide, before you leave my presence here today, whether you are a fool and a dupe, or whether you are part of the machinations and strategies of your court at home!'

To Warwick's astonishment, the king stood up from his seat and raised a finger to point at him, the king's face darkening with every appearance of rage. The man of silks and philosophical musing had vanished into spittle-flecked fury.

It was so appallingly sudden, Warwick had to struggle with every nerve and muscle in his body not to laugh. There was something magnificently comical in the swollen royal bladder before him, for all Warwick's life hung in the balance.

The wild urge to destroy himself faded, leaving him weak and shaking.

'Your Majesty, I do not understand . . .'

'Dupe, then? You know, that is not your reputation, Richard Neville – a man who has walked a failed king to his cell in your Tower of London. Does your King Edward think to intimidate me with you? Does he intend me to read some threat from your presence?'

Warwick swallowed in discomfort.

'That is *not* his intention, I swear it. If you had met King Edward, Your Majesty, I think you would find he is not a man for such games, for such a labyrinth. By my name and my honour . . .'

King Louis held up a hand, clean and white.

'I have sent gifts of gold and silver cups to you, milord. I have demanded of the merchants in Paris that they make no charge on any of your party, not one! That even the whores make themselves available to your men without a single coin in return. I have had the most skilful seamstresses and weavers and dyers in France take the measurements of every man who rode with you from the coast. Why not, milord? They will return home in better clothes than those they brought from England. My master tailors will have shown their wares to English families wealthy enough to order more. You see? Trade is the thread that joins us, not war. The English cry out for better wine than your own poor vineyards, better cloth, better cheese. In return, who knows, there must be something you have that we might want?'

'Archers?' George, Duke of Clarence, replied.

Whether his intention was to defend Warwick from the tirade or just a response from insolence and sensitivity to insult, Warwick had no idea. He gripped the young man's arm briefly, quick as a thought, to quieten him.

'Your Majesty, I do not understand the source of this anger,' Warwick went on hurriedly. 'I suspect there has been some confusion, perhaps a message misconstrued, or some enemy with spite on his lips . . .'

King Louis squinted at him, looking into his eyes and sighing.

'I do not believe you have been told, Richard. That is why I am angry – in part on your behalf. What will you do now? Now that your king has made you a fool for a second time? He has you negotiate for a French princess and, *swip*, snatches it all away from you, saying, "I am married." And now, milord, he sends you to me once again, to bring about a treaty worth . . . well, no matter. And while you are in France, he makes his *own* treaty with the Duke of Burgundy, for trade and more, my lord. *More!* It is my information that he has agreed a *pact* with milord the Duke of Burgundy, dear Philip! A pact of mutual protection against France! Such a betrayal . . . and yet, and yet I fear for you, milord. To be betrayed so by your king! Infamous! Will it be war now between us, do you think? Would that be King Edward's intention?'

Warwick had stood very still, barely aware of the shifting, gaping young man at his side. He had no cause to suspect a lie from the French king. It was too outlandish, too appalling, to be anything but true. The knowledge showed in his face.

'Ah, as I said, the dupe,' Louis went on, almost sadly. 'I thought so, despite your reputation. Your King Edward risks a great deal in offending me twice, perhaps less so with you.'

'My brother will have had reason . . .' Clarence began.

Warwick rounded on him, snapping out a command to be silent, so that the young man bit off the remaining words.

'My lord Clarence,' Louis said, his eyes full of pity. 'Of course your brother had a reason, as all men do. Burgundy will know you are in Paris, in negotiation with me. I do not doubt spies will report even this conversation, just as they did yesterday and the day before. Pigeons fly all over Paris, all over France. Your brother will have secured excellent terms for his country's trade and protection, I am certain. The fact is that Burgundy and I have not enjoyed a peaceful friendship in recent years. Perhaps I pushed him into the arms of England. I do not know. Your King Edward has gained his trade route to the whole continent – and in return, he has risked making an enemy of France and perhaps of Warwick and Clarence, eh? Who knows? Kings reach and grasp and then reach again like children, until they find they no longer have the strength. It is the way of things.'

The king's gaze flickered over Warwick, assessing the complete destruction of his expression, the slack features and eyes lost in inward thought. Louis nodded to himself, his conclusions all confirmed. Warwick had not known.

'You may keep your gifts, my lords. Are we not still friends? I am desolated, for you and the trust I felt was beginning between us. I saw glories ahead, and now there is only wilderness. I am truly sorry.'

Warwick understood he was being dismissed, but could find no words, no line of argument to continue. He breathed out slowly, his mouth tight. As he and Clarence bowed, King Louis held up his wagging finger once again.

'I thought . . . no. My lords, I had intended to make a final gift to this fine young man, a suit of armour made by the best master of Paris. Master Auguste has brought all his best designs. He wishes only to take your lengths and then . . . ah well. No, it is such a *waste*! Perhaps I could still have it sent to you even so, as a token of my respect and friendship.'

The sullen mood that darkened Clarence's brow cleared

completely at hearing this. He glanced at Warwick, trying to see if he dared to accept.

'With my lord Warwick's permission, I would be very pleased to see such a thing. Why, only yesterday, I was describing the armour I had seen in your training grounds. I was envious . . . Your Majesty, it is a princely offer. I am overwhelmed!'

Louis beamed at the pleasure in the young man.

'Go, go then, before I change my mind or count the cost. Follow this gentleman here and he will show you to Master Auguste. You will not be disappointed.'

Warwick gave a slight nod when Clarence turned to him questioningly.

'Don't worry,' Warwick said. 'I will discover the fault in this business.' He found himself smiling as he spoke. The young man's enthusiasm was infectious, the gift truly a royal one.

As the door closed behind the Duke of Clarence, Louis settled himself in the high-backed chair once again. Warwick turned to him with one eyebrow raised and the king chuckled.

'Yes, my lord, I thought it might be better to distract the young fellow for the next hour. Oh, he will have his armour – and Master Auguste is a genius – but this is not about your king using you so poorly, just to get better terms. There is another matter, one I wished to witness.'

As Warwick frowned in confusion, King Louis gave a signal to Chancellor Lalonde, who gestured in turn at another set of doors on the opposite side of the room. Warwick had the strong impression of standing at the heart of a hive, with each door opening on to whatever Louis wanted shown, or closed on what he would keep private. For all the king's goodwill, Warwick had seen the fury and the sharp intelligence of the man. He would not treat him lightly . . .

Warwick froze, his hand dropping to where his sword would usually rest on his hip. The blade had been taken from him as he entered, of course, a matter of simple courtesy in a foreign court. His fingers twitched for it, recalling the slender dagger he had under his waistband. It could be reached in a moment if need be.

Derry Brewer limped through the doors. He walked with the aid of a heavy cane that spread into a carbuncle under his clutching hands and bore more resemblance to a mace than a cripple's stick. Warwick felt some of the tension go out of his frame as he noted the man's trailing leg and missing eye. He tried not to show discomfort as the lurching figure crossed the polished floor and came right to his side. The spymaster was dressed in a brown leather coat over jerkin and cream hose, good, thick wool that would keep the chill from his bones.

Warwick drew himself up unconsciously, determined not to show fear or to be intimidated. He realized he was afraid, even as he struggled to hide it. The man was his enemy, and Warwick could feel the burning gaze of the French king on the side of his face, watching the meeting with unashamed fascination.

'Good morning, my lord Warwick,' Derry said, 'You will excuse me if I do not bow, with this old leg o' mine. It took a battering. A few years ago now, but the scars are tight, still.'

'What you do want, Brewer? What could you possibly believe you could have to say to me?'

'King Louis has been very kind, Richard. I asked to

meet you first, in case you were likely to take out that little dagger against your ribs and start waving it. Before I risk my mistress in your presence, you see.'

Warwick grew cold and still, overwhelmed. He could feel the knife pressed against his skin under his arm, the leather sheath damp with sweat.

'Queen Margaret?' he asked, giving her the title from long use, though it made Derry smile to hear it.

'I do not think you will run mad, will you, Richard? All she wants is to ask after her husband. Is that too much? It is said you walked Henry to his cell, and that you have visited him there. Will you let a man's wife ask you about him, my lord?'

Warwick knew Derry understood his every twisting thought. Margaret had been responsible for the death of his father. She had watched while York and Salisbury had been executed, their heads taken to be spiked on city walls. If he agreed to speak to her, he would look into eyes that had seen his father's head cut free to roll on the earth. It was a hard thing to ask.

'It would honour me, my lord Warwick,' King Louis said behind him. Warwick half-turned, trying to keep Derry Brewer in sight. 'Margaret is my cousin,' the French king went on, 'and, well, you were here in Paris. She is, of course, under my protection. It seemed churlish not to grant her request, you understand?'

Warwick wondered. To be informed of another humiliation by King Edward – and then to meet his enemy in the space of moments. He wondered how many hours of planning he had missed to be brought to that place at that very instant of time. He shrugged to Derry Brewer.

'Bring her in, then. You can have my dagger, if you'd like. I don't seek revenge on women, Master Brewer, though I would be willing to take that staff of yours and give you a new set of lumps with it.'

'I would be delighted, my lord Warwick, if you wish to try,' Derry replied with a grin that showed half his teeth had gone. He had clearly been beaten with extraordinary violence. Still, he seemed strong, his hand on the staff thick with corded veins. Only the twisted leg and empty eye showed what he had suffered.

Margaret entered without fanfare or servants, sweeping into the room in a dark-blue dress that trailed over the ground behind her. She was not the broken figure Warwick had imagined, instead standing straight-backed and bright of eye. The greater surprise was the young man at her side, dark-haired and slim at the waist under wide shoulders. Edward of Westminster raised his head in greeting and Warwick decided her son was around fourteen, perhaps fifteen years of age. The boy was already taller than his mother and had the look of a swordsman about him. Warwick realized he was fascinated.

'Thank you for agreeing, Richard,' Margaret said.

'It was a courtesy to my host, no more,' Warwick replied. Despite himself, he bowed slightly, making her smile.

'I regret the loss of your father, Richard. I give you my word. I stood against York and he stood with his friend, but I was never an enemy to your house.'

'I cannot believe you, my lady.'

To his surprise, Margaret turned her head as if he had hurt her.

'I still remember when you and I were on the same side,

Richard, against Jack Cade and his rebels. Do you recall? We have served enemies, it is true. I do not believe we must always be enemies ourselves.'

'Ah, gentlemen, my lady,' King Louis said, rising. 'My steward, who is gesturing at me like a child, has prepared a little lunch.' The king strolled down the hall past them. 'If you are brave, I suspect we can find some dish to please even that wonder of the world, the famous English palate. Follow on!'

'Where would I be without you?' Edward murmured. He buried his face between his wife's breasts. 'Without *these*!'

His hot breath tickled her and she shrieked, pushing him off the rounded curve of her belly.

'You would be dressed an hour ago,' she replied. She rolled over in the bed and gasped at the sight of her mastiff waiting patiently, the great black-and-white dog tall enough for his entire head to appear over the edge of the bed and stare at her.

'How long have you been there, Bedey? Away now, outside.'

She turned to her husband as he sat on the side of the bed, reaching up to his shoulder and curling around him.

'Without me you would not have seen the hold those Nevilles had on you. I saw it from the first, as fresh eyes. In every house, in every single noble line.'

'As you have pressed your Woodvilles forward,' Edward teased her.

She blew air from her lips, making a coarse sound that made him chuckle.

'We have but trimmed the vine before it choked you,

that is all! Either way, it is not the same. My family are solid country stock, not these devious cutpurses and conspirators! We know cattle and we know men, whereas these Nevilles, well, they are even more cunning than I understood at first. I think, in time, they would have had you fenced around like a bull in a pen, unable to see over to the next field.'

Elizabeth ran her hands across the expanse of his shoulders, wondering again at the power in them, after an entire life wielding sword and mace. The muscles writhed as he moved, each one shifting under her hand until he squirmed at her attention and reached for his shirt.

'I am not sure about John Neville, Elizabeth. He has not harmed me and it is a low thing to consider taking away what he prizes most in the world.'

Elizabeth sat up straight, one hand across her breasts as she drew up her knees.

'It is not harm, Edward, but a balance, as we discussed. The Nevilles are still too strong, so that the policies of the throne are always what benefits the Nevilles, more than you or England! I did not ask for a Woodville as your chancellor, only that you should deny that vital role to the archbishop, with his loyalties to his family and to Rome.'

'He did not fight, as you said he might,' Edward murmured. 'He went like a lamb.'

'I'm sure it was because you brought strong men and found him with just a few servants. What choice did he have, Edward, but to meekly hand over your seal? No, it was well done, a redress. You are the York line. If you prune them back now, your daughters and your sons will not have to face another war in thirty years, or your grandchildren after that. We will find the balance once again, with no single family too strong for all the rest – unless it is your own!'

'The Percy family supported King Henry, you know. If I brought their heir out of the Tower and put him in Northumberland, I could make an enemy of John Neville for nothing.'

'The "King of the North"? That is what they call him. From Northumberland, that Neville controls the entire north – with his brother George, the Archbishop of York – from the border of Scotland to the River Trent. Do you see it now? You cannot rule but half a country, Edward! The Percys and the Nevilles fought for a generation. There are some who say this entire struggle was caused by their feud. And you gave *Northumberland* to the Nevilles. My love, you have a great heart. You are generous and trusting – more than a man should be, more than a king should be. Northumberland is too big a prize.'

'I could make him a marquess, perhaps,' Edward said, in thought. 'It is not oft used, but it is a grand title. It would be small recompense for losing Northumberland.'

'England cannot have two kings,' Elizabeth said. 'Of all men, you should feel that in your bones. I fear for the future if you let a Neville tree take root in the north.'

Edward waved a hand, tired of her arguments.

'Enough, enough. I will consider it, for peace from you. I just . . . The Nevilles have served me well.'

'They have served their own cause,' Elizabeth murmured. Her pregnancy made her groan as she rolled away. 'Oof! You will have to use the maids tonight, my love. I am too heavy with this child.'

Edward nodded, deep in thought, with his chin resting on his hand.

27

'What would you have me *do*, Brother?' Warwick said. '*Demand* King Edward stop granting permission for Wood-villes to marry? Return to us our lost honours? Edward has not taken so many blows to the head that he would choose my goodwill over that of his wife!'

Summer had aged into autumn, with Warwick's return from France two months past. From the windows of Middleham Castle, both he and John could see the golden fields of wheat being scythed down, sweep by sweep, baled and collected by hundreds of local men and women, entire villages come to gather the harvest and then celebrate with drink, music, bonfires and stolen kisses out in the stubbled fields.

John Neville was once again Lord Montagu, made a marquess and told that it was somewhere between an earl and a duke. He had raged about it for a time in private, to his brothers, though thankfully not in the hearing of those who might have wished him harm. Warwick understood his brother's anger, of course. John had been given his heart's greatest desire and they had taken it from him. Once more, a Percy ruled in Northumberland, as had so many generations before him. It had been a little odd returning Henry Percy to the Tower of London just so he could be walked out again, but King Edward had been pleased to find the young man in good health, as he might not have been after years in a cell. Warwick knew Henry

Percy felt a loyalty to him for his treatment. Their parting had not been too far from father and son. Middleham was a good deal quieter with just the king's brother living there as his ward. Richard of Gloucester still suffered some pain from a twist in his back, but they had pushed him through so many hours with axe and sword that entire new sets of armour had had to be made for a shape that had become lean and strong. Warwick no longer faced him in the training yards, at least. He had grown too slow, while the younger Richard was quick and sure.

John Neville, Marquess Montagu, had not responded to his questions, preferring instead to pull a chicken leg from a carcass on the table and accept a cup of wine. When he felt Warwick's gaze still on him, he gestured irritably. John Neville had personally executed a dozen men for King Edward. His loyalty had been absolute, unquestioning. His reward for it had been to have his title taken away and given to a Percy son. When he dwelled on the unfairness for too long, he dared not speak his thoughts aloud, even to Warwick. His brother Richard seemed prepared to suffer any humiliation rather than do what they all knew would come, in time.

Edward and his wife would have them all out with the pigs and geese before they were finished, John was certain. He burned too for his brothers, aghast at the unfairness of their treatment. Warwick sent to France, only to be humiliated and used as a pawn. George with the Great Seal taken from him over a sword's length – and John's precious title stolen and given to a boy. It was a campaign, far beyond a grudge. The architect was Elizabeth Woodville, that was the only certain heart of it. It was a shame that Warwick had known two women prepared to go to the ends of the world to damage his family. If their interests had ever coincided, John suspected they could have had a Neville on the throne of England.

George Neville entered, alone, crossing the room to grip hands with both of his brothers.

'Uncle Fauconberg has arrived,' he told them. 'Shall I have him brought in?'

'He did not send word he was coming,' Warwick responded, frowning. He looked from one to the other of his brothers. 'Ah. What is this?'

'Mother,' George replied. 'She thought perhaps it would be wise to gather Nevilles in one place. God knows we are not what we once were. Six cousins wait on your pleasure, Richard. A pitiful number, though they do hold some good land. We *are* diminished. We are rags made from fine banners, but you are still the head of the family.'

'Mother thought we should at least discuss the years ahead,' John Neville added, 'perhaps before King Edward fathers a son and heir. Three daughters now, but then that fertile little mare has had boys before. Another will surely come. Will the Neville men be banished entirely then, do you think? I do not imagine we could survive one more season of her ill will.'

There was no need to explain whom he meant, not in that company.

'I will not discuss *treason* with you,' Warwick hissed furiously to his brothers. 'I would be pleased to see my cousins and Uncle Fauconberg, but not to talk of plots or anything that might give King Edward cause to call our loyalty into question. Would you have me set this house on fire? That is what you risk. My God, the king's *brother* lives here!'

'I am not a fool, Richard,' John Neville spoke up. 'He was sent to the market to buy brandy, hours ago. If he'd spy for the king, he won't have a chance until this evening or tomorrow. Either way, he's not a boy any longer. I would send him home to his mother. You've filled your obligations there and more.' He shook his head, anger simmering. 'I don't understand why you would hold back *now*, after what we have suffered.'

'He waits on the petition,' George Neville said.

'Ah, of course,' John Neville said sourly. 'You have the right of it. Our brother still hopes for it to be granted, to have his Isabel wedded to a Plantagenet. I tell you, *she* will never allow it – and King Edward has shown he puts more weight in her word than all his council of lords who have served him so well. The man was made a weakling in her bed, that is the truth of it.'

'I do hope, yes, that my daughter will find her husband in George, Duke of Clarence,' Warwick retorted. 'Isabel is pleased at the match. He is but a year older than her and they . . . are well suited. She will be a duchess and Clarence will gain her estates, in the fullness of time.'

'How long is it now since you asked the king?' John muttered.

Warwick shook his head.

'No, you will not make me worry. It has been a few months; what of it? Such a joining of houses is not to be decided on a whim, but slowly, studiously, with care and an eye for each way the wind might change.'

John looked at his older brother, knowing that Warwick was blind, or chose not to see. He shrugged.

'You are the head of the family, Richard. Wait until winter, then, or next spring if you wish. It will not make any

344

difference, not with Elizabeth Woodville guiding the king's hand. She'll want your estates for her sons.'

Edward watched his baby daughter suckle at Elizabeth's breast. The fire was crackling, piled on with enough logs to make a man sweat in that Westminster room. The mastiff, Bede, lay stretched out on the tiles across the heat, so close that Edward had to prod him back with his foot before the old dog burned himself. Beyond the crackle of flames and the fussing of the child as it warbled and fastened on, there was no other sound, with even the personal servants dismissed.

Elizabeth felt her husband's gaze and smiled up at him, seeing his contentment.

'I didn't imagine this when I saw you first,' he said, 'all leaves and dust, scrambling down to save your dog from wolves.'

'And falling! Though I recall a great oaf of a man who did not catch me!'

He smiled at her. Over the years, the words had become a recitation between them, with no real sting. He enjoyed the closeness such things seemed to bring about, rattling through shared memories and seeing again that Elizabeth enjoyed his company.

'You know, I have seen too many men who have to demand respect from their wives.'

'That is not so very strange, husband, with Eve made to be Adam's helpmeet. That is the natural order of the world, as ewes follow the ram.'

'Yes, but . . .' Edward gripped a spot between his eyes, seeking the words. 'Men *need* to be adored, Elizabeth. Even the weak ones, the poltroons, the cowards and the fools.

Those are pitiful creatures, whose wives screech and rail at them. They are not masters of their homes.'

'Some women have not the first idea how to treat their men,' Elizabeth said, with a trace of self-satisfaction. 'All they cause with their complaining is resentment and their own misery. They are fools to themselves.'

'Not you, though.' Edward smiled. 'You treat me as if you have found a wonder of the world. I want to deserve it, do you see? I want to be called master in my home, but only because I damn well *am* one. Not because the laws of man or God would have me so, but because I am made to lead.'

'Made to be my king,' Elizabeth said, her voice soft. She raised her head to be kissed and he crossed the room in three strides, pressing his lips on hers. The baby girl began to fuss and snuffle, losing the nipple.

'I would like to call this one Cecily, to honour your mother,' Elizabeth said, responding to the joy she saw in him. 'If she lives, she will make you proud.'

'My mother will be pleased, though I confess I would have been happier with a son, Elizabeth.'

'You'll need daughters to adore you in your old age – and to marry away to keep the kingdom strong and bring you allies. You will not regret these darling little girls in the years to come, not a single one of them.'

'I know, I know. It's just, with a boy, I could show him how to fly a falcon against pigeons and rabbits, how to hunt boar with just dogs and a knife, how to build the strength to fight in armour.' He shrugged. 'I have . . . *been* a boy. I remember the years fondly. I would make him squire to a knight, perhaps one of your brothers, so that he learns how much work it takes to keep a man in royal service.'

'I would like that,' she said. 'And you will be a fine teacher to a son, Edward. The next one, I promise. I only hope your training will be enough protection, if your heirs are challenged by your brother's sons.'

Edward took a step away from her, hissing air.

'Again? I have not been rash, just as I said. I have given it time and months of patience, and still I cannot see the error in bringing all of Warwick's estates and wealth into my own family, under my own roof!'

'Edward, this is important. I wish it were not. If you allow George to marry this Isabel Neville, he will inherit *hundreds* of manors and estates, not dozens. Castles, villages, towns. Warwick and Salisbury are combined now – and that inheritance is the single greatest fortune in England.'

'Which I would give to my brother! He and Isabel are matched in age. They even love each other, so he says. Who am I to refuse a brother his love, when it will also bring him half of England as a dowry?'

Elizabeth pursed her lips, controlling her temper with difficulty. Tucking her breast away, she called for a servant and handed the child over even as the girl began to squall. A wet nurse would continue the feed in the kitchens.

When they were alone once more, Elizabeth leaned forward on her chair, clasping her hands on her lap.

'You know, my husband, I do adore you – and you are master in our house, or wherever we find ourselves. If you give me your final word on this, I will accept it, I swear to you I will. Think only this, though – yours is not the royal line.' She held up her hand as Edward rounded on her in growing anger. 'Please. Your great-grandfather was Edmund of York, the *fourth* son of a king. He was not in reach of the crown you wear now, but he had wealth. He married well and his son and grandson were both clever and strong. They built great estates and gathered titles by marriages and honours, until your father was strong enough to challenge for the throne.'

'I understand,' Edward said. From the set of his jaw, she suspected he did, but she chose to say the words even so, to be certain he heard.

'Your brother George of Clarence is your father's son as well, Edward. He has the same wit and strength. If you let him marry into Warwick's vast fortunes, he will live to challenge you – or his sons, or his grandsons. You will be storing up trouble for another day, or another war between cousins and brothers. Please. As much as it will hurt George, you must deny this suit for the sake of your own children.'

'That is not a reason I can give him,' Edward said. 'I can hardly say, "George, I do not want you and yours to *prosper*, in case your sons ever threaten mine." This is a coward's response, Elizabeth. You'd have me worry about my own brothers? About George and Richard? My mother Cecily did not raise weak men, but she did not raise turncoats either. I do not fear them – or their sons.'

'No, though you rose from a lesser line. You are a king now, Edward. You should look further, to a thousand years, beginning with the little girls I have fed on my lap. George of Clarence has been made a duke by your hand. Let him be content. I will find him another wife, and if he chooses later to take Isabel Neville as a mistress, that will be up to him, of course. These are decisions and choices a king must make, Edward. Your brother will understand that.'

'And when he asks my reason?' Edward said.

Elizabeth smiled at him.

'Tell him you do not trust the man who would be his father-in-law, if you must. Or that the Neville girl is barren, or that the moon was dark when you heard the news. It does not *matter*. He gave an oath on his immortal soul to obey you in all things. If he asks you, remind him of *that*.'

Warwick found himself panting, though he had walked only five or six miles in the cold. Middleham estate had been made quiet by the winter. Half the great house had been locked and barred away, with all windows sealed against bats and birds roosting. No doubt the odd owl or sparrow would find its way in. They always did, so that the first job of spring was to clear away the little corpses, always lighter than they looked.

'We could rest here for a moment,' he said. 'More for you, Isabel, than for me, obviously. I could walk all day.'

'I should hope you could, Father,' his daughter replied, utterly oblivious to the fact that her father was suffering a stitch and was weary. If he had told her, she would not have believed it of him, either way. He leaned on a wooden stile-post and looked over the hill of dark earth touched with the first frosts, stretching away across a valley. In that cold, half the birds had gone. For a time, the only sound in the entire world was his own breathing, surprisingly loud as soon as he noticed it.

His daughter was beautiful, Warwick was certain, long-necked and bright of cheek, with teeth white and even, sharpened on the apples she adored. She had grown up at Middleham, just as he had, though most of her year was in the company of his mother and her own, three

349

women fussing around the estate together and, to his everlasting gratitude, getting on well almost as sisters or friends. His brother John had made a comment about the three ages of women that he had come to regret, but Isabel was every inch the virgin, just as his wife Anne was the mother and his mother Alice had become a crone, withered by the death of his father, as if the old man had taken some vital part of her to his grave.

Whenever Isabel awoke each morning, she looked for some letter that might have arrived in the night. Each time it broke Warwick's heart anew to see her disappointment when there was none. It had been hard enough when he spent his days in London with the king. At least then his returns had been accompanied by news and odd sweets or gifts from the city.

He had not left Middleham for three months, not since the autumn. The late sun had given them so much fruit that drunken wasps plagued the house, wandering along the inside of every window for weeks. All that time, Warwick had stalked the estate grounds, losing himself on long walks and yet returning with an even deeper glower. Letters came for him from London, some with the Privy Seal of King Edward. Not one had contained the king's permission for Isabel to marry Clarence, or any mention of the subject at all.

Though Warwick did not know it, Isabel was watching him carefully, judging his mood and his unhappiness. She had heard him rage about his brother losing the Great Seal and, worse, her uncle John's title being taken from him. In private with his wife, Warwick gave vent to outrage and disappointment, unaware or uncaring that his daughters heard.

The sky was a sharp blue, with no sign of rain. The world was touched with frost and the coldness of the air made both father and daughter aware of their breaths, the winter cutting into them. Isabel chose her moment.

'Do you think the king will ever respond to his brother?' she said. 'George has not paid me a visit here since the harvest and his letters make no mention of the suit, as if there is no chance at all. It has been so very long now and I confess I lose hope.'

Her father looked down at her, seeing the quiver at her mouth where she struggled to hide just how much his answer meant. His fist gripped hard on the icy wood of the post, the knuckles showing.

'No, Isabel, I am sorry. I have waited for six months, longer. All my letters have gone without answer. I do not believe King Edward will grant his permission, not now.'

'But he has sent for you, has he not? The messenger I saw? Perhaps King Edward has agreed to the marriage and all it would take is for you to go to London.'

'Isabel, every time I enter his presence, he finds some new way to take something I prize. It is as if there is some spite in him against me. Undeserved by any measure, I swear it. I do not know whether that great clod of a man is jealous of me or afraid of me, or just the plaything of his wife, but these last few years have been a trial. It is . . . better for me to remain on my estates, to tend them and the people on them, away from the intrigues of the court.' He took a huge breath of air that scoured out his lungs. 'There! That is what I need, not whispers and lies.'

His face fell as he saw her grief and he stepped closer so that he could put his arms around her.

'I am sorry. I know this is harder on you than me. I have lost a king's trust, while you have lost your first suitor.'

'My first love,' she said, her voice muffled. 'There will not be another.'

'Oh, Isabel,' he said sadly into her hair.

'Will you ask again for me?' Isabel said. 'I know that George is meant to be the one to speak to the king, but I don't know if he has. If you ask, I will have an answer – though if it is no, I don't, I can't . . .' She sobbed, burying her head in her father's coat.

Warwick made his decision, long unable to resist her entreaties.

'I will ask, of course. I can be there and back in a week. As you say, it is better to know for certain.'

He stroked her hair as she leaned on him. Christmas was almost upon them and a trip to London would help make it a more festive occasion at Middleham, with market hams spiked with cloves, roast geese and roaring fires.

Warwick rode out to London with Richard of Gloucester riding alongside and Isabel's fears and hopes weighing him down. The young duke often accompanied him to the capital, more so perhaps as they both realized his time at Middleham was coming to an end. They wore leather coats over mail and thick hose, with swords on their hips and enough dust kicked up from the road to make it look as if they wore masks.

The first day south was spent in near silence, with Warwick settling into a grim anticipation of what he would find in London. He ate some poor stew in a roadside inn and muttered a goodnight to his ward as they found rooms. Both of them missed the light heart and chatter of Henry

Percy that had made conversations flow easily between them. Without Henry, both Warwick and Richard felt the silence was oppressive.

In the morning, Warwick woke with an aching head, though he had drunk only a cup of wine. He growled and grunted his way through a bowl of hot oats and honey, snapping at the inn servants and then growing angry at his own lack of control. He found that Richard had saddled his horse and brushed the animal down, so that it gleamed once more. Warwick stepped on to the mounting block and swung over his leg.

'Thank you, lad,' he said. 'I have a great deal on my mind today. I fear I am a poor companion.'

'I understand, sir. You fear my brother will refuse you.'

Warwick looked up, caught between surprise and worry.

'What do you know about it?'

Richard smiled weakly, sensing the anger in a man he wanted to impress.

'Isabel has talked of little else these past months. And George is my brother, sir. He writes to me.'

Warwick blinked, closing his mouth over the desire to ask for the young man's opinion. It would not do. Instead, he tugged the reins and turned his horse to face the gate of the inn yard, where the London road ran alongside, some thirty yards away.

'I hope the king grants the petition, sir. I would like to see Isabel made happy.'

'So would I,' Warwick muttered.

He cracked his neck back and forth and trotted out on to the road. Richard followed, wishing he could give something back to the man who had been so kind to him.

*

Warwick was granted an audience with the king without any delay. He rode from private lodgings to the Palace of Westminster along the river. Richard of Gloucester stayed with him as far as the doors to the king's own apartments. They stood side by side there, waiting to be admitted. Warwick took a moment to look the young man over and brush dust from his coat. The gesture made the king's brother smile as the doors swept open and they went in.

Warwick's expression tightened as he saw Edward and Elizabeth seated together, with their children around them. It was an intimate family scene and it somehow rang a false note. Warwick wanted Edward to consider his petition as a king, not as a husband and father. In that place, with a doting wife and gurgling little girls at his feet, he could not be both.

Warwick and Gloucester each went down on one knee before the royal family, rising as Edward stepped forward to greet them. He embraced his brother hard enough to make him gasp.

'You look strong!' Edward said, reaching out to squeeze his brother's right arm like a prize calf. 'I have you to thank for it,' Edward went on, nodding to Warwick.

Warwick shook his head, still tense.

'He has worked hard, Your Highness. Sword, lance and pollaxe, horsemanship, Latin, French . . .' He trailed away and Edward's brother broke in.

'Law and tactics, too Edward. It is my desire to be useful to you.'

'You will be, I do not doubt it,' Edward replied. 'My mother asks after my brother, Warwick. Will you release him to me now, as your ward?'

Warwick blinked and cleared his throat, buying time.

'Your Highness, I had not thought . . . I did not plan to excuse him from his duties today.'

'Still, I am pleased at what I see in him. You have my thanks. Wardships come to an end, Warwick, and you have done well.'

Embarrassed under the stares of the king and queen, Warwick and Gloucester shook hands and embraced awkwardly and briefly. Warwick opened his mouth to say something to mark the years, but the young man bowed stiffly to the king, turned on his heel and left the room.

Warwick turned back to feel their eyes still on him. Only the young children were oblivious, gathered up by a nursemaid when they wandered too far. His breath shuddered in his chest as he realized the moment was upon him and would no longer be denied.

'Your Highness, it has been many months since I petitioned for my daughter to marry your brother, George of Clarence. As we are friends, may I have an answer?'

'I have given it much thought, Richard,' Edward said. 'My brother George is just nineteen. I do not doubt he believes he is in love, but I will choose a wife for him in a few years. My answer is no, to your petition.'

Warwick stood still. Though the arrangement of his expression changed hardly at all, his anger was written as clearly as his control. Behind Edward, Elizabeth sat forward a fraction, fascinated. Her mouth was slightly open, the edges rising as if she drank in his discomfort.

'Thank you, Edward. Your Highness,' Warwick said with perfect courtesy. 'I would rather know, and be disappointed, than not know. Now, if I could be dismissed, I would like to visit the London fairs and purchase geese for Christmas at Middleham.'

'Of course. I *am* sorry, Richard,' Edward said.

In response, Warwick inclined his head, his eyes tight with pain.

Isabel waited for Warwick on the road, taking up a spot each morning and evening and standing there for hours, desperate for news. When she saw him, she knew from his face, before her father could say a single word. She retired to her room for three days then, weeping for the young man she loved and could never have.

Warwick spent that time in private discussion with a stream of visitors, all riding to Middleham to pay their respects to the head of the Neville clan. For an age, the Nevilles had suffered reverse upon reverse. They had lost land, fortunes, titles and vital influence. For all that time, Warwick had insisted they endure and stay silent, without one cry or murmur against the king. He had changed his mind. As January was born in darkness and cold, he decided to let them rise.

28

Winter was a time of darkness and of death. In any house, a fine, frosty morning could reveal the stiff body of an old man, or a child too young to survive a fever. The bitter season meant stews of blood in oats and the earthy taste of old vegetables, months or years after they had been picked. Carrots and onions and turnips all went into broths with hard blue cheese or curds of lard to help keep out the cold. With bread and eggs and ale, the king's subjects endured, waking halfway through the night to talk or mend, then sleeping again until the sun brought the return of the day.

Spring meant far more than green shoots and snowdrops in the hedgerows. The rebirth showed in a sense of purpose, in the waking from slumber with new life in the veins. There was laughter to be heard, and the last of the preserved food could be devoured now that they had reached the end of another winter. Fresh meat and greens appeared again in the town markets. Graves were dug in softening ground, small or long, with bodies carried out from where they had lain in barns and cool cellars. Men and women who might want to find a husband or bride greeted the season with clean clothes and a bath. They broke their first sweat with a day's labour, making things to sell or preparing the ground for the first planting.

Edward Plantagenet could feel the sap rising with the dawn light. Spring meant the first hunt since riding out at New Year, with hot blood and breathless speed and drunken revelry far from towns and villages. The hunt brought anger and fear to the surface, revealing the man. Edward smiled to himself as he watched his horse being saddled in the royal stables at Windsor. The hunter's coat had been brushed, but it was still shaggy with winter growth. He patted a flank and grinned at the cloud of hair and dust that lifted into the air.

Around him, the stables were busy and loud with squires rushing to prepare their masters for the royal hunt. Thirty knights and the same number of servants would ride out to beat game for the dogs and birds. Edward smiled at the energy of it, scratching his horse's neck and making the big stallion snort and flick its tail at him.

Over the years of his reign, he had assembled a group of stalwarts to accompany him on such days when the sun held a little warmth and the sky was clear. Men like Anthony and John Woodville, who could match him for reckless-ness, if not the king's skill with his falcon.

Edward's great bird sat hooded on an ornate stand, turning its head to every sound. He heard it make a chir-rup and reached out to stroke the dark wings, more for his own pleasure than any sense that the bird enjoyed his touch. Gyrfalcons were savage killers, taking what looked very much like delight in their ability to dominate and ter-rify ducks, grouse or hares, stooping from a thousand feet up, smashing into running prey at incredible speed, then ripping through flesh with a razor beak. Edward mur-mured a greeting to the bird. She had hunted with him for six years and turned to his voice instantly, recognizing it. It amused him that she could turn to face him wherever he was, even in the hood. As he watched, the bird clacked her beak and made a questioning sound. The falcon was hungry and Edward felt his heart beat faster at the thought of sending her into the air.

He looked up at a clatter of hooves as a horse came crabbing down the length of the stables, held on a tight rein but still trotting almost sideways with rolling eyes. The animal had been startled by something and it made the others whinny and stamp, reminding them of predators attacking the herd.

Edward stared in irritation at the wiry fellow who had brought the gelding in to unsettle the rest. He did not know him, though it was not possible for a stranger to reach the stables and the person of the king without having been challenged. Edward liked to pretend he had no interest in the care his guards took, but as he eyed him, he was still pleased to know the man had been searched. Edward watched, frowning, as the stranger dismounted and went down on to one knee. He wore mail and a tabard over leather and wool, all well worn and about as dusty as the horses. Edward guessed he had come a long way and was not surprised when the man spoke with a rolling accent of the north.

'Your Royal Highness, my master Sir James Strangeways, sheriff of York, has sent me to you. I am to report an uprising among the weavers in villages around the city, with riots and alarums, my lord, too great in number for the sheriff's men there to put down. Sir James asks for a few dozen men, sixty or eighty, no more, to ride north. In the king's name, he would remind the weavers that they do not decide what taxes they will pay and what laws they will obey.'

Edward raised his eyebrows and rubbed the bristles on

his jaw. He no longer wore a beard, having shaved for spring. He had been cooped up in Windsor and Westminster for months of cold and darkness, eating and drinking too much, so that he had put on fat like a dormouse. He patted his stomach as he thought, while the messenger waited.

'Go to the kitchens and tell them I said to feed you well,' Edward said to the man.

As he bowed and hurried off, Edward stared out to the sunlight, past the horses and men and noise. He made his decision, chuckling to himself. The country was at peace. The winter had given way to spring, with all the promise it brought.

'I believe I will go to York,' Edward muttered to himself with a grin. He imagined the faces of the rebellious weavers when they saw no less a man than the king of England riding up with his men. He might have to hang the leaders or flog a few of them; that was often the case. He would match his falcon against the new goshawk the Woodville brothers had raised from a chick. Edward knew he would enjoy showing his wife's brothers how fast a royal falcon could fly, once the weavers had slunk back to their homes.

'Anthony!' he called.

The knight looked up from where he was standing nearby, having watched the messenger enter and leave. The Woodville men were always quick to respond when Edward called.

'Yes, Your Highness,' Anthony Woodville said, as he halted and bowed. His right wrist and forearm was splinted and wrapped so tight the fingers were fat and red.

'How is your hand?' Edward asked.

'Still broken, Your Highness. I believe it will mend well enough. Perhaps I will then be granted a chance to redeem my honour.'

'If you wish,' Edward said with a smile. As he was the one who had broken the man's wrist in tourney practice, it was only fair to agree. 'Though I am sorry you cannot accompany us today. Your brother can fly your hawk; it will make no difference in the end.' He grinned as the other man raised his eyes in mock frustration. 'I believe I will take the hunt out a little further than I had planned.' Edward looked around him, counting under his breath. 'Now, I will certainly need these fine fellows here, but then another forty knights ahorse . . . and a hundred or so of the best archers as well.'

'There are only a few master bowmen in the barracks here, my lord,' Sir Anthony replied. 'I can find another dozen at Baynard's, more from the archery school . . .' He broke off at Edward's impatient gesture. 'Yes, Your Highness, I will have them assembled immediately.'

He clattered away, leaving Edward to tempt the gyrfalcon from the perch to his forearm. He could feel the bird's claws flexing, even through thick layers of leather.

It was a pleasure to sense the growth and green all around him. Edward would leave Windsor and all the damp and chills of winter behind, to hunt, to seek, to punish, as he saw fit. It was a heady feeling and the falcon sensed it in him, flaring its wings and screeching out a call to hunt.

By noon, the whole town of Windsor knew the king was riding out. Anthony Woodville had run the king's stewards ragged, seeking out archers from villages all around

Windsor and London. They had ridden as far as they dared and the results came in by threes and fours, adding to the number of bowmen with the king until there were two hundred of them with bows and quivers ready, bright-faced and beaming with the sense of adventure. It was an honour to accompany the king, and Edward could be seen at the stable yard, cheerfully bantering with his knights and squires. He would hunt as a king of England, with his falcon on his arm. At the last minute, he had decided to wear heavier plate and changed horses for his great destrier, now sixteen years old and in its prime.

In the same way that the number of archers had doubled, his hunting party had attracted any man who thought he might find advancement under the king's sight. At least a hundred milled and curbed their mounts, while about as many dogs chased and barked. It was all clatter and shouting and laughter, and Edward was at the heart of it, content to shrug off the cobwebs.

'Hold fast!' Edward heard called. He turned his horse on the spot to witness his wife's father come trotting out on a fine mare, wrapped in coats and cloaks, with a boar spear held high. Edward chuckled in amusement at Earl Rivers. He had grown to like the old fellow well enough, though he greeted him with a warning shake of his head.

'These fine lads won't hold back for age, my lord Rivers. Youth will prevail, once the horns are blown.'

'Your Highness, I am content just to ride out once more. After such a winter, it is good to feel the sun on my face once again. If I cannot stay with the main group, I will drift back and be tended by my servants. Have no fears for me, lad.'

Edward chuckled at being called 'lad' by his wife's father,

though the man was sixty-four years old and a life of punishing the wine and ale had left him red-faced and bleary-eyed. Still, he was good company when the drink and wild tales began to flow.

The earl's mention of servants had Edward frowning and looking over the assembly as it swirled around him. His original plan to bolster his hunting party had grown unrecognizably. With servants and knights and archers, he was looking at around four hundred men. He saw Anthony Woodville utterly forlorn at what he would miss. It was noisy, joyous chaos and Edward realized the numbers would only grow if he remained where he was. It was the power of a king once again – men wanted to follow him.

Edward raised his hunting horn from its cord around his neck and blew a long note. By the time he stopped, the men had fallen silent, though the dogs still yelped and snapped in excitement.

'I am informed of unrest around the city of York,' he called to them. 'The weavers, gentlemen! They have forgotten they owe their livings to me. We will remind them of their duty. Away now! North and the hunt!'

The baying of the hounds rose in intensity, becoming an almost constant wail. Horns blew and hundreds moved off, trotting and laughing, waving to loved ones and those left behind. Spring had come.

Warwick strode through the great hall of Baynard's Castle on the bank of the Thames in London. The last time he had passed that fireplace had been on the night Edward had declared himself king in Westminster Hall. Warwick shook his head at the memories, feeling no regret. It had been the right thing to do then, without a doubt. Edward could never have triumphed at Towton without the peculiar aura of royalty. For all the young man's talent, Edward could not have brought in enough men without the crown, not in the time they'd had. That had been Warwick's great contribution.

His reward had been a series of assaults on his family's holdings – and on its honour. It seemed Edward was willing to use the crown to act beyond the law, without thought to consequence. Warwick set his jaw as he walked. So be it. He might have endured all the disappointments if they had come from Edward himself, yet it was clear to Warwick that for the second time in his life, a queen's spite was behind the reverse in his fortunes. Margaret of Anjou had been bad enough. It was too much to expect him to suffer it again!

George, Duke of Clarence, came into the hall, wiping his face with a steaming cloth as he had been called and interrupted while about to be shaved. He looked in astonishment at Richard Neville approaching.

'My lord Warwick? What's afoot, for you to seek me here?' The young man suddenly grew pale. 'Is it Isabel? My lord, is she unwell?'

Warwick halted, bowing to the man's more senior rank.

'Isabel is with me, George. Outside and full of life.'

'I don't understand,' Clarence said, wiping his neck and tossing the cloth to a steward to snatch out of the air. 'Shall I come with you, to see her? Sir, you have me at a loss.'

Warwick glanced at the servant, reminded that they were not alone. He gestured to a door he knew led to stairs up to the iron roof of the castle, where an observatory had been built. It would be quiet and protected from the ears of those who would report his words to the king.

'What I have to say is for you alone, my lord Clarence. Come with me, if you please. I will make it clear.'

The young duke followed immediately, his face without a trace of suspicion as they ascended flights of iron stairs and shoved open the hatch to the open air. Anyone climbing to listen behind them would be heard and Warwick breathed more easily than he had in days, smelling the river and the city as gulls swooped and shrieked overhead.

'Do you put your trust in me, George?' Warwick said as the younger man came to stand by him.

'Of course, sir. I know you supported my suit to the king. I know you argued for me and I am grateful, more than you know. I am only sorry it came to nothing in the end. Is Isabel well, sir? I have not dared to write to her these last months. May I see her at the carriage when you leave?'

'That will be your choice, George,' Warwick said, with an odd smile playing across his mouth. 'I have come to take you to the coast, if you wish to come. I have a ship waiting there, a fine little cog to carry us to the fortress of Calais. From there, I have papers to go through the gates and into France.'

Clarence shook his head. 'With Isabel, sir? I don't understand your meaning.'

Warwick took a deep breath. This was the heart of it and part of what he had planned over the winter months.

'Your brother cannot *unmarry* you, if you are bound, George. If you marry my daughter, there is nothing Edward can do to prevent it, not then. You are his own brother and it is my feeling that he will see it is the best thing for you.'

George of Clarence stared, the wind at that height flicking his hair across his forehead and wide eyes.

'You would allow me to marry Isabel? In France?'

'My lord Clarence, it will be done before sunset today if you gather your wits in time! I have made it all ready for you. The question is only whether you want the marriage and are willing to risk your brother's wrath.'

'To marry Isabel? A thousand times over!' the young man replied, gripping his future father-in-law by the arm, hard enough to make Warwick wince. '*Yes*, my lord. I thank you. Thank you! Yes, I will come to France and, yes, I will marry your daughter and protect her and give her my honour as her shield.'

The young man stared out across the boats on the Thames in a sort of dazed wonder. His eyes darkened suddenly and he looked back.

'What of you, though, sir? My brother will forgive me, of a certainty. He will, of course, forgive my wife. Did he not marry for love himself? Edward will rage and break pots, but he will not hold me to account, I think. For you, though, his anger will be . . .' He trailed away, aware that he did not want to dissuade Warwick from going ahead.

'I am his foremost earl and a member of his council,' Warwick said gently. 'He named me companion after Towton and my family has supported both Edward *and* your father from the very beginning. He may rage, George – yes, I am sure he will – but he and I are friends and the storms will blow out.'

Warwick spoke easily, though he no longer believed any of it. Whether by the poison Elizabeth Woodville dripped into Edward's ear or the king's own sense of betrayal and childish temper, Warwick had a very clear sense of the breach that would follow. He had spent a number of dark nights planning for it.

George of Clarence heard what he wanted to hear, that the wedding could go ahead and it would all be to the good with the passage of time. He embraced Warwick, surprising the earl, before making his way down the steps at such a speed Warwick thought he would surely fall and break his neck.

Warwick could not keep up with the duke as he galloped through the halls. The older man reached the outer doors of Baynard's Castle just in time to see George of Clarence leap up on to the side of the open carriage. The duke gathered a weeping Isabel Neville into his arms, scandalizing the coachmen, two guards and a gaggle of passers-by. Warwick found himself flushing in embarrassment and he cleared his throat noisily as he drew close, sending the pair springing apart with matching expressions of guilty passion.

Richard, Earl Warwick, climbed up and sat deliberately between the two of them, staring woodenly ahead as the duke and his daughter tried to look round him.

'Away, coachman!' Warwick called, pulling up furs over their knees.

The man snapped a whip across the pair of black horses and they broke into a trot through the muddy streets. Warwick could see people stopping to point at the strange sight, but the news could not travel as fast as they could. By the time anyone understood what they were about, the marriage would have been made and he would have the king's brother for his son-in-law.

They passed rapidly across London Bridge, where the head of Jack Cade had been taken down years before. Warwick shuddered at the row of iron spikes there, remembering darker days and the fate of his own father. It was possible for a man to reach too far. God knew, it was hard to dispute that. Warwick clenched his fist unseen on his lap. He had suffered enough without response. Saints would not have had the patience he had shown, but that had come to an end. The die was cast, the plan begun. Neither King Edward nor Elizabeth Woodville would stop him, not then. He reached out and touched the wooden side of the carriage for luck as they turned on to the ancient road to the south coast, some sixty miles away. As they travelled on, the sun was still rising over the capital.

29

The weather had held, with no rain and a mild sun, so that it had given the royal party almost perfect hunting skies. As importantly, King Edward's falcon had made the Woodville goshawk look slow. Sir John Woodville flew his brother's bird well enough, but the fault was in nature not his skill. The goshawk screeched in rage when it could not pursue, an emotion as clear as any the men felt themselves. In turn, the king's falcon appeared to take pleasure in showing its mastery, pulling tight turns and dives right across the face of the Woodville knight, so that the hawk went stumbling in the disturbed air of its wake.

There was prey for them both, flushed by the dogs from cover, so that hares went racing or grouse flapped madly into the air, with squires yelling and pointing out their course. The archers competed among themselves to take birds on the wing or, at one point, even trout from a river, with silver wagered by those who said it could not be done. Between them, the entire group took enough to feed themselves each night, with servants building spits and firepits. Those who missed their shots went hungry for days at a time, until their friends took pity on them. It helped that they had brought horses laden only with flasks and amphorae of wine. In the evenings, the drink flowed and the men jostled and competed to amuse the young king.

Edward was content. He would have preferred more

challenging prey, but there would be no sign of wolves or deer so near to the road. The animals were too used to the sounds of men and knew when to run and keep running. With great fondness, he recalled his hunts in the deep woods or the wilds of Wales, where the animals were not so used to the scent of man.

It had not been a rush north, to bring king's justice on rioting weavers. Edward and his knights had enjoyed the hospitality and feasts arranged for them in too many manor houses and market towns. There had been days when they'd been so taken by groaning, drunken illness that they had barely made five miles. Earl Rivers had suffered a terrible bout of loose bowels for two entire days, until Edward thought they would have to leave him behind, or perhaps get him a new horse.

The young king laughed at the memory of the old man's mortified expressions. His father-in-law was riding a little way over and looked up in suspicion, not quite seeing the humour that had reduced some of the knights to tears.

Ahead lay the city of York and, at the sight of those walls and the thread of the River Ouse, Edward lost his desire to smile. There were too many savage memories bound up in the stones of that place ever to call it home. The worst of it was the damned Micklegate Bar, open to the south. He thought he might have those towers and walls there taken down, or rebuilt so as not to overwhelm him every time he saw them.

Edward was staring ahead when he saw a darkening line appear on the horizon around the city. He squinted and leaned forward, shading his eyes. He had no scouts out and, for an instant, he felt his stomach clench, before his natural belligerence reasserted itself. He would not fear rioters.

'Sir John!' he called back. 'Ride ahead and scout for me. Who are those men there?'

His wife's young brother dug in spurs and his horse bunched and lunged into a gallop, a fine display from a man whose hawk was too slow. Edward watched him go and, for the first time, cast an eye over his men as an armed force rather than a huge hunting party. What he saw did not please him, as one who had known the disciplined ranks of Towton. The knights and men-at-arms who had accompanied the king into the north were a little ragged for the experience. His archers still looked keen though.

'Thank God for that,' he murmured. With a whistle, he summoned a captain to his side and gave a string of orders, bringing something resembling structure to the disparate group.

Sir John Woodville rode back some time later and looked with interest over the steady ranks of knights and wings of archers that had formed around the king at the centre. For all his faults, Edward Plantagenet would have made a fine captain; there had never been any doubt about that.

Sir John began to dismount and Edward held up his hand, irritation showing.

'Stay in the saddle, lad. What could you see?'

The dark line around the city was clearly made of distant figures by then. They did not look like any rioters Edward had seen before, nor labourers, weavers or not.

'Two thousand, maybe three, Your Highness. I saw perhaps a hundred ahorse, eight hundred archers. The rest are marching here, now that they have seen us.'

'Banners? Who commands them?'

'I saw none, though they formed like soldiers. It could be Lancaster rebels.'

'Which? There are none left.' Edward had a terrible thought then, that the Percy earl he had restored might have turned against him. The thought sickened him, not least because of how Warwick would look when he heard.

'Whoever leads them, we are sorely outmatched, my lord,' Earl Rivers said, riding up to Edward's side.

The Woodville father exchanged a worried glance with his youngest son, seeing the tension in him. They could both see the young giant tapping the hilt of his sword as he stared away to the horizon. If any man in England could turn the trap into a victory it was Edward, but Earl Rivers knew their lives – his son's life – hung in that decision.

'I believe your father sallied out against Lancaster forces, Your Highness,' Earl Rivers murmured. 'You have armies who would fight for you.'

'I have two *hundred* archers here, now,' Edward replied. 'I have seen what they can do. For all we know, these others are false bowmen meant to make us run. Men with axe-handles and twine, my lord. My two hundred could tear them apart for their insolence and trickery.'

'Yes, Your Highness. Or this is a plot to kill you and put Lancaster back on the throne of England. You won at Towton, my lord, but you had your army with you. *Please.*'

Edward looked askance at his wife's father, then back to those he had brought into the north. They were as fine a hunting party as he had ever known, but no kind of army. They looked afraid as the lines widened ahead of them.

'Very well, Rivers. Though it breaks my heart, I will choose good sense and caution over rash action and giving the bastards blow for blow. Away south, gentlemen! With me, at your best pace now.'

It did not escape Edward that they were a long, long way from the forces he needed to answer the threat, or that the hunters had become the hunted. He heard horns sound behind him and the king shivered, feeling the cold.

Spring had come to France, with the fields a deep, vivid green as far as the eye could see. Warwick's papers had been old permissions to land, with the dates sanded away and new ones inked. The harbourmaster who had been rowed out to them and then the captain of the fortress had barely glanced at the vellum and the seals. Both men remembered Warwick and Clarence from their previous visit and were visibly embarrassed in the presence of a beautiful young woman, radiant with happiness.

Warwick had brought only his coachman and two guards with him, preferring speed to a real display of force. The small group had borrowed horses from a mystified king's captain, promising to return them the following morning. The English officers all suspected some romantic scene was being played out before them, but they kept their questions to themselves.

The small group had not ridden far from Calais, just a few miles down the road to the village of Ardres. There, Warwick greeted a white-haired country priest and explained what he required in fluent French. The priest beamed at them all, seemingly delighted at their mere presence in his humble church, though Warwick also passed over a pouch of silver coins.

For his part, George of Clarence could only stand in wide-eyed joy and clasp Isabel's hand, hardly believing that what they had desired for so long was happening right then and there. Warwick's men had smoothed their hair down and brushed their jackets with water from the well. They would be the witnesses and they bristled with pride.

Warwick held up his hand when he heard the approach of horses outside. His daughter looked at him in alarm, but he winked at her. No one had followed them from the coast, he was certain. There was only one other who might have come at his private request.

'Isabel, George. If you would wait for just a little time . . .' he said over his shoulder to them, walking along the nave to the wooden doors.

They opened before he reached them and two guards in armour entered, with swords held ready. Behind them came King Louis of France, bare-headed and in simpler clothes than Warwick had ever seen him wear.

'Your Majesty, you do me a great honour,' Warwick said.

Louis smiled, looking around him at the stupefied priest and the young lovers waiting to be joined in marriage.

'Ah! I am not too late, it seems. Such a place to find, this little Ardres. Carry on, carry on. I told milord Warwick I would attend if I could. Why not? A marriage in France is perhaps the best of all, no?'

The king accepted the bow of Warwick's men and the priest himself, who wiped his forehead and seemed to have forgotten the service he had planned.

As the sun set outside, the priest rolled through the Latin vows, with Warwick repeating them in both English and French for Isabel and George of Clarence to say to one another. The little church was silent and dusty, but the day had been warm and spring was a time for love and new lives. There was a sense of happiness in that place, felt even by King Louis and his personal guards, so that they beamed and twinkled at the bride and groom as they turned with their hands clasped tightly together. Warwick led the cheers and they echoed well enough in that empty church as the small group clustered in to congratulate and kiss cheeks.

'Milord Clarence, I have a wedding gift for you,' King Louis announced, his chest swelling. 'The armour I promised, from Master Auguste of Paris. He said he has never made a finer set and it is measured to you with room to grow across the shoulder and chest, so you will never need another.'

George of Clarence was overwhelmed, by Isabel, the ceremony, the presence of the French king in that strange setting. He laughed as the priest handed him a square of rough cloth to wipe the perspiration from his brow, then followed them out.

Warwick fell in beside King Louis a few paces behind the married couple, exchanging the smiles of more worldly men.

'Your daughter is exquisite,' King Louis said. 'I assume her mother is an extraordinary creature.'

Warwick smiled.

'There is no other explanation, Your Majesty. Thank you for coming to this. It is such a small thing to witness, but they will remember you were here for the rest of their lives.'

'We are friends, are we not?' King Louis said. 'You and I understand, I think. Peace does not matter – man will always fight and shed blood. My lords rebel and chafe under my laws. Even honour comes to an end. But love? Ah, Richard. Without love, what is the point of anything?'

'I could not have put it better, Your Majesty,' Warwick

replied, bowing. 'You have given me great honour here today. I will not forget.'

'I should think not, milord!' Louis said with a smile. He swept forward, ducking under the low lintel.

Outside, Isabel was standing in blushing embarrassment, glowing. George of Clarence was exclaiming at the sword he had drawn, a blade marked with finely carved figures. The rest of King Louis's gift lay in saddlebags on two mules.

'It is almost dark now. Will you race back to your fortress of Calais, milord?' King Louis said. 'Scurry scurry, like little mice?'

The French king's eyes had crinkled in joy at the sight of Isabel once again, her long dark hair bound in a silver clasp and falling to her waist.

Warwick glanced at the king, wondering, not for the first time, how much the man truly understood. It was not something he would say aloud, but it was important that the young couple consummate their marriage. He would spend a night in a tavern near the Calais fortress, giving them a room to themselves. After that, no man or indeed king could annul the union.

'It is just a few miles, Your Majesty, though it has been a long, *long* day. Perhaps we will spend the night in comfort. To think, this morning I was in London! The speed of the world is extraordinary.'

'Then I will bid you adieu, milord – and good luck. We will meet again as friends, I do not doubt.'

King Louis waited courteously for the little group to mount and arrange themselves, remaining in the churchyard until they had vanished into the night, safe back on the road. He did not know yet whether they would prosper or fail, but he had laid down good, solid stones, unseen but present nonetheless. The king sighed to himself. She had been very beautiful, so much in love that she only had eyes for the young duke at her side.

'Oh, to be young!' he said to himself. 'When life was so *simple*.'

'Your Majesty?' one of his men said cautiously, well used to the king's murmurings.

'It is nothing, Alain. Lead me to shelter. Lead me to warmth and good red wine.'

Edward pushed on, though the moon was a slender reed and the stones of the road were hard to see. He could hear the army coming behind him, closer with every mile and every jingling step. There was still no sign of banners, even if there had been enough light to make them out. Edward grimaced, preferring to remain silent rather than speculate. It did not matter who they were, only that they had dared to attack his royal party and that they were so many he was in real danger of being taken. His knights simply could not ride a hundred miles without stopping. It was impossible, for both the men and the horses. They had already ridden a full day by the time they'd first caught sight of the city of York, and Edward had intended to rest within its walls. Instead, he had been forced to turn and ride away, the horses already blowing, the men weary. Behind them came fresh ranks, marching and riding, pressing as fast as they could go to close the gap, stretching a mile across the road in greater numbers than he could believe. No weavers these! This was an armed insurrection against royal authority, his enemies in the field.

As the stars turned overhead, Edward's men urged him

to ride on alone. If his horse had been fresh, he might have done, but the animal's head was drooping. His hopes soured into vinegar. The army behind was not content to herd him south. They were pressing on at their best speed, coming closer and closer. Edward and his men could see the dark, trudging lines blotting out the natural lie of the land behind them. There were thousands in his wake.

The London road swung south-west for a time, taking Edward and his men past the rolling valleys where he had fought the battle of Towton. Those who remembered crossed themselves and said a prayer for the dead. No one ever rested a night there, not with so many ghosts and so much blood soaked into the clay.

The image of being captured in such a place spurred Edward on. He called to his men to take heart and wait for dawn, all the while thinking furiously of where he might bolt and who he could reach in time to aid him.

By the time the sun showed first light, Edward was grimly accepting. He had not a quarter of the men stalking him – and his men and the horses were spent, their stamina gone. The archers were pale and stumbling in the dawn light, halting the moment they saw Edward rein in.

He turned his warhorse back to face those coming down the road. With sharp commands, his knights sent the archers out in a wide line in case fighting began. Two hundred of them could do terrible damage, though those on horseback would never survive an exchange of shafts.

The light was too dim at first to see more than the rows of archers spreading out on the other side in answer to his own. Edward shook his head irritably. He was the king of England, and beyond the inner fury that lay banked, his main emotion was curiosity. There were not many enemies who would have had the nerve to trap him in such a way. He felt a touch of fear as well, causing him to recall his father's fate. He pressed that away with an effort, determined to show only contempt.

A small group of armoured men rode closer, with a herald out in front to call for peace. Edward turned to his men, patting the air with a mailed glove.

'Keep your swords down,' he told them. 'You cannot defend against so many and I would not have you throw your lives away.'

There was a palpable sense of relief on his side of the battle lines. His four hundred faced many more and they knew they were yawning and weak with hunger. It would not have gone well for them if the young king had ordered them to fight to the last man.

'Surrender to my custody, Edward. You will be fairly treated, on my honour.'

The voice came from the centre of the armoured men, making Edward peer. His eyes widened a fraction in the dim light as they made out the features of George Neville, Archbishop of York. In armour rather than robes, the man was as burly as any warrior.

'Treason, then?' Edward asked, still trying to understand what was happening. Alongside the archbishop, he saw John Neville, or Marquess Montagu as he had made him. Edward's confusion faded and he nodded to himself.

Seeing the king resigned to his fate, the archbishop chuckled and brought his horse up close. To Edward's astonishment, the man levelled a sword at him, the point unwavering.

'Now, surrender, Your Highness. Say the word or I will

give you to my brother and he will take your head. As you took his title.'

Edward stared back for an age, his expression reptilian.

'So the Nevilles have turned against me,' Edward muttered.

Despite the archbishop's breadth of shoulder, the man was no true warrior. Edward wanted to smack the sword aside and lay about him in fury. He knew if he did they would kill him. He clenched his fist and then unstrapped his sword, handing it over and watching as it was taken out of his reach. He felt weaker without the weapon, reduced.

'Warwick, too?' Edward asked suddenly. 'Ah. His daughter's marriage?'

'You *have* given us cause, Your Highness,' the archbishop replied. 'I will ask you for the last time now.'

'Yes, very well. I surrender,' Edward snapped. He saw the tension leave some of the men facing him and he sneered at them.

'What a mark of courage to hide your banners! Or is it that you know of all men I do not forgive my enemies? I understand your fear, lads. Were I in your position, I would feel it myself, most cruelly.'

He watched in scorn as archers fanned out around him, arrows nocked on the cords to draw and shoot at the slightest provocation.

'Your Highness,' the archbishop said. 'I must bind your hands. I do not want you tempted into running. I would not see you hurt.'

Edward breathed harder as a strange knight approached to wind twine around and around his wrists, taking some small satisfaction from the way the man flinched as their eyes met. There was a promise of retribution in Edward's gaze that was unpleasant to look upon.

'There, Your Highness. You have a long ride ahead of you to the place we have prepared. You need not fret about your men. They are no longer your concern and my brother John will sift them well.'

Edward's gaze met that of his father-in-law. The older man shrugged at him, an admission that there was nothing to be done. Edward clenched his jaw and allowed his horse's reins to be taken. The road led south and some sixty horsemen rode out with him. He could see his men had been almost swallowed up, encircled. He forced himself to turn away and consider his own fate.

'Does your brother Warwick know of this? Is he part of this conspiracy of treason?' Edward asked again.

'He is the head of the family, Your Highness. If you cut one of us, you cut him. Perhaps he'll come to see you at Warwick Castle. Is it not strange to think my brother has *two* kings of England in his custody: Henry in the Tower and now you?' The archbishop tutted to himself in awe at the very idea.

Edward shook his head.

'You are a fool to say such a thing to me. I will not forget it, nor anything else. And there is only one king.'

Warwick smiled, breathing the soft air of morning. On the Dover quays, the first catch of the day was already laid out to be bought by merchants willing to seek higher prices inland. The earl had always loved ships and the sea, taking more pleasure in the lash of spray and white-crested waves than a perfect spring morning. Yet his carriage and driver were trundling along the wooden quays towards him, and his daughter and her husband were arm in arm, walking and murmuring to each other as they went. Warwick had to whistle to catch their attention and bring them back to his side as he clambered in. With a moment's thought, he took a seat at the far end, so that the newly married couple could sit together.

His daughter Isabel was blushing, always finding some way to have a hand or a knee touching George of Clarence. She looked up at him adoringly and Warwick considered that the young man had obviously been kind to her the night before.

As the open carriage trundled away with a snap of the whip over the horses, Warwick saw that his son-in-law was looking pensive.

'Are you well, George?' Warwick said.

'Never better, sir, though I confess I cannot keep from considering my brother's reaction to the news. I only want him to accept what he must accept and for us to speak of it no more. It is as you said, sir. Isabel and I are married now. That cannot be changed. Do you think Edward will accept it?'

Warwick turned, looking out to the road stretching dustily away.

'I'm sure he will,' he replied. 'We must all accept what we cannot change. I am not worried, George. Not worried at all.'

30

'Go home now,' John Neville said. 'My men shall witness justice here.' He glared at the bedraggled remnants of the royal hunting party, just daring them to refuse. Once King Edward had been taken away, Neville men-at-arms had gone amongst the group, using axe-handles to enforce their masters' will. Bows, swords and any valuable piece of metal had all been removed. More than a few fine purses and baubles had been taken as well, the action enforced by sudden blows. There was no question of resisting, once they were surrounded. The king's knights endured the rough treatment with stoic indifference for the most part. The archers had little of value on them beyond their bows, so they made a show of tossing the weapons on to a pile as if they meant nothing. It was a fine gesture, betrayed by the way their eyes followed the bows as they were unstrung and wrapped.

The bravest of the king's party shouted in protest when the Woodvilles were singled out. Earl Rivers and his son were forced to dismount and had their hands bound, taken away from the rest of Edward's knights and companions. As those men continued to shout and complain, John Neville's temper frayed. With a sharp gesture, he sent his men in with cudgels to quiet them. The beating was brief, but it left two dead and four witless and bloody.

The remainder of the hunters were shoved and kicked

on to the road, dragging their dead and wounded between them. John Neville watched them go with murder in his eyes and few of them dared to look back.

When the last of the hunting party had vanished into the trees and fields, John Neville called for a camp to be set up, not far from the road. He sent some of the remaining horsemen into the nearby town to enquire about the use of their courtroom and their gallows.

'You have no authority,' Earl Rivers called. The white-haired old man was deadly serious by then, fully aware he had fallen amongst enemies. 'We have surrendered, sir, in expectation of good treatment. Let there be no more lives lost. Ask what ransom you will, in time-honoured fashion. Speak not of courts and gallows to threaten me. You are a man of honour, are you not?'

'I am many things, my lord,' John Neville replied with a twisted smile. 'And I have been more than I am today. They called me Edward's dog, when I was a-killing lords for him. Somerset was one of mine, a duke I stretched on a stump and whose head I took.' He nodded in satisfaction, sucking at a broken tooth as Earl Rivers paled. 'And I was Earl Northumberland for a time as well. Your daughter didn't like that, though, did she? She asked her husband to take my land and my home away from me.'

'And in return, you have broken your oath of fealty. A treason that will see you burn in eternal flames.'

John Neville laughed at the threat, a dark clatter that was almost like sobbing.

'You ought to have said that to my brother, my lord. It troubles his mind something terrible. Me? I will make confession and be washed clean as a babe. But I will see justice on you first. My men will witness.'

The Woodville son stepped closer then, free to walk though his arms had been bound behind him.

'There is no path back for you, sir, not if you kill the queen's own family. Do you understand? No redemption, no peace, not ever again. If you release us now, we can bear your demands to my sister. Is it Northumberland you want? It can be yours again, with such papers and seals so it can *never* be taken from you!'

'Well, by Christ, aren't you a lawyer, boy?' John Neville responded, his eyes glittering. 'I never knew you could make me such a fine offer! I would trust your word, o' course, after having had it taken from me once before!'

With a growl, he kicked the young knight's legs away and watched as he fell flat.

'It is *Marquess* Montagu now. Though I fear I am left with scrapings, it is yet all I have.' He looked up at the startled faces all around. 'Bring me an axe here – and some more fellows to witness.' While father and son looked stricken with fear, John Neville raised his voice to carry. 'What better court than God's green grass? On English soil? Is there more justice in oak? In iron bars? No, lads. We are honest men here. I need no judge but God above and my own conscience – and I declare this court in session.'

His men gathered all around and John Neville forced Earl Rivers to kneel alongside his son, pressing him down on to the damp ground.

'You two Woodvilles, of no great line, are accused of being poor counsellors to the king of England, of making your nests in fine velvets and furs, while doing down a finer family and better blood.'

All around, men pressed in, standing and watching in silence. John Neville leaned in to Earl Rivers. '*You* are complicit in stealing a good man's titles and pushing yourself forward in their place. *Treasurer, Earl.*'

He made the names sound like accusations with his scorn. With a shove, John Neville pushed the old man on to his back. The son cried out in fear as their tormentor came to stand over him in turn. The young man looked around at the hard faces on all sides, still hoping it was cruel sport.

'And *you*, who married an old duchess just to steal away her title. In my day, a knight was a man of honour. Shame on you, son.'

He too was sent over on to his back.

John Neville gestured and one of his men strode up smartly, with a billhook over his shoulder. The Woodvilles scrambled painfully back to their knees, not daring to rise. Father and son eyed the heavy blade with equal parts terror and disdain in their expressions.

'I find you both guilty, of dishonouring your titles and sharp practice,' John Neville said. 'I sentence you to death. I suppose it's not fitting for the judge to execute you, so I'll be witness to't. I'll let your families know, don't worry. I'm a fine hand with letters for the families.'

John Neville nodded to the crowd.

'One of you run into town after the other lad. We won't be needing the court, not now. And bring back some hot bread and a ham. I find I have an appetite.'

He gestured to the burly man who had stepped forward.

'Go on with your work, son. Justice will be done. As for you two, may God have mercy on your black Woodville souls.'

*

Though Warwick Castle gave him the name he used most often, it was not one of Richard Neville's favourite homes. Built right up to the banks of the River Avon, it was damp and cold in the mornings, the huge structure rambling around a courtyard almost too large for the scale of man. Unlike some of his other estates, the vast castle was too clearly a fortress built for war rather than any human comfort.

King Edward was confined to a room high in the western tower, guarded by two men at the door and another pair at the foot of the stairs. There was no danger of him escaping, though his great size and strength made him a threat to any man within reach. The king had given his parole not to escape, though it would not be honoured if they made no attempt to bargain with him or arrange for a ransom to be paid. In that, at least, Warwick knew the king would not believe a word. Warwick had no need of a king's ransom.

Two guards stood close behind Edward, giving him great honour in the way they watched for him to lunge at Warwick. It was hard to relax under those steady stares, though Edward seemed to, leaning back in his chair and crossing his feet at the ankles. Warwick looked for some sign of discomfort at his captivity, but found none.

'You have no complaints, then?' he asked. 'My men have treated you with courtesy?'

'Beyond keeping the king of England a prisoner, yes,' Edward said with a shrug. 'Your fat archbishop brother crowed that you had two kings in cells. I told him then it was only one. I imagine you are already discovering there is a *difference* between holding Henry of Lancaster and holding me.'

387

Edward was watching him closely and Warwick kept his face blank, trying hard to give nothing away. It irritated him to have Edward lean back once again and smile as if he had seen something of note.

'The days pass slowly here, with just a bible to read. What has it been, two months? A little more? A beautiful spring missed, as I cannot leave this tower. It is hard to forgive a man for that, Warwick, for making me miss a spring like this one. How much longer before you release me, do you think?'

'What makes you think I will?' Warwick said. 'Your brother George is my son-in-law. I could put him on the throne if I wished – and go on from there.'

To his irritation, Edward chuckled and shook his head.

'Do you think he would trust you if you did? I know him rather better than you do, Richard. He is a fool, yes, and too much a follower, *yes*, but he will not be king while I live – and he will not forgive you if I am killed. I think you know that very well, which is why I must endure long days here, while you try and put right the terrible mistake you have made.'

'I have not made a mistake,' Warwick replied peevishly.

'No? If you kill me, you will never sleep again for fear of my brothers. Sooner or later, some follower of theirs will offer one of them your head. By now, the whole country knows you took the king of England prisoner. Whispers, Richard, right across the land. Did you think it would be as it was with Henry? I believe you did! A weak and feeble child no one had even seen for how many years? The lords and the commons did not care when Henry was captured. Only his wife stung them into fighting for him, or they

388

would have kicked a few stones and looked away and done nothing at all.'

Edward's gaze hardened, so that Warwick could sense the roiling anger beneath the surface. The king's hair had grown overlong, matted thick as a mane. There truly was something lion-like in him as he lounged there, insolent and strong.

'I am not Henry,' Edward said. 'I imagine you have found keeping me is a little more trouble than you expected. Yes, I can see it in your face! How many counties have risen by now, to call for your head? How many sheriffs have been murdered, or judges or bailiffs or men of the law? How many members of Parliament have been chased through the streets by angry mobs? I am the *king* of England, Richard! I have blood ties and allies in half the noble families in England now – and I smell smoke in the air.'

Warwick could only stare as the young man sniffed, his gaze unwavering, drawing in a great breath.

'Yes – *there* it is, Richard. England in flames. So . . . how long before you release me now, eh?'

It galled Warwick that Edward's predictions were wrong only in the magnitude. The young king had not exaggerated them enough, that was the appalling truth of it. The reaction to Warwick capturing the king had been riots and unrest in the entire country. His brother the archbishop had been chased by a mob and had to barricade himself inside an abbey or be killed. A dozen Neville manors had been burned to the ground and entire towns had rioted, hanging their law officers and looting any and all – but always Neville holdings first.

The guiding hand was to be seen in the accuracy of the attacks, but Warwick thought they had run beyond even the best hopes of Elizabeth, as a fire will spread out of control and leap across from one forest to another. In the years since her marriage, she had clearly charmed or flattered every man of influence who had waited on King Edward. Her call had gone to a thousand throats and was still doubling every day, spreading from estate to estate, village to village, from the south ports into Wales and up to the border of Scotland. The worst of it was that Warwick's capture of her husband fitted so neatly with what she had whispered before. The Nevilles were proven traitors, just as Elizabeth Woodville had claimed. No one could deny it, now that they had captured Edward on the king's own road and stolen him away.

Margaret of Anjou had never had a tenth of the support Elizabeth had gathered in just a few months, Warwick thought. That said, she had never had Edward for a husband. Everything the king had said was true – and much more. Henry had never won a battle, while Edward had been seen by half the country's fighting men at Towton, leading from the front. Those men who had fought for York that day still lived. They remembered Edward's wild ride to crush the flank attack. They had seen the king ride for them and they came out for him in return, to burn and hunt Neville lords.

Henry of Lancaster had hidden himself away in priories and abbeys, while Edward went hunting and toured the courts and towns, enjoying himself as a young man and buying lavish gifts for his family. Poor Henry had never had the wit to charm men who would willingly have followed him. It was more than Edward's giant frame, or his skill with hawk and hound. He was a rough sort of king, but still much more the idea of one than Henry had ever been.

Warwick looked at the younger man's self-satisfied expression and wanted to dash his confidence. He shook his head and smiled as if to reprove a child, knowing it would infuriate Edward.

'I could bring Henry out of the Tower. His wife and his son are well, in France. An entire line – better, the *true* line, the true king restored. I have heard Edward of Westminster is a fine young man, grown tall now.'

Edward leaned forward at that, his mocking humour vanishing.

'You . . . no, you would not.' He spoke again before Warwick could ask. 'Oh, I am sure you would put Henry on my throne, if it could be done. Now follow my reasoning, Richard. I have had long enough alone here to think. You've had the chance to kill that pale saint. You did not. I do not complain, Richard. I live as well, so I am thankful! Yet the truth of it is that you are not a cold-hearted killer. You would have to be one to put a crown on Henry's head once again. Do you understand that? I suspect you do, or it would already have happened. You would have to wade through blood to do it – to cut out every Woodville, including my own daughters. You would not do such a thing. Not the man I have known and respected since I was a boy. It is not in you.'

Warwick looked at him long enough to catch the edge of worry behind the young man's bluster. He understood it, considering his own two girls. Children were hostages to fortune, vulnerable to enemies. Just by existing, they could make a strong man weak, who might otherwise laugh in scorn at his own demise.

'No, that is all true,' he said. Edward grunted in poorly hidden relief, leaning back once again as Warwick went on.

'It is true I could not dip my hands in so much blood. Yet I do have a brother. John Neville. How many did he kill on your orders, in the years after Towton?'

Edward's head dipped, a hand rubbing the bristles around his mouth. He sensed the truth in the words and he tried not to show fear. Warwick nodded to him, almost sadly.

'Earl Rivers is cold in the ground now. His son John is dead. My brother's anger, Edward. Did you think you could take his title with no consequence at all? Even a loyal dog will bite if you pull a bone away too many times.' Warwick shook his head sadly. 'Did you think I would hold every knife myself? If I must choose one path over another, I would not leave my enemies alive! No, if I were you, I would pray I can control the damned riots before I have to make a decision about your fate!'

Warwick stood up then, angry with himself for letting slip the snippet of information to the king, who sat with his mouth open. It had all been guesswork and supposition before, but now Edward knew there truly was unrest over his capture.

'Set me *free*, Richard!' he shouted, raising his clenched fists.

'I cannot!' Warwick snapped.

He left the room and as Edward surged to his feet, his path was blocked by the two soldiers, glaring and pressing hands against his chest. For a moment, Edward considered knocking them aside, though they carried iron thumpers to addle his brains if he tried – and there were other guards below.

'I am the *king*!' Edward bellowed, at such a volume that both his guards flinched. 'Set me free!'

Warwick left him roaring as he reached the sunshine and mounted his horse to ride back to London, his face as grim as winter.

The heart of the Tower of London was its oldest part, a tower of white Caen stone that was higher than the outer walls, so gave a view of the city and the Thames running alongside. In the night, Elizabeth had climbed up through a tiny hatch, to emerge on a roof of ancient tiles, bird nests and lichen. From the first moment, her hair and clothes had been tugged by the wind as she looked over the dark city. The moon gave the barest of sheens to some of the houses and the river itself, but the only other light came from the torches of rioters, marching all night, for she had heard the tramp of their feet even in restless dreams. They roared for Neville blood and they hunted Neville men, that was the satisfaction and the terror of it.

She had known her husband was loved and held in awe, of course. Elizabeth had gained some inkling that England's merchants and knights and noble lords had all shown joy in Edward winning through, banishing the scholar king to a cell and allowing his French wife to run home to her father. Even then, she had not appreciated the degree of their loyalty, the extent of their outrage at his capture.

The news had spread on the angry words of town gatherings, all shouting and smashing down the doors of official houses, looting the most valuable items and then setting fires to conceal their crimes. As each town or village heard, they sent runners to the next and the next, until there were great marches of ten thousand, bearing torches and billhooks. Orators and captains who had stood at Towton all called for Neville traitors to be hunted down.

Elizabeth's lips pulled away from her teeth, though it was an expression of pain more than satisfaction. The wind filled her, making her feel light as the freezing air. The only bridge across the river was not far from the Tower. From where she stood, she could see a line of torches coming over it from Southwark, cheering, savage men coming back to their homes – and in the distance over the river, a dim glow against the darkness as some great house burned in its grounds.

Elizabeth had summoned loyal lords and called for vengeance, hot-eyed and empty of tears. The Nevilles had begun the fires and they would grow now to a conflagration that would consume them all. She panted in the wind, feeling its touch like cold hands pressing into her.

She had known from the beginning how deeply the Nevilles had eaten their way into the country, like worms in an apple. She had found more and more evidence wherever she looked. Her dear trusting husband had been blind to it all. It had been the merest sense to try to break their grip before they ruined him.

'I was right,' she whispered into the wind, taking comfort as the words were spoken and immediately lost in the air. 'I saw it, but they were stronger than I knew, and more cruel.'

Her tears were blown back into her hair as the wind increased, moaning as if it suffered the same wrenching pain. Her father and her brother had been murdered by Nevilles. There would be no mercy for them after that. They had drawn a line in her family's blood and she would not rest until they were smears of ash.

There were some who had called her a witch over the first years of her marriage, for how well she had snared her husband and the court. It was no more than the malice of womanly men and manly women. Yet in that gale, she wished it were true. In that moment, she would have given her immortal soul for the power to seek out her enemies and dash out their brains upon stone. Her father had not deserved his fate. She had brought him to court and it had cost him his life. She clenched her fists, feeling the nails dig in to her palms.

'Let them all die now,' she whispered. 'Let the Nevilles *suffer* as I have suffered, as they deserve. If God and the saints will not answer me, O spirits of darkness, hear my words. Bring them down. Return my husband to me and let them all *burn*.'

31

They came after sunset, marching along empty country tracks in single file. They appeared in taverns to wash away the dust of miles on the road, making themselves known to those they trusted. When the night came, they tied cloth around their faces and they carried oil and dark lanterns, shuttered against the wind.

Sometimes the servants ran and were allowed to escape. Others chose to stay, to warn the household after years of loyalty. They were not spared then, the families or those who served them. Fire destroyed them all.

They called themselves 'Burners' and their dark business showed on their skin. They were always red-faced and stained with old soot, their inflamed eyes making them fearsome to look upon. They lit their torches and set the horses free to run, then burned the stables. When those inside rushed out, they found a ring of men with cudgels or billhooks, their faces covered against being recognized. They battered any man who came out, sometimes past healing with a broken pate. The burning went on then, building by building, barn by barn, until the whole countryside was lit by the red-gold flicker and the cold air was made into a warm breeze carrying the smell of char and destruction. By the time local farmers and the bailiffs came riding up, the fires had too much of a hold to be brought under control. Ancient manors were reduced to black timbers, burning for days and nights. Then, forty or eighty miles away, the Burners would appear again out of the night, standing in their ring with torches crackling.

There had been uprisings before, great and small, against cruel treatment, or for a hundred reasons. The people of England had always been slow to rouse, in part for fear of what they felt within them. They had endured cruelty and poverty in sullen anger, drinking hard and spending their resentment in bloody sports or boxing. They had suffered taxmen taking their coins, though Christ knew they were the lowest of all sinners. They had felt the lash of laws that left them swinging in the breeze – and those who had loved them had gone out to burn and murder in revenge. Some were always caught and hanged each generation, as a warning to anyone else who might think of grabbing the stick that struck them down. It was the normal, ancient way of things, and the deep countryside was far darker in some ways than city streets. There were villages that were places of silence and sin, with simmering rage amidst the cattle and the peace. Hard lives bred hard men and women, who could carry a torch or a blade when they saw the need. After all, they cut and killed and worked themselves to the bone just to live.

That year was different. The Burners came to places that had never known them before. They grew more cruel as well, as the months passed with King Edward still held by traitors. Manor houses went up in flames with the doors nailed shut by great spikes. The screams went unheeded. Castles of stone were set afire by their own servants, with noble families murdered by their retainers, loyal for a lifetime, until they were not.

There were exceptions, as villages older than Christ took advantage of the unrest to settle old scores. There were new bodies in every street and every village square, and some of them were just grudge killings or drunken murders, with the men of the law shivering in their homes, waiting for the hard knock. The rest, though, the greatest portion of the destruction, was all of one clan, one family – in particular, the holdings of one man. Neville herds were slaughtered. Warwickshire coal mines were set ablaze. Neville ships were burned at their moorings and the great houses of Richard Neville made ash and bitter char, with blackened bodies burned to the bones.

As the months wore on without news of King Edward's release, the attacks and the burnings became ever more open. Men kicked in the doors of Warwickshire taverns and shouted questions. When the answers were not the right ones, they threw in pots of oil and lit torches, standing outside with pitchforks to keep them in. The Burners had their leaders, three separate, killing men, *all* known as Robin of Redesdale. Between them, they were the voice of the soldiers at Towton. They were the voice of the king in captivity, crying out on his behalf.

As the summer fled, the harvest was poorly taken, for fear of full barns attracting the Burners, and also because workers stayed away from the Neville estates to avoid being beaten on their way home. Crops rotted in the fields and entire herds were made to vanish or, worse, found with their throats cut. The coal mines could not be put out and smoked a funeral pyre into the air that could be seen right across the county and might burn until the end of time, the flames reaching deep into the bones of the land to seethe on, hidden.

Fauconberg pressed two hard fingers into his stomach, making himself grunt in pain. He sat in the kitchens of

Middleham Castle, with all the staff dismissed so as not to view his humiliation. The chair Warwick had ordered brought down for him was padded and soft, but the elderly earl could not find a comfortable position.

'It grows worse, Richard,' he said, putting down a bowl that swam with swirls of milky vomit. 'I hardly eat now – and when I do, it all comes back. I cannot believe I have much longer.'

Warwick leaned against a huge wooden table with legs thicker than his own. He tried not to show his shock at how much weight his uncle had lost. Fauconberg had never been a large man, but his bones were clearly visible in the dark planes of his face, and his legs and arms had grown frail-looking. Even his hair had thinned, so that it hung in wisps around his shoulders. Something was eating him from the inside and Warwick agreed with the assessment, though he would not say so.

'And who will advise me when you are not here? Eh, Uncle? Come on, old man, I need you. It's not as if I have shown such great wisdom or cunning in my choices recently.'

Fauconberg tried to chuckle, though the movement hurt him and made him gasp. Putting the bowl down with its noisome contents, he pressed his hand into his side again, finding some relief.

'You will find a way through, Richard, for the family. God knows we have struggled past thorns before.' Even in his pain, Fauconberg glanced at his nephew, wondering how to persuade him. 'I suspect you know the best choice even now, if your pride would let you say it aloud.'

'You'd counsel me to release Edward?' Warwick asked glumly. 'If I could go back and make a different decision, I tell you I would. I did not understand then what would happen when I put the king behind bars and oak.' Warwick grimaced to himself in bitter memory. 'You know, Uncle, he even *said* it to me. Edward, when I visited him. He said I had seen Henry captured and failed to understand that he was not loved, that he was a weak king. And he was *right*, though it burns me. I thought I could push them like pieces across the board. I never saw that the entire game could be kicked over if I touched the wrong king.'

Fauconberg did not respond. His own estates were north of the city of York and even he had suffered barn burnings and the murder of a local judge, far away from the cities and the riots. Each month had brought worse news and the fire still seemed to be spreading. He thought his nephew had only one choice, but Fauconberg knew he would not live to see it. His stomach held a hard ball of some ridged foulness, like a creature that lived off him. He had seen such things when livestock had been slaughtered in the past, brought to him as curiosities. Whatever it was, it had curdled his blood. His largest veins had grown dark with the thing's poisons and he knew he would not survive it. All he could hope was that Warwick would keep the family safe. It was hard not to tell him what he had to do.

'What were your true hopes, though, Richard? I was there while we planned it, but all the talk was of how we might get Edward into the north with only a few men, or of how you would go to France with his brother and your daughter. You were busy with the excitement of a thousand little details, but there was not so much talk of what came after that.'

'There should have been more,' Warwick admitted. 'Yet I was so angry I thought only of showing Edward how badly he had treated his most loyal men. I still saw him as the boy I helped train in Calais. Not as a king, Uncle, not really. Of all men in the country, I was the only one who was blind to what he had become. I was the one who misunderstood.'

Fauconberg shrugged.

'You were not alone. Your brothers thought the same, as I recall.'

'We all saw the wilful boy, though I fought at his side at Towton. We saw the *man*, not the king. Either way, the decision was mine. I could have told John and George to endure and be still.'

'John? There is so much anger in him, I think it would have spilled. He might have been hanged by now, or lost his head for some rash act.'

Warwick sighed, reaching for a jug of wine to pour two cups.

'Can you hold wine down?' he asked.

'If you bring me my bowl, I will try,' Fauconberg replied.

Hiding his disgust, Warwick emptied the vomit bowl into a slops bucket and wiped it out with a clean cloth before handing it over with a cup of claret. With a wry expression, Fauconberg raised it in toast to him.

'May we see this only once,' he said, and drank, smacking his lips. 'And I think his wife's family played their part in rousing the country. Some of our troubles were bought with her coin, Richard. Those damned "Burners". I'd wager her purse jingles behind every barn or house in flames.'

'I thought perhaps I would offer the throne to Clarence. I say this to you knowing you will take it to the grave, Uncle. Yet to do it, I would have to have Edward killed, not just held. I am not even sure I can hold him as a prisoner for much longer. There are too many calling for his release, and if he escaped . . .' He broke off, imagining the great wolf, enraged and free. Warwick shuddered. 'He *is* the king, Uncle. That is the strangest thing. I see it now and I am filled with fear for the mistake of capturing him. All I want is to find a way to put him back on his throne that will not mean the immediate destruction and attainder of every Neville house.'

'That might have been a thought *before* John executed the queen's father and brother,' Fauconberg croaked.

His throat was pulsing and as Warwick watched, he held the bowl to his mouth and dribbled a stream of milky red into it. Warwick looked away rather than witness his discomfort. He waited until the sounds had come to an end and glanced over to see his uncle pale and wiping sweat from his face.

'Not so very pleasant,' Fauconberg whispered. 'As I am dying anyway, perhaps I should take an axe to the king's neck as my last act. You could blame the whole plot on me and recover some honour with Clarence.'

'And see your name trampled in the mud?' Warwick said. 'No, Uncle. He told me I would hold back from murders and he was right. Killing him would call for another and a dozen after that. I will not go so deep into blood. No. Anyway, as things stand, we would not survive the fires lit for Edward's death!'

'There is no one else,' Fauconberg replied, his voice strengthening. 'Neither of the king's brothers would trust the man who killed Edward! If you raise Clarence or Gloucester, you will be putting your own head on the block. No, you must make peace with the king. It is the only thing left.'

'I have thought of it; did you think I would not? You

have not been to see him, Uncle. He is *insane* with anger. Three months in a cell and he has broken through the door twice and killed one of the guards. I had to have the doors repaired while he stood and lunged at bare swords, just daring me to kill him. On other days, he sits and eats and calmly tells me what I should be doing in the realm. He is bored and angry and vengeful, and you would have me turn him out? I wish I could.'

'If it were not for the Woodville dead, I would say yes, you can release him. I have never known Edward break an oath, not once. He has a code, from his father or perhaps from you, I don't know. You keep saying he is no longer the boy you knew, that he is a king. Well, trust in that! Have Edward sign an amnesty for all your crimes, a protection from the law and all retribution, sworn on his immortal soul, on the lives of his children, whatever you would ask!'

'You think I can trust his word? *Truly?*' Warwick asked, his desperation showing in the strain on his face.

'I think if the rest of the world went up in flames, you would still be able to trust his word, yes.'

'The rest of the world *is* going up in flames! What about John's title?' Warwick said.

Fauconberg shook his head.

'I would not reach too far, Richard. It was Edward's gift to take back. If you can see another way, I would be delighted to hear it, perhaps before my pain grows much greater.'

'I am sorry, Uncle,' Warwick said, slumping in defeat. 'Very well. Edward *is* king. I will have him sign an amnesty and pardons. He is not the angry boy I knew, not any longer. I *have* to believe in his sworn oath. I don't have any other choice at all.'

32

Richard Neville reined in at the massive gatehouse of Warwick Castle. He held a lance up over his head, with his
banner of a bear and staff embroidered into the cloth that
hung from it. A light drizzle dampened his spirits further,
making him cold and weary. He was three days out from
London, though it might as well have been another country. It was a miserable day in the middle of England and
the place looked about as bleak and sullen as he had come
to expect.

At least the Burners had not spread their whispers there.
As the attacks had grown in number and savagery around
the country, Warwick had ordered this most vital stronghold shut tight, going to shifts and siege orders. No one
entered or left and there was no contact at all with the local
population. Warwick had given clear commands to show
crossbows to man or woman approaching the walls, with
an order to fire on anyone who did not retreat.

It would mean the local poachers emptied his forests of
deer and grouse, of course, but there was no help for that.
With the country so close to complete insurrection and
chaos, he could not let the news creep out that King
Edward was there, held prisoner.

The guards on the high walkways stared down without
expression as he showed them the signal. A tabard on a
lance was clear enough and Warwick stopped waving it
when his arms began to ache, waiting for the crossbowmen

to call a serjeant. It was a serious decision to open the main gate while under siege orders. Warwick waited as the rain increased and began to drive across him. His horse shivered, the great neck and flanks rippling in response to the cold. By the time the first crack of light showed within, he was blue-lipped and he barely nodded to the guards as they recognized him and stood back. The doors were closed and barred behind him, the iron portcullis rattling down into holes with a clang. He shook rain from his face and hair as he walked his horse on a long rein through the killing path. It was only forty paces or so, but he was overlooked by ledges and walkways that could have been filled with archers. As he reached the end of it, he closed his eyes for an instant, breathing in the smell of damp stone and cold. The castle was cut off once again. With the river running by, they had a never-ending supply of clean water and enough salt meat and grain to make bread for years. The world, with all its troubles and grief, had become a place outside those walls.

Warwick felt himself relax. He handed his horse over to a lad and walked through the inner gate to the great courtyard. He could not help the way his eyes looked up to the tower where Edward had his cell. Warwick was aware of the castle steward droning on about some part of the estate or the rents. He did not trouble to listen, looking instead at where he would go. The steward dried up as Warwick thanked him, his attention clearly elsewhere. The man fell behind as Warwick crossed the huge inner yard, surrounded by windows of the great house beginning to gleam gold as lamps were lit to welcome the master home. As he went, he patted the satchel he wore over one shoulder, feeling the heft of the papers within.

Edward had not changed in any particular way over the summer of his captivity. Warwick had heard he spent hours every day throwing himself around the room and lifting chairs and his bed, or pushing himself up and down in odd positions. They had refused him a sword, even a blunt training weapon, for fear of what he would do with it. Edward had also been denied a razor and as a result he had grown a great black beard that made him look like a wild hermit.

As he was still in his twenties, at least the king's fitness would not have suffered too badly, Warwick thought with a twinge of envy. He could smell Edward's sweat as he entered the room, a rank odour that was musky and not completely unpleasant, like urine on a dog's paws.

Edward had on the same shirt he'd worn at his capture, though Warwick could see it had been cleaned and even had a seam resewn. The steward and the staff had no cause to mistreat him and would have been fools if they had.

Without a word, Warwick gestured to a large stuffed chair, sensing a difficult meeting might go a little better if Edward was not allowed to loom over him. The king enjoyed being taller than other men. He always had.

With a curl of his lip, Edward dropped into the seat. There was nothing relaxed about him. Every muscle was tensed and he looked ready to leap up at the slightest provocation.

'Now why would you be here, now?' Edward said. Warwick opened his mouth, but the king went on before he could reply. 'You can be told I am well in a note, by pigeon or rider. No, you are here now for one of two choices.'

Edward had leaned forward as he spoke, his hands gripping the arms of the chair. Warwick was aware of the threat in the younger man. He rose to his feet and put his own seat between them, and nothing about the action was unconscious. Edward's eyes were coldly assessing, a man near the end of his patience. Perhaps it was the odour of perspiration, but Warwick felt as if he was the one being stalked. He glanced back at the two guards who waited, watching the prisoner for the first sign that he might attack. They had good solid maces of iron to bring down on Edward's head and shoulders. Warwick made a show of stretching his back and sat himself down once again, facing the young giant who made his chair look small against the frame.

Edward smiled at him infuriatingly, reading the nervousness.

'Not to kill me, then, or you would have given the order to my guards.'

His gaze dropped to the satchel Warwick wore, the brown leather scuffed and shiny from long use. Edward's eyebrows rose.

'What do you have in there, Richard?'

'In all the time I have known you, I have not seen you break your oath. You remember when we talked about it? Before Westminster, when you asked me what they wanted from a king? I said he would be a man who kept his word.'

'Not you, then,' Edward murmured. 'You broke your oath to me. You may have damned your soul, Richard, and for what?'

'If I could take back what I have done, I would. You have my word, if it is worth anything at all.'

Edward was surprised by the intensity in the man across from him. He stared, then nodded.

'I believe you mean what you say. Ask me for

forgiveness, Earl Warwick. Who knows, it could be granted to you.'

'I will ask,' Warwick replied.

He felt like a supplicant, rather than the one demanding terms. There was something powerful in the presence of the king, as if he had been born to wear the crown. Warwick felt it as a tide and he wanted to kneel. The fate of his brothers held him steady, anchoring him.

'I will ask you for an amnesty and a pardon, for all crimes, all sins, all broken oaths. For me and for my family. I trust your word, Edward. I have known you since you were thirteen years old and wrestling with Calais soldiers. I have never known you to break an oath, and I will accept your seal on the papers my scribes have written.'

Without looking away from Edward, Warwick reached into the satchel and fumbled for the silver halves of the king's Great Seal. Edward looked down as he heard them chink together.

'A pardon for holding me prisoner,' Edward said. 'For breaking your oath to me. For your brothers George and John Neville, in breaking their oaths.'

Warwick coloured. The wound could be cleaned, if they forced a heated blade to the root of it and let out all the poison.

'For *all*, Your Majesty. For all past mistakes and sins and errors.' Warwick took a deep breath in through his nose. 'For all the deaths of loyal men. For the execution of Earl Rivers and Sir John Woodville. For the marriage of your brother George, Duke of Clarence, to my daughter Isabel. Amnesty for everything, my lord. I would take almost all of it back if I could, but I cannot. Instead, I must make it the price of your freedom.'

Edward's gaze had narrowed and the sense of danger came off him like heat.

'You would have me pardon the men who killed my wife's father?'

'You are the king, Edward. I have told you what must be. I cannot take back one word of it. If I could return to the morning at Towton when we found the bridge cut down, before the snow began to fall, I would. And I would stand with you again. I ask your forgiveness now, for me, and for my family.'

'And if I will not, you will leave me here,' Edward said.

Warwick flushed under his scrutiny.

'I must have your seal and your name on the pardons and the amnesties, Your Highness. There is no other way. For you see, I know you will honour them, even though they are the price of your freedom. Even though your wife will rage when she hears you have granted pardons to men she has hated since she arrived at court.'

'Do not speak of my wife,' Edward said suddenly, his voice grown deep and hard.

Warwick inclined his head.

'Very well. I have ink and wax. I have a quill and your seal. I ask for your pardon.'

Warwick handed over the satchel with its contents, feeling a touch of shame at the tremble he saw in Edward's hand, the young man still hardly daring to believe he would be released and not killed. Warwick prepared himself to remain still, almost holding his breath. He saw Edward unwrap the sheaf of vellum sheets, reaching into the satchel and seeking the quill and the metal bottle of black squid ink. Without reading them, Edward scrawled 'Edward

Plantagenet Rex' on each page, then tossed the quill over his shoulder.

'You have my seal. Finish the rest of it yourself.' He rose with Warwick and passed the papers into his arms.

'There. You have what you wanted. Shall we see now if you are able to redeem any part of your honour, of your word? Will I be allowed to leave this castle?'

Warwick swallowed. He was desperately afraid he had loosed his own destruction on the world. It troubled him terribly that Edward had not read the pages he had signed. The king had forced the test of his honour, finding by instinct the very crux of it all. Did it matter how well Warwick had worded the documents to be signed and sealed? What mattered most was Edward's word. Warwick could only gesture to the guards, so that they stood back from the door. For the first time in seven months, it lay open.

Edward crossed the room in three quick strides, his speed making the guards tense and exchange glances. In the doorway, the king hesitated, looking down on dark steps descending away.

'I think you should walk down with me, Richard, don't you? I don't want your guards to put a bolt through my chest in an accident. I would prefer a horse, though I will walk if I must.'

'Of course,' Warwick said, suddenly so weary he could barely think at all. God knew, he had made mistakes before. Edward had forced him to understand that it came down to trust. He crossed to the stairs and Edward turned to him.

'I think, after this, I will not summon you to court, Richard. Though I will be bound by the amnesties and pardons, I cannot say we are friends, not now. I think it would be safest for you if you do not cross my wife's path for a time either. Where does she lay her head now? I would see her again, with my children.'

Warwick bowed his head and felt both shame and loss.

'In the White Tower, I swear by her own choice. There has been no ill treatment. I have not seen sight nor sound of her for months.'

Edward nodded, his brows drawn down over a glower.

Warwick accompanied the king to the stables, where the horse master selected a fine broad-chested gelding to carry the king. Warwick offered Edward a cloak, but he refused it in his impatience to leave the place of his confinement.

In darkness, the great gates opened once more and King Edward cantered out, back straight, into the night.

The rider was filthy with road dust, his beard thick with it. The grime lined every seam of his face and clothes, though he wore no cloak and his arms were black to the elbow like a smith's. The sheer size of him made people wonder and stare as he passed. Not one in a thousand had seen the king in person, when Edward had stood on the steps of Westminster Hall and summoned them to march north. He had been resplendent then in a cloak and cloth marked in gold. He had been shaved cleanly and his hair had been shorter, not the straggling mass of dirt and knots this rider had tied back with a strip of cloth torn from his jerkin.

Edward rode the gelding at a slow walk, the animal's head drooping along with its master. The evenings were long then and the light was fair as, one by one, men and women stepped out into the street behind him, wondering in whispers, asking out loud, daring to believe it.

A young monk ran up alongside the weary rider, resting

a hand on the thick mud clotted on to the stirrup. He stared up, panting and jogging along, straining to see through the beard and the filth.

'Are you the king?' he asked.

Edward opened one eye and stared at him.

'I am,' he said. 'I have come home.'

The monk fell back at his words, standing with an open mouth in the road until he was surrounded by a crowd.

'What did he say, then? Is it King Edward?'

'Who else could it be? The size of him!'

The monk nodded, an incredulous smile pulling one side of his mouth.

'It *is* him. King Edward. He said he had come home.'

They roared at that, raising their hands into the air. As one, the Londoners began to race after the lone rider still making his way towards the Tower, gathering more and more from every street and shop and house they passed. By the time Edward reached the gatehouse of the Tower of London, a thousand of his subjects stood at his back, with still more flooding in behind. Some of them even carried weapons, ready to be commanded in anything.

Edward knew he had ridden fast enough to outpace any messenger. He had driven his horse to lame exhaustion. As a result, he was not certain whether the guards at the gatehouse would have been told of his freedom. He set his jaw. He was the king and his people stood at his back. It would not matter what they had been told. Summoning his confidence, he strode forward and thumped his fist on the wood, then waited with the sense of eyes crawling over him.

'Who is it down there?' a voice called.

'King Edward of England and Wales and France, Lord of Ireland, Earl of March, Duke of York. Open this gate.'

Edward saw flickers of movement as men leaned over the high wall. He did not look up and merely waited impassively. Bolts and chains began to sound on the other side, then the rattle of an iron lattice being raised. Edward looked back to the sea of faces waiting around him.

'I was held, but now I am free. It was your loyalty that freed me. Take heart from that.'

As soon as there was enough room under the rising spikes, Edward ducked under it, pulling away from the trailing touches of the crowd on his back. He strode across the stone yard within, towards the White Tower and his wife, Elizabeth.

33

Edward watched his children play, his oldest daughter waving a piece of apple out of reach of another. Elizabeth's two boys by her first marriage were competing to carry the girls through half a dozen rooms at Windsor, charging in and out of open doors with hoots like hunting calls. Edward felt no particular affection for the boys. He had appointed swordmasters and tutors to instruct them, of course, so they would not embarrass him. After that, he took no more interest than he would in the get of any other stranger.

As for his three girls, Edward had discovered he adored them when they were not actually in his presence, as if the idea of them was somehow more of a joy than the reality of their shrieks and constant demands on his attention. He loved them best in their absence.

Elizabeth looked sidelong at her husband, smiling as she read his thoughts about as easily as her own. As soon as Edward began to frown, she shooed all the whooping, neighing children out of his presence, closing a door on their noise.

As the clamour died away, Edward blinked in relief, looking up and understanding when he caught her smile. Elizabeth was solicitous in her care of him, though not in a way that made him weak, or so he hoped. Edward smiled back at the thought, though her own expression had grown serious. As he looked at her, she bit her lower lip, halfway along its length.

'I have not troubled you with this, just as you asked,' she said. 'Not for a month now.'

He groaned at the words, understanding on the instant. Though his wife claimed to have remained silent on the subject, he had seen it in her eyes every day, a silent reproof.

'And I give thanks for that!' he said. 'Be *ruled* in this, Elizabeth. It will become a sourness between us if you cannot turn away from it. I have granted pardons, for all crimes. Amnesty for treasons. There will be no attainder, no executions, no punishment, no reprisals.'

'*So,*' Elizabeth said, her mouth a thin pale line, 'you will let the weeds grow again. You will do nothing as the vines thrive to strangle your own children!'

As she spoke, she ran a hand over her womb, protectively. There was not yet a true swelling there, though she knew the signs. The vomiting had already begun in the mornings, so violent this time that it had left her with broken veins on her cheeks. It gave her hope of a son.

Edward shook his head, unaware of her thoughts and showing only a stubborn anger as she pressed him.

'I have made my ruling, Elizabeth. I have told you. Now *be* told. This will come between us if you don't let it go. I cannot change what is in the past. My brother is married to Isabel Neville and they are expecting their first child. Can I unplant that seed? Your father and your brother John are dead.' He pursed his mouth. 'I cannot bring them back, Elizabeth! Your brother Anthony is Earl Rivers now. Would you have me take his title away from him? That is a path to madness. Let it be enough that I have forbidden the royal court to the Neville men. You do not have to see them, in your grief. The rest . . . the rest is in the past and I will not pick and pick and *pick* at it until the blood flows again!'

He heard how far his voice had risen in volume and anger and he looked away, red-faced and abashed.

'I think you have spent too long moping and sighing about the palaces of London, Edward,' his wife said, gentling her voice and touching him on the arm. 'You need to ride out, perhaps to bring the king's justice where the sheriff and bailiffs have not yet been replaced. There are many villages wanting those now. My brother Anthony was telling me of one place not twenty miles to the north. Three men are accused of murder, caught with the red knives on them – and the jewels they stole from a great house. They left a dead father and daughter behind. Yet they sleep well in their cells and laugh at the local militia. The people there have no king's officers. There were bloody riots a few months back and they are afraid. They dare not try the scoundrels without a judge in attendance.'

'What is this to me?' Edward retorted. 'You'd have me pass judgment on every thief and brigand in the land? Why, then, do I even have judges and sheriffs and bailiffs? Is this some comment on my treatment of the Nevilles, Elizabeth? If it is, you are too subtle for me. I do not see your point.'

His wife looked up at him, standing as tall as she could, with both palms pressed against his chest. She spoke slowly and with an intensity he found chilling.

'Perhaps you need to blow the froth off your maunderings, to ride hard and tear through the webs that have made you so slow and thoughtful. You will *see*, Edward, when you speak to the men and deliver judgment upon them as their feudal lord. You will see in the way those villagers look to you, as a king. Anthony knows where the place lies. He will show you.'

'No,' Edward said. 'I don't understand this, but I will not go rushing off just because you have something planned with your brother. I have had enough of plots and whispers, Elizabeth. Tell me what it is or I will not move from this place, and those men can rot in a cell until new judges are appointed and they are brought to trial.'

Elizabeth hesitated, her eyes wide. He could feel the tremble of her hands through his shirt.

'The murders were just two weeks past,' she said. 'Those men claim Richard Neville as their lord: Earl Warwick, in treason against your offices.'

'Christ, Beth! Did you not hear me before? I have *pardoned* them.'

'They accuse Warwick – and Clarence too, Edward! My brother Anthony put them to the question, with fire and iron. There is no doubt. They name Warwick in conspiracy: to murder you and put Clarence on the throne! These are *new* crimes, Edward, not covered by the amnesty, nor the pardons. Do you understand? My father knows no rest, has had no vengeance. Do you understand, Edward?'

The king looked at his wife, seeing the way hatred and grief had added lines to her, stealing away the last of her youthful bloom. She had never seemed too old for him before, but she did then.

'Oh, Elizabeth, what have you done?' he said softly.

'Nothing at all. These men named two of your foremost lords as traitors, conspiring against you. Anthony had them questioned and, in fire and iron, the truth was given. They do not lie.'

'You will not tell me the truth, even now?'

Elizabeth clenched her jaw, her gaze fierce.

'These are *new* crimes, Edward,' she said. 'You are not

forsworn. Your precious amnesty was for all that had gone before. It is unbroken.'

Edward looked away, saddened.

'Very well. I *will* ride to them, Elizabeth. I will hear their accusations, against Warwick and my own *brother*.' He took a slow breath and she recoiled from his anger, stepping back. 'I promise nothing beyond that.'

'That is enough,' she said, suddenly desperate to heal the rift that had sprung up between them. She pressed kisses and tears against his mouth. 'When you hear what they have to say, you can arrest the traitors. Perhaps then we will see such an ending as they deserve.'

Edward bore the kisses, feeling a coldness between them. She had not trusted him and he could not quite recall the way he had looked at her before his imprisonment. It reminded him of the times he had left a dog behind and returned months later. The animal had looked the same but somehow slightly off, in its scent and the touch of its fur. It took time to find the old easy comfort, and until it came back, it always felt like a different hound. It was, perhaps, not the sort of thing he could discuss with Elizabeth, though it felt very much the same. Her father's death had hardened her, or drawn some softness out that he had taken for granted before.

He left her with tears shining in her eyes, though he did not know if they were from relief or sadness. Edward went down to the stables and scowled to find her brother Anthony waiting with Edward's warhorse, ready to be ridden. The man's broken wrist had healed many months before. As with Elizabeth, Edward had not recovered his ease of manner with the Woodville knight, though he thought the cause might have been the same. He had lost his mind for a time when his father had been killed. Perhaps it was not so surprising that the Woodvilles had grown harder and more bitter at the loss of their own.

Edward stepped up on to the mounting block and swung into the saddle, feeling the old strength coil and gather. He held out his hand for his sword, strapping it on over the jacket tails at his waist. The last time he had ridden from that place had been to his own capture. He shook his head at the memory, as if a wasp had brushed his skin. He would not be afraid. He would not allow it.

'Show me this village,' he called to Anthony Woodville, as the man crossed the yard and mounted his own horse.

Elizabeth's brother dipped his head, then cantered out with Edward into the sun, the gates opening before them.

Warwick was outside, working up a sweat with sword exercise at Middleham Castle, enjoying the sun and the thought of fruit pies and jams all autumn, with every sticky treat from apples, plums, greengages, strawberries, a host of fat fruits. It was never possible to preserve them all in chutneys, brine or vinegar, and so the local villagers would gorge on them until they could not face another mouthful, then put the rest in cool cellars or send them away to command high prices at the markets. It was, perhaps, his favourite time of year and he thought again of the London court he had left behind as a sort of fever dream. In his forties, Warwick could consider the years of intrigue and war safely behind him. He hoped as much. There would not be another Towton in his lifetime, though he touched a wooden window frame and made the sign of the cross just at the thought. Men older than him had fought in battles. He could still remember the first Earl Percy, well into his sixties when he had fallen at St Albans.

Warwick found himself shuddering, as if a cloud's shadow had crossed the sun. His uncle Fauconberg was gone, found cold in his bed just a few days after Warwick had last spoken to him. It had surprised him how hard that loss had been. Warwick had spent so long finding his father's brother an irritation that he had not realized how close they had become by the end. Or perhaps it was just that his father's death had hollowed him out.

He saw two riders coming along the main drive, seeing the dust they raised. It blurred the air behind them and caught his eye, so that he fixed his gaze on them, watching the dark figures racing closer with a feeling of tension. Such speed and urgency had never been the harbinger of good news. He almost wanted to go back inside and shut the doors. It could be the axe falling at last, the blow at his neck he had been dreading and expecting ever since Edward had returned to London.

An entire month had passed without a word of any unrest, though Warwick had servants and listeners all over the houses of the capital to warn him if the king took to the road with an armed force.

He swallowed uncomfortably. At his back, he could hear men and women calling out in alarm as they spotted the riders. His guards would already be gathering kit and horses, braced to protect him or to ride out at his command. Warwick stood alone before the great house, his eyes narrowed. He had an old short sword on his hip, though it was a tool more than a weapon, a cleaver on a leather thong, hanging from his belt. He used it in the gardens to hack at old wood, but its hilt was a comfort. On impulse, he tugged it free and laid it against a bench close by, ready to be snatched up.

His worry swelled to panic when he saw that one of the riders was his brother George, the other Richard of Gloucester, already a much better horseman than the archbishop. Warwick's brother bounced and hung on for dear life, lucky not to have been thrown.

Warwick could feel his heart thumping as George Neville and the king's brother came to a halt, bringing a cloud of ochre dust that bloomed around and past them as they dismounted. Warwick coughed into his hand, his stomach clenching as he read their expressions.

'Is it the king?' he demanded.

Bishop George Neville nodded.

'Or his wife. Either way, they have found men willing to accuse you of treason. I believe we are ahead of the warrant for your arrest, but it cannot be more than a few hours behind us. I'm sorry, Richard.'

'George of Clarence is named as well,' Gloucester blurted out, his voice cracking. 'My brother. Will you take word to him?'

Warwick glanced at the young man who had been his ward. No longer a boy, Richard of Gloucester was grim-faced and pale, in a dusty shirt.

'How can I trust you, Richard,' Warwick said softly, 'with your brother's hand turned against me?'

'He brought the news to me,' the bishop said in reply. 'If not for him, the king's men would have reached you first.'

Warwick rubbed sweat from his face, making a quick decision. He had planned for disaster, even before releasing King Edward from his captivity. Ships and chests of coins had been taken to lands he owned in France, unknown to a soul on this side of the Channel and all ready for him to bolt if the word came. He had not expected his daughter's husband to be included in the accusation.

With his brother and Richard of Gloucester staring and waiting, Warwick forced himself to breathe and think, standing still. The coast was a two-day ride, to a fine sixty-foot boat he had waiting there, crewed by four men and ready at all hours. His daughter and her husband were at a beautiful estate house thirty miles to the south, waiting for Isabel's confinement to end and their first child to be born.

'Clarence has not been told?' he asked. His brother shook his head. 'Right. We can fetch him here, with Isabel. She will want her mother to be there as well, with the baby so close. It is not too far and there is more than one road. If the king has sent an army, they'll be slow. If he has sent just a few, we'll fight our way past them.' He held up a palm as the bishop began to reply. 'No, I won't leave my wife or my daughter to the mercy of Elizabeth Woodville. Have you sent a message to John?'

'I have,' his brother retorted, 'and I was not suggesting you leave Isabel or Anne. Send a rider to Clarence now, on a fresh horse. I have been hammered black by this saddle and I could not ride another thirty miles – a day on the road and the same back again? Lord, Richard, Edward's men will be here by then.'

Warwick cursed, trying to think.

'The quickest way would be to sail down the coast and then ride in to fetch them. I'll send a messenger on a fast horse even so, in the hope of gaining them a few hours of warning before I'm there to take them off. What about you, George? Are you coming?'

His brother glanced at the young Duke of Gloucester and shrugged.

'Neither Richard nor I have been named. My amnesty still holds. I don't think Edward cares much about me, though I dare say his wife still takes an interest. She is the Eve in this English garden, Richard. You should be wary of her.'

'I have had she-wolves snapping at my throat my whole life,' Warwick said. 'Good luck then, George. I would take it kindly if you would look after Mother. She is half-blind now and I do not know how much she still understands. She would appreciate your kindness, I am certain.'

The two brothers looked at each other, very aware that once they moved they might not see each other again for years, if ever again. George opened his arms and they embraced, gripping tightly. Warwick winced at the rasp of stubble over his cheek.

Richard, Duke of Gloucester, was standing nervously, an outsider with a deep colour to his cheeks. Warwick extended his hand and gripped his arm.

'For your part in bringing me this warning, you have my thanks. I will not forget it.'

'I know you for a good man,' Gloucester replied, looking at his feet.

Warwick blew air out in a great sigh.

'Not good enough, I think.' He smiled at the bishop for the last time. 'Your prayers would be very welcome, Brother.'

George Neville cut the sign of the cross into the air and Warwick bowed his head, then raced away back into the estate house.

*

For all the endless hours he had spent planning for the catastrophe of Edward hunting them, the result was nowhere near as smooth as Warwick had imagined. His boat crew had mysteriously been away from the craft and had to be roused out of a local tavern, half-drunk and sheepish. It seemed that so many weeks of readiness without actual duties had been too much for their discipline.

Once they were out at sea, Warwick's nerves had settled a little. No one knew where he was and he had only to reach his great ship *Trinity* in berth at Southampton to have a crew and soldiers, supplies and coin. It was no hardship to collect his daughter and her husband and then spend two days at sea in fine weather.

Isabel and Clarence had been waiting on the docks when the yacht dropped anchor. Warwick could only gape at the sheer size of Isabel as she was handed up from a tiny rowing boat over the side. His wife made her a place on the open bench, though there was no shade or protection from the spray. Isabel gripped her mother's hands and looked about her with dark, bruised-looking eyes, clearly terrified of the boat. Her husband had brought two great bags and not a single servant with them in his panic to get away. The young Duke of Clarence fussed around his wife and mother-in-law with blankets, making Isabel as comfortable as it was possible for her to be, so close to the end.

The crew of four were still abashed by their lack of readiness, though they'd had the sails rigged and bellied out in the wind in no time at all. The little boat left the shore behind once more and tacked back and forth down the coast. They were out and safe, with gulls screeching overhead and Isabel huddled against the breeze and spray, looking pale. Warwick tried to relax, but he found himself staring ahead as the crew settled down in turns to sleep. The sun dropped beyond the hills on his right side and he watched the moon rise and the stars turn for a long time. He had planned for it all and yet, as it unfolded before him, he dared not allow himself to feel the despair and anger it brought. Whether it was his own fault, or King Edward's or the Woodvilles', or his brother John's spite, it meant a breach. It meant an ending. Whatever else happened, he had lost more than he dared to dwell upon.

He had not sat still since the first news had reached him. Yet on the boat there was nowhere to go and nothing to do except wait for the sun to rise again. He could hear someone leaning over the stern and vomiting helplessly. In the darkness, unseen, Warwick closed his eyes and felt tears come.

34

In the morning, the little boat rounded the eastern edge of England and tacked against westerly winds down the coast to Southampton, to what was perhaps the best harbour and river mouth in the world for great ships. The Channel was busy as soon as there was light enough to see, with merchant cogs crossing from the continent and coming from as far off as the coasts of Africa. To gain entrance into the deep ports, they had to negotiate frightening shoals that required the services of an expert pilot. Small boats came out under sail to every merchant cog, ready to guide them in to the markets of England.

Warwick felt his spirits lift at the clusters of white sails, tight triangles and squares on a thousand different vessels. His own small yacht would surely go unremarked amongst so many, and he waited for the crew to tack in past the Isle of Wight.

The most senior of his men came clambering back to Warwick, moving easily with the roll of the yacht as the wind freshened. The sailor had the accent of Cornwall, one of that breed who knew the ways of the sea better than the land. He raised his voice to be heard, leaning close to Warwick and pointing into the body of water between the Isle and the mainland.

'Those ships at anchor there, sir, I know them. The black one is *Vanguard*; other is the *Norfolk*.'

Warwick's heart sank. He had heard the names before.

'Are you certain?' he said.

The sailor nodded. 'I am, sir. Before this jaunt, I was in *Trinity* at Southampton for six months. I know every ship on this coast, and those two are under the command of Anthony Woodville, king's admiral.'

'Can't we slip past them? This yacht could show them her heels.'

'See those boats in the water, my lord? They have the whole Solent blocked there. It's my feeling they know we might try to get in. They haven't picked us out from the other boats and ships, not yet. I believe they have men up in the yards looking, my lord.'

Warwick swallowed drily. It took no great imagination to see Anthony Woodville would move heaven and earth to capture them. With a better understanding, Warwick could see then how the smaller boats were rowed or sailed across the mouth of the Solent. Nothing afloat could pass through to the port of Southampton without being challenged and stopped, then boarded.

As he stood there, with a hand on the mast, staring across the blue, Isabel gave a great cry. Warwick jerked round, but his wife was there before him, pressing a cup of water to her lips and resting a hand on the swell of her womb under the cloth. As Warwick stared in dismay, he saw his wife snatch her hand away, as if something had bitten her.

'What was it? Did the child kick?' Warwick asked.

His wife Anne had gone ashen and shook her head.

'No, it was a tightening,' she said.

Isabel groaned, opening her eyes.

'Is it the child? Is it coming?' she asked plaintively.

Warwick forced himself to chuckle.

'Not at all! There are pangs sometimes, long before the

birth. I remember your mother was just the same. Isn't that so, Anne? For weeks before the day of birth.'

'Y-yes, yes, of course,' Isabel's mother said. She pressed her palm against Isabel's forehead and turned to Warwick where the daughter could not see, her eyes wide with alarm.

Warwick drew the crewman as far away as he could, right to the bowsprit, where they could see foaming waters rushing past.

'I need to get to a safe port,' Warwick murmured through clenched teeth.

'Not here, sir. The admiral's men will give chase the moment they know who we are.'

Warwick turned, looking over his shoulder. It was a clear day, but the coast of France was too far off to be seen.

'The wind is fresh enough. Can you reach Calais?'

As if to spur them on, Isabel gave another great cry then, her voice rising to a shriek like the gulls overhead. It seemed to make the crewman's mind up for him.

'If the westerly holds, I'll get you there, my lord. Twelve hours, no more.'

'Twelve!' Warwick said, loud enough to make his wife and Clarence look up questioningly. He dropped his voice, leaning in very close. 'The child could be here by then.'

The sailor shook his head in regret.

'At our best speed, we are as fast as anything afloat, but I cannot put on more sail than she can bear. Twelve hours would be a fine run, my lord – and that's if the wind blows steady. If I can better it, I will.'

'Are we going back to land, Richard?' Warwick's wife called. 'Isabel needs a safe, warm place.'

'There is none, not in England, not now, not with the

king's hand turned against us!' Warwick snapped, overcome with the demands on him. 'We will sail for Calais.'

The steering oar was pressed hard over and the sails
flapped as the prow swung, until they bellied out once
more on to the new tack.

Warwick took a turn steering, feeling the life in the craft as
it strained under his hand. Isabel's cries had grown more
pitiful with every passing hour, the effort of the contrac-
tions exhausting her. There was no longer any doubt as to
what they were. The baby was coming and the green coast
of France loomed ahead. The crew had been busy for the
entire day, tightening ropes and adjusting the twin sails by
the tiniest fraction to gain a little more speed. They cast
nervous glances at the red-faced young woman as they
passed, having never seen anything like it.

Ahead of him, Warwick saw the dark mass he knew as
well as his own estates. Indeed, Calais had been his home
for years before, when King Edward had been just a boy.
He could look over the fortress and the town with something like nostalgia. The day had remained clear and the
Channel had narrowed as they'd headed back up the coast
from Southampton, so that he could see the white cliffs of
Dover on one side, with France and freedom on the other.
Every passing moment took him closer to safety and yet
further from everything he loved and valued.

He was shaken from his reverie by his daughter as she
cried out, the sound sharper than before and longer. The
sailors did their best not to stare, but there was nowhere truly
private on that open boat. Isabel sat on the boards with her
legs apart, panting and holding her mother's hand on one
side and her husband's on the other. She was mortally afraid.

'It will not be long now,' Warwick said. 'Get in as close as you dare and drop anchor. Put my banner up high on the mast, so we are not delayed.'

'There is no deep keel on this craft, my lord,' the Cornishman replied. 'I could take her all the way in to the quays.'

Warwick looked across the crowded waters in desperation. Beyond them, the fortress rose in stone walls. He knew the exact number and weight of cannon shot they could fire. The fortress could not be besieged from the land side, because they could be supplied from the sea. They could not be attacked from the sea, because of the great cannon. Calais was the best-fortified English possession in the world and any craft daring to scorn her defences would be smashed into firewood. Even so, he considered it, wondering if he could shelter their approach behind other vessels and then dart for the docks before anyone guessed their intention.

'See those wisps of smoke?' he said bitterly. 'They have iron shot, heated to dull red in braziers, ready to be heaved out with tongs and dropped down the barrel on to a wet plug. They can strike a mile out to sea, and whatever they strike burns. We must wait for the harbourmaster.'

As he spoke, one of the crewmen hoisted his colours. The wind was growing stronger and the banner snapped out as the waves began to crown with white. The yacht rocked and dipped, snubbing the small anchor and wrenching at them all. Warwick held on to a rope that was like a piece of iron and stood on the railing, waving one arm back and forth to the shore to convey the urgency. Behind him, Isabel wept and cried out, biting her lip until blood showed and her cheeks were speckled with broken spots under the skin.

'The child is *coming*, Richard!' his wife called. 'Can't you land? Sweet Jesus and Mary preserve us. Can't you take us in?'

'They are coming out! Hold fast, Isabel. The master can signal the fortress guns and the wind is still in the right quarter. I'll call for a doctor to attend you . . .'

He turned to give new orders to the crew, but they were ready to cut the anchor rope and drop the sails once more. It would be crude work, but they were ready for his signal.

The yacht gave a great lurch and the wind howled, rising every moment and sending spray across them all. Dark clouds went scudding overhead and Isabel screamed. Warwick looked down to see his daughter's bare legs splayed wide. He caught a glimpse of the baby's head crowning and swallowed. His wife had given up all pretence of privacy and knelt on the boards, shivering in the sea spray, but determined and ready to take the tiny scrap of life into her hands.

Warwick watched the harbourmaster's boat making its slow way towards him. He imagined they could hear Isabel's cries, though they seemed in no hurry at all. Surely the sounds would carry across the water. They seemed so piercing to Warwick's ear that he thought the entire garrison would know there was a child being born.

When the harbourmaster's boat came within hailing distance, Warwick roared at the top of his lungs. He pointed up to the bear and staff at the tip of the mast, then called through cupped hands for a doctor to attend a birth. It was done and he sagged, panting and seeing white spots flash before his eyes from the effort. The wind was gusting like a mad thing, sending the ropes shivering and the tethered yacht surging up and down in great lurches, so that the horizon seemed to plunge and rise sickeningly.

Warwick started in confusion as the harbourmaster's skiff

kept coming, with no sign of a signal flag raised to the watchers in the fortress. He shouted again, pointing and waving, while the little boat came on under a scrap of sail, great sheets of salt water breaking over her prow. Warwick could see a man standing just as he was, holding on to a rope and swinging dangerously as he gestured in turn. The wind had risen still further and Warwick could not make out all the words. Rather than wait, he called again for a doctor, saying over and over that he was Warwick and there was a child being born. In the midst of his fury, he heard a high wail, stuttering and shrill. The wind dropped for a moment, fluky and gusting. He looked back and saw one of the sailors standing abashed, holding out a horn-handled knife for Isabel's mother to cut the cord and throw the caul into the sea.

Warwick stood swaying, his mouth open and his mind blank. There was blood on the deck, spreading with the spray that hammered at them, so that it ran into the cracks of the old wood and raced down the planks. Isabel had been covered up again under blankets. He watched as Anne pushed the tiny child under Isabel's shirt, not to feed, but just to feel the warmth and get out of the biting wind and damp air.

'A girl, Richard!' his wife called back. 'A daughter!'

It was a moment of wonder and when he turned once more to the port, he saw the harbourmaster's skiff had come dangerously close. There were only four men on board and he recognized the fellow who had welcomed Clarence and Isabel once before, when they had come to be married. The man had been all smiles and gentle laughter then. In the cold, his stare was hard.

Warwick called to him even so, now that they were close enough to speak over the wind.

'A child has been born, sir. I will need a doctor to tend

my daughter. And an inn with a good fire and hot mulled wine as well.'

'I'm sorry, my lord. I have orders from the new Captain of Calais, Sir Anthony Woodville. You may not land, my lord. If it were up to me, I would allow it, but my orders were sealed by King Edward. I cannot go against them.'

'Where *would* you have me land?' Warwick demanded in despair. Wherever he turned, it seemed the queen's brother had been there before him. Warwick was close enough to see the Calais man hunch his shoulders at the pain in his voice. He filled his lungs and howled again across the waves and spray. 'Listen to me! We have a child born on deck not minutes past, my grandchild! No, King Edward's *niece*! Born at sea — your orders be damned, sir! We are coming in. Cut that damned anchor!'

His sailors sliced the line and the yacht turned immediately, going from a bobbing piece of flotsam on an anchor rope to a live thing the instant it parted. Warwick could see the harbourmaster gesturing, waving him off, but he nodded to his men and they heaved out enough sail to give them steering way. The yacht's motion steadied as she sliced through the waters.

A double crack sounded from the dark mass of the fortress on the shore, for all the world like a crow crouched over a corpse. Warwick could not see the flight of the heated shot, but he saw where they fell. Both smacked into the sea around them, aimed no doubt when they had made such a fine target at anchor. He knew the cannon crews practised on anchored boats bought as hulks. He had overseen such work himself.

The second ball came close enough to make Anne shriek and Clarence clutch his pale wife to him in fear. The

433

ball missed the yacht but they could hear a furious bubbling as it gave up its heat. Around them came a strong smell of hot iron, rising from the depths.

'*Richard!*' his wife called. 'Take us away, please! They will not let us land. We cannot force our way to the dock. *Please!*'

Warwick stared out, knowing the next shots could smash the yacht to pieces and kill everyone on board. He could still not believe they had fired upon him, with his banner on the mast. His men were waiting on his word, their eyes wild. He raised his hand and they moved, the yacht swinging round and the sails going slack. It might have saved them as the cannon sounded again, the report cracking across the sea. The dull red balls fell short, with plumes of steam hissing upwards while Warwick's crew heaved them back and the yacht steadied once more.

'What course, my lord?' the Cornish sailor called.

Warwick walked the length of the boat, looking back as Calais began to dwindle behind them.

'It seems there is no loyalty left in England now,' he said bitterly. 'Follow the coast to Honfleur and then the river into Paris. I believe I have one or two friends there who might aid us in our hour of need.'

He started as Isabel gave a wail, a sound of such pain that was as much the moan of a wounded animal as anything he had heard before. Warwick crossed to her and saw how she had opened her blouse to see the tiny babe within. It was unmoving, the wrinkled skin faintly blue. Isabel had felt the coldness grow against her skin and now she tried to feed her breast into a mouth that was still. She put her head back and shrieked out her grief until George of Clarence pressed her into his shoulder and held both the mother and his dead daughter, tears wracking him in great heaves.

Epilogue

Warwick could smell the city of Paris as he waited in the corridor. Unlike the Palace of Westminster, built along the river from London so that it would benefit from sweeter breezes, the Louvre was right at the heart of the French capital. The result was that it was practically unusable in summer months, when poisonous miasmas rose from the overcrowded streets and the entire French court packed up and moved to the country. There was still a sense of chaos in the hundreds of rooms he had passed, as staff polished and swept, opening windows to let light and air flood back into shuttered cloisters.

He sat on a bench in a small alcove, resting his head against a statue much older than Christ, of some Greek with a tightly curled beard. His daughter had withdrawn into herself, hardly speaking even to her husband Clarence. The two of them had been inconsolable as they buried the tiny child in a French field, a niece of an English king. The grave had been marked and Warwick had sworn to bring the box back to England when they were free to do so, for a proper tomb and service. It was all he had been able to offer.

A door opened, interrupting his thoughts so that he sat straight and then stood as King Louis came out, looking for him. Warwick knelt as the French king wiped his hands with a cloth. The king's fingers were dark with ink and he eyed them dubiously as he took Warwick's arm.

'Richard, I have heard of your tragedies. I left my work with these new presses, these printing machines that replace a dozen monks with just three men and a contraption! I am so sorry, both for you and your son-in-law, for your daughter. Did she name the child?'

'Anne,' Warwick said, in a whisper.

'It is a terrible thing. I have experienced it in too many ways, too often to bear. The dead children who cannot even go to heaven without baptism! It is a cruelty, too much. And your King Edward! To allow such accusations to stand against his earl and his own brother! It is incredible. I offer you my hospitality with my sympathy, of course, anything you require.'

'Thank you, Your Majesty. That means a great deal to me. I have funds and some small property . . .'

'*Pfui!* I will sign a thousand livres to you for your expenses. You and your companions are my guests, friends to this house. There are entire floors unused in this palace, my lord. There are worse places to grieve than Paris, I think. It is up to you, of course. I merely offer and advise.'

Warwick was genuinely touched and bowed once again to show his pleasure at such generous treatment. The king bowed back, solemnly.

'I hope you will take up residence in this place, Richard. You would not be alone.' The king paused, pressing his finger across both of his lips. 'I should tell you, perhaps. You were a gentleman before, when I was so crude as to presume on your good manners. It was wrong of me to force you into the presence of one who might have made you uncomfortable.'

'Queen Margaret, Your Majesty?' Warwick asked, following the stream of words with a little difficulty.

'Of course, Margaret, with that brigand she calls Derry Brewer, who claims to speak no French at all, but listens most acutely to what is said in front of him.'

'I don't follow, Your Majesty,' Warwick said.

King Louis faced him squarely.

'Milady Margaret of Anjou is once again my guest, Richard. I would not want you to be uncomfortable, though she spoke well of you after you met here before. Her son accompanies her also. Perhaps you will find it in you to tell the boy another tale or two about his father.' The king stared at Warwick's eyes as if he could see through to the man behind them. 'If it is not possible, I understand. You have suffered as much as any man. Betrayed by your king, a granddaughter dying at sea before your eyes. Would the child have lived if you had not been forced to run? Of course, of course. It is too cruel.'

King Louis wiped at his eyes, though Warwick had not seen a trace of tears there.

'You know, Richard, there are some who never truly accepted Edward of York as king. A king must lead, of course, but not just on the battlefield, do you see? It is his role to encourage his lords, to create a rising tide that lifts all the ships, not just his own. Perhaps I should arrange another fine lunch for you to tell Margaret and her son all that has happened. Would that be agreeable, my lord? It would please me. King Henry is still alive in the Tower, yes? Still well?'

'He is the same,' Warwick replied. He felt a surge of anger at the manipulation, then shrugged it away. He had been cast out of England, left to rot like Margaret of Anjou before him. What if there was a way back?

'Ah, I am pleased,' King Louis said. 'His wife tells me

that he has no will of his own, poor man. Such tragedy. Yet you have met his son. Quite the Tartar! If you agree to see the lad again, I think you will be amazed at how he has grown in just a few years. He has a more royal bearing, if you follow me. If you agree, Richard?'

Warwick bowed a third time. Margaret was responsible for the execution of his father. He had imagined her death a thousand times, though less so in later years, when she had been so far from his thoughts. He nodded, finding that the embers had grown cool and he could put aside an old anger at last. Now that he had discovered a new one.

He had felt despair as he buried the body of his grand-daughter. The French king's words brought a lamp into that deep and inner darkness, giving him hope.

'Of course I will meet Queen Margaret and her son,' Warwick said. 'It would be a great honour.'

Louis was peering closely at him, and whatever he saw brought a gleam to the king's eye.

'Who could bear a life without challenge, without perils, Richard? Not I! I sense it in you also. While we are all young, why should we not live? Like birds of prey, without regret or too much fear of what lies ahead. I tell you I would rather reach and fall than sit and dream. Is it not the same for you?'

Warwick smiled, feeling his black depression begin to ease, affected by the man's sense of delight in the world.

'It is, Your Majesty,' he said.

Historical Note

Gens Boreae, gens perfidiae, gens prompta rapinae

'Northern people, treacherous people, people
quick to steal.'

Abbot Whethamstede, turning a neat
Latin phrase to describe Margaret's army

After the battle at Sandal Castle in December 1460, known
now as the battle of Wakefield, four heads were taken to be
spiked on the walls of the city of York. The Duke of York
was one, wearing a paper crown to show his empty ambition.
The second was Earl Salisbury, father to Warwick. The third
head belonged to York's son, the seventeen-year-old Edmund,
Earl of Rutland. Finally, with terrible symmetry, the fourth
head belonged to Salisbury's son, Sir Thomas Neville. Sir
Thomas was also seventeen and, for plot reasons, I chose not
to place yet another young Neville man in the same battle.
The danger of this period is always that there are too many
cousins, daughters, sons and uncles to keep a main line of
plot moving. Some, who play no major part, must fall away. It
is interesting to note, however, how many of the lords at
Towton had *very* personal reasons to seek vengeance.

Salisbury's two main titles passed to his sons: Salisbury
to Warwick and Montagu to John Neville. John Neville

became Earl Northumberland for some time, but was later forced to return that title to the Percy heir by Edward IV. The Montagu title was bumped up to a Marquess to compensate John Neville, though I suspect nothing ever really could. The rank of marquess, somewhere between an earl and a duke, is a rare creation, little known in England – with notable and famous exceptions such as the Marquess of Queensberry, who codified boxing, and the modern Marquess of Bath, who owns the stately home of Longleat, Cheddar Gorge and around ten thousand acres.

John Neville was indeed captured by Queen Margaret's forces for a time, but was still a prisoner in York until Edward entered the city after Towton, so did not fight in that battle.

In regard to the extraordinary event of 1461, when London refused entry to the queen, the king and the Prince of Wales, the key to it does appear to be the fear of northerners. It is true that Margaret's army had been allowed to steal and butcher and burn their way down the country – without pay, the leash was off. At that time, northerners spoke a thick dialect that would have been almost unrecognizable to London ears. (Abbot Whethamstede described it as sounding like dogs barking.) Londoners would have feared the Scots in Margaret's army even more – true 'savages' from what was then an unimaginably distant and unknown country. The sense of a foreign invader is difficult to comprehend today, but having Scots in her army did Margaret no favours in public perception.

Sir Henry Lovelace did in fact play a part in the run-up to the second battle of St Albans. Warwick created the most ornate defences, all facing north, only to have the queen's army swing west to Dunstable and then strike Warwick's army in the rear left square, working their way to the centre force. Although Derry Brewer is a fictional character, once again, someone like him must have existed to have gathered this sort of useful information. Lovelace may have been promised an earldom for passing on the details. It is true that he was one of Warwick's close retinue. I changed his name to Sir Arthur Lovelace as I had another Henry in Earl Percy, one more in Henry Beaufort, the Duke of Somerset – and, of course, King Henry himself. With all the Richards and quite a few Edwards, it does seem at times as if the noblemen of medieval England chose their names from just half a dozen, in a hat.

After the second battle of St Albans in 1461, that disastrous rout, the Yorkist side had lost their control of King Henry – and with it, a large part of their authority and how they were perceived. They needed another king and Edward Plantagenet was in the right frame of mind to reach for a crown. As daring military decisions of history go, it would be the turning point in the York fortunes. It took slightly more careful managing than I have described, led by Bishop George Neville, who became a vital player for his show of support from the Church. It was Bishop Neville who declaimed Edward's rights to rule in London on 1 March. Excited captains ran across the city, carrying the news that Edward of York was to be king. A slightly more formal 'Great Council' met at Baynard's Castle on the bank of the Thames on 3 March. The entire process was put together in an incredibly short time and owes its success to sheer audacity – and London's rejection of the house of Lancaster. The city had chosen sides when they refused to let King Henry enter. They had no choice at all but to back York.

On 4 March 1461, Edward made his coronation oath in Westminster Hall. From that moment, supporters and vital funds flooded in. London bankers lent him £4,048 to go with a previous £4,666 13s 4d. Individual loans were also made, from private individuals and religious houses in the city. Soldiers expected to be paid, fed and equipped.

On 6 March, Edward sent proclamations to the sheriffs of thirty-three English counties, as well as major cities such as Bristol and Coventry. Lords and commons came to fight for Edward Plantagenet at the same time as even greater numbers and twenty-eight lords were joining King Henry and Lancaster in the north. As nothing else, this explains why Edward declared himself king. From that day on, he assumed the power and authority of the Crown over feudal lords and their followers.

The speed at which such large armies gathered is impressive by modern terms. By the much slower medieval standard, this was a vast and *furious* rush to battle. It would have taken Edward's army eight or nine days to march one hundred and eighty miles to Towton. The first skirmish was on 27/28 March at Ferrybridge, involving Edward, Fauconberg and Warwick – and the death of Clifford as he tried to reach the safety of the main force and was run down and killed by an arrow in the throat.

On 29 March 1461 – Palm Sunday – in a driving snow-storm, the battle lines of Towton came together. What followed is certainly the bloodiest battle on English soil. Historical estimates run as high as twenty-eight thousand dead, as reported by George Neville, bishop and chancellor, in a letter written nine days after the battle. That is around eight thousand higher than the first day of the Somme in 1916. It is worth noting that in the First World War, modern weapons existed, such as the mounted machine gun. At Towton, every man who died was cut by arrow, or sword, or mace, or billhook, or axe. The river ran red for three days afterwards.

Reports of the numbers fighting vary enormously, from the most likely estimates of sixty thousand to hundreds of thousands. The death toll was around one per cent of a population of just three million. In impact on the society, then, it would be the equivalent of a battle with six to seven *hundred thousand* dead today. In all the extraordinary tapestry of English and, later, British history, Towton stands out.

The name of Towton comes from the village nearby. The old road to London ran through it and it was better known than Saxton, though the battle was fought about halfway between them, in a place now known as 'Bloody Meadow'. I recommend a visit. It is a bleak place. The steep flanks of Cock Beck are daunting enough on their own. In snow, for men in armour, they would have been an impossible obstacle for Lancastrians trying to retreat. Towton has become the established name of that terrible slaughter, though in the past it was known as York Field, Sherburn-in-Elmet (a town to the south), Cockbridge and Palm Sunday Field.

Note on weapons: billhooks, pollaxes and swords. The word 'broadsword' was not used at all in the fifteenth century. It came in much later to distinguish medieval swords from eighteenth- and nineteenth-century duelling swords.

With individually crafted weapons such a key part of a knight's kit, there were almost as many descriptive names as blades.

One medieval weapon in common use was the falchion, a single-edged cutlass very much like a modern machete, in that it was wide-bladed and top-heavy. Untrained working men called by Writs or Commissions of Array would do better with good, solid weapons of this sort.

The billhook and the pollaxe (or poleaxe) are similar in many respects, though the main blade of a billhook usually had a single point to pierce armour and the pollaxe used a crescent axe blade, and often a hammer on the opposite side. Both weapons often bore bayonet-style spikes and they are similar in the sense that they were three to five pounds of sharp steel bound to an axe-handle or longer pike-handle. Nicely weighted, they would have been devastating in the hands of untrained farmers and townsmen – men who were very familiar, however, with chopping tools. The billhook was used more in England than the pollaxe, though both found their way into the hands of the armies at Towton. Some of the crushed and broken skulls found in burial pits in that area can only have come from multiple, enraged blows – six or ten delivered with a pollaxe, say, to a body long dead. The level of savagery is comparable to a frenzied stabbing. Violent killing is clearly difficult to stop, once begun.

I hope I have described the main events of Towton accurately. Lord Fauconberg's contact with the Lancaster lines is an example of how a good commander needs to respond to factors like changing weather and terrain. Under Fauconberg's orders, archers loosed thousands of shafts and then immediately fell back out of range. In heavy snow, with visibility down to almost nothing, the Lancaster lines replied blind, wasting precious shafts. Fauconberg's men gleefully collected those shafts – and sent them back. The Lancastrian lines suffered brutal losses in that one action – certainly thousands. They were stung into attack and the two armies crashed together.

Fauconberg used both wind and poor visibility to annihilate enemy positions, even before the main forces came together. His name is almost unknown compared with his nephew Warwick, but it is not too much of a stretch to say that Fauconberg was probably the better tactician. He lived just a few years after Towton, though I kept him alive a little longer into Part Two, for Warwick to consult, and also because I liked him.

As is so often the case with turning points of history, luck and the weather played a vital part. In the case of Towton, fortune favoured Edward of York. Norfolk's right wing getting lost and falling behind turned out to be the key factor in breaking Lancastrian spirit. Norfolk never claimed to have planned the action, so we must assume it was as it seemed – a complete disaster, turning into a late arrival that was every bit as decisive as Blücher turning up at Waterloo. Eight or nine thousand fresh soldiers appearing on a flank would have been crushing to the fighting spirit of those who thought they were holding well. In the snow and the dark, it broke the forces of Lancaster – and the routed men drowned or were slaughtered as they tried to escape, crushed and beaten.

Historical fiction is often a struggle between the desire to tell the main story and the desire to reveal extraordinary side stories – at least in my experience. It is very common for me to learn of some scene which I simply cannot fit into the story arc. A novel must not bog down. My Part Two begins in 1464 and, in doing so, omits the attempt by Margaret in 1462 to take back the kingdom. It could easily be a book on its own. In exchange for mortgages on Calais, Margaret brokered with the French king for forty-three ships and eight hundred soldiers to support troops still loyal in England. She picked up King Henry from Scotland, made an armed landing and retook castles like Alnwick in Northumberland. Moving swiftly, Margaret took her fleet back to sea – where it was wrecked in a sudden storm. Margaret's ship limped into Berwick and she escaped once again to France. Her father, René of Anjou, allowed her to live on a small estate in the Duchy of Bar, and she remained there with some two hundred supporters in poverty: the pitiful remainder of the Lancaster court. Margaret never lost hope, despite the sort of setback that would have broken many.

After betrayal, Henry was eventually captured in 1465 and taken to the Tower of London by Warwick. There is no record of him writing letters or poetry or anything at all. I suspect Henry was a broken figure by that time, an empty vessel. Five members of Edward IV's household were paid well to wait on King Henry and others were brought in as needed. A priest, William Kymberley, celebrated Mass with him every day of his confinement. Henry's solace, as always, lay in faith and prayer.

There is also no record of ill-treatment. A later text suggested the king endured torture, as part of an attempt to have Henry recognized as a saint. There is no proof either way, but records do exist of new clothes being fitted as well as wine sent from the royal cellars. At a later stage, there is a suggestion that Henry had become unkempt, possibly filthy, but it is most likely that he was by that point seriously mentally ill and unable or unwilling to look after himself. How that affects the judgement of Margaret in leaving him behind is a matter for discussion. It has turned some against her in the intervening centuries. It is only my own opinion, but I do not judge her too harshly for not loving a man who brought her so much pain and was never truly a husband to her.

Elizabeth Woodville came to court in 1465, with five brothers, two sons and seven unwed sisters. Older than Edward, of no great house, a widow with sons, it is true that Edward married her in secret and admitted as much to Warwick only while he was in the process of negotiating for a French bride.

Like the Nevilles before her, Elizabeth Woodville set about seeding her family into every noble house in England, so creating and shoring up support in the most powerful families of the realm. The marriage of John Woodville (nineteen) to the Dowager Duchess of Norfolk (sixty-five) was obviously an attempt to gain the title, part of the seven great marriages arranged by Elizabeth Woodville in the two years after being crowned queen consort. The Duke of Norfolk who had fought at Towton had died in 1461. He did in fact have a son, who was alive at the point of the 'Diabolical Marriage'. That duke died suddenly, however, leaving only one daughter, so the title fell into disuse. If John Woodville had survived the Wars of the Roses, he could well have ended up as the duke and been free to marry again.

Beyond the seven great marriages, various titles came

flowing down from the generosity of King Edward to his wife's family. Her brother Anthony Woodville married the daughter of Baron Scales, the man who had poured wildfire on to the crowds of London. In doing so, Anthony Woodville inherited the title. Under Edward, he also became a knight of the Garter, Lord of the Isle of Wight, Lieutenant of Calais and Captain of the King's Armada, to name but a few. Elizabeth Woodville's father became the king's treasurer and Earl Rivers.

King Edward was a man given to grand gestures and extraordinary generosity. He had made John Neville Earl of Northumberland, but as part of the trimming of the Neville vine, he forgave and then restored the Percy heir, taking the young Henry Percy from the Tower and returning him to his family estates. The idea that Henry Percy might have passed some of the intervening time with Warwick is my own invention. However, Richard of Gloucester, later King Richard III, spent some years growing up at Middleham and was apparently happy there.

It is interesting to note that the removal of the Great Seal from Archbishop George Neville went as I have described it, with the king and armed men riding to an inn at Charing Cross to demand it. It is unlikely that King Edward expected an armed response, but it does show how far his wife's influence had turned him against the Neville family. The name 'Charing Cross' may be a corruption of 'Chère Reine' (Dear Queen) Cross, named after the commemorative crosses raised by Edward I after the death of his beloved wife Eleanor. Or that story could have been conflated with 'Cierring', an Anglo-Saxon word for a bend in a road or river. History truly is a collection of stories – and sometimes a mingling of fact and fiction.

It is also true that Edward sent Warwick to France and then concluded a deal of trade and mutual military support with Burgundy, then an autonomous dukedom, while Warwick was away. It can never be known if Edward might have accepted King Louis XI as his ally. From the start, the English king seemed to favour the dukes of Burgundy and Brittany – anyone, in fact, who was willing to snub the French court. It is speculation, but Edward had been successful on battlefields in Wales and at Towton. It is not beyond belief that the warrior-king of England dreamed of another Agincourt and winning back lands so recently lost.

A Burgundian delegation came to England and were there much flattered and praised. Anthony Woodville fought a famous, violent, two-day demonstration joust with their champion, the man splendidly named 'the Bastard of Burgundy'. In Paris, Warwick was humiliated once again – and more importantly, King Louis had been publicly scorned. The French king who had earned his nickname of 'the Universal Spider', began to consider the problem of Edward and how to solve it.

It is true that Margaret of Anjou spent some time in Paris around this period. It is not known if she and Warwick had any contact at this stage.

For Warwick, the years of Edward's marriage to Elizabeth Woodville had resulted in a string of personal and public humiliations. The final straw was King Edward forbidding George, Duke of Clarence, from marrying Isabel Neville. From Warwick's point of view, it was a perfect match, a rise in status to offset the extraordinary wealth of his

449

daughter's inheritance. For King Edward, it was a union that could have produced sons to threaten his heirs. The house of York had risen to rule over an older line: he could not possibly let George, Duke of Clarence, create *another* royal bloodline that was wealthier than his own.

In addition, it is reasonable to suppose that Elizabeth would rather have found a Woodville for Isabel Neville, perhaps one of her sons. Age difference was clearly not an issue and letting such a plum as the Warwick fortune fall into another's hands was never going to happen with Elizabeth's consent. The only way left was for Warwick, Clarence and Isabel to defy King Edward. They travelled to Calais and Warwick's daughter married George of Clarence in 1469, against Edward's wishes and command.

In the first two books, I have tried to explore the sheer awe felt by some for the person of the king of England. It is the only thing that explains why King Henry remained alive despite being captured by York and held for months at a time. Yet it is also true of human nature that 'awe' is less likely when one has witnessed a boy growing up and becoming king. No man is a prophet in his own home – and Warwick was sufficiently exasperated with Edward and his wife to throw it all into the air and arrange Edward's capture and imprisonment. The history is slightly more complex, though the essence is that they incited and encouraged rebellion in the north to draw Edward out – and then ambushed him. George Neville, Archbishop of York, was indeed part of that capture, as was John Neville, then Marquess Montagu. It is true that Elizabeth Woodville's father, Earl Rivers, and her brother, Sir John Woodville, were both executed after a rough mockery of a trial. The Neville family had been robbed and battered. Their revenge was both spectacular and savage.

The exact length of Edward IV's captivity is unknown, but for the summer of 1469, Richard Neville, Earl Warwick, had *two* kings of England in his custody. Henry of Lancaster was in the Tower of London; Edward of York was in Warwick Castle and Middleham Castle. That unbelievable situation was what earned Richard Neville, Earl Warwick, the name of 'Kingmaker', above all else. He must have assumed he would benefit from imprisoning Edward, though his true intentions can never be known. Was it to put George of Clarence on the throne? To restore King Henry? There were a number of options and Warwick chose none of them because the country went up in flames. After an entire life seeing Henry reduced to an unloved and useless pawn, it is not so surprising, but Warwick *completely* misjudged the public response.

Rebellions, murders, arson and civil unrest spread across the country with extraordinary speed. Elizabeth Woodville had something to do with it, without a doubt, but there were also tens of thousands of soldiers who had fought with Edward at Towton. Only nine years later, they were still alive and did not take kindly to Edward being imprisoned.

Warwick had vastly overreached. In September 1469, he came to Edward and offered him his release in exchange for a complete pardon and amnesty for everything that had happened before. Edward had always been a man of his word and Warwick clearly trusted him and believed the deal would hold. To a modern reader, it is quite surprising that he honestly thought it would, or perhaps he just had no other choice.

I suspect the extent of anti-Neville unrest would not have been recorded by Warwick or anyone else. He could easily have been at his wit's end and in fear of his life. For once, his huge number of estates estates proved a burden, impossible to protect against organized attacks, vulnerable to night burnings and local unrest. I imagine Warwick had few choices left when he decided to trust Edward's word and release the king.

It is to Edward's credit that he did *not* break the pardon and amnesty he granted. From five centuries on, it is impossible to know if what happened next was a plan to find a loophole in the pardon, or something new. After a few months of peace, Lancastrian rebels apparently named Warwick and George of Clarence as traitors, though we will never know for sure if those were true accusations. The country was still simmering with unrest and dozens of small uprisings. This was new information – and potentially a crime not covered by the amnesty Edward had agreed before. He duly ordered the capture of both men – and they chose to run for the coast with Isabel, then in the last stages of pregnancy. Warwick's first plan was to reach his great ship *Trinity*, berthed in Southampton. He was blocked from reaching it by Anthony Woodville, by then an admiral for Edward of York. Warwick, his wife Anne, George, Duke of Clarence, and Isabel, Duchess of Clarence all took a smaller ship to France. Crucially, Edward had already sent word to far-flung commanders that Warwick and Clarence were to be refused all aid, vital letters that were sent to both Ireland and the fortress of Calais.

They were forbidden entry to Calais by the garrison

there. The four of them were left stranded, trapped at sea with both England and France blocked to them. Isabel gave birth on board and it is true that the infant girl was either stillborn or died in the spray and the cold, Warwick's first grandchild. His reaction and his rage over these events would drive him into the arms of Margaret of Anjou – and shake England to the foundations.

Conn Iggulden
London, 2015

The Paston Letters

The Paston Letters are a collection of over a thousand letters and documents from the fifteenth and early sixteenth centuries. The majority concern the work and personal relationships of generations of the Paston family in Norfolk, but amongst them can be found strange and intriguing gems such as the will of Sir John Fastolf (the inspiration for Shakespeare's Falstaff), otherwise unknown poems of the period and letters between key figures involved in the Wars of the Roses. Altogether, they are an endlessly fascinating resource, from the earliest surviving Valentine letter in the English language to the grim report of the dead at Towton.

The Paston family themselves were upwardly mobile in a way that is quite recognisable. They were all hard-working and clever – famously so, in fact. Not for nothing is it said in Norfolk: 'There was never a Paston poor, a Heydon a coward, or a Cornwallis a fool.'

The grandfather, Clement Paston, was a peasant farmer in Norfolk, working just a hundred acres. Though he had very little income, he paid for his son William to be educated. William Paston became a lawyer, then a Justice of the Peace, a Member of Parliament and a Norfolk landowner in his own right. His son, Sir John Paston Senior, also became a London lawyer. He attended the court of Edward IV, managed estates for Sir John Fastolf and was a man of some influence himself. Descendants of the original Pastons would become earls and one would marry a daughter of King Charles II.

The letters begin just after the 1415 battle of Agincourt and end with the reign of Henry VII and the Tudors. Their range,

1422–1509, covers the Wars of the Roses, from the outbreak of violence at St Albans in 1455, to the crown changing hands at Bosworth in 1485. As an insight into the society and values of the day, they form a priceless bank of information and evidence: of fifteenth-century language and vocabulary, of manners, laws, sermons, clothing and furniture – and occasionally gossipy commentary on some of the key events of the century. At times, they are the only source.

In the intervening centuries, the Paston Letters passed through the hands of a number of individuals. The first printed selection of letters was published in 1787, with more complete editions produced in the nineteenth century. The famous six-volume set edited by James Gairdner was published in 1904. Most of the originals are held today by the British Museum in London and can be viewed on a day pass.

As a personal side note, one of the difficulties encountered in writing a series about the Wars of the Roses has been the small field of names. There are simply too many Johns, Edwards and Richards for comfort. Sir John Paston Senior was not a major player in the Wars, but he must have noticed the lack of variety in names. He would not be outdone. He had five sons who lived to adulthood. He called two of them John. Both of those John Pastons fought at the battle of Barnet – though, as a slight consolation from my point of view, only one had been knighted.

What follows is a short selection of the letters. For the most part, I have rewritten the spelling and found more easily recognisable alternatives to archaic words such as 'wete' for 'know'. I have also added breaks and paragraphs. When paper was a luxury, original lines were usually crammed in, with little spacing. There will always be indecipherable references, of course, when two people who know their own business and friends well do not go to the trouble of explaining a note or a name. Some of the letters also concern matters of law being undertaken by the Pastons – wills and deeds and so on. These are of less interest. Yet despite the gaps, despite the *unbelievable* spelling, they present a very personal picture of a distant century, sometimes obscure and sometimes surprisingly familiar.

I have left the last letter untouched because I find the spelling intriguing, with its clues to the Norfolk accent of the time, and because I know I have readers who will enjoy reading the originals, perhaps aloud.

1. William Paston and Thomas Players to John Paston. 4 April 1461[1]

Despite it being the bloodiest battle ever fought on British soil, there are actually very few fifteenth-century sources that mention Towton. Each one is therefore immensely valuable when it comes to understanding what happened on that brutal day, in the snowstorm of 29 March 1461.

To my master, John Paston, in haste.

Please you to learn of such tidings as my Lady of York[2] has, by a letter of credentials under the seal of our sovereign lord King Edward, which came to our said lady this same day, Easter Even [4 April] at 11 o'clock and was seen and read by me, William Paston.

First, our sovereign lord has won the field[3], and upon the Monday next after Palm Sunday, he was received into York with great solemnity and processions. And the Mayor and Commons of the said city made their request for grace for the city to Lord Montagu and Lord Berners. Before the King came into the city, they desired of him mercy for the city, which he granted them.

On the King's part is slain Lord Fitzwater, and Lord Scrope is sore hurt. Sir John Stafford and Sir Robert Horne of Kent were killed; and Humphrey Stafford, William Hastings made knights with others; Blont is knighted &c [etc].

1 Letter 450 in Gairdner 1904.
2 'Lady of York' was Duchess Cecily, mother of King Edward IV.
3 At the battle of Towton.

On the contrary part is killed Lord Clifford, Lord Neville, Lord Welles, Lord Willoughby, Antony Lord Scales[4], Lord Harry, and to be supposed the Earl of Northumberland, Captain Andrew Trollop, with many other gentlemen and commons to the number of 20,000.

Item: King Harry, the Queen, the Prince, Duke of Somerset, Duke of Exeter and Lord Roos have fled in to Scotland and they be chased and followed &c. We sent no sooner to you because we had no certainties until now; for unto this day London was as sorry city as might. And because Spordauns had no certain tidings, we thought you should take them at their worth till more certain.

Item: Thorp Waterfield is yielding, as Spordauns can tell you. And Jesus bring you success. We pray that these tidings my mother may know.

By your Brother, W. PASTON
T. PLAYTERS

On a piece of paper attached to the above letter is the following list of noblemen and knights slain at Towton.

Comes Northumbriae [Earl of Northumbria]
Comes Devon [Earl of Devon]
Dominus de Beamunde [Lord or Baron Beaumont]
Dominus de Clifford
Dominus de Nevyll
Dominus de Dacre
Dominus Henricus de Bokyngham [Henry of Buckingham]
Dominus de Welles

4 This is incorrect – an early report, revised in the next letter. Anthony Woodville, Earl Rivers and Baron Scales, died in 1483.

Dominus de Scales: Antony Revers.
Dominus de Wellughby
Dominus de Malley: Radulfus Bigot Miles

Knights
Sir Rauff Gray
Sir Ric. Jeney
Sir Harry Bekingham
Sir Andrew Trollop
With xxviij ml [28,000: i and j interchangeable until 18th
    century] nomberd by Harralds [Numbered or counted by
    Heralds]

2. THOMAS PLAYTERS TO MASTER JOHN PASTON. 18 APRIL 1461[5]

With no mass communication of any kind, private letters are
sometimes the only surviving reports of major historical
events. Here, two weeks have passed since Towton and the
country is still rife with rumour and gossip. Thomas Playters
struggles to confirm or deny the tales he hears.

To my master, John Paston, Esquire.

Please your Mastership to know, that I have spoken with
Essex, in the matter you know well, and find him well disposed
to the idea, not withstanding he will not allow an ending, till
the chief baron[6] be come to London, and that he be made
privy to the matter, which we look after this second Saturday

5 Letter 451 in Gairdner 1904.
6 The 'Chief Baron' was the Foremost Judge of the Exchequer – the Court
of Common Law.

after Easter – and as for Nottingham, he has not yet come to London.

Item: As for news, it is said in truth by worshipful men that the Earl of Wiltshire is taken prisoner. Doctor Morton[7] and Doctor Makerell were also brought to the king at York. Master William spoke with a man who saw them.

Item: Sir, I heard from Sir John Borceter and Christopher Hanson that Harry the sext[8] is in a place in Yorkshire called Coroumber, or something like it. And there is siege laid about and diverse squires of the Earl of Northumberland who gathered together five or six thousand men to interfere with the siege, that meanwhile Harry the sexte might have stolen away by a little postern gate around the back side – at which clash 3,000 men of the north were killed.

Sir Robert of Ocle and Conyrs lays the siege on our side. Some say the Queen, Somerset and the Prince should be there.[9]

Item: It is now told as true that the Earl of Northumberland is dead. Item: The Earl of Devonshire is dead by justice [beheaded]. Item: My Lord Chancellor is at York. Item: The King and the Lords won't come here until Whitsuntide[10], so they say. Item: Sir, upon the arrival of the chief baron, I shall send you a letter, with God's grace, who preserve you and have you in His blessed keeping.

Your, THOMAS PLAYTERS.

---

7 Dr John Morton would later be Cardinal for King Henry VII and a mentor to St Thomas More.
8 Henry VI.
9 This was all rumour. Henry VI, Queen Margaret and their son had escaped to Scotland.
10 Seventh Sunday after Easter – later May/June.

[PS] At Cockermouth was the Earl of Wiltshire taken and those doctors. Item: Some men say Lord Welles, Lord Willoughby and Scales are alive. Item: Sir Robert Veer is slain in Cornewayll, which is believed to be true.

3. Dame Elizabeth Brews to John Paston. February 1477[11]

In this letter, a young John Paston's future mother-in-law is writing to him about his relationship with her daughter Margery. She refers to her daughter's enthusiasm for John – and follows that with a request that he be reasonable on the subject of his expectations. John Paston hopes for a good dowry settlement to accompany Margery. Her parents, meanwhile, would prefer it not to be excessive.

Additional note: Geoffrey Chaucer (1343–1400) wrote the following line in his poem *The Parliament of Fowls*: 'For this was on Seynt Valentyne's day, When every fowl cometh then to choose his mate.' Though the customs are older, that is said to be the first mention of St Valentine's Day in English as a special day for lovers. Such things can never be known for certain, but it's possible Chaucer's line is referenced without explanation in the letter below, suggesting the works of Chaucer were already well known and quoted, seventy-seven years after his death.

To my worshipful cousin, John Paston, be this bill delivered &c.

Cousin, I recommend me unto you, thanking you heartily for the great cheer that you made for me and my folks, the last time I was at Norwich; And you promised me that you would

11 Letter 896 in Gairdner 1904.

not raise the matter with Margery until such time as you and I were at an agreement. But you have made her such an advocate for you, that I may never have rest night nor day, for calling and crying upon me to bring the matter to an end &c.

And, cousin, Friday is Saint Valentine's Day, and every bird may choose himself a mate; and if you would like to come on Thursday night and so present yourself to stay with us until Monday, I trust to God that you shall so speak to my husband; and I shall pray we shall bring the matter to a conclusion. For, cousin,

> It is but a simple oak,
> That is cut down at the first stroke.

For you will be reasonable, I trust to God, which have you ever in His merciful keeping &c

By your cousin, DAME ELIZABETH BREWS,
otherwise shall be called by God's grace.

4. MARJERY BREWS TO JOHN PASTON. FEBRUARY 1477[12]

The fourth letter was written in the same month by young Margery Brews. The tone is altogether more passionate and is considered the earliest surviving Valentine's Day letter in English.

12 Letter 897 in Gairdner 1904.

Unto my right well-beloved Valentine, John Paston, Squire,
be this bill delivered &c

Right reverend and worshipful, and my right well-beloved Valentine, I recommend me unto you, full heartily desiring to hear of your welfare, which I beseech Almighty God to preserve unto His pleasure and your heart's desire. And if it please you to hear of my welfare, I am not in good health of body, nor of heart, nor shall I be till I hear from you.

> For there knows no creature what pain I endure,
> And for to be dead, I dare it not discover.

And my lady mother has brought the matter diligently to my father, but she can get no more than you know about, for which God knows I am sorry.[13] But if you love me, as I trust that you do, you will not leave me for that; for if you had not half the livelihood you have, for me to labour harder than any woman alive, I would not forsake you.

> And if you command me to keep true wherever I go,
> I know I will love you with all my might and never
>   know more.
> And if my friends say that I do amiss,
> Or that they shall not let me so to do,
> My heart bids me ever more to love you
> Truly over all earthly thing,
> And if they be never so enraged,
> I believe it shall be made better by passing time.

13 A reference to the dowry – property and land given with a young bride. Marriage is said to have been primarily a business transaction in the fifteenth century. However, troubadours sang of romantic love by this period – and Margery clearly had strong feelings towards her future husband.

No more to you at this time, but the Holy Trinity have you in keeping. And I beseech you that this letter be not seen by any earthly creature, saving only yourself &c.

And this letter was written at Topcroft, with full heavy heart &c.

By your own, Margery Brews.

Margery Brews and John Paston married later that year. With a population in England of only three to four million (down from four and a half million just before the Black Death of 1348), marrying a cousin was not particularly unusual, though a union between first or second cousins might require special dispensation from Rome.

5. Margaret Paston to John Paston. 19 May 1448 [an extract][14]

The first John Paston married a Margaret Mautby in 1443. She dictated this letter in 1448. James Gloys was a senior Paston servant. The Wyndhams were a local, newly risen family and avowed enemies of the Pastons.

Right worshipful husband, I recommend me to you and pray you to know on Friday last, while the Parson of Oxened was raising the Sacrament at Mass in the Parish Church, James Gloys was in the town and coming homeward by Wyndham's gate, when he was attacked by Wyndham, who had two of his men with him, and driven into my mother's place for refuge. With the noise of this, my mother and I came out of the

14 Letter 77 in Gairdner 1904. Longer versions available.

church from the Sacrament and Wyndham called my mother and me 'strong whores' and said you Pastons and all your kin were . . . [A hole in the paper where a word or phrase was torn out] . . . ingham said he lied, knave and churl as he was.

After noon, my mother and I reported this to the Prior of Norwich, who sent for Wyndham and Pagrave came with us. While Wyndham was in with the Prior and we at home, Gloys was assaulted again in the street, as he stood in the Lady Hasting's chamber, by Thomas Harris, one of Wyndham's men. This last assault the Parson of Oxened saw.

6. John Northwood to John, Viscount Beaumont. 28 May 1448[15]

Life was hard and dangerous, on the field of war or sometimes just in the street. The sixth letter is interesting for the picture of a fatal encounter between enemies. It was written by a rather obsequious servant, John Northwood, to his master, John, Viscount Beaumont. [At times like this, it's easiest just to assume everyone involved is called John.] It is included in the Paston Letters presumably because it was part of the records for the case in law.

To my worshipful and reverent lord, John, Viscount Beaumont.

Right worshipful and my reverent and most special Lord, I recommend me unto your good grace in the most humble and lowly ways that I can, desiring to hear of your prosperity and welfare, to my most singular joy and special comfort.

15 Letter 78 in Gairdner 1904.

And if it please your Highness, as touching the sudden adventure that fell lately at Coventry, please it your lordship to hear that on Corpus Christi Evening just passed[16] between eight and nine o'clock after noon, when Sir Humphrey Stafford[17] escorted Sir James of Ormond to his inn, from Lady Shrewsbury. Returning, he met Sir Robert Harcourt, coming from his mother towards his inn, and in doing so, passed Sir Humphrey – and Richard, his son, came a little way behind and when they met together, they struggled and Sir Robert smote him a great stroke on the head with his sword – while Richard, with his dagger, went at him in haste. And as Richard stumbled, one of Harcourt's men smote him in the back with a knife; who knows how badly hurt he was, it showed so red. His father heard the noise and rode towards them – and Harcourt's men ran. But the horse went down, no one knows how, while someone behind him smote him on the head with a hedge tool, some unknown weapon, so that he fell down with his son lying before him, as good as dead.

And all this was done, as men say, in a Pater Noster while.[18]

And forthwith, Sir Humphrey Stafford's men followed after and slew two men of Harcourt's – one Swinton, one Bradshawe, and more were hurt, some fled and some are in the jail at Coventry.

And before the coroner of Coventry, upon the sight of their bodies, were indicted, as principal for the death of Richard Stafford, Sir Robert Harcourt and the two men that had been killed. And for the two Harcourt men who had been killed, he indicted Sir Humphrey as principal.

16 22 May.

17 This Sir Humphrey Stafford was killed fighting against the rebels of Jack Cade in 1450.

18 In the time it takes to say the 'Our Father' – i.e. very little time at all.

And there has been nothing brought before the Justice of the Peace of Coventry for this riot, because the sheriff of Warwickshire is dead[19] and the JP cannot sit to hear the case until there is a new sheriff.

And all this mischief came about because of an old debate that was between them for taking an offence, as it is told.

And Almighty Jesus preserve your high estate, my special Lord and send you long life and good health.

Written at Coventry on Tuesday next after Corpus Christi day &c.

By your own poor servant, JOHN NORTHWOOD.

7. MARGARET PASTON TO JOHN PASTON. 28 SEPTEMBER 1443 [AN EXTRACT][20]

To complete this Paston selection, here is the opening of one of the personal letters reproduced without any changes to the spelling or style – from Margaret Paston to her husband concerning his recent ill-health. It is helpful to read it aloud and consider different vowel sounds. I have made a few notes, to help. It remains a somewhat dusty pleasure when a cryptic phrase suddenly becomes clear – but it is a pleasure, nonetheless.

To my rygth worchepful husbond, John Paston, dwellyng in the Inner Temple at London, in hast.

Ryth worchipful hosbon, I recomande me to yow, desyryng hertely to her of yowr wilfar, thanckyng God of yowr a mending of the grete dysese that ye have hade; and I thancke yow for

19 Thomas Porter was sheriff of Warwickshire and Leicestershire. He died the day before this letter was written.
20 Letter 47 in Gairdner 1904.

the letter that ye sent me, for be my trowthe[21] my moder and I wer nowth in hertys es fro the tyme that we woste[22] of yowr sekenesse, tyl we woste verely[23] of your a mendyng. My moder be hestyd[24] a nodyr[25] ymmage[26] of wax of the weytte of yow[27] to oyer Lady of Walsyngham[28], and sche sent iiij. nobelys[29] to the iiij. Orderys of Frerys[30] at Norweche to pray for yow . . .

21 By my word/my troth.
22 Knew.
23 Verily – as truth.
24 Asked for – at her behest.
25 Another.
26 Image.
27 Of the weight of you.
28 Walsingham is a Norfolk place of pilgrimage to Mary, the mother of Jesus.
29 iiij = 4. Nobles were gold coins.
30 Friars, showing the Middle English/French root of 'Freres'.

Read on for an extract of

RAVENSPUR

The Rise of the Tudors

The epic conclusion to the Wars of the Roses series.

I

1470

The river bent a tail around Pembroke Castle. Winter sun shone red against the walls and the keep rose above the rest, tall as a cathedral, and about as proud.

On the path by the gatehouse, the stranger rested his hands on his saddle pommel, rubbing a thumb along a line of broken stitching. His horse was tired, the animal's head drooping as it found nothing to eat on the stones. Compared to the guards staring down, Jasper Tudor was as dark as a shepherd. His hair was thick with road-dust, like matted cloth. It hung to his shoulders, keeping his face in shadow as the sun set and the day began to die around him. Though he was weary, his eyes were never still, watching every movement on the wall. Each time a guard turned his head to the inner yard, or glanced at an officer below, Jasper saw and listened and judged. He knew when the news of his presence had summoned the master of the castle. He knew how many steps that man had to climb to reach the outer gate, barred in iron and just the first of a dozen defences against an attack.

Jasper counted under his breath, distracting himself from the anger he felt just at being in that place. He imagined each turn of the stone steps within and his mouth quirked when he saw William Herbert arrive on the crenellation. The young earl looked down at him, strong emotion making him mottled. The new master of Pembroke was just seventeen years old, a red-faced brawler, still reeling from the death of his father. It seemed Earl Herbert did not much like the sight of the dark and wiry man looking up at him. That much was clear from his expression and the way he gripped the stone with his thick hands.

Jasper Tudor had been the Earl of Pembroke once, a dozen years before. He had called that castle home and he knew and loved those stones as well as anywhere in the world. It was hard not to bristle when a man half his age looked down upon him in arrogance from his own walls.

Earl William Herbert merely stared for a time, his eyes pinched small as if he lacked the long sight or had swallowed something that irked him. The younger man had a wide head, not fat but broad, topped by sleek hair cut straight across. Under that gaze, Jasper Tudor inclined his head in greeting. It would have been hard enough to deal with the father, had the man lived.

The older Herbert had not died well, giving no new honours to his family line. He had not lost his life in some valiant action but had been cut down without thought when Warwick had captured King Edward. That small loss, ignored at the time, had been eclipsed by the greater sin of Warwick laying hands on the king. In Pembroke, it had meant an entire town in mourning.

In the gathering gloom, Jasper Tudor swallowed nervously. Glints of light appeared and vanished in stone along the walls, as men in armour shifted their weight. He knew he had gained no advantage by spotting them. No one could outride a bolt.

Clouds drove across the sky, lit from beneath by the last of the sun. Above, the new earl lost patience at last with the silence. For all it cost him a slight advantage, for all his grief and dominance, there were not many seventeen-year-olds who could have matched the stone-like calm of a man at forty.

'*Well?* What do you want here, Master Tudor?' The young earl seemed to find some small pleasure in the lack of a noble title. Jasper Tudor was King Henry's half-brother. He had been raised high by the house of Lancaster, and in return he had fought for them. He had taken the field against the eighteen-year-old Edward of York, the giant still weeping in rage for the death of his father. Jasper repressed a shudder at the memory of that monster in red armour, carmine as the sun on Pembroke walls.

'I give you God's good day and recommend me to you. I have sailed from France to this coast, running ahead of all news. Have you heard yet from London?'

'Does it so stick in that Welsh throat to call me lord?' William Herbert demanded. 'I am the Earl of Pembroke, Master Tudor. If you're at my gate to beg for food or coin, you will be disappointed. Keep your news. Your Lancaster mobs and your ragged *prisoner* king have no claim on me. And my father gave his life in defence of the *rightful* king of England, Edward of York.' The young man's mouth turned up on one side, twisting his face. 'While you, Tudor, I believe you were *attainted*, losing all honour, titles, property. I should have you struck down at this moment! Pembroke is mine. All that was my father's is *mine*.'

Jasper nodded as if he had perhaps heard a point worth considering. He saw bluster in the young man, covering weakness. Once more, he wished he could have dealt with the old earl, who had been a man of honour. Yet that was the way of it, when wars began. Good men died and left their sons to follow them, for better or worse. Jasper shook his head, swinging the clotted locks of his hair. He was one of those sons himself, perhaps a lesser man than his father, Owen. Worse, in the years of his exile, Jasper had found no wife nor made sons of his own. If the French king hadn't granted him a stipend as his cousin, Jasper thought, there was a chance he would have starved to death, alone and penniless. Yet he had remained loyal, to King Henry, and to Queen Margaret of Anjou, in all her despair and her fall.

Jasper looked down for a moment, his hopes fading under the earl's scorn. Yet he stood before Pembroke, and that old place had been his. It still rang with an aching familiarity and gave him some strange comfort just from being there, tempting him to reach out and touch the stone. He could not allow himself to be shamed in sight of those walls. He raised his head once more.

There was still one whom he loved within the fortress, as well as any father loved a son, both the reason for and purpose of his visit. Jasper Tudor had not come to Pembroke to make accusations or vengeance. The tide of men's affairs had called him home from France and he had asked permission of Warwick to take the time for a private errand. As the great fleet braved the open sea, his ship alone had set off into the west.

Jasper looked along the length of the battlements and saw no sign yet of his brother's son, kept for fourteen years as a ward, or a prisoner.

'I used to think Pembroke was a different world from all the busyness in London, all the doings and the trade,' Jasper said, raising his voice to carry. 'Two hard weeks on the road, with a string of horses. It can be done, but it is no easy task. And in the winter, the roads are such a quagmire, it is better to sail round the Cornish coast, though it takes at least as long and is more perilous. For myself, I fear those winter storms that can tear a ship's hull open and drown all those who risk their lives on deep waters, God bless their souls.'

The words flowed from him, making the eyes of the earl grow glassy until the young man shook his head in confusion.

'You will not enter here, Master Tudor,' Earl Herbert snapped, losing the last threads of his patience. 'Play no more of your Welsh games; I will not open my gate to you. Say what you have come to say and then go back to your damp woods and your camps and your poaching of hares. Live like the grubby, starving brigand you are, while I enjoy Pembroke and roast lamb and all the comforts of King Edward's trust.'

Jasper rubbed his jaw with the back of his thumb to keep a flash of anger from showing. He loved Pembroke still, every stone and arch and hall and musty storeroom, filled with wine and grain and preserved haunches of sheep and goats. He had hunted the land all around and Pembroke was home to him in a way that had a greater claim than anywhere else in the world. It had been a dream as a child that he might one day own a fine lord's castle. When it had actually come true, Jasper Tudor had been satisfied. There was no greater dream, not for the son of a soldier.

'Whether you have heard or not, *my lord*, the tide is turned. Earl Warwick has come home with a fleet and an army.' Jasper hesitated, searching for the right words. The young earl watching him had leaned right out on hearing that name, gripping the stones so hard it looked as if he wanted to break a piece off and hurl it at him. Jasper went on slowly, making the words fall far from the gatehouse.

'They will restore Lancaster, my lord. They will lay a hot iron over the wounds, ending York. I speak not to threaten, but to give you the good word so that you may choose a side, perhaps before anyone asks again with iron in their hands. Now, I have come for my nephew, my lord. For Henry Tudor, son of my brother Edmund and Margaret Beaufort. Is he well? Is he safe within?'

As the Earl of Pembroke opened his mouth to reply, Jasper saw movement along the wall at last, a white face, surrounded by thick black hair. The boy, surely, not yet with a man's growth. Jasper gave no sign he had seen.

'*You* have no claim on him,' William Herbert snapped, showing his teeth. 'My father paid a thousand pounds to gain a ward. I can see the ragged edge of your cloak, Tudor. I can see the grease and dust on you from here. Can you return that thousand pounds to me?' The young man's sneering grin vanished as Jasper Tudor reached behind him to a parcel of canvas and leather strapped to the small of his back. He pulled it out and shook it to jingle the gold coins within.

'I can,' he said, though there was no triumph in his voice. He could see the scorn in the earl and he knew it would not matter.

'Oh yes? Do you also have . . .' William Herbert's mouth worked as if some thick clot of rage had closed his throat '. . . *the years* spent on his training in that bag of yours? Do you have my father's time? His trust?' The words spilled out faster, his confidence returning. 'It looks too small for all of that, Tudor.'

The young earl's will would prevail, no matter what was said, or who had the better of the exchange. One man could not force the door of Pembroke. Ten thousand could not.

With a sigh, Jasper shoved the parcel out of sight once more. At least the French king would not own him once he had returned the loan. He rubbed his forehead as if in tiredness, hiding his eyes from the man thirty feet above him so he could flick a glance at his nephew. Jasper did not want the boy seen and sent away. If he addressed him directly, he sensed enough spite in William Herbert to make his nephew's life a misery, or even put it in peril. When Jasper spoke again, it was as much for the ears of Henry Tudor as it was to the new earl in Pembroke.

'This is a chance to earn a little good will, my lord,' he called up. 'The past is the past, all our fathers gone to tombs. You stand now where once I stood as earl – and Pembroke is yours. The years turn, *my lord*, and we cannot take back a day, or return one *hour* to make a better choice when we had the chance.' He took heart from the earl's silence, feeling that the young man was at least not yelling curses and threats.

'Edward of York is away in the north, my lord, far from his armies and palaces. And now it is too late for him!' Jasper went on proudly, making his voice ring out for all ears. 'Warwick is returned to England! With a vast host raised in Kent and Sussex, aye and France. Men such as he have even kings bend close to listen when they speak. They are a different breed from you and me, my lord. Look you, Earl Warwick will bring Henry of Lancaster from the Tower to rule again. *There* is your rightful king – and he is my half-brother! Now, I would like to take my nephew to London, my lord. I ask you to pass him into my care, in good faith and in trust of your mercy. I will repay your father's investment in him, though it be all I have.'

While they had spoken, torches and shuttered lamps had appeared along the walls, seeming to snatch away the last of the day's light. Lit by a flickering gold, William Herbert waited only an instant when the entreaty came to an end.

'No,' he called down. 'There's my answer. No, Tudor. You'll have nothing from my hand.' The earl was enjoying his power over the ragged man at his gate. 'Though I might have my men take your coins from you, if that was not one of your lies. Are you not a brigand on my road? How many have you robbed and murdered to gather so much coin, Tudor? You Welsh hedge-lords are all thieves, it's well known.'

'Are you so much a *fool*, boy?' Jasper Tudor roared up at the younger man, making him splutter in outrage. 'I have told you the tide has turned! I came to you with an open hand, with a fair offer. Yet you bleat at me and threaten me still, from behind the safety of your walls? Is that your courage then, in the stone under your hands? If you will not give up my nephew, then open your ears, boy! I will put you under the cold ground if you harm him in any way. Do you understand me? Deep under the earth.' Though he spoke in apparent rage, Jasper Tudor shot a glance to the fourteen-year-old nephew watching him from the battlements further down the wall. He held his nephew's gaze until he sensed William Herbert craning round to see what had caught his attention. The face vanished. Jasper could only hope his message had been understood.

'Serjeant Thomas!' the young Earl of Pembroke called in imperious tones. 'Take half a dozen men and ride down this brigand on my road. He has not shown sufficient respect to a king's earl. Be thou *ungentle* with this Welsh bastard. Spring a little blood from him, then fetch him back to me for punishment.'

Jasper cursed under his breath as great thumps and cracks sounded within the castle gatehouse, along with the rattle of enormous chains. Soldiers raced up to the walls on all sides to check the environs for any force in hiding. Some of them carried crossbows and Jasper Tudor could feel their cold gazes crawling over him. It did not matter that one or two might have been his own men, from years before. They had a new master. He shook his head in anger, wheeling his horse and digging in his heels so that the animal bunched and lunged down the open road. No bolts sprang after him into the darkness. They wanted him alive.

Leaning out as far as he dared between the stones, Henry Tudor had stared at the rider, thin and defiant before the gatehouse of Pembroke, sitting like a beggar on a dark horse and yet daring to challenge the new earl. The black-haired boy had no memory of his uncle and would not have been able to pick him from a crowd if William Herbert hadn't called him Tudor. All he knew was that Uncle Jasper had fought for King Henry, for Lancaster, in towns so distant they were just names.

Henry had drunk in the sight of his blood relative, risking a fall to hear every word, gripping the rough stones he knew so well. He had been born in Pembroke, both he and his mother coming close to death, so they said. He'd heard it was surely a miracle that a woman so tiny had survived at all. Not twenty feet from the gatehouse wall where William Herbert stood, Henry had come into the world, his mother just thirteen years old and half-mad with fear and pain. He had been given to a wet nurse and little Margaret Beaufort had been spirited away to marry again, her only child and dead first husband to be forgotten and left behind. When the Yorkists took Pembroke and his uncle Jasper had been hunted as a Lancastrian traitor, Henry Tudor had been left utterly alone.

He was convinced it had made him strong, that isolation. No other lad had grown up without a mother, without friends or family, but instead with enemies on all sides to hurt and scorn him. As a result, in his own mind, he had been made about as hard as Pembroke. He had suffered a thousand cruelties from the Herberts, father and son, but he had endured – and he had watched, all the years of his life, for one single moment of weakness or inattention.

There had been shameful times, when he had almost forgotten the hatred and had to nurse and blow upon it to keep it alight. Before the old earl had been killed, there had even been days when Henry had felt more like the man's second son than the mere coin he truly was, to be hoarded and spent at the right time. He'd found himself wanting to earn some word of praise from William, though the older boy never missed a chance to cause him pain. Henry had hated himself for his weaknesses then, and clutched anger to his breast as he slept, curling in on it.

On the road below, he heard his uncle grow stern. The man's stream of words caught at Henry like a barbed line snatching across his throat. '. . . under the cold *ground* if you harm him.' It was the first concern for his well-being that Henry could remember, and it shook him. At that instant, as he understood in wonder that a man cared enough to threaten an earl, his uncle Jasper looked directly at him. Henry Tudor froze.

He had not known his uncle had spotted him creeping closer. He was pierced by the gaze and his thoughts shook suddenly, skipping a beat ahead. *Under* the earth. *Deep* under it. Hope soared in Henry's chest and he ducked back inside, away from his uncle's eyes – away too from a Herbert earl who had long taken out his hatred of Lancaster on the weakest end of a distant line. Henry Tudor had taken no sides in the wars, at least beyond the colour of his blood, as red as any Lancaster rose.

The boy ran, clattering along the walkways that rested on beams beneath the battlements. In the flickering torchlight, one of the guards put out a hand to stop him, but Henry knocked it away, making the man swear under his breath. Old Jones, stone-deaf in his right ear. The Tudor boy knew every man and woman in the castle, from those who lived within the walls and tended to the Herbert family, to the hundred or so who came up from town each morning, bringing supplies and carts and their labour.

He leaped down steps, throwing himself against the outer post with all the carelessness of youth so that he thumped hard into the rails but lost no speed. He had raced across the castle grounds a thousand times, building his wind and his agility. It showed then, coupled with a purpose that had him casting off all caution and running like a scalded cat through Pembroke grounds.

In near darkness, he scrambled through a workshop erected on the main yard, raising himself on his arms as he jumped across piles of crates, thick with the briny green smell of the sea. On another day he might have stayed to see the silvery fish or oysters unpacked, but he had a path to follow and a burning need to know that he had not been mistaken. Across the open ground, he could see the setting sun had dropped beyond the walls, casting an odd light as he reached the stone halls around the keep, the massive tower that stretched five storeys above the rest of the castle and could be sealed against an army. Pembroke had been built for defence, though it had one weakness to those who knew it, one secret, kept well hidden.

Henry skidded as he reached the lower feast hall. He saw the earl's Constable there, a florid man in earnest conversation with one of the castle factors, both poring over a scroll as if it held the meaning of life and not just some record of slates broken or hundredweights of oak and beech. He slowed to a stiff-legged walk as he crossed the end of the hall farthest from them. Henry could sense the men looking up, or perhaps he imagined it as they did not call out. Without even a glance at them, he reached the door and opened it on the heat and steam of the kitchens beyond.

Pembroke had two dining halls, with the kitchens running beneath the grander of the two. Staff and unimportant guests ate in the first. Henry had spent many evenings chewing bread and meat in near darkness there, begrudged even the cost of a tallow candle. He'd sat alone, while reflected light and laughter spilled from the windows above, from the greater hall where the earl entertained his favoured guests. Henry would have risked a beating to even enter that place, but that night he was concerned with the kitchens themselves – and what they concealed.

The maids and serving staff barely looked up as he entered, assuming the skinny boy was bringing back a bowl, though he usually ate off a trencher and took the slab of hard bread away with him to gnaw or to feed to the jackdaws on the towers. Even so, Henry was familiar to them and he could not see the cook, Mary Corrigan, who would have shooed him away with her big red hands and a flapping apron. In the heat and steam from bubbling pots, the air was thick and there was bustle on all sides as the staff dug into piled ingredients and measured them out. The sight made him lick his lips and he realized he had not eaten. Should he wheedle a little food from the cooks? His gaze flickered over a pile of peeled apples, already turning a honey-brown. Slabs of cheese bobbed next to them, in a pot of watery whey. And how long would it be before he ate again?

As he stood there, with the clamour and smells and sheer hard work of the kitchen going on all around him, he could sense the door on the far side. Set into the stone wall, it was narrower than a man's chest, so that a soldier would have to turn to pass through. An oak plank blocked the doorway, resting on thick iron braces in the mortar. Henry could feel it there as he looked anywhere else but directly at it. He knew every stone of Pembroke, in winter and summer. There was not a storeroom or an attic or a path he had not walked, though none of them had gripped his attention as had that single door. He knew what lay beyond it. He could feel the dampness and the cold already, though his skin was sheened in sweat.

He walked across the kitchen and the staff parted before him like dancers, carrying pots and trays, clattering and calling to one another. They would feed six hundred men and some eighty women that evening, from the high table in the great hall and those closest to the young earl right down to the falconers and the priests and in a later sitting, the guards and the boys who mucked out the stables. Food was a vital part of the compact between a lord and his people, a duty and a burden, half symbol, half payment.

Henry reached the door and lifted the bar with a heave that had him staggering under its weight as it came free.

He spent precious moments steadying the plank against the wall. Breathing hard, he took the key from where it hung and as he inserted it, he felt a hand on his shoulder. He turned to see Mary Corrigan peering at him. She was no taller than he was himself, but seemed three times his weight in meat and bone.

'And what are you after?' she said, wiping her hands on a thick cloth. Henry could feel himself flushing, though he did not stop working the key until the ancient lock clicked open.

'I'm going down to the river, Mary. To catch an eel, perhaps.'

Her eyes narrowed slightly, but in disdain rather than suspicion.

'If Master Holt or the Constable saw you using this old door, they'd skin you, you know that don't you? Honestly, *boys*! Too lazy for the long way round. Go on with you, then. I'll lock it behind. Be sure you put the keys back on their pegs. And come back to the gatehouse. I won't hear you knocking here, not with all this noise.' To Henry's surprise, the big cook reached out and ruffled his hair with fingers strong enough to bend an iron ladle.

He felt his eyes threaten tears, though he could not remember the last time he had wept, not in all his life. There was a chance he would never set foot in Pembroke again, he realized. What passed for his family were all within the walls of that castle. It was true Mary Corrigan had beaten him three times for stealing, but she had once kissed his cheek and slipped an apple into his hand. It was the only act of kindness he could remember.

He hesitated, but recalled the dark figure of the rider. His uncle had come for him. Henry's resolve hardened and he nodded to her. The door opened with a draught of cold air and he closed it on Mary's bright perspiring cheeks, hearing the lock click and the woman grunt as she lifted the bar and put it back. Henry steadied himself, feeling the cold seep into him after the thicker air of the kitchen.

The stairs turned immediately, so that no one who came up them would ever have room to brace himself and swing an axe. They dropped away into the cliff under Pembroke, twisting sharply. The first few steps were lit through cracks in the door, but that dim gleam lasted only to the second turn. After that, he was in blackness, thick as damp linen pressed against his face.

No one knew if the cave had been discovered after the castle was built or whether it was the reason the first wooden fort had been raised in that spot, centuries before. Henry had seen chipped flint arrowheads recovered from the cavern floor, formed by hunters from a past too distant to know. Roman coins too had been found, with the faces of dead emperors set into blackened silver. It was an old place and it had delighted Henry when he'd found it first, during a winter of solid rain when every day had been a misery of tutors, bruises and damp.

Some change in the echoes of his steps warned him before he struck the door below. It too was locked, but he felt for the key there and found it on a leather cord. It took all his strength to force the door open after he'd unlocked it, thumping his shoulder against the swollen doorjamb over and over until he fell into a much colder darkness. Panting from exertion and not a little fear, Henry shoved the door closed behind him and held the cold key in his hand, wondering just what to do with it. It didn't seem right to take such a vital thing. He could sense the huge cavern overhead – a different world, though he stood directly under Pembroke. The silence was broken by flutters of pigeons on the high stones, reacting to his presence in their mindless way. He listened harder and heard the river's gentle breath.

The darkness was complete as he stepped out, immediately knocking his shin on the keel of a rowing boat, no doubt dragged into the cave to be repaired. The existence of the cave was not the secret of Pembroke. The secret was the hidden door back in the gloom, that led to the heart of the castle above. Henry cursed and rubbed his leg, feeling the key once again. He hung it on the prow of the boat where it would be found and edged his way past on a floor that was as smooth as a riverbed.

The last barrier to the river was of iron, a gate set into stone walls built over the natural mouth of the cave. Henry collected another key and worked it in the lock until he heard a click. He stepped through and stood outside in the darkness with his back to the river, relocking the gate and tossing the key back beyond reach. He did not do that for William Herbert, with all his scorn and cruelty. He did that for Pembroke – and perhaps for Mary Corrigan. He would not leave Pembroke's secrets to be discovered by others.

He could not go back. Henry heard himself breathing hard before he summoned his will and slowed his heart, forcing calm like cream poured into bubbling soup, so that all became still. The heat was still there, but hidden, or drowned.

He turned to the river then and understood that he had been hearing the muffled sounds of a boat, somewhere close. Though there was no moon and the river was almost as black as the cave, he thought he could still make out some deeper blot, barely twenty feet long. He whistled in its direction, hoping he was not wrong.

Oars plunked and creaked, sounding loud in the night. The boat came gliding across the current and Henry Tudor stared in fear. Smugglers, fishermen, poachers and slavers – there were a number of men with reason to go out on the waters in the dark. Not many of those would take kindly to being hailed by a boy.

'Well done, lad,' came a voice from the darkness. 'And didn't your tutors say you were clever?'

'Uncle?' Henry whispered. He heard the man chuckle and began to scramble down, half falling into the boat until a dark figure grabbed him by both arms and proceeded to crush the air out of him with surprising strength. Henry felt the man's stubble rasp against his cheek and he could smell sweat and green herbs, and the odour of horses driven deep into his uncle's clothes. There were no lamps lit, not with Pembroke's walls looming above. Yet after the blackness of the cave, stars and the moon were enough for Henry to see surprisingly well as he was guided to a thwart to sit.

'Well met, lad,' Jasper Tudor said. 'And I only wish my brother could have lived to see this. Half the guards seeking me in the town, the rest following one of my men with a burning brand, while I am here – and you remembered the cave under Pembroke. Your father would be so proud of you.'

'He would not know me, Uncle,' Henry said, frowning. 'He died before I was born.' He felt himself retreating from the warmth of the man, his tone and his embrace, pulling back in all senses, finding an old comfort in coldness. He inched a fraction clear along the plank, feeling the boat rock. 'Delay no further for me, Uncle. There must be another boat, a larger one. I heard your words to William Herbert. Are we to London?'

Henry did not see the way his uncle Jasper stared, obscurely deflated. They were utter strangers, both becoming aware of it in the same moment. Henry had never known a mother or a father. Waiting in strained silence, he supposed it was not so strange that his uncle might retain some family feeling for his brother's only son. He felt no answering need in himself, only a black chill as deep as the river under them. Yet it felt like strength.

Jasper cleared his throat, shaking off the stillness that had held him.

'To London, yes. Yes, boy! My ship is moored at Tenby and this little bark is far too frail for the open sea. I have horses though, waiting a mile up the river. Can you ride, son?'

'Of course,' Henry said curtly. He'd had the training of a knight, or at least as a squire to William Herbert. It was true he'd had more in the way of cuffs and scorn than proper instruction, but he could stay in a saddle. He could handle a sword.

'Good. Once we are out of sight of the castle, we'll mount up and ride to the coast. Then London, boy! To see your namesake, King Henry. To see Lancaster restored. By God, I'm still taking it in. We are out! To roam like free men, while they search the woods for us.'

The boat moved on the current, the oars employed with little noise. For a long time, the only sounds were from the water and the harsh breath of working men. Jasper shook his head at the continuing silence of the boy. He had expected a chattering jackdaw. Instead, he had rescued a little owl, watchful and still.